Also by Mervyn Jones

FICTION

John and Mary (1967)

A Survivor (1968)

Joseph (1970)

NON-FICTION

The Antagonists (1962)

In Famine's Shadow (1966)

Lord Richard's Passion

LORD RICHARD'S PASSION

by Mervyn Jones

ALFRED A. KNOPF
New York
1974

THIS IS A BORZOI BOOK
PUBLISHED BY ALFRED A. KNOPF, INC.

Copyright © 1974 by Mervyn Jones

Library of Congress Cataloging in Publication Data

Jones, Mervyn.   Lord Richard's Passion.

I. Title.   PZ4.J777Lo3   [PR6060.056]   823'.9'14   73–20765
ISBN 0–394–49220–X

Manufactured in the United States of America

FIRST EDITION

Contents

Contents

Lord Richard's Passion

CHAPTER 1

A Weekend
at Longmarsh

HE ALWAYS THOUGHT OF HER in the midst of pure and delicate colours: white, green and grey. White was her dress—she was lovely in white. White too, that first morning at Longmarsh, was the mist resting on the lawn, the rose gardens, the ornamental lake and the home park. It promised a beautiful June day, the warmth growing surely but gently, the sunlight saved from harshness by its misty beginnings. Green was the well-mown grass, a fresh and light green after a rainy spring. Grey was the old stone of the house; his room was in the east wing and he looked across to the west wing, touched almost to silver by the sun. He opened one casement window to the full extent of the latch and rested his hand on the stonework. His fingers reached a fragment of lichen; he broke it off and looked at it. It was all of these colours, tender-green and silver-grey and silver-becoming-white. He was sorry about breaking it off. It could have been there for a long time.

The mist, which must have risen from the lake, didn't cover the fields of the tenant farms. There, the green had three shades: pale in the growing corn, rich in the meadows, darker in the hedgerows. The village lay almost hidden among trees—old oaks and beeches—but he could see some chimneys, a few already smoking although it was Sunday, and the church tower. So the same colours were repeated: white for the smoke, green for the trees, grey for the church.

He felt the beauty of this country of his, this England—felt it as a poet feels, and would have put it into loving verse had he been a poet, which he certainly could never be. (But the poem about "this England," or rather the speech from the play, he did know by heart.) This beauty—embodied in houses like Longmarsh, lawns and rose gardens, oaks and beeches—had taken a long time to make or to grow, was now in a state of perfection, and was happily everlasting. His life had a meaning in devotion to this country; this gave him a deep contentment, an assured sense of belonging.

These feelings were not original, nor did he wish them to be so. They were the natural feelings of a young man like Lord Richard Somers, twenty years old in 1875.

Long afterwards, he remembered as an integral part of this moment that Ellie was there. He didn't see her come out of the house; she was there when he brought his eyes back from the village to the foreground. It was as though a landscape artist, having sketched the outline of the scene, had sensed that something was missing—some touch of charm and movement—and had put in Ellie. She wore a white dress with a green sash and bow, and a white hat which shaded her face but left her golden tresses free over her shoulders. The mist surrounded her, as if Nature were reluctant to expose her with too much clarity.

She moved timorously, like some small animal—a rabbit, perhaps—aware that it was safe only when unobserved. Richard couldn't guess what she was doing out before breakfast, until he realised that she was looking for something. She found it on a seat in one of the arbours, made by trees trimmed to form a recess, which were placed at intervals round the lawn. It was a book, he saw. Picking it up with relief, she returned to the house. She must have left it there

the day before and been afraid of a scolding for letting the
dew warp the leather. He wouldn't tell anyone, Richard
thought with a smile.

Later, when he was in love with Ellie—hopefully, hopelessly, joyously, miserably, passionately, carnally, in all the
ways a man could be in love—Richard sometimes longed to
regain the lightness of heart that had been his when he first
saw her. His feelings about her then, he was certain, were
pure. They were scarcely about her at all, so mingled were
they with his feelings about the June morning, about Longmarsh, about England. She was a child, and he saw her as
a child. She was fourteen, as a matter of fact; she hadn't put
her hair up, she didn't dine with the adults. Richard had
been introduced to her, as to all the Colmores whom he
didn't already know, when he arrived on Friday. But, had it
not been for this glimpse from his window and Ellie's unaware completion of a perfect picture, he wouldn't have been
able to say afterwards whether she had been at Longmarsh
that weekend or not. Lord and Lady Farnham had a large
family—three sons and five daughters. Since the occasion for
the house party was the announcement of an engagement, all
of them were there except the second son, who was at Eton.

Celia, who had become engaged to Richard's friend Ralph
Ashton, was the second girl. The eldest, Charlotte, was a
problem, being regrettably plain and plump. The third
daughter, Fanny, would clearly be no problem at all—or the
problem, if any, would be to stop her making an unsuitable
runaway marriage. She was extremely pretty, vivacious and
amusing; Richard had greatly enjoyed dancing with her, and
even more sitting out with her in a flow of lively talk, at
two or three balls during this season. Then there were two
younger daughters, Eleanor and Anne.

So far as the marriage market went, Richard understood
that he was destined to be a valuable catch. This he didn't

attribute to any personal attractions, though he couldn't help knowing that he was good-looking, but simply to his being the son of the Duke of Berkshire. The younger son—but blood was blood. If the girls, or their mothers, hadn't started to pursue him seriously, there were two reasons. He wasn't of age yet; and he was under orders to sail for India with his regiment, so it wasn't to be expected that he would tie himself down, even in a vague understanding, until he returned from the three-year tour of overseas duty.

It was partly the thought of India that made England so beautiful on a soft, misty summer morning. True, Richard looked forward to India with some excitement. There would be polo, pig-sticking and tiger-shooting. There might be, the Colonel had hinted, a chance of action; on the ever-restless frontier, the Afghans were giving trouble. But there would also be torrid heat, which Richard didn't stand very well, flies, scorpions, tummy troubles—apparently everyone got tummy troubles—and filthy thieving natives. There would be dusty plains and untamed jungles. For three years, only memory would give him the beauty of fresh green meadows, beech coppices, murmuring trout streams, downland bright under scudding white clouds: the beauty amid which he had lived, never thinking how lucky he was, since childhood. Nor would there be delightful girls like Fanny, or gracious and hospitable ladies like Lady Farnham. Some of the senior officers were taking their wives—it had become the thing to do since the opening of the Suez Canal, which meant that the ladies could go home quickly if they couldn't stand the climate—but they couldn't be expected to entertain as in England.

Richard rang for hot water and told the man to lay out Sunday clothes. Ralph Ashton said that the Farnhams were easy-going and it wasn't necessary to dress formally for church. While shaving, he noted that his moustache was growing nicely. It was brown with a hint of red, like his hair —the Somers shade. He took his scissors and trimmed it carefully.

He dressed and went down to the breakfast room. What he liked about Longmarsh, where he hadn't stayed before, was that it was easy to find one's way about. At Severalls, the country home of the Dukes of Berkshire, guests sometimes got lost and had to ask the servants the way. It was treated as a joke, but it was really a nuisance. To Richard's mind, Severalls was far too big. Although of course it was his home, "at home" was just what he didn't feel in the picture gallery, the great ballroom, the larger dining room, and other rooms which were there to be admired and were used only two or three times a year. There were even bedrooms which were never used at all, the furniture resting permanently under dust-sheets. Longmarsh, on the other hand, was probably filled every weekend and an occasion like this, Richard guessed, was a bit of a tight squeeze. It had a cosy feeling— the feeling of a real home. No doubt it was mainly the big Colmore family that created this atmosphere; the family at Severalls—Richard's parents, his brother and himself—looked rather thin-spread even in the smaller dining room which they normally used. Besides, Longmarsh was more to Richard's taste as a building. It was a Tudor manor-house, built by a gentleman who wasn't yet an Earl, while Severalls was a palace built by a Duke. Longmarsh had an air of having acquired dignity, without strain or show, across many generations. Severalls, with all its grandeur and opulence, gave an unseemly effect of ostentation, even of intrusion on the English landscape. After all, it was not much more than a hundred years old.

Going down the stairs, which were of wood and not of marble and creaked pleasantly, Richard decided that his brother was welcome to Severalls. When he married, he would look for a place in the style of Longmarsh. Of course, if he married Fanny Colmore he would be more or less at home at Longmarsh itself. But Fanny wouldn't be on the shelf in three years' time—not likely.

There were two men already in the breakfast room, Ralph Ashton and a person called Sharp. Ashton was in Richard's regiment and they had become firm friends, although he was five years older and a captain while Richard was the junior subaltern of the mess. It was as Ashton's friend that Richard had been invited to Longmarsh, and he would have been best man at the wedding if he were not going to India. Ashton had been appointed aide-de-camp to a General and was not going with the regiment.

As for Sharp, Richard gathered that he was a distant relative of Lord Farnham's or possibly Lady Farnham's. He was a curate, just down from Oxford, and Lord Farnham was proposing to find him a living. He wore rimless glasses and had protruding teeth, just like a curate in *Punch*. Having him in the house party, Richard thought, was typical of the Farnhams' kindness.

"Morning, Ashton. Morning, Sharp," Richard said heartily.

"Morning, Somers. Try the kidneys, they're first-rate," Ashton suggested.

"Have a general reconnaissance, I think."

The hot-plates offered a good range: eggs, bacon, haddock in milk, kippers, chops, kidneys, mushrooms. Richard helped himself to a chop and kidneys and sat down.

"Another beautiful day, I think we may safely assume," Sharp said. He had a reedy voice, already with the monotonous rhythm of a parson.

"A scorcher, I shouldn't wonder, after that mist," Ashton rejoined. "Glorious morning, anyway. Rotten having to waste it in church, isn't it, Somers?"

"Good for a snooze," Richard said.

"Yes, I was up early. I've given Celia fair warning, she's not going to laze in bed half the morning when we're married."

"When you're married? You'll leave her in a fit state to do nothing else, that's my guess."

Ashton smiled, but didn't laugh. Richard wondered if the remark was a bit strong—all right for the smoking room, but not for breakfast. He had taken the hint from his friend to bait Sharp, who blushed and concentrated hard on his boiled egg.

"Shocking fellows, these cavalry officers, what?" Ashton said for Sharp's benefit.

"I'm not your chaplain, Captain Ashton," Sharp replied mildly.

Lady Farnham came in, with her habitual air of being slightly late for an appointment. The men stood up.

"Don't move, gentlemen, please. I always tell myself I must be in the breakfast room before my guests, but I never manage it. Are you taking kidneys, Lord Richard? We're rather proud of our kidneys. Mr. Sharp, you don't propose to face the day on a boiled egg, I trust? I won't have it, I positively won't have it."

Gradually, the room filled up. There was the Earl, and Arthur Colmore, and Charlotte, and the other guests: two more young men—the Farnhams, naturally, were filling the house with eligible young men—two married couples, and a widow with her daughter. Celia and Fanny didn't appear until it was almost time for church. The younger Colmores —Ellie, Anne, and little Tommy—had breakfast in the nursery.

Church, and the civilities by the lych-gate afterwards, occupied most of the morning. As the guest of the highest social rank, Richard was seated in the family pew between

Lady Farnham and Charlotte, so he was careful not to snooze. Charlotte mumbled her Amen's as he did and didn't speak the prayers. He had imagined her to be devout; evidently she wasn't. Plain girls were not invariably devout, he supposed, though it could be assumed that pretty girls invariably were not.

Luncheon was generous and excellent, and kept them indoors during the heat of the day. It didn't turn out to be a scorcher, however; it was perfect for England in June.

"Now," said Lady Farnham, "we old people are going to rest, and you young ones are going to walk off your luncheon. You must see the barrows. They're our only local distinction —it's positively a duty. Arthur, gather your company and lead the way."

It was Fanny who led the way, walking with an energy that would have been unfeminine but for her charm. Two young men placed themselves on either side of her. Richard wasn't practised enough to secure this position in time, so he walked with Charlotte. Arthur was with the widow's daughter, with Sharp vaguely in attendance. Ashton and Celia brought up the rear and were tacitly allowed to fall farther and farther behind; indeed, they never reached the barrows.

The barrows were about a mile and a half from the house, not far enough to tire the ladies. They were whale-backed mounds, standing undisturbed in rough pasture and covered with the springy turf of the Downs. Charlotte explained to Richard that, according to antiquarians, they were the graves of ancient British chiefs. It must have been a lot of work making them with primitive tools—a labour of piety. He liked the gentle contours, softened doubtless by time, and the way that the barrows seemed almost to grow out of the land. How old were they? he asked. Probably two thousand five hundred years, Charlotte said; they would have been antiquities to the Romans, as medieval castles were to the nineteenth century. Richard was impressed. It was good to think of men living and working in England all those centuries ago: men who, savage and uncouth though they might have been, had tilled the soil, loved and defended their land, buried their great men with honour, and left a heritage to the generations.

Somehow or other, he and Charlotte found themselves lingering near the barrows after the rest of the party had started to walk back to the house. Her company was congenial, or at least it suited the place and the mood. He wasn't obliged to keep thinking of jokes and pleasantries as he would have been with Fanny. Indeed, Charlotte seemed perfectly content with silence. But after a while he felt called upon to make some remark, and said: "I'm afraid this outing isn't much of a novelty for you, Miss Colmore."

"I don't mind that," she answered. "I like it. But as you saw, it has always figured in Mamma's orders. When we were younger, we were sent off to sketch the barrows whenever she wanted to get rid of us."

"You must let me see your sketches."

"They're nothing much. I'm just good enough to enjoy trying. Do you sketch, Lord Richard?"

"I've tried. Very little talent indeed, I fear."

"I trust you'll find time to sketch some of the antiquities of India."

"Oh, I hope to," he said, though he hadn't thought of it. "But no barrows, alas. Don't the natives burn their dead?"

"Yes. The dead, and the widows."

Richard had heard of this, but considered it an unpleasant topic for a lady. "I believe we've pretty well stamped that out," he said.

"Perhaps." Charlotte began to walk back, lifting her skirts above the untended grass. "It's only the Hindoos who burn their dead, I think. The Muhammadans have graveyards, like us."

Richard wasn't sure. She was probably right, though he wondered where she could have picked up the information.

"Yes, the Muhammadans are the more advanced," he said.

"No, the Hindoos are the educated classes."

"Ah, yes. Of course." The flat contradiction jolted him; it was new to his experience of conversation with ladies. Like her mother, Charlotte was very positive.

"Three years is a long time to spend in a country," she said. "We shall expect you to be an authority on India when we see you again."

"I hope indeed that we shall meet again, Miss Colmore. One can easily forget a weekend guest in three years."

"Oh, but surely you won't lose touch with Captain Ashton and Celia?"

"No, no. Of course not." She had put him right again, deuce take it. "But three years bring changes," he said. "Your sister and her husband may well be a settled couple with a growing family. Funny to think of, what?"

"Why is that funny, Lord Richard?"

Quite astonished this time, he looked straight at her. She returned the look; her eyes examined him seriously, like a man's. Rather fine grey eyes, despite her unprepossessing features. Confused, he looked away.

"I don't exactly mean funny," he said. "Chose the wrong word. I mean—I'd have to get used to it."

"So will they, won't they?"

"Well . . ." He could only treat this as a joke, though Charlotte wasn't smiling. "I suppose so. I daresay a young lady sometimes has to pinch herself to convince herself that she's a wife."

"Do you think Celia is doing well to marry Captain Ashton, Lord Richard?"

"Certainly. Splendid fellow. Been like an elder brother to

me, you know." Extraordinary question, he thought. Extraordinary conversation.

"I'm glad you say that. I didn't imply anything to his disadvantage. Only, I know very little of him. Celia knows very little of him, really."

"Enough to accept him, surely, Miss Colmore."

"And that can be little enough. Never mind, though. She's getting married; it's very gratifying to the family."

"Ashton and your sister are marrying for love, though, aren't they? Don't you think—if I may be so bold as to ask—don't you think one should marry for love?"

"We're always told so." She spoke as though it were open to question.

"Well . . . I can only look at it as a man, Miss Colmore. If I proposed marriage to a young lady whom I didn't love, I should consider myself guilty of deception."

"I needn't expect you to ask for my hand, then, Lord Richard."

There was no way, that he could see, of responding to this. He mumbled something indeterminate, cleared his throat, and hoped that the subject was closed. Charlotte walked steadily on, apparently unaware of any embarrassment. Poor thing, Richard thought; she had probably reconciled herself by now to getting no proposals and was facing it with sardonic courage.

She said in a steady voice (but her voice was always steady): "What d'you make of those clouds? It couldn't rain, I hope, after this lovely day."

It didn't rain. The evening, indeed, was so mild that Richard and Ralph Ashton were able to take a stroll on the lawn before bed. Richard moved in a serenity whose components were good food, claret, old port, and the aroma of one of Lord Farnham's excellent cigars. Beside him, his friend's pace matched his own. For several minutes they didn't speak —felt no need to speak. There was a concord in a stroll like this, easy and undemanding. Easier with a friend, Richard found himself thinking, than with a woman.

But it was their last evening together, for three years at least. Ashton was staying at Longmarsh for another fortnight; Richard had only one more week's leave, and naturally it would be spent with his parents at Severalls. After that he would be with the regiment, immersed in the bustle of preparing for embarkation.

And when they met again, it would not be quite the same. There would be other evenings, in town or at Severalls or, Richard hoped, at Longmarsh. But, after the port and the cigars, the natural ending of Richard's day would be sleep, while Ashton's would be—Celia.

What was it like, Richard wondered—marriage, or rather that very private aspect of marriage? Did one look forward to it with a renewal of the desires that one had felt before they were first satisfied? Or did it become a mere habit, an obligation? He would never be able to ask his friend. They had talked about women, of course, as young men do. Talking about a fellow's wife was another matter.

He imagined Celia as she would be for her husband. She wasn't the beauty of the family—Fanny was that—but she was a fine-looking girl. Unusual, rather fascinating large eyes. Silky brown hair, probably very long when it was unpinned. Quite a bosom. Excellent figure, altogether. Richard checked his thoughts; in Ashton's presence, they seemed almost as indecent as if they'd been put into words.

"Think I'll turn in," he said, throwing away his cigar. "Up early tomorrow. I looked up the trains—I'd better catch the nine-five."

"I shall be up, don't worry."

"Goodnight then, Ashton."

"Goodnight, Somers."

Richard undressed slowly, standing by the window and gazing down at the lawn, which now glistened in the moonlight. Then, rather reluctantly, he went to bed. He didn't fall asleep for a good half-hour; for him, it was most unusual.

CHAPTER 2

Champagne
and Its Consequences

Although the feeling was unworthy, Richard was impatient to get through his farewell stay at Severalls. His friends —the other subalterns in his squadron—were in London enjoying a final fling. There had been talk of feminine company, champagne by the magnum, and high jinks of every kind. The feminine company was guaranteed by Harry Fielding, an acknowledged expert in such matters. There wasn't much time; they had to join the regiment at the weekend— on Saturday, indeed, because it was at a place without Sunday trains. Richard hoped to get to London by Wednesday, or Thursday at the latest, but his mother was prostrated by migraine when he should have been receiving her parting kisses, and he had to stay until Friday. To make matters worse, the fine weather collapsed into thundery rain (storms were the worst time for migraine, the Duchess often said) and Richard could scarcely get out of doors. In the vast rooms with their high ceilings, it was even chilly.

The Duke, Richard's father, was a robust and broad-shouldered man in his early fifties, still without a grey hair and an energetic Master of the Berkshire Hunt. He had succeeded to the title only eight years ago. Richard could well remember his grandfather, the fifth Duke, a survivor of the

Regency era who took snuff and said "Demme"; he had fought in the Peninsula, voted against the First Reform Bill, and died at the age of eighty-three.

The sixth Duke had married young and emphatically for love. Richard's mother had been one of the leading beauties of her time; Severalls had a dozen portraits of her by distinguished artists. She was petite, dark—a colouring which she hadn't transmitted—and delicately shaped; when she felt faint, her husband carried her about like a child. As far back as Richard could remember, she had been a martyr to palpitations, migraine, and mysterious internal ailments, never exactly dangerous but calling for regular medical attention and constant rest. From occasional hints, Richard gathered that childbearing had ruined her constitution. She had endured agonies for his brother and himself, with a series of miscarriages in between. Though she didn't ride and never went out in uncertain weather, country air was a necessity for her and she spent as little time as possible at Berkshire House, the London residence in Park Lane. The Duke, who liked spells of town life, maintained what was virtually a bachelor establishment there. The Duchess was extremely pious and insisted on the highest moral standards; housemaids had been dismissed for allowing themselves to be kissed, not even in the corridors of Severalls but in the village on their free days. Inclined to tolerance, and no more religious than his position required, the Duke thought this a bit hard.

The Marquis of Wantage—Richard's brother, George—was not at Severalls, being detained in London by the parliamentary session. Eight years older than Richard, he was still unmarried despite paternal promptings. He didn't shine in society, and his favourite company was his own. His main interest was farming and he had definite ideas about estate management.

Last year, at the 1874 election which gave Disraeli a healthy

majority, George had become Member of Parliament for
West Berkshire. He hadn't the least desire to go to Westminster; he disliked London, he had little interest in politics, and
the idea of making speeches appalled him. But it was a firm
tradition that a Somers should occupy the seat. A cousin of
the Duke's had held it for twenty years until, stricken by gout,
he had been flatly unable to stand again. For George, as the
Duke made clear, there was no choice. Resigned to his fate,
he found that it wasn't too bad. One wasn't compelled to
speak, and he overcame his reserve enough to explain his
views on agriculture to men of influence in the smoking
room. Still, he counted the days until the House rose. When
in London, he lived quietly in a set of rooms in the Albany.

Friday morning came at last. Below the double stairway
that mounted from the entrance hall of Severalls, the staff
waited to say goodbye: footmen, housemaids, cooks and
kitchen maids, gardeners, coachmen, grooms and stableboys.
Richard moved along the line, chatting for a couple of minutes with those of higher status—the butler, the Duke's valet,
the head gardener—shaking hands with the other men, pausing while the women made their curtseys. He had to bite his
lip at the thought that there were some whom he might
never see again. Old Jenkins, who had taught him to ride
his first pony, was well over seventy. Prescott, the kennel-
man, coughed uncontrollably and was thin as a rake; the
next hard winter could carry him off.

The stationmaster hurried out to the road when he heard
the carriage. The Duke chatted to him amiably as they
strolled toward the platform, while the porters took charge
of Richard's boxes. The Duchess decided to stay in the carriage; too much excitement, and loud noises like the whistling and puffing of the engine, were a strain on her nerves.
She lifted her veil and Richard kissed her, feeling her little
hands tremble as they touched his face. He could think of

nothing to say except: "Don't cry, Mater, please." Her tears had always embarrassed him when he went off to school.

There was a crowd on the platform—some tenants, the gamekeepers and occasional staff, and a few people who were actually travelling. The stationmaster kept looking anxiously at his watch, but the train was dead on time. Richard saw his boxes safely loaded in the van, trying to behave as if no one were watching him. Then he walked briskly to his reserved compartment, where the stationmaster was holding the door open.

"Goodbye, Richard," said the Duke.

"Goodbye, Pater."

"Mind you write to us."

"Of course, Pater."

"Well, mustn't keep the train waiting."

They shook hands. The Duke's grip, as always, was strong to the verge of being painful.

Richard shook hands with the stationmaster, got into the compartment, and lowered the window.

"Three cheers for Lord Richard!" shouted the stationmaster, raising his top hat in the air. The hurrahs resounded; Richard smiled and raised his own hat in response.

"Three cheers for his Grace!" Again the hurrahs, merging this time with the thudding of the engine. The train began to move. Richard stayed at the window, moving, until he saw his father turn away. Then he sat down and lit a cigar. He was on his own, he was a man—he couldn't help feeling elated.

From Paddington he went to Berkshire House and left his luggage. There was a note from Harry Fielding: "mighty plans" were on foot for the evening, and they were to meet at a famous West End restaurant. Meanwhile, Richard had just time to get to the House of Commons, where George was giving him a farewell lunch.

George's conversation, as usual, wasn't scintillating. He asked after their parents, and talked a little about the wet weather and its effect on the crops, and about farming in general. Considering that "our side" was in office, not enough was being done for the landed interest, in his opinion. This reflection plunged him into deep thought, which Richard was happy to leave undisturbed.

After the meal, George took Richard on a tour of the House. It was a surprisingly big place—echoing corridors and wide staircases and mysterious corners, quite like Eton. Today it was more like Eton on a half-holiday; as it was Friday, most of the Members had started their weekends. A few greeted George in the Members' lobby. They didn't exactly strike Richard as the flower of the nation. The House was spoken of as the best club in London, but Richard suspected that this phrase dated from before the First Reform Act, certainly the Second. No doubt most of the Members were gentlemen, the Liberals as well as our side—it was wrong to be prejudiced. But there were also the Radicals, loud-mouthed fellows with no ideas except to turn everything upside down and come out on top; and the Irish Nationalists, who were not even loyal to the Crown; and at the last election the Liberals had brought in a few labouring men—colliers, Richard believed—who probably felt embarrassed at being so out of place. No, it wasn't a club that he would have cared to belong to.

He said goodbye to George and spent half an hour in the gallery. One Member was speaking almost inaudibly to about a dozen others. Richard had hoped to see some celebrities— Disraeli himself, with luck—but he was disappointed. There seemed to be no point in staying; besides, he had to visit his banker and make some last-minute purchases during the afternoon.

In the end, he had only just time to take a bath and change —and put down a quick whisky, which he somehow felt to be necessary—before taking a hansom to the restaurant. When he went in, he couldn't see Fielding or the others. He consulted his watch; he was dead on time. The manager approached.

"Excuse me, sir—are you one of Captain Fielding's party?"

Richard said that he was. Presumably all military gentlemen were captains to this fellow.

"If you'd be so kind as to come this way, sir."

There was more to the restaurant than one might have suspected. As well as the ground floor, which was open to anyone, and the first floor, which could be reserved for banquets and club dinners, there was an upper floor with a long corridor, lined with numbered doors. The manager conducted Richard to number six, at the far end.

He paused for a moment. A gay medley of voices, male and female, came from number six. Richard gave a pat to his hair, adjusted his tie, and opened the door. There they were—Fielding and Smythe and Robertson-Haig. And four young ladies, or girls, or whatever one said.

Unlike other dining rooms in Richard's experience, this one had no chairs. Two walls were lined with upholstered benches, and a table fitted into a right-angle. The rest of the room was just big enough for serving tables, and one of them was already loaded with ice-buckets containing, doubtless, champagne.

"Here he is!" Fielding shouted. The men set up a cheer, in which the girls joined, as if Richard were arriving at a cricket club dinner after scoring the winning boundary.

"By Jove, I was afraid you were going to miss the festivities. Allow me to present some friends of the regiment. The gorgeous Jenny, pretty Polly, the delectable Kitty, and the splendiferous Lucy. Ladies, needless to say this is Dick whom you have been so eagerly awaiting."

The girl called Kitty, who was sitting on Fielding's left, said: "I think he looks sweet. Come and sit next to me, Dicky-boy. Come along, don't be frightened. I'm quite easy to get along with really."

Richard obeyed. The girl called Lucy had to stand up for him to take his place between Kitty and her. He mumbled an apology as he edged past her; she replied with a friendly smile.

Kitty started to chatter to him. Easy to get on with, she certainly was. She kept on calling him Dicky—ridiculous, really. To the few people entitled to use his Christian name, he had always been Richard; presumably Fielding had decided that "Dick" suited these surroundings. Richard found that he quite liked it, and also liked the curious way in which everyone called everyone else by Christian names. The feeling of being incognito stressed that this was an adventure; it was a world away from Severalls and "Three cheers for Lord Richard!"

Had he just come up from the country? Kitty asked. What part of the country? Berkshire—wasn't that on the river? She adored the river; she'd spent days on the river last summer with some fellows who had a boat—a launch, was that right? —once gliding along all through a moonlit night and seeing the dawn come up—glorious!

Lucy interrupted to say that she didn't trust boats; once she'd been sitting up at the front end, the bow or whatever you called it, and the wretched boat had tipped up and thrown her into the water. Both the girls laughed and laughed. Kitty shrieked with laughter—there was no other word—but Lucy gave a kind of delicious throaty gurgle.

Fielding hadn't been boasting about his knowledge of the fair sex, Richard thought. All four girls were absolute stunners. Kitty, in particular, was what he imagined in a girl of this type. Her features were irregular, to the point perhaps of being rather common, but in the other sense of the word most uncommon: eyes that slanted intriguingly, a little upturned nose, a mouth simply made for kissing, and a chin that oddly vanished away. A face that wasn't to be taken seriously, but charming—absolutely charming.

Lucy was different. Her face was a perfect oval; in any drawing room, she could have passed for a young lady of breeding. Only her twinkling black eyes might have betrayed her. Her skin was a rich olive colour, and there was a good deal of it to be seen, as there was of all the girls. Her arms were bare, her shoulders were bare, and her dress was cut so low that Richard wondered how it stayed up. Just where revelation was imminent, she wore a rose at the transient perfection of rosehood.

Richard asked her if she had Italian blood.

"Oh, you are a good guesser. Yes, Italian's what I am. Born there—came to London as a baby. I'm Lucia really, but Lucy's easier for English people to say."

"Lucia is beautiful. As beautiful as you."

"Oh, I say, Kitty, he does know how to tell the tale, doesn't he?"

The waiters began to serve the meal. They progressed through oxtail soup, shrimps, Dover sole, roast veal, devilled eggs, pancakes and cherry tart to strawberries and cream, ending with Welsh rarebit as a savoury. Richard tucked in heartily, but the girls took only a few mouthfuls of each course.

"You're starving yourself," he told Lucy.

"It's for your sake," she answered. "I'm sure you appreciate a nice waist." She grasped his hand and held it for a moment at the point in question. A delicious slender waist—and no sign of a corset.

Meanwhile, they drank champagne and nothing but champagne. Every now and then the waiters came in with fresh buckets, or the girls screamed in mock terror at an exceptionally loud pop. Richard hadn't the least idea how many bottles they were getting through. Of course, nobody who was anywhere near being a gentleman would count.

He couldn't help thinking of what the evening might lead to. The girls weren't ladies, obviously, but they weren't like street-walkers either. Were they prepared to yield utterly, or did they stop at providing company for a jolly evening with a bit of flirting and kissing? Perhaps it depended on whether a girl liked you; perhaps you had to persuade her. Richard wasn't sure if he was up to that.

But if everything was possible, ought he to make a set for Kitty or Lucy? Each was entrancing in her own way. However, when dinner was cleared away Fielding put his arm round Kitty and began to stroke her slender arm with a habitual air, as a man might stroke a favourite dog. She leaned back on him, smiling happily; he bent and kissed her cheek. Richard remembered that there had been other evenings while he was stuck at Severalls. All right, he thought; it wouldn't be at all the done thing to compete with Fielding. And he decided that Lucy was the pick of the bunch, really.

He tried to think of a seductive remark, but nothing occurred to him. A silence had fallen between them; any remark would be better than nothing. He said: "That's a lovely rose you've got there, Lucy, honestly it is."

She gave him a sly, provoking smile and said: "Oh, but the scent's the best of it."

He bent down and smelled the rose. His head swam—not with the champagne, surely—and he had to make a distinct effort to regain his balance.

"D'you like it, Dick?"

"Magnificent."

"It's yours."

She unpinned it and fastened it to his lapel. He didn't trust himself to look where the rose had been.

The manager appeared and asked: "Was everything to your liking, gentlemen?"

"First-rate," Fielding said. "Good enough for Royalty."

"Royalty isn't unknown here, Captain." They all chuckled at this. "Would you care for some brandy? I have a brandy, if I may make a guess, that's older than anyone at this table."

"Let's stick to fizz, Harry," Kitty said. "Always dangerous to mix."

"That's right, my dear. Stick to good old fizz."

"Champagne then, gentlemen?"

"Yes, just keep it flowing."

More bottles arrived and were emptied. Robertson-Haig said: "Give us a song, Polly, do." The suggestion was applauded; evidently Polly's voice was among her attractions. She sang "The Enniskilling Dragoon," quietly and melodiously, still reclining in Robertson-Haig's arms. The song created a languorous, faintly melancholy atmosphere. Richard thought of how long it would be before he enjoyed another evening like this, and knew that all his friends were thinking the same.

He realised that he was the only man who didn't have his arm round a girl, and hastened to put this right. Lucy smiled up at him.

"I must tell you, Dick—you have the darlingest moustache."

"Oh, dash it, scores of fellows have moustaches."

"I'm not talking about scores of fellows, I'm talking about you. You know what the song says?"

"What?"

She chanted in a light, pretty voice: " 'Kissing a man without a moustache, Is like eating an egg without salt.' " Then her eyes twinkled, and she said demurely: "I like salt."

He wasn't sure what happened then. Positively, he'd intended to kiss her on the cheek. But somehow his lips found hers; or hers found his; or a kind of magnetism was at work, irresistible, magical, intoxicating.

After the kiss he sat quite still, content for the present with the nearness of Lucy. He felt tremendously well and happy, full of vigour and confidence, ready for anything and superlatively wide awake. It seemed to him that any sensation, from a gallop over the fences to kissing this entrancing girl, would yield a keener pleasure now than ever in his life. It was the champagne, he thought—just the right amount of light, foaming, dancing fizz. One couldn't feel like this sozzled with brandy, nor cold sober. There was nothing like champagne, he decided.

Suddenly there was a noise in the corridor. A woman was screaming, and a man was shouting: "Come here, blast you! I'll teach you, damn your eyes!" Fielding pushed the table away, strode across the room, and opened the door. The woman—a girl like these girls, though not so pretty—was trying to escape to the stairs, but the man was clutching her wrist. Her dress was torn, and while she struggled she was trying to cover her bodice with one hand. The man wore impeccable evening-dress, but something about him—the bull neck above his collar and his red bulbous nose—showed at a glance that he was no gentleman.

The door of number four was also open. Other men were shouting, either at their friend or at the girl, and other girls were screaming too. Richard couldn't see how many there were—it seemed to be a large party.

Fielding stepped up to the man and said: "Let that lady go, sir, d'you hear me?"

"Mind your damned business, sir," the man retorted.

"This is anybody's business. You're a cad, sir."

"He's a beast," the girl cried. "He's trying to rape me."

"Here, I say, that's a whopper," interrupted another man from number four.

"It's the truth," yelled a girl. "He tried to strip her, in front of everybody."

"Let go of her wrist, anyway. You're hurting her," Fielding said.

"Step aside, sir. I warn you."

"I shan't step aside unless . . ."

Suddenly releasing the girl, the bull-necked man struck Fielding on the jaw with his closed fist. He was a powerful fellow—a pug for all they knew, Richard thought. Fielding reeled and fell against the wall.

Richard didn't hesitate. He put up his guard automatically and landed a punch on the bully's nose. It was splendid to feel the swollen flesh crumple and see the bloodshot eyes contract. Just as he'd thought, every sensation tonight was raised gloriously above the normal.

In a matter of seconds, there was pandemonium. Richard caught a stinging blow across his ear and replied with a punch that achieved nothing except to bruise his knuckles on a stiff shirt. Robertson-Haig, coming to his rescue, was seized by two men and thrown through the doorway into number four. Smythe dashed after him. Tables thudded to the floor, plates and glasses smashed. The girls scurried about, and most of them managed to get down the stairs. In the corridor, Richard had his back to the wall, defending himself against three men. Fielding, still dazed, wasn't able to help. Richard was still exhilarated and not in the least afraid, but he was aware that the cavalrymen were outnumbered.

Then, mysteriously, he was alone and no one was attacking him. For what could only have been a few moments, he was baffled. Someone tugged at his arm—it was Lucy.

"Come on! Come on!"

"What d'you mean?"

"It's the peelers. Didn't you hear the whistle? Come on!"

She dragged him through a door at the end of the corridor, which he hadn't noticed because it was set flush in the wall. She knew her way here, evidently. They went through what must have been the manager's private apartment, down some stairs, and out of a door that gave on to a back yard. A maze of evil-smelling alleys led them to a street—not the same street as at the front of the restaurant.

"Where are we, Lucy?"

"That's Leicester Square down there. We'll easily get a cab."

"By Jove, I hope so." Richard was acutely conscious of having left his hat in the restaurant and of Lucy's low-cut dress.

They found a cab. While Richard was trying to think of where to go—could he risk taking Lucy to Berkshire House? —she spoke to the driver. He leaned back against the leather.

"Are you hurt much, Dick?"

"Not a scrap."

"You were wonderful. I've never seen anything so brave."

"Oh, nonsense."

"You're sure you haven't cut your lip?"

He felt it. "No."

"Why don't you kiss me, then?"

He was aware, briefly, of clattering hooves and the gleam of gas-lamps; then of nothing but Lucy's lips, and Lucy's bosom pressed to his shirt-front, and Lucy's bare shoulders.

The cab stopped. He gave the man a sovereign and waved away the change. They went in a short, narrow street—a mews.

"Where's this?"

"Home."

She had two rooms over a stable; the smell of hay and horses reached him pleasantly as he followed her upstairs. The rooms were small and low-ceilinged, but delightfully done up: gaily striped wallpapers, armchairs and sofa with chintz covers, two stuffed dolls on the mantelpiece, a Swiss cuckoo clock. It was more like a young girl's nursery than the home of a— well, what Lucy was.

She lit the gas, came close to him, and said: "You have got a bruise, you know."

"It's nothing, really."

"Oh, look what I've done to my dress in that filthy yard. I must change. Sit down there, Dick. Have a brandy—you certainly deserve it. It's in that corner cupboard. And smoke if you like, I don't mind."

She disappeared into the other room—it must be a bedroom. He felt happier than ever. The brandy was welcome, the cigar even more so. When she came back, she was wearing a dressing-gown that showed her ankles and a tantalising few inches of leg. She stood in the middle of the room for a moment, then settled on his knees. He realised that there was nothing between the dressing-gown and the delicious promise of her flesh.

"You must finish your cigar," she said five minutes later.

"No, dash it, never mind about the cigar."

"Come along, then."

He'd never thought before how awkward men's clothes were—evening-dress particularly—and how irritatingly long it took to deal with all the buttons and studs and cuff-links. She lay in bed, only her face visible, gazing dreamily at the ceiling; she must have tactfully slipped out of her gown and slid between the sheets in a moment when he was looking the other way. Tactfully, too, she didn't look at him while he took off his combinations. He got into bed, but didn't touch her. Her nakedness and his own nakedness were two strange and enormous facts. He wondered how one began—should he kiss her as he'd kissed her in the other room, or didn't kissing belong to what was done in bed, or ought he to say something? Nothing occurred to him. Then he felt her hands on his body, first one and then the other.

"It's your first time, darling, isn't it?" she murmured.

"What? What the deuce d'you mean?"

"You're sweet. Don't worry, it's going to be lovely."

And it was lovely. It was a wild excitement, a release and triumph of the body, transcending all excitement he had ever known. Yet somehow, at the same time, it was soft and tender and beautiful, as Lucy's body beneath him was soft and tender and beautiful.

When it was done, he lay on his back, proud and contented, fully a man. She snuggled beside him, her face buried in his neck and her hair strewn across his chest, breathing gently. A lamp at the corner of the mews cast a delicate light, and the smell of the stable came faintly through the window. It was very quiet and peaceful, but once he heard the distant rhythm of hooves, and then the cuckoo clock sounded and he counted the strokes to twelve. He cast his mind back over the evening. High jinks, indeed. He wondered if the other fellows had got away. At all events, the police wouldn't make trouble for officers under orders for India.

"Are you asleep, Dicky?" Lucy whispered.

"No, I'm not asleep."

She gave a deep sigh, and her hands moved on his body again. He felt surer of himself this time. It was as wonderful as before—more wonderful. But after it, he dropped straight into sleep.

The sun woke him. He almost dozed off again, but realised that he must find out what time it was. He had to get back to Berkshire House and change—he absolutely mustn't miss his train. Lucy was still asleep, but she had moved away from him and he was able to get out of bed without disturbing her. To his relief, his watch showed only a quarter past six. He hesitated; breakfast with Lucy and parting kisses would be a further pleasure. But if he got back into bed, he might oversleep —it was too much of a risk. Besides, it wouldn't do to be seen, in evening dress and hatless, by anyone he knew. As quietly as he could, he dressed.

Before he left, he very gently pulled back the bedclothes. Lucy lay on her back, arms bent and hands on the pillow, like

a child. All over her body, her skin had the same softly lumi-
nous colour as her face, as if sunlight ran in her veins. Her
breasts had blue circles round the nipples. Extraordinary thing
—or did all women have that, he wondered? The hair between her legs was jet black, tightly curled, and very short.
Perhaps she trimmed it as he trimmed his moustache. He enjoyed the moment, a last instalment of loveliness. But it wasn't
the thing to do, looking at a woman like this, even a woman
of Lucy's kind. She stirred, and he hastily covered her again.

Some people—ladies like his mother, of course, and some
men too—would take a high moral tone about Lucy. She was
a whore, Richard supposed, if one wanted to use such words.
A harlot, as the Bible said. But he couldn't think of her like
that. He couldn't quite work it out, but it seemed to him that
evil couldn't belong with such beauty. There was a beauty of
the London streets as well as a beauty of the unspoiled countryside; and there was a beauty of girls like Kitty and Lucy as
well as a beauty of pure young ladies like his future wife—
whoever that might be. It wasn't at all the same, of course.
Yet it was all a part of the wonderfully varied beauty of England, the heritage and delight of Englishmen.

He left a fiver on the dressing table—that was right, he
thought. Then he tiptoed down the stairs, remembering not to
slam the doors. It was a calm, perfect morning. He still felt
superlatively well and hadn't a trace of a thick head. He
walked a short way and reached a main street—Notting Hill
Gate. It wasn't a district where he often found himself, but he
realised that he could walk to Berkshire House through Kensington Gardens and Hyde Park. No one would be likely to see
him at this hour, or no one who mattered.

On the Serpentine Bridge, he paused and leaned on the bal-
ustrade. There was beauty here too: the calm of the lake, the
trees in full leaf, the curious turrets of the India Office, the

proud tower of Big Ben. Through the trees, he caught a glimpse of a troop of Life Guards from Knightsbridge Barracks exercising their mounts in Rotten Row. He was glad to take this memory, too, as he said farewell to England.

CHAPTER 3

The Strange Behaviour of Mrs. Ashton

As Lady Farnham was often to say in tones of honest bewilderment, no one could have had a happier childhood and youth than Ellie. The Farnhams were easy-going parents, not exactly indulgent—knowing themselves inclined to it, they resisted the temptation to spoil their children—but averse to rules and prohibitions that were not clearly necessary. They genuinely liked children, were glad to have so many, and created an atmosphere of affection without any conscious effort. Ellie received even more affection than the others, because she was what the Farnhams considered to be an ideal child—that is, a child who finds the golden mean between being a goody-goody and being naughty. She wasn't lacking in liveliness and fun, but she was never wilfully disobedient. You could count on your fingers, Lady Farnham also said, the times when Ellie had to be punished.

Like her brothers and sisters, Ellie was allowed to do as she pleased within reasonable limits. The grounds of Longmarsh were a wide world for a child; there were bluebell woods, hedgerows thick with blackberries, streams where they could fish for tiddlers, hills down which they raced in summer and tobogganed in winter. Ellie had everything a girl could want —her pet rabbits, her spaniel, her pony. She always seemed grateful, and always contented; it was a pleasure to give her pleasure. And she was good at occupying herself. Fanny, as a girl, used to hang about asking "What can I do next?" but Ellie never minded being left to her own devices. On a wet day, she didn't grumble if an outing had to be cancelled; she was quite happy with her paint-box or her crotchet-work, happiest of all curled up in a chair with a book. Often she surprised everyone by being quiet for hours at a time. Longmarsh was on the whole a noisy house, and it became a family joke to say: "Somebody go and see if Ellie's fallen down the well."

Ellie was clever, too—not too clever for a girl but, as with her other qualities, just right. Miss Frayn, the governess, put it very well: Ellie made the best use of the brains that God had given her. And that, as Miss Frayn told the Vicar's wife in confidence, was by no means true of all the Colmore girls. Fanny was hopeless—she had enough intelligence if she cared to use it, but she never did care. If she chose to play and laugh her way through life, Miss Frayn couldn't help it. Celia, and later on little Anne, were simply not cut out for book-learning. It was no tragedy for them, but it made teaching them a joyless chore from Miss Frayn's point of view. Only Charlotte and Ellie rewarded Miss Frayn's efforts. Charlotte had to try hard, poor thing; she doubtless realised that she might never find a husband and her brains would be her best friend. Ellie just happened to have had all the good fairies round her cradle.

So Miss Frayn was able to give consistently good reports: for spelling and handwriting, for Bible knowledge, for sums, for French. Ellie could well have thought of a profession had she been a boy, in Miss Frayn's opinion. Miss Baldwin, who came three times a week to teach the piano, was equally pleased with her pupil. Not only this: from about the age of twelve, Ellie enjoyed reading grown-up books. She devoured Dickens and Thackeray and Mrs. Gaskell, as well as Sir

Walter Scott's and Lord Lytton's historical romances, and she amazed her father by reciting long poems like "The Ancient Mariner" and "The Charge of the Light Brigade." Her mother cautioned Miss Frayn not to encourage this passion for reading to excess. One didn't want Ellie to turn into a bookworm; and, with her looks, it would be disastrous if she strained her eyes and had to wear glasses.

For, on top of everything else, Ellie was beautiful. So long as she was a child, it was generally said in the county that Fanny was the beauty of the family. But when Ellie was sixteen and came down to dinner in grown-up dresses, anyone with half an eye could see the difference. Fanny was bewitching when she smiled, and had half the young men for miles around dying for that smile; but older women noted that when the smile was absent—still more, when she wore her sulky expression—her features were unremarkable. On the other hand, when you looked at Ellie, whether she was reading a book or placidly listening to a conversation, you were looking at the true beauty that depends neither on art nor on expression. It was English beauty at its finest—the beauty of golden hair, limpid blue eyes, a clear and healthy complexion, a pure brow, a head poised finely on a graceful neck. The Colmores were agreed to be the oldest family in the county, tracing themselves to a union between one of the Conqueror's barons and a Saxon princess. Maturing through nine centuries, the inheritance had reached perfection in Ellie.

Afterwards, Lady Farnham traced her first anxieties about Ellie to that summer of 1877. Sixteen was a difficult age, of course. After the carefree joys of childhood, a girl faced the adult world with an unavoidable awareness of her inexperience. Men, for the first time, were men to her and not merely friends of her parents or of her older brothers and sisters. She couldn't yet accept compliments from them or think of them as suitors, but she couldn't help seeing the admiration in their glances. From older girls—in Ellie's case, the irrepressible Fanny—she was likely to hear remarks and stories that stimulated unsuitable thoughts. An awkward, in-between period, Lady Farnham recalled from her own memories.

It affected Ellie in several ways. She had always been modest, but now she was shy. She stammered when she answered questions from strangers, whereas her speech hitherto had been exceptionally clear. She no longer enjoyed weekend house parties, and was downcast when she heard that guests were expected. She avoided the company of young men—not only avoided being alone with one, which was of course proper, but was reluctant to join in an outing that included young men in the plural, which to Lady Farnham's mind was excessive. More than ever, she was happiest with a book and liked to be alone. Yet, puzzlingly, there were also times when she couldn't bear to be alone. If she woke up early in the morning, she sometimes knocked on her mother's door, or on Charlotte's, and sought company like a little girl.

Lady Farnham didn't worry much about these growing pains, as she considered them to be. But she might have paid more attention to Ellie, she thought later, if she hadn't been worrying about Fanny and Celia.

During the London season, the family was divided. Lord Farnham stayed in the country with the younger children; Lady Farnham was at the town house with Charlotte and Fanny. The season was a painful time for her. While Fanny—nineteen this year—was drawing the young men like flies and rejecting proposals every week, Charlotte's hopes were as dim as ever. After the last June dances, Lady Farnham prepared with relief to reunite the family, only to find that Fanny was invited to stay with her uncle and aunt (Lady Farnham's sister) at their place in Staffordshire. There was no plausible reason to forbid the girl to go, and Lady Farnham had every confidence in her sister. Still, Staffordshire was a long way off, she knew very little about her sister's set, and as the visit lengthened beyond the original fortnight she became positive that Fanny was carrying on some quite unsuitable flirtation. Letters, as one might expect with Fanny, there were none. Her thoughts often turned on ways of summoning Fanny home, or finding a reason to visit Staffordshire herself, but she wasn't an inventive woman and nothing occurred to her.

If the worry about Fanny arose because she wasn't at Longmarsh, the worry about Celia arose because she was. She ought, clearly, to have been with her husband. About four months ago, Ralph Ashton had gone to Ireland, the General whom he attended as aide-de-camp having been given the Irish command. Celia, down at Longmarsh for a weekend, complained bitterly. She didn't know a soul in Dublin, she said, and it was ghastly to be torn away from London with the season just coming on. She had gone to endless trouble to get her house as she wanted it—the Ashtons had a charming house in South Audley St.—with the right furniture and satisfactory servants, who were none too easy to find nowadays. Now she would have to close it, or let it, or sell it—really, she had no idea, and Ralph expected her to make all such decisions. It was terribly vexing.

Lady Farnham didn't sympathise with these complaints. Surely one could live very comfortably in Dublin, she said to her husband; it wasn't as though Ralph had been ordered to India, or even Gib or Malta. Anyway, if Celia couldn't face such upheavals she shouldn't have married a soldier. Celia's behaviour heightened this disapproval. She delayed following her husband as long as she could, and then she didn't close the house or dismiss the servants. After spending some weeks in Dublin, she was back again—just to see friends and have a few dresses run up, she said. However, this took her most of May and June. And then she announced that she would like to stay at Longmarsh for a while. Ralph would be able to get leave and come over, she hoped. So far, this hadn't happened, and Celia didn't appear noticeably distressed.

From various signs, not to be ignored by a woman of experience, Lady Farnham suspected that all was not well between Celia and Ralph. She blamed her daughter unequivocally; Ralph was a model husband, the soul of courtesy and consideration. Whereas Celia had revealed a strange vein of wilfulness and flightiness—after marriage, somehow, rather than as a girl. Motherhood, of course, was what she needed to settle her; but of this, after eighteen months of marriage, there was still no sign. Her expenditure on clothes and jewellery, considering that Ralph wasn't a wealthy man, was excessive. Her enthusiasm for the season, and her appearance at parties to which admittedly she'd been invited, but which in Lady Farnham's view a married woman shouldn't attend without her husband —this kind of thing was unbecoming. Her long stay in England without him was selfish, even disloyal, and could well set idle tongues clacking. All this was bad enough—if only, Lady Farnham prayed, there was nothing worse!

One morning in June, Lady Farnham looked out of the window of the house in Berkeley Square and saw that summer was at its most beautiful. She suggested to Charlotte—Fanny wouldn't be up for hours, of course—that they might order the carriage and take a spin in the park. They set off without delay, feeling rather adventurous since it was barely nine o'clock; but, as Charlotte agreed, these fine mornings often clouded over and the early hours were the best. Naturally, the park was deserted. Lady Farnham had just remarked that one might almost imagine oneself in the country, when two horses cantered past. The first rider turned her head away sharply, but not before Lady Farnham—and, she feared, Charlotte too—had recognised Celia. The other rider was a man who had been pointed out to her at a charity ball as a visitor from Poland, Count Rokossowski. Lady Farnham had heard enough about him to entertain the keenest suspicions. To put it flatly, if he was a Count then she, Lady Farnham, was the Empress of China.

In the circumstances, if Celia didn't return to Dublin it was at least a mercy that she came to Longmarsh. All the same, Lady Farnham felt that fate was subjecting her to trials that she hadn't deserved. One expected to worry about daughters, but surely one had a right to hope that the worries would end when they married.

Celia had scarcely arrived at Longmarsh when she asked at lunch: "Whom are we inviting, Papa?" To which Lord Farnham, good-tempered as ever, replied innocently: "Well, my dear, whom would you suggest?"

Although Celia's suggestions were perfectly proper, the mere prospect of a house party set Lady Farnham a problem. She didn't propose to tell her husband, who imagined that all was serene between Ralph and Celia, what she had seen in Hyde Park. But, as hopes of finding a match for Charlotte were still entertained, she couldn't put a ban on inviting single men. After much pondering, she compiled a list including two men who were as unlike Count Rokossowski as possible. One was a Fellow of an Oxford college and author of a historical work; this Mr. Pickering seemed to be a confirmed bachelor, but he might with luck find an affinity with Charlotte. The other was a widower, a Major in a good county regiment. He had recently lost his wife in childbirth and was said to be inconsolable.

At dinner, Ellie was seated next to Major Falconer. She was terrified of him. He was an extremely tall man, and everything about him seemed to be enormous. Enormous head, enormous moustache and whiskers, enormous mouth which gaped cavernously as he ate, enormous hands. She couldn't take her eyes off his hands, which were covered with long black hairs. At one time, between courses, he rested his right hand on the table beside her, and it was as if some huge and dangerous spider—such as she had seen illustrated in a book about the tropics—had landed on the white cloth, mysteriously unnoticed by anyone but her, and was waiting to bite. Altogether, the Major had a great deal of hair. To say nothing of the moustache and whiskers, it sprouted out of his ears and, she saw when he leaned forward, on the back of his neck. Ellie wondered how she could survive sitting next to him at every meal through the weekend. Yet how silly she was!—his manners were perfect, he was doubtless a most estimable gentleman.

Major Falconer told her how much he admired the house, and how pleasant it was to be in a real family atmosphere, and asked whether she was the youngest, or were there any more? He had a loud voice; this frightened her too, but she supposed it was natural to him, like his size. She stammered when she had to answer, and he had to bend his head down to grasp what she said, which increased her confusion. Luckily, he conversed for most of the meal with his neighbour on the other side, a Mrs. Granger, or gazed in silence across the room—thoughtfully, perhaps sadly; Ellie had heard about his tragic loss.

On Saturday, she didn't see Major Falconer except at luncheon and dinner. In the morning, the ladies played croquet and the gentlemen went for a little rough shooting with her father. In the afternoon, everyone set out on the obligatory walk to the barrows, but Ellie pleaded that she had a headache—it was true—and retreated to her room. She sat by Charlotte in the evening; she always felt safe with Charlotte. Charlotte was telling her that bracken was growing round the barrows and it would have to be cleared, when they were joined by Mr. Pickering. He talked about antiquities, and doubtless it was very interesting since he was a real scholar, but Ellie couldn't concentrate and found herself staring across the room at Major

Falconer. Her headache came on again; she kissed her parents and went to bed.

She had a terrible dream. She didn't remember exactly what she had dreamed, which made it all the more frightening. She thought afterwards that Major Falconer must have been in it, but perhaps she thought this only because of what happened later. All that she was sure of, when she woke up, was a ghastly fear—nameless, mysterious, yet utterly devastating. Something had pursued her, gained on her, cornered her, and was going to inflict on her a doom that she was helpless to escape. So extreme was this fear that she couldn't free herself from it even when she was wide awake and sitting up in bed.

It was light—thank God for summer!—but it was far too early to dress and go downstairs. Ellie knew that she couldn't bear to be alone. She hurried into the corridor just as she was, in her nightdress. Out of the room where the fear had seized her, she felt a little better already. But where was she to go? She didn't dare to wake her mother at this hour; she had already been scolded for this childish habit of being afraid to be alone in the mornings. Charlotte wouldn't scold her, but Charlotte's room was in the other wing and she felt that she lacked the strength to reach it. So she went to Celia's room, just along the corridor, and knocked on the door. There was no answer. It didn't matter, she thought, if Celia was asleep; she would sit quietly in a chair, her sister's presence would be enough. She opened the door and went in.

This is what she saw:

All the bedclothes on Celia's bed were thrown back, and an enormous creature was bouncing up and down on it—up and down, up and down, with a rhythm that was ferocious, frenzied, yet also systematic, determined, ruthless. She grasped—within seconds, but by distinct stages of understanding—that the creature was a man, and that the man was Major Falconer. His face was pressed into the pillow, but no other man could have a body like this—so enormous, and so hairy. He had a line of hair down his back, hair on his behind, thick hair on his legs. Later, Ellie wondered if all men had hair in these places. Probably they did, but not so much as Major Falconer.

Celia was underneath him, pinned down and pounded by his thudding weight. Her eyes were wide open and staring at the ceiling, her mouth was wide open too, and her expression was so strange that, if Ellie hadn't known that this was Celia's room, she might scarcely have recognised her. It was an expression of—was it intense pain, was it fear like the fear in Ellie's dream, was it madness or some mysterious trance? A low, throaty gasping escaped from her in time with what the man was doing to her. This sound too was strange, as if a voice that wasn't Celia's were coming from Celia's mouth. As the man had taken possession of her, so he had transformed her.

Ellie ran. She never knew how she managed it, but she ran all the way to Charlotte's room. And Charlotte was awake, or woke up at once.

"Ellie darling, what's the matter?"

"I'm sorry . . . don't be cross, please . . . I'm so frightened."

"Of course I'm not cross. Have you had a bad dream?"

"Yes—an awful dream."

"Come on, dear, I'll cuddle you."

She felt herself gathered into the warm bed and pressed comfortably to Charlotte's plump, reassuring body.

"Tell me about it. Tell old Charlotte."

"I can't . . . I can't."

"It'll make you feel better."

"No, please. Anyway, I can't remember. Honestly I can't. I just know it was frightening."

"Well, it's all over now. And it wasn't real, whatever it was.

It's only things that really happen that you ever need to worry about."

Charlotte went on talking, consoling, making gentle fun of Ellie, distracting her with all kinds of irrelevances. When enough time had passed for the servants to be up, she rang her bell and sent a maid for tea and biscuits. After that, Ellie dropped into an exhausted sleep and didn't wake until everyone in the house had finished breakfast.

Questioned by her mother, Charlotte said that Ellie was unwell and ought to stay in bed all day. But Lady Farnham felt that Ellie's moods were being indulged too much. She took Ellie's temperature, found that it was normal, and told her quite sharply to get dressed; she would only just have time to swallow some breakfast before church.

In the hall, as they all prepared to set out, voices reached Ellie as if through a mist.

Celia: "Have you seen my white gloves, Mamma? I know I put them on this ledge yesterday."

Lady Farnham: "We haven't time to search the house now, Celia. I'll lend you a pair."

Celia: "Oh, it's so tiresome, these servants are always moving things."

Lord Farnham: "I trust you slept well, Major."

Major Falconer: "Like a log, thank you, my lord. But then, I always do."

How could they be so composed? How could they change back so easily into their familiar public selves? Ellie tried to believe that it hadn't really happened. Perhaps it had been part of her dream; perhaps she was beginning to have hallucinations. But it had happened—she knew.

In church, she could hear Major Falconer's loud voice clearly from two pews behind. He spoke the prayers firmly: the collect, the prayer for the Royal Family, the Lord's Prayer

at the end of the service. "Our Father . . . thy will be done
. . . lead us not into temptation . . . deliver us from evil . . .
forgive us our trespasses . . ." He sounded perfectly sure of
himself, like a man with a clear conscience. Celia only mumbled, but that was all she ever did.

Ellie's ordeal lay ahead: sitting next to Major Falconer at
lunch. If she could get through that, she would be safe. She
had heard him tell her father that he would have to leave by
an afternoon train, because he was on duty on Monday morning.

Until the pudding, it seemed that he wasn't going to speak
to her. His gaze was fixed straight ahead—not into vacancy, as
she had innocently supposed, but at Celia who sat opposite.
However, he suddenly said: "I'm sorry to hear you weren't
well, Miss Colmore." The booming voice made her jump, like
a roll of thunder, and then she sat frozen, unable to move a
finger. But the words, once again, seemed to come through a
barrier; it took her several seconds to realise that she would
have to answer.

She stammered something.

"The hot weather, possibly. D'you suffer from hay fever?"

He was looking at her now, she felt, though she didn't dare
look up. She couldn't speak again—she was sure to stammer.
She tried to shake her head, but she was petrified.

"Pardon? You look pale, Miss Colmore. I hope you're not
still indisposed."

Ellie burst into tears. Everyone fell upon her—her mother
and Charlotte calling her name, Mrs. Granger leaning over
her with a glass of water, the Major booming out: "I say, Miss
Colmore!" She stumbled to her feet, seeing nothing, and fled.

From this time, a new label was attached to Ellie: highly
strung. She didn't know quite what it meant. Evidently it was
an affliction, which she had carried within herself unknowing

from birth, and which was destined to stay with her throughout life. She wasn't to be blamed for it, she gathered. One could be highly strung and still be a member in good standing of the family circle, cared for, loved—perhaps cared for and loved rather more than before.

She thought constantly of what she had seen in Celia's room. The shock and the horror turned gradually into bewilderment. The act itself—there was much that baffled her about that. She supposed that it was what husbands did to their wives. It was very secret, never spoken of—of course, because it was so nasty—but she realised that it was done, although she felt sick when she imagined her father doing it to her mother. It must be what was meant, or a part of what was meant, by the obedience that a wife owed to her husband. It was hard to understand that something could be shameful and also necessary, but apparently it was. An overheard remark came back to her mind. Lady Farnham, referring to a lady recently widowed, had said to a friend: "My dear, what she must have endured from her husband!" The lady had been married for forty years—endurance indeed. But then, Lady Farnham herself had been married for over thirty years and showed no obvious marks of suffering. Perhaps it wasn't always so horrible as what she'd seen. Perhaps it was only certain men, like Major Falconer, who did it in that ruthless, frenzied way. Perhaps men—good men, at least—did it less cruelly to their own wives. But nasty, more or less, it must always be.

It was necessary, and had to be endured by a wife, because it had something to do with having children. But Ralph had presumably done it to Celia, and she wasn't having a baby. Some wives never had babies; was this because they refused to obey their husbands? Celia had been heard to contradict Ralph at the dinner table and was perhaps lacking in obedience.

Then why did she let Major Falconer do it to her? Could she have a baby because of Major Falconer, or could only husbands and wives have babies?

Ellie had heard references to unfaithful wives; that must mean wives who did this thing with men who were not their husbands. It was, she thought, what the Bible meant by committing adultery, though Miss Frayn had never explained the word clearly. Such women, if they were found out, were dragged through the divorce courts, disgraced, and never again allowed to show their faces in decent society. Ellie was horrified to think of this happening to Celia. But why do the thing with another man, if it was bad enough—a duty to be endured—having to do it with your husband? Morality apart, it didn't make sense.

It was a great sin; that surely was true. It invited the most dreadful and eternal punishment, the punishment of Hell. Celia must know that. Major Falconer must know it too. Although Ellie could reconcile herself to the thought of Major Falconer burning in Hell, the idea of Celia suffering this fate was appalling. But on Sunday, after it had happened, Celia had got up and dressed, fussed about her white gloves, gone to church, eaten a good lunch, and laughed at a funny story told by Mr. Granger, all as if she hadn't a care in the world. Sometimes Ellie wondered whether religion had anything to do with the way people lived. It was hardly ever spoken of, except in church. When someone did wrong, and her father said: "He'll suffer for that, mark my words," what he meant was that the man would be cut in society, or dismissed from his employment, or at the worst sent to prison, not that he would go to Hell. If the Bible was true—and any sane person knew that it was true—how could it be so ignored? What could be more important than Heaven and Hell, when one could die at any time, like Major Falconer's wife? If Major Falconer had loved his wife, as people said, how could he do the thing he'd done to Celia while she—his wife, that is—looked down at him from Heaven? Especially as she had died in childbirth, which in a sense was his fault. But Major Falconer too had gone to church, eaten a hearty lunch, and laughed at Mr. Granger's funny story.

Ellie was also distressed by the thought that Celia might have heard her coming into the room. She couldn't remember closing the door when she ran off; perhaps she'd left it open, perhaps she'd slammed it. The thing was very secret, even when a husband and wife did it. Celia might imagine that Ellie had seen the Major going into her room and come to pry. In the ensuing weeks, whenever Celia spoke to her crossly, as she not infrequently did, Ellie trembled and thought that Celia must know. But when Celia spoke to her kindly, this might mean that they shared a secret, that Celia was making sure of her silence. And indeed, whether Celia knew it or not, Ellie had the burden of a terrible secret.

What was her duty? Perhaps God had directed her to see the horror for some good purpose. Perhaps she ought to plead with Celia to feel remorse; but she hadn't the courage, Celia might merely get cross, and she was sure to stammer and lose her words. Perhaps she should tell her mother or Charlotte. She would dearly have liked to do that for the sake of her own peace of mind. But she knew that she could never bring herself to do it; the thing was too dreadful to be put into words. Perhaps she ought to write to Ralph. She could sign the letter "A Well-wisher" or something of the kind. That would mean the divorce courts—shame for the whole family. How could she bring disgrace and misery on Celia, whom she loved?

She saw that, if the secret came out, Celia would suffer more than Major Falconer. And this she couldn't contemplate; for, deep in her mind, she believed that it wasn't really Celia's fault. Pinned on the bed like that, crushed, hammered, Celia was clearly the victim. Perhaps this was what was meant by rape.

True, Celia could have screamed or rung her bell, and she hadn't. This was hard to understand. It seemed to Ellie that, somehow or other, men had the power to frighten women into submission. She herself had been petrified by Major Falconer, merely at the dinner table. Her voice had choked in her dry throat, she had been unable to move. So, how petrified she would have been if he had advanced on her as he must have advanced on Celia—a thought that made her feel faint even in imagination. If a man appeared in one's bedroom, pulling off his clothes, showing his terrible hairy body, intent on doing the thing, how could one think straight, and how could one act? How could one escape? Then, when it started, surely one was under a kind of spell. One was, almost literally, not one-self. She remembered Celia's strained, staring face: no, that hadn't been the Celia whom Ellie knew. And if Celia had been quite composed afterwards, it was the composure of someone emerging to become herself again.

In those summer weeks, musing in her room or taking soli-tary walks in the grounds, Ellie thought often of what it meant to be a woman. One learned to make polite conversa-tion, to play the piano, even to do sums and speak French. But what one would become eventually was a wife. When one was engaged—chosen, secured—it was cause for celebration. To be passed by, like Charlotte, was to be pitied. Someone to whom that happened remained a woman, but not a proper woman. A man, even a reasonably good-looking man, could decide to be a bachelor, like Mr. Pickering, and no one minded. A woman didn't decide to be a spinster, an old maid. It hap-pened to her, because of her defects.

And what was it, this being a wife? It was managing a household, taking one's full place in society, bearing and bringing up children. Yet at the core of it was this thing that everyone knew of and no one spoke of: this lying on one's back under a man, this submission, this ordeal, this endurance. In the end, that was what women prepared for as they smiled and blushed and pleased the men. If one pleased many men, like Fanny, then one could choose to end up lying under one man rather than another. But to refuse—that wasn't possible. Fanny knew this. She didn't exactly refuse her suitors; she told them that they must wait, she was still young, they could hope.

But they didn't simply hope, Ellie thought. They pursued. She had seen them, weekend after weekend for years, descending on Longmarsh like raiders on a fertile coast. Sometimes, looking for a lost croquet ball or merely strolling about, she had seen one of them with Fanny, or with Celia before she was engaged to Ralph. They contrived opportunities for seclusion, they spoke earnestly in low voices, they seized hands. Ellie realised now that she'd always known what it was about, though she hadn't admitted it to her conscious thoughts. She saw Longmarsh—her home, where she had always felt free and safe—as a place of danger, a place where her future fate waited for her inexorably. She saw men as cunning hunters, waiting in cover, blocking ways of flight, stalking, revealing themselves to close in when the prey was helpless. Then there was a ritual of capture: the ring, the first kiss, the announcement to the smiling family, the wedding. But at the core of it all, once again, was the terrible secret. For they knew what they really wanted, the men. There, lurking in their minds from the first glance and the first word, was the thing they meant to do. Gentlemanly, courteous, kindly they might seem, and might indeed be in the daytime, in the public world. But a man was a man when his time came—his time of mastery and triumph, with his woman held down beneath him. And then, not one of them would have mercy.

At last, at the end of July, Celia departed for Ireland. Ralph had leave and they were to join a house party in County Waterford, which she hoped might be amusing. Fanny came home; another young man had proposed to her. She had told him to wait, but regarded him with some favour and wanted to think about him. In August, therefore, Lady Farnham invited no more young men.

For Ellie, it was a welcome relief.

CHAPTER 4

A Satisfactory Arrangement

RICHARD WAS EAST OF SUEZ for four years, not three. India was dull, except for the polo and the shikar. The cantonment at Lucknow was a closed world of which he soon knew every corner; the summer heat was dreadful, with troopers regularly fainting on parade; everyone longed for the day when the regiment would entrain for Bombay and home. But just when the time was near, the call to action came instead. Shere Ali, the treacherous Emir of Afghanistan, was intriguing with the Russians and refusing British protection. A strong force was mustered to teach him a lesson, and Richard's regiment—to his delight—was ordered to take part in the campaign. Rare experiences were packed into the three months of fighting before General Roberts rode into Kabul and Shere Ali fled to an ignominious death in a remote province. There were days of danger and hardship, and bitter nights shivering in tents pitched amid the snow. There was loss and sorrow when Harry Fielding fell to a sniper's bullet and the bugles sounded over a lonely grave. But there was also a glorious cavalry charge, when the squadrons swept through the Shutargardan Pass and cut the tribal levies to pieces with the sabre.

After a summer devoted to the pacification of the country and to enjoyable patrols among the stupendous mountains, the

regiment came home in October 1879. Richard had three
months' leave, and of course he went straight to Severalls. His
father was the same as ever, looking not a day older. His
mother was in reasonably good health, or—as she said—Richard was the best of tonics. And the great house was more lively
than he remembered it, for there were two new members of
the family: George's wife, Maud, and their little girl, Elizabeth.

Richard liked Maud at once. "Dashed sensible, capable girl,"
said the Duke, and so she was. She was no beauty, but she had
a pleasant, open face and a smile to which one couldn't help
responding. Brought up in the country—her father was a Scottish Earl—she was just the right wife for George, and it was
obvious that they were devoted to each other. The child, a year
old and beginning to toddle, was adorable.

"We mustn't keep you here, my boy—sure you're longing to
see Piccadilly Circus again," the Duke said after a fortnight.
Richard admitted that he was. It wouldn't be necessary to open
up Berkshire House on his account, he said; he could take a
set of rooms somewhere, and join a club as soon as it could be
arranged. But the more Berkshire House was lived in, the
Duke said, the better. When he stayed there himself he usually took Simmons—the head footman at Severalls, a most reliable fellow—and Simmons could go with Richard now. A
small staff was kept permanently at the house.

Once in London, Richard's first thought was to look up his
friend Ralph Ashton. An enquiry at the War Office told him
what he needed: Captain Ashton had a staff appointment at
Aldershot, but kept a house in town. It was practically round
the corner from Berkshire House, so Richard strolled along
the same afternoon. A housemaid answered his knock. The
Captain was at Aldershot until the weekend, she said.

"Very well, I'll leave my card."

"Mrs. Ashton is at home, sir. Shall I send your name up?"

Why not? "Yes, do. Lord Richard Somers."

He remembered Celia as a fine-looking girl, and a fine-looking woman she certainly was now. She greeted him with a warmth that was more than hospitable.

"Lord Richard—what a delightful surprise! Ralph will be so pleased. He was saying just the other day that you must be home by now."

"Back about a fortnight, Mrs. Ashton. I had to stay with my people, of course. As soon as I got to town, I made this my first call."

"I know you were always Ralph's greatest friend. I hope I'll make your acquaintance properly now. It's such a shame, you were off as soon as I'd set eyes on you. Four years ago—it seems an age."

"I haven't forgotten that weekend at Longmarsh. Delightful place. Your parents are well, I trust?"

"Oh, gracious yes, they're hardy annuals. I'm sure they'll wish to see you. Now you must tell me all about everything while I've got you to myself. You were in the Afghan campaign, I believe?"

"Yes . . ." Richard began, but she interrupted: "Oh, how could I forget?—you're quite the hero. You were mentioned, surely?"

"Can't imagine why," Richard said, but he was glad she knew. It wasn't every subaltern who was mentioned in despatches after his first battle. He gave her a brief account of the Afghan war, playing down his personal experiences and describing the ferocity and cunning of the tribesmen. She gazed at him, enthralled. There was something a trifle disconcerting about her fixed look, the large eyes that scarcely left his face even while she poured the tea. Perhaps she was the romantic type, he thought.

He stayed for over an hour; once he tried to leave, but she detained him pressingly. When they finally shook hands, she asked: "Can I lure you to dinner on Saturday?" Again her eyes held his, and he felt that "lure" was the appropriate word.

"It's most kind of you, Mrs. Ashton. But I fear I'd be upsetting your plans."

"Oh no, quite the contrary—I'm short of a man. It's nothing grand. Very much of a family party. A Longmarsh reunion, shall I say?"

"Nothing could be more delightful."

He understood on Saturday why she'd been short of a man. Two of her younger sisters were there; one wore a ring and was introduced as Madame de Chaumont, but her husband wasn't with her. Arthur Colmore, Lord Farnham's eldest son, was there with his wife. A staff officer called Campbell, who had come up from Aldershot with Ralph, was the only other guest from outside the family.

The atmosphere was relaxed, as if indeed they were gathered for a country weekend. Longmarsh (Campbell knew Longmarsh, evidently) was frequently recalled. Madame de Chaumont—Fanny, Richard remembered—told a story, and told it very amusingly, about a guest who had been instructed by Lady Farnham that he must see the barrows, and had gone off to inspect the wheelbarrows in the gardeners' shed. Both Celia and Fanny chattered a great deal. It wasn't quite what one expected of ladies, but it was an informal family occasion, and Richard had been starved of feminine voices and feminine laughter for so long that he thoroughly enjoyed it and was quite sorry when the ladies rose. Only the youngest sister, whose name he couldn't call to mind, scarcely opened her mouth. Seated next to her, he made a few efforts at conversation, but without success. Of course, she was the youngest person at the table and had that excuse for being shy. She didn't look more than eighteen; he wondered what she was doing in town, apparently without her mother.

"Well, this is a famous occasion," Ralph said when the port was set on the table and the cigars lit. "It's splendid to welcome you home, Somers. And you know, Colmore's not long back from abroad."

"Really? Where have you been?" Richard asked.

Arthur Colmore assumed a deprecating look. He was a tall, clean-shaven man, probably about thirty; his hair was slightly receding and he had a grave, or at least thoughtful, expression even when he smiled. The brains of the family, Richard remembered that Ralph had said of him.

"Not very far," he replied. "I'm in the Diplomatic Service, and I've been at the Embassy in Paris for the last three years."

"By Jove, that must have been fun."

"Not for Colmore," Ralph said. "He was a married man before he went there."

"Fanny's visits provided most of the excitement," Arthur remarked.

Fanny, Richard learned, took advantage of her brother's posting to descend on Paris and soon made herself as popular there as in London. The man who secured her hand, after so many others had failed, was the Vicomte de Chaumont. Arthur described him as a very dashing fellow, a true match for Fanny. The circumstances were dramatic to the verge of being scandalous. They turned up in Nice, having travelled together on the overnight train, and demanded to be married by the British Consul. Telegrams flew between Nice, Paris and Longmarsh. With Fanny and the Vicomte staying at the same hotel, Lord Farnham was obliged to give his consent, though it was months before he would receive his son-in-law. Now everyone was on good terms and Fanny paid visits to London, staying with the Ashtons, and to Longmarsh. Her husband was reluctant to cross the Channel, saying that the food in England was impossible.

Richard asked about the rest of the family. Robert was at

Oxford, intending to take Holy Orders. Ellie—ah yes, that was the name, Ellie—was living with an aunt in London and studying the piano, really studying it seriously. The youngest girl and boy were still at home. Richard noticed that Arthur didn't mention the eldest girl, the plain one. No good news about her, presumably.

The port went round again. After a brief silence, Campbell said: "I say, Somers, you were in Afghanistan. D'you think, if the need had arisen, we could have pushed on into Russian territory?"

"That's one for you staff fellows," Richard answered. "But I'd say at a guess, when you think of the distances—no railways, mind—the supply problems would be the difficulty, not the Russians."

"You know we were almost at war with Russia last year," Arthur said.

"Well, I couldn't follow the news, of course, but I believe it was pretty close."

"Damnably close, I can tell you. I doubt if anyone but Dizzy could have made them pull back in the Balkans and avoided war too."

"I don't know anything about politics," Richard said. "But most people in India—my Colonel, for instance—were pretty sick when we did avoid war. We'll have to thrash the Russians sooner or later, shan't we? Or are you saying they're too strong for us to thrash them?"

Arthur tapped the ash from his cigar reflectively. Then he answered: "I should say that they are too weak for us to thrash them safely."

Richard repeated this in his mind, but couldn't make sense of it. "Could you explain that to a simple regimental soldier, Colmore?" he asked.

"Yes, I mean something like this. The civilised world is made up of units, which we call the Powers. It's dangerous to hit any of them so hard that it collapses, because then you simply leave a hole, and a hole can't be filled from outside. France was very hard hit in '71, and the mess was awful. Now France has made a remarkable recovery, which I've watched with admiration, and Bismarck is wise enough to see that it's all to the good. At present, the weakest unit is Turkey. We risked war last year, quite rightly, because Dizzy knew that Turkey must not be allowed to collapse. But if Russia collapsed—and another defeat like the Crimea might have that result—it would be the biggest disaster of all, because it would leave the biggest hole."

There was a long silence. Then Ralph coughed and said: "Well, that's very deep stuff. Shall we join the ladies?"

In the drawing room, Ellie played the piano. Richard knew even less about music than about politics, but he felt sure that she played very well. The speed, the sureness, the number of notes she hit in a minute, and all from memory—it was simply astounding. The music was by some German composer; Celia mentioned the name, but it meant nothing to him. Though there wasn't exactly a tune, it had a gay, lilting rhythm that took his fancy greatly. Everything went well together: the music, the handsome furnishings of the drawing room, the lamplight enriching the golden hair of the girl at the piano, the company of good friends and charming ladies. It was all that he had missed in India, all that he had defended in the Afghan wilds and now deservedly regained. He was in a contented mood when he said goodnight and walked back to Berkshire House.

At the corner of Curzon Street, a lady of the town accosted him. It was the hour when they swarmed about Mayfair, sallying from their base in Shepherd Market. He gave her a smile and a cheerful: "Not tonight, my dear."

Smoking a small cheroot as he prepared for bed, he thought about women. He could count on invitations that would lead to his meeting any number of young ladies, for the word would soon go round that the twenty-four-year-old son of the Duke of Berkshire was in town. He would enjoy the smiles and the charming prattle, but he wasn't inclined to look for any attachments. About marriage, certainly, there was no hurry. The sensible course was to wait—though not necessarily as long as George—and be sure that the choice was the right one.

The more immediate question was what to do, on a different level, about the natural needs of a young man. He remembered the night before he had said goodbye to London —a pleasure that he was more than ready to repeat. But he didn't know how one got hold of girls like Lucy. Fielding had known the ropes, and Fielding would never drink a glass of champagne or fondle a slender waist again. There was always Shepherd Market, but the frank commercialism was distasteful and the risk to health was an unknown quantity. Keeping a mistress—a pleasing, man-of-the-world phrase—was more the thing. But how the deuce did one set about finding a potential mistress?

He would see what turned up, he decided. In the metropolis, something was sure to turn up. And, only a few days later, chance solved his problem.

He had spent the afternoon at his tailor's, discussing the replenishment of his civilian wardrobe, and come in with a little time to spare before going out again to a stag dinner with two fellow officers who lived in London. He went up to his room to change, but decided that a whisky would go down nicely and rang for Simmons. Instead of Simmons, however, a housemaid appeared.

"I rang for Simmons," Richard said.

"It's Mr. Simmons's afternoon off, my lord. I thought I'd better answer, if your lordship will excuse me."

"I wanted a whisky and water. D'you know where to find the whisky?"

"Yes, my lord."

She was back quickly. "Shall I pour, my lord?"

"Yes, do."

A trim little bottom, he thought as she bent over the table. And a trim little profile under the cap.

"What's your name?" he asked.

"Alice, my lord."

"That's a pretty name."

"Thank you, my lord."

"A pretty name to suit a pretty face."

She stood quite still, accepting this without any silly simpering. She must know she had a pretty face, of course.

"Will that be all, my lord?"

"No, there's one more thing."

He kissed her soundly, holding her close to him and resting his hand on the trim little bottom.

"Well, Alice," he said as he released her, "you know your way here, don't you? D'you think you could find it in the dark?"

"Yes, my lord." Her voice was perfectly steady. Her speech, though not lady-like, wasn't the common Cockney accent.

"Eleven o'clock, shall we say?"

Still no simpering, no affected confusion. "Is that an order, my lord?" she asked calmly.

Richard was amused. "No, it's not an order, Alice," he said. "I've made a suggestion to you—I think you understand my meaning. I'm not the man to threaten you with dismissal or anything like that. I shall be here at eleven o'clock, that's all."

"Very good, my lord."

He was there at a quarter to eleven. Surprising himself, he couldn't get the girl out of his mind throughout dinner, fretted when he couldn't find a cab for a few minutes, and then told the driver to hurry. In his room, he smoked a cheroot almost nervously, paced aimlessly about, and twice looked at the second-hand on his watch to make sure that it was going. At eleven, he felt like kicking himself. He should have told her it was an order—what the deuce, one ought to make these things clear. Now she wasn't coming, and it would be awkward to ask her again.

There was a gentle, scarcely audible knock at the door. He found himself running to open it.

She undressed behind a screen, quickly and silently, and darted into bed while he was putting away his cuff-links. Her face on the pillow, framed by dark-brown curls, looked quite different—not like a servant's face at all. After he was finished with her, she dressed as quickly as she had undressed and remembered to take a prudent peep at the landing before she left the room.

As he found her that first night, so she continued—willing, self-composed, intelligent and discreet. When he came in, as he usually did, between eleven and twelve, he saw her leaning over the rail of the stairs to the servants' attic. He would nod to her or shake his head, as he preferred. If he came in very late, there was naturally no sign of her. Once, after particularly enjoying himself, he suggested that she should stay until morning, but she replied very sensibly that it wouldn't be wise.

She would have been content with the mere physical transaction, but Richard felt that it was too much like going with a street-walker. So far as the gulf between their stations in life permitted, he wanted to treat her as a person. He gave Simmons a standing order to leave a decanter of port in the bedroom. Simmons brought one glass, naturally, and Alice used Richard's toothbrush mug. They had a drink—she wouldn't accept a second—and chatted for a while. She was capable of shrewd comments on the other servants (she had been in the household for over a year), on London life as she knew it, and on the crimes and scandals reported in the ha'penny papers.

He didn't like to give her money. Once a week or so, he made her a present: a brooch, or a silk scarf, or a tortoiseshell comb. If she sold the things, that was her business. She wasn't grasping, and never asked for anything, but she had a sound sense of the value of money. Sometimes she asked Richard what he'd paid for a new tie or a pair of shoes, and told him that he'd been overcharged.

He was sure that she was quite faithful. When he offered her a couple of tickets to a show for her evening off, she said that she had no one to go with. Then she looked thoughtful—he liked her thoughtful expression—and said: "I'd only like to go with you, if I could."

"I'm afraid that wouldn't do."

"No, of course not."

"Would you like me as your young man, if things were . . . you know, different?" he asked.

"Yes, I would. I was glad when you kissed me, the first time."

As Richard had suspected, Alice didn't come from the servant class. Her father had owned a small print-shop, and a run of bad luck had driven him into bankruptcy. The shame had killed him, Alice said. Her mother had died before this, so she was left alone in the world. "I hadn't much choice, except service."

"Do you mind service very much?"

"I mind being ordered about. Not by the gentry, I mean—by people like Mrs. Tindall." Mrs. Tindall was the cook. "I'd like to be on my own."

"On your own—how?"

She had this all worked out. Her dream was to set up as a dressmaker and seamstress. She had the skill, and she believed that she had the business sense. But she had no capital, so she said calmly that it would never be more than a dream.

Richard asked how much capital would be needed.

"Well, for the treadle-machine, and the other things you've got to have, and for getting a place and meeting the rent till custom builds up—say fifty pounds."

"That's not much," he said instantly.

"Not much for you, my lord." She sometimes called him "my lord" even when she was sitting on his lap, with a touch of irony. "I could never save it out of my wages."

"Why, how much are your wages?" He had no idea.

"Twenty pounds a year."

When Alice had left him that night, Richard got out of bed and thought the matter over with the aid of a cigar. He could see no reason not to give her the money—it was nothing for him, true enough. From every point of view, it looked like a highly satisfactory arrangement. She would be independent and contented, restored to her original social level. Her affection for him would be reinforced by gratitude. When he visited her, there would be no more talking in low voices and separating in the middle of the night; he would, in fact, have a real mistress. Ultimately, when he married and had no more need of her, she would be making an adequate living. On the other hand, if he didn't make this arrangement, he would be losing her as soon as his leave was over and he no longer lived at Berkshire House. He could see no snags. He went back to bed, his mind made up, in the happy mood natural to anyone who is in a position to show his generosity and do himself a favour at the same time.

He told Alice of his decision the following night. She kissed him rapturously. For once, he had to caution her to keep her voice down instead of the other way round.

She gave in her notice without delay. Richard supposed that another housemaid arrived, but didn't notice. He suggested to

Alice that she should look for a place in the Camden Town district. It would be convenient; after his leave was up, his squadron would be in the barracks in Albany Street.

He didn't see her for a couple of weeks, and then she wrote to say that she had found a suitable place and was ready to move in. There was a large room on the ground floor where she would work, a sitting room and bedroom above, and a good attic for storage.

Richard went to see her, and she showed him her equipment with pride. She had left cards in the neighbourhood and secured her first order. He fixed an evening for a celebration. As the kitchen was in the basement, they dined in her work-room—curious but amusing surroundings. She was a good cook, among her other virtues, and served up a succulent roast fowl and an apple tart with pastry that melted in the mouth. Richard had ordered champagne to be delivered. In cheerfully fizzy mood, talking and laughing loudly, they went to bed in the cosy upstairs room and watched the firelight flickering on the low ceiling. In the morning, Richard breakfasted with a woman for the first time in his life. That, in a way, was the greatest pleasure.

Those three months on leave, he thought afterwards, were the most pleasantly carefree in his life—and not only because of Alice. He went about like a free spirit, always at leisure but never with time heavy on his hands, savouring the best that both London and the country had to offer. A golden autumn melted gradually into a crisp, stimulating winter. He went to Severalls when he felt like it for a week at a time— a week of shooting, a week of hunting, and of course for the family Christmas. He spent a week at Aldershot, staying in the headquarters mess and swapping memories with Ralph until all hours of the night. Everyone there was anxious to hear his account of the Afghan war. The staff officers were admirable fellows, he thought—the eternal antagonism between staff and regimental officers was really absurd. It even crossed his mind that, instead of following a regimental career as he had always assumed that he would, he might have a shot at becoming a staff man. Going through Staff College took brains, and he'd never considered himself gifted in that line; but he hadn't been exactly a duffer at Eton, though he'd made far more effort to get into the First Eleven than to pass exams. If he set himself a purpose—one did, he thought, need a purpose in life—hard grind might make up for his limitations. However, there was plenty of time to think about that. He had his whole life ahead of him.

He was out of London every weekend; indeed, he had more invitations than he could accept. Friends of his parents were eager to offer their hospitality—the most eager, of course, being those with marriageable daughters. When Alice was established in Camden Town, he took her for an incognito (he hoped) weekend in Brighton, and part of the fun was that it meant declining an invitation to Chatsworth. He stayed at Goodwood, at Trentham—in an enormous house party which included the Prince of Wales—at Blenheim and at Hatfield. Yet, at the end of the three months, he felt that the most enjoyable weekend had been at Longmarsh.

There, in the old Tudor house which was more friendly than ever with log fires blazing, one was drawn from the first moment into the happy, easy life of a true English family. He helped Lord Farnham prune the roses, he sat with Lady Farnham looking through the family album, and he almost missed changing for dinner through telling little Tommy one more story of the Afghan war. The Ashtons weren't there, but he saw plenty of them in town. Ellie was there; she went home every weekend, he gathered. She was quiet, as usual, but not quite so shy as in London. He strayed into the music-room while she was practising a new piano piece, and she accepted his offer to turn the pages. As he couldn't read the music and had to watch for her nods, he had a good excuse to keep his eyes on her lovely profile. Recalling it the last thing at night, he thought that he had never seen such a beautiful girl. But at that time—although later, when he was in love with her, it seemed incredible—he only contemplated Ellie's beauty with tranquil enjoyment, as one contemplates the beauties of Nature.

The eldest girl was still at home and still unmarried. She helped her father to manage the estate, as the eldest son would have if Arthur hadn't taken up a career. She was reconciled to her lot in life, Richard supposed. He noticed that there was a special sympathy between her and Ellie. Once at dinner, when a guest asked Ellie a question that she found difficult to answer, she threw Charlotte a look of mute appeal, and Charlotte swiftly turned the conversation.

In London, too, Richard was overwhelmed with invitations. He seemed to be always about ten minutes late as he went about the West End to lunch here, tea there, back to Berkshire House to change, and on to a dinner party or a box at the theatre. If he dropped in at his club for a quiet hour alone, someone was almost sure to call out: "Ah, there's Somers—just the fellow!" and drag him off to the card-room or the billiard-room. Naturally, he told himself, hostesses liked a spare man, families with daughters liked an eligible bachelor, and everyone liked the son of a Duke. But he did get the impression, without undue vanity, that quite a number of people liked him for himself. "Of course they do, the same as I do," Alice said.

The house that Richard came to know best was the Ashtons' house in South Audley St. He often dined there when Ralph was in town; but Celia too was making a favourite of him and used to ask him on evenings when she was alone. Not literally alone, of course—that would have been impossible, though Celia was decidedly unconventional—but presid-

ing over a quite informal buffet supper, with guests summoned casually by telegram and not even the right numbers
of ladies and men. You could meet rather odd people at South
Audley St.: artists, poets, foreigners whose reason for being
in London wasn't very clear, ladies whose presence without
their husbands wasn't clear either, and men who had done
out-of-the-way things like exploring the Upper Amazon or
fighting as volunteers in Balkan insurrections. Still, the talk
was always amusing and Richard also saw people whose position in society was beyond question, so he decided that it was
all right.

He saw Fanny once, over from Paris again. And twice he
saw Ellie, who had been prevailed upon to come and play the
piano, though only—Celia said—when it was a very small
party consisting entirely of people she knew. She came with
her teacher, a strange old man with fuzzy hair and a strong
German accent. Except for visiting Celia, Richard gathered,
Ellie didn't go into society at all. During the last season she
had been presented at Court and gone to the usual dances, and
had found it an agony.

It was strange—everyone at South Audley St. was striking in one way or another, and yet it was Ellie, if she was
there, whom one noticed as soon as one entered the drawing
room. Something about her was rare and precious, making
everyone else appear commonplace. She was like a pure shaft
of white light amid gaudy colours; like a draught of clear
water after cloying liquers: like the note of a piano against
the blare of a brass band. Such phrases didn't come to Richard's mind until later, when he was in love with her. But he
had always been aware—so he believed, looking back—of that
special quality in her, that unique beauty.

CHAPTER 5

Lord Richard's
First Proposal

AFTER HIS RETURN to military duty, Richard was seen much less in society. True, he was living in London and there were only two nights a week when he was orderly officer and had to stay in barracks, so he could have accepted almost as many invitations as before. But for a professional soldier—and he sincerely wanted to be that—there were disadvantages in being the son of a Duke. It was important to give the impression of taking the Army seriously, not of being a man about town with a cavalry commission as an extra social adornment. Besides, he liked the quiet evenings with Alice. Her little house was a kind of home for him, where he could relax with a brandy and a cigar while he listened to her stories about her customers and neighbours. So, when he left the mess in the evening, it was for his mistress or his club more often than for a drawing room.

Spring in 1880 came early, with a scattering of warm days that promised a good summer. Given a week's leave, Richard went down to Severalls and found the quiet countryside in a state of unusual animation. Parliament had been dissolved, and the Liberal candidate for West Berkshire, a bustling barrister, was dashing about the constituency as if he really had a chance. He had none, of course; most of the voters felt it vaguely improper that anyone should stand against the Marquis of Wantage. George confined himself to his adoption speech and a few appearances at social functions, and was returned as safely as before. However, in the general election as a whole the Liberals triumphed. The Queen would have to send for Gladstone. "She won't like that," the Duke remarked.

It was a wrench to leave Berkshire just as the lambs were frisking and the daffodils coming out. Back in London, Richard got into the habit of taking a daily walk in Regent's Park, which was handy to the barracks. It was new to him, and he was delighted to find that it was as large and as pleasant as Hyde Park. One wasn't likely to meet people one knew, but he didn't mind that.

One morning, as he crossed the little bridge over the lake, he saw a young lady standing by the edge of the water. The golden hair, the sweetly serious face, and the graceful figure were unmistakable—it was Ellie Colmore. She had a paper bag of bread or rolls and was feeding the ducks. The picture was so charming that Richard paused on the bridge. But it wouldn't do to stare. He approached her, raised his hat, and said: "Miss Colmore—what a delightful surprise!"

She looked round, astonished or even—one might think from her expression—frightened, as if she had imagined the park to be a private garden.

"Lord Richard! You quite startled me."

"May I be forgiven? It's months since I had the pleasure of seeing you."

"I don't see many people," she said in her quiet voice.

"Then the pleasure is more to be prized. Is Regent's Park your favourite haunt, may I ask?"

"My aunt lives in Clarence Terrace."

"Just overlooking the park? What a splendid choice."

"I must go now," she said, giving the swiftest of glances up at him, then down at the ground again.

"Perhaps we may meet again in these charming surroundings."

"Perhaps . . . yes . . . Good morning, Lord Richard."

"Good morning, Miss Colmore."

He watched her as she left the park and crossed the carriage-drive. Strange, he thought, this shyness of hers. Yet he couldn't regret it; it went with her beauty.

A few days later, he met her again. This time she was walking purposefully along the Broad Walk, near the side entrance to the Zoological Gardens. He was puzzled, partly because this was a long way from Clarence Terrace and partly because it was much earlier in the morning.

She saw him before he approached her and looked round, almost as if she were searching for a way of escape.

"Good morning, Miss Colmore. I see that you're exploring the whole park."

"Lord Richard," she whispered, almost inaudibly.

"I hope you don't suspect me of waylaying you."

"No . . . of course not." But she looked as if she did.

"My barracks are just over there. I take a stroll whenever I can."

"Yes, I see."

"If you're going this way, perhaps I may accompany you?"

"I . . . yes."

They walked along the Broad Walk, at first in silence. Richard thought of a couple of possible remarks, but they struck him as inanely superficial—with this girl, anyway—and he felt that she would say something to him if he gave her time to recover her composure. This she did. As they reached the carriage-drive, she explained that she was going to her piano lesson. Dr. Pfaffer, her teacher, lived in Prince Albert Road.

"You walk right across the park and back, Miss Colmore? And alone?"

"I like to be alone." She blushed, gave him another timid glance, and said: "I'm sorry . . . I don't mean . . ."

"Of course, Miss Colmore. But since chance has caused us to meet twice, there is something I ought perhaps to say. If I may sometimes walk with you, here in the park, I shall esteem it more than an honour. But if you prefer that I shouldn't —if I intrude—your wish will be my law."

"You're very kind," she said faintly. "No, I don't wish to avoid you."

"I'm deeply grateful."

"Dr. Pfaffer will be waiting for me."

He saw her across the carriage-drive and across Prince Albert Road, not venturing to take her arm but touching it gently. When she had gone into the house, he turned quickly and strode—almost marched—back to the park. A curious elation possessed him, which had to be worked off in energy.

It was a Friday; he had to wait through the weekend. She wouldn't be back from Longmarsh in time for a Monday lesson, he supposed. The time seemed very long. He kept thinking of her, even when he was with friends in the mess and even at Alice's house. The shy girl seemed to represent, indefinably as yet, something that had been lacking in his life.

On the Tuesday, he was in the Broad Walk at twelve o'clock, which he judged to be the time when her lesson ended. When he saw her crossing the canal bridge, that same elation took hold of him. She greeted him with a smile—a small, momentary smile, but the first he'd had from her.

Yes, she said when he asked her, she had been home for the weekend. The country was looking beautiful.

"I'm surprised you weren't tempted to stay there. It's the best time of the year."

"Oh, I am tempted. But I can't miss my lessons."

"I trust they're going well?"

"I don't know. Dr. Pfaffer seems quite pleased with me."

"You work very hard, Miss Colmore."

"I want . . ." She hesitated; Richard had the feeling that she was trusting him with a confidence, with something very important to her. "I want to do something—one thing—really well. Anyone should want that, don't you think so?"

"Oh, I agree. I want to be a good soldier." The principle was sound, undeniably. But it was a singular thing to say, for a girl.

Some people were riding along Chester Road: a Major in Richard's regiment with his wife, and their little boy on a pony.

"Do you enjoy riding, Miss Colmore?"

"I'm afraid not. Horses rather frighten me."

"There are gentle horses, you know."

"Yes . . . I must try."

They walked, mostly in silence, across the inner gardens and down to the lake. Silence was easy with her; she didn't mind it, and he had no fear of being thought a dull dog. She had her bag of bread again. He enjoyed the opportunity to gaze at her while she fed the ducks.

"There's a greedy fellow," he remarked. "No consideration for the fair sex among these creatures."

"No. But then, the drakes are the fair sex, aren't they?"

"It's no excuse. At least, I don't think so."

"I've no more bread," she said. "Oh, some of them didn't get any. Oh, it's such a pity."

And, while the ducks quacked demandingly, she turned to him with a look of pleading that went straight to his heart.

"I tell you what," he said. "I'll go and buy a loaf."

"Oh, I couldn't give you the trouble. And it's so silly of me."

"No trouble at all. I'll be back in a jiffy. Must be a baker in Baker Street, what?"

He found a baker a few doors past The Volunteer public-house. He felt like a fool buying a loaf of bread—had never bought one before, hadn't the faintest idea what it cost. But, going back to the park, he had to restrain himself from breaking into a run.

Ellie was gazing at him. As he approached, he held up the loaf like a trophy. She smiled, and in that smile was a world of feeling—relief, and gratitude, and all her pure goodness.

He stopped a couple of yards from her, unable to speak and somehow reluctant to come closer. How beautiful she was! How beautiful, at this moment!—for it was, strangely, as though he had never before grasped the full wonder of her beauty, or never been moved by it as he was moved now.

He said to himself: I am in love with Ellie Colmore. It seemed to be a fact about himself, essential and eternal, of the same order as: I am Richard Somers. It was not something that had happened, but something that he should always have known.

He broke the bread and helped her to feed the ducks. He walked with her to her aunt's house. He raised his hat and bowed as she went in. All this time, he scarcely knew what he was doing, and yet had a feeling that he was doing something of high significance: a ritual, a dedication.

The next day, it poured with rain. He assumed that Ellie went to her teacher's in a carriage, or didn't go. In an obvious sense, it was a disappointment; in another way, he was glad of the respite. He was able to think about her calmly, or as calmly as a man in love can ever think.

What was absolutely clear, as a starting point for his reflections, was that he must make Ellie his wife. It was a necessity to him. To be with her meant perfect happiness, to live without her meant utter misery. It was, beyond all comparison, the most important thing in his life. If he had to choose between marrying Ellie and succeeding in his career (though fortunately there was no reason to envisage such a choice), he would choose Ellie without an instant's hesitation.

Setting aside for the moment the central question of whether she would accept him, there were surely no obstacles. He wasn't likely to be ordered overseas again for a considerable time, so he could offer her a home. His parents would be charmed with her, and he could count on the consent of Lord and Lady Farnham. In terms of social position, it was a most suitable match.

But when he came to think of winning Ellie's hand, he felt far from confident. She was infinitely too pure of soul to accept him without loving him, for the sake of a good marriage; rank and wealth meant nothing to her, he was certain. And she wasn't in love with him—why on earth should she be? Very likely she wouldn't even have let him walk in the park with her if he hadn't been a friend of the family.

People might think him a catch, an eligible young man; but that had nothing to do with trying to win the love of a wonderful being like Ellie. Richard began to reflect sadly on his inadequacies. He was reasonably good-looking, but Ellie's beauty deserved far more than that. He was popular in society —a fault rather than a merit in her eyes, probably. He certainly wasn't clever, nor serious-minded in the way that she was. Quite possibly, she was silent in his company because she found his conversation commonplace and trivial. He hadn't read many books, and he couldn't read a note of music. Perhaps he could put that right, at least.

Gloomier thoughts followed these. Even if his qualifications had been ideal, it couldn't be easy to coax Ellie into love. She was so innocent, so shy, so much the opposite of flirtatious. She had detested the season, which was a pleasure to almost any girl who attracted admiration. If she guessed, tomorrow or the next day, what Richard's feelings for her were, it was all too likely that she would take fright. Fright, that was it—

she was like a loveable but timorous little animal which one had to approach gently, advancing one's hand by inches, lest it should take fright and scuttle away. He couldn't imagine why Ellie had this tendency to fright (it certainly didn't run in the Colmore family) but there was no doubt about it. Since he was in love with her, it added to her charms. However, it also added considerably to his difficulties.

His only chance, he decided, was to guide her toward love by stages. First she would get used to his company, then she would place her trust in him as a man who respected her and sincerely desired her happiness, and at last the idea of being able to love him would seem a natural growth from what had gone before. At all costs, he must not spring his own love on her as a shock. He mustn't rush her. "Easy does it," he muttered to himself.

It might be wise, he thought, not to press his company on her too constantly. She liked being alone; she must not be made to feel that she couldn't cross the park without meeting him. Twice or at most three times a week would be the limit. It would be a sacrifice, but unless he made this kind of sacrifice he couldn't begin to be worthy of her.

Through April and May, Richard kept to this self-imposed rule and began every day by debating whether to go to the park or not. He did feel that Ellie was glad to see him—at least, she always had a little smile for him, though never again the radiant smile that had brought him to awareness of love. He tried, by gentle questions and assiduous catching of hints, to enter her world. When she told him which composers she was studying, he consulted the regimental bandmaster and got some information about them. When she mentioned a liking for the poems of Wordsworth, he bought a copy and pored over it, even memorising a few lines which he was able to quote on a suitable occasion the next week. Often, however, they walked in silence. She was grateful to him, he hoped, for not forcing her into continual conversation. For him, to be with her was joy enough.

"What do you do in the afternoons, Miss Colmore?" he asked once.

"I practise. Or I read."

"Your aunt doesn't entertain?"

"Oh yes, there are callers sometimes."

"May I call, do you think?"

"Please do, Lord Richard. My aunt would be delighted to meet you."

"I should be delighted to meet her," Richard said. "But really, Miss Colmore, I should be calling on you."

She cast down her eyes and made no reply, but he felt that she wasn't displeased. He called and took tea with Ellie and the aunt, Mrs. Fairfax. By great good luck, she was the widow of a Hussar Colonel and Richard was a Hussar. He would always be welcome at Clarence Terrace, she indicated. She didn't entertain lavishly, but a couple of weeks later she gave a musical evening and Richard was invited. Ellie played, Dr. Pfaffer also played, and a niece of Dr. Pfaffer's sang in German. The music went on rather too long for Richard's taste, but a whole evening in the same room with Ellie was precious.

"Were you bored last night?" Ellie asked next morning in the park.

"Certainly not. It was splendid," he replied.

"I had an idea that your thoughts were wandering during the Brahms," she said with one of her quick glances.

He decided on a gamble and said: "My thoughts never wander far from you, Miss Colmore."

No reply, of course. But no signs of fright.

He was consumed with love for her. Every day, though he wouldn't have believed it possible, his love seemed to be deeper, more compelling, more passionate than the day before. Her face appeared before him on the parade-ground, in the mess, in the streets, first thing in the morning, last thing at night. A day when he didn't see her was a day without meaning, a day lost from his life.

Meanwhile, his feelings for Alice were unchanged. Apart from the obvious difference between a housemaid turned dressmaker and a lady, between his mistress and the girl he hoped to marry, the cheerful, easy affection and the haunting love existed on different planes. Except, he had to recognise, that both Ellie and Alice were women and he was a man. For it wasn't only Ellie's face that appeared to him; he had persistent and uncontrollable visions of the undiscovered beauties that must surely match the beauty on which he had gazed. These visions seemed to him a shameful offence, a wicked outrage on her purity. But, after much heart-searching, he came to the conclusion that carnal desire could be a part of love. What he longed for, after all, was to marry Ellie—to make her fully his own. Marriage would satisfy many kinds of longing and yield many kinds of happiness; the bodily side of it, surely, was as legitimate an aspiration as any other. At all events, his manly passions seemed to be reaching a new intensity since he had been in love. When he slept alone, he felt the same frustrated urges as in his schooldays or in India. It was lucky that he had Alice for relief, or he might have betrayed this aspect of his desires to Ellie. He vented his cravings on his mistress to their full extent, pressing her to come to bed early in the evening and sometimes taking her three or four times in a night.

As spring became summer, he began to think seriously of declaring himself to Ellie. He bore in mind that he had promised himself to move gradually and that premature action might be fatal; still, making all allowances for his own eagerness, it did seem to him that the right moment was approaching. Ellie was innocent, but she was not stupid—far from it. Surely she realised by now that his feelings for her went beyond friendship. As to her feelings for him, he could only hope for the best. Several times, a glance from her blue eyes or a quivering of her delicious lips encouraged him to think that she was coming to love him, though he could never be sure. Naturally, she couldn't show it before he made the opportunity. Sooner or later, he must resolve on the supreme venture.

Though he still didn't go out in society much, he accepted every invitation to the Ashtons' house in the hope—which had so far proved vain—of meeting Ellie there again. One evening, when he had strolled to the far end of the drawing room to admire a painting (and to escape from one of the more dubious guests), Celia followed him.

"Lord Richard, you seem to be preoccupied," she said.

"I'm very struck by this picture."

"I don't think that's it."

Her eyes were fixed on him with their peculiar devouring stare.

"I believe you're sweet on my little sister, isn't that so?"

He answered stiffly: "Your sister is admired by everyone who has the honour of her acquaintance." Celia shrugged, laughed, and urged him to take another glass of Madeira.

He was very disturbed by this incident. He couldn't risk making Ellie a subject of gossip, especially in the raffish South Audley Street circle. And if rumours came to Ellie's own ears, she would never speak to him again.

In any case, time was pressing. No one stayed in town after the beginning of July. He would be going on manoeuvres with the regiment, and then getting a month's leave which he would be expected to spend mainly at Severalls. Ellie would presumably go to Longmarsh for the summer, and it wasn't certain that she would return to London in the autumn.

He concentrated his mind on finding an occasion to propose to her. The park seemed to be the right setting; they would always associate it with the burgeoning of their love. But would she think it indelicate to broach such a personal matter in a public place? And, although Regent's Park was quiet on weekday mornings, anyone might come along at just the wrong moment. Richard couldn't decide. It was like the daily decision whether to join her in her walk, magnified a thousand times.

Celia was not the only one who found him preoccupied. One evening, Alice leaned over his chair, stroked his moustache, and said: "Richard, d'you know I've spoken to you twice and you haven't heard me?"

"I'm truly sorry, my dear."

"I don't want to disturb your thoughts. I think I'll go to bed, and you may come when you wish."

She kissed him gently, perhaps wistfully. Later, when he took her, she seemed to be moved by some unusual emotion.

Over breakfast, she said suddenly: "I don't mean to interfere in your affairs, but . . ."

"What is it, poppet?"

"There's someone else, isn't there?"

"Yes," he said. "There's a young lady." He stressed the noun slightly, lest she should think that he was setting up another mistress.

She poured the tea with a steady hand, looked directly at him, and said: "You needn't imagine that I'd try to hold you, even if I could."

"You're a sweet little thing," he said, touched.

She was indeed a sensible, tactful girl, he reflected later. There would be no tears when he dropped her; she would look forward, not back. Her little business was a success and she was able to stand on her own feet. Besides, like any other woman, she doubtless hoped to have a husband and children some time.

Then, like a gift from the gods, he received an invitation for a weekend at Longmarsh. Of course—that was the place! He would speak to Ellie at her home, where she felt safe, where Colmore engagements and weddings were as natural as the flowering of the roses. Later, it struck him that the invitation wasn't exactly a gift from the gods: more likely, a scheme of Celia's. At all events, the Ashtons were there. With Arthur and Grace Colmore too, it was a fair muster of the family.

Detained by being orderly officer, he couldn't go down until Saturday morning. It was the last Saturday in June and a scorching day, more like a day in India than in England. He took a cab to Waterloo through empty streets and caught an early train. He wasn't expected until later, so there was no one to meet him at the station and he hired a fly. The countryside was breathlessly still, the Downs blue and hazy.

The drive to Longmarsh, after passing the lodge, crossed a bridge over the little stream that fed the lake. From the crest of this bridge, Richard saw someone in a white dress seated on a bench under an old copper beech. It was Ellie.

He stopped the fly, and told the man to take his valise on to the house and say that he was taking a stroll.

She was reading, and didn't see him until he was within a few yards of her. Then she looked up, not with a smile but with her startled expression.

"I couldn't resist taking the earliest train," he said. "I shouldn't have wished to miss an hour here."

"It is a lovely day," she said.

"Would you care to walk down to the lake with me? I always think it's the most beautiful spot in the grounds."

She rose silently, put down her book with the marker in place, and began to walk with her eyes on the ground. He had the curious impression that she was walking like a prisoner under guard. She was nervous, certainly—either because of his sudden appearance or because she guessed his intentions. He was a little nervous too, but also excited, elated, borne up by the thrill of the risk and the challenge. His heart thudded as it had thudded when, far away in the Afghan hills, the bugle sounded the charge.

They reached the shore of the lake. The water was as still as in a glass. Rhododendrons, thick and luxuriant, screened them from the house.

"I have something to say to you, Miss Colmore," he began.

She looked up at him and down again, in her quick troubled way.

"You must have seen, in the time since we have known each other, that my feelings for you are of a special nature. I have tried to disguise them, I have tried to restrain them, but they are too strong and ardent for that. I love you. I love you with my whole heart, a heart that has no other desire than to offer you my devotion. I love you for your beauty, for your purity, for your goodness, for your utter perfection."

She stood motionless—yet not quite motionless. One hand picked nervously at a fold of her dress.

He resumed. "When I speak of my devotion, that word can have only one meaning. I ask you to be my wife. I have little to offer you—nothing that is worthy of you. All I have is my love, a love that will cling to you and surround you, a love that can never weaken or waver through all the years ahead. And now, my whole happiness is in your hands."

He waited. He had gazed at her while he spoke, but now he didn't dare to; the longing to seize her in his arms would have been too strong. But he was aware of a strange glance that she gave, a glance not up and down this time but to right and left, as if she were looking for a way of escape. The rhododendrons, curving to the lake, enclosed them except along the path they had followed.

"Lord Richard . . . it's s-s . . . s-s-s . . ."

Sudden? So sudden? Surprising? Whatever it was, she couldn't get it out.

"Ellie," he said gently, "you must let your heart speak, as I have mine."

She made a visible effort. "I didn't mean to stammer. I th-th . . . thought I'd got over it. It's s-s . . ." She gave up "silly," if that was the word, and said: "It's foolish, I know."

"I understand. This is a difficult moment. But all will be easy, all will be happy, if you will accept my love."

"Oh, what am I to say?" she cried. "I believe you love me. I thank you—I must thank you. But I don't know . . . I don't know . . ."

Richard felt a surge of joy. She loved him, after all—this confusion could mean nothing else. It was her shyness that wouldn't allow her to admit it. He took her hand; it was trembling.

"You have only to say one word—one short, wonderful word," he said.

"Let me th-th . . . let me think."

"Dear, dearest Ellie, I should be ashamed to press you or to cause you any distress. You will answer me later—so be it. But this I must say: whatever your answer may be, I can never love you the less, I can never love anyone else, I shall love you until the day I die."

"Oh, don't say that," she said in a low pleading tone. It was, strangely, as if he had spoken a curse on them both, instead of a promise.

"Ellie, beloved, I must say it. It is God's own truth."

"Let me go, please!" she cried. She was taking fright now, he thought, checking a smile. He released her hand. She turned and hurried away, stumbling as her feet caught in her dress, like a hunted creature.

Richard lit a cigar and walked slowly round the lake. Reason told him that he had done well. She was startled, more startled than he had expected, but it would be all right when she had calmed down. Perhaps she would consult her mother, and that would load the scales in his favour. Yet he couldn't feel the confidence that was logical. Something was against him: something that he didn't understand.

He walked up to the house. They were playing croquet on the lawn; Celia, delighted to see him, claimed him as her partner. He achieved a show of composure, but he played badly.

At luncheon, Ellie did not appear. Richard sat between Grace and an empty chair.

"Collins, go and knock on Miss Eleanor's door," Lady Farnham ordered.

Richard intervened. "I met Miss Colmore as I was walking up the drive. She told me that she was feeling unwell from the heat, and she thought it would be unwise to take any food."

"One should always eat," Lady Farnham said firmly. "Take her up a tray, Collins."

After the meal, Richard asked for a private word with Lord Farnham. They went into the library.

"What I said about Miss Colmore wasn't quite true, I'm afraid. It was my fault she didn't come to luncheon. We had an interview by the lake."

"You did, what? I think I know what you mean."

"I asked for her hand, sir. You may not be aware that I've seen a good deal of her in town. I am deeply in love with her. I hope I may ask for your consent, if I secure hers."

"Did she accept you, then?"

Richard explained what had happened.

"She's a funny girl," said Lord Farnham. "Not a bit like the others, you know. Don't worry, my boy, I'm sure she'll come round. As for my consent—I don't know anyone I'd be happier to have as a son-in-law."

Richard saw no more of Ellie in the afternoon. While he was dressing for dinner, a servant brought him a note.

Dear Lord Richard,

I write to thank you most sincerely for the honour you have done me, and to apologise for my foolish behaviour. I fear that I must apologise, too, for what I now have to tell you.

Richard closed his eyes for a moment, then forced himself to read on.

I do not feel able, at this time, to accept a proposal of marriage. I am young, perhaps younger than my years, perhaps still childish. I cannot blame you for seeing me as a wife, but I cannot see myself as that—yours or any man's. Such love as yours only makes me conscious of my unreadiness to make the response that it deserves. I cannot accept your hand, nor do I refuse it, for that too would be beyond my powers. I can only ask you to wait, though of course I can place you under no obligation to do so. When I am older, I hope to know myself better. I have told my parents of the terms in which I am writing to you. Pray do not speak of the matter to anyone else in the house.

With renewed thanks for your honourable offer, and with sincere regret for the course that I feel bound to follow,

Eleanor Colmore

Ellie was not at dinner. Richard spoke to Lord Farnham again, and said that it would be best for him to leave by the first Sunday train. Lord Farnham promised to invent a suitable story. "Don't worry, my boy," he repeated. "She'll come round in time, depend upon it."

CHAPTER 6

A Change of Career

"Your father has suffered serious accident. Come at once. Maud."

The telegram was handed to Richard as he was watching a sword-drill practice. He hurried to the mess, secured leave from the Major, and sent a man for a hansom while he changed hastily into civilian clothes. George was already at Paddington. His telegram had reached him at the House of Commons; he was in a frock-coat and top hat, quite unsuitable for the country.

"Do you know what's happened?"

"Serious accident—that's all. I suppose we got the same message."

It was a miserable November day. A yellow fog hid the houses, and the train crawled until it was out of London. The fog lifted after Reading, but the countryside looked grey and sad under a solid bank of low cloud. Richard was thinking, and doubtless George was thinking too, of the happy mood in which they had expected to make their next journey to Severalls. Maud had recently given birth to a son, and the christening was due this week.

The Duke's valet met them at the station and gave them the news. The poor fellow was as affected as if disaster had struck his own father. Out with the hounds this morning, the Duke had rashly mounted an untried blood-mare, a new purchase. It had fallen at a fence. The Duke hadn't been able to get his feet out of the stirrups in time, and the mare had rolled on top of him. It had been necessary to carry his crushed and bleeding body in through the tradesmen's entrance, lest the ladies should see it.

The Duchess and Maud—already the new Duchess, perhaps —were in the drawing room. The lamps had not been lit, although the short day was fading. Richard had a piercing sense of a familiar scene thrown into disorder.

"The doctor is with him now," Maud said.

They waited in silence. The Duchess sat like a statue, controlling herself nobly. Then, hearing a door close upstairs, the brothers glanced at each other and went to the hall.

The doctor halted on the stairs, looked at them gravely, and shook his head.

Poignantly, the funeral and the christening took place on successive days. It was by the special wish of Richard's mother —now the Dowager Duchess—that the latter was not postponed, and she found the strength to go to church for both ceremonies. The child was named Frederick after his grandfather.

Then, having done her duty, the Dowager Duchess collapsed; one appalling attack of migraine followed another. Guiltily, Richard was relieved to be back with the regiment. He had loved his father, and routine was the only salve for grief. People, of course, had the tact not to send him social invitations. He spent his evenings quietly with Alice, somewhat consoled by her sweetness and tenderness. "He was a fine gentleman," she said of Richard's father. All who had set eyes on him, from peers to housemaids, agreed on that.

About a month later, Richard received this letter:

Dear Lord Richard,

You will not know my name and I apologise for the intrusion which this letter represents. I trust that

*you will understand my situation, however, when I
mention that for upwards of ten years I have been in
receipt of an allowance of £200 p.a., paid monthly,
from your late father the Duke. This has now ceased
with the winding up of his affairs. I have no other
means of subsistence, having retired from the stage on
the Duke's account. Though having no legal claim, I
hope you will consider me deserving of continued assistance. I am certain that the Duke would have wished
it so, and would have made provision had his death not
been so sudden.*

*I have not written to the present Duke lest a letter
should fall into the hands of the Dowager Duchess and
cause her distress. You are a young gentleman who
cannot be ignorant of how such situations occur, and I
cannot believe that you will withhold your sympathy
and assistance. I presume to say that I was faithfully
devoted to the late Duke and that his happiness, to
which I believe I contributed, was my sole and constant
thought from the moment of his first attentions to me
until his death. Your reply, on which I count with a
confidence based on your reputation for generosity,
may be directed to this address.*

*With sincere assurances of my respect, I remain
your obedient servant*

Rose Hopkins (Miss).

Richard was surprised, but not shocked. He couldn't imagine himself keeping a mistress if he succeeded in marrying
Ellie, but it was impossible to lay down universal principles
in these matters. His mother had been a semi-invalid for
many years, and his father had never ceased to be a robust and
vigorous man—even more of a man, Richard felt, in the light
of this letter. Miss Hopkins seemed to be a woman of some

delicacy, as such women went; the disclosure would certainly have been a terrible blow to his mother. He couldn't help smiling at the phrase about his reputation for generosity. Could Miss Hopkins know about Alice? There was a grapevine in London, he supposed.

Strictly, he thought, the financial obligation rested on George. But George was a sobersides of a fellow; he might be wounded, though less cruelly, in the same way as his mother. Richard instructed his banker to make Miss Hopkins an allowance of a hundred a year—a sum, the banker assured him, on which a single person could live quite reasonably. The banker obviously thought that Miss Hopkins was a mistress whom Richard himself was dropping, but Richard didn't mind about that.

Then something else happened, something of infinitely greater importance. During his Christmas stay at Severalls, George said to him one afternoon: "Come into the library for a chat, there's a good fellow." He had a premonition that it was a serious moment for him. George's manner, deceptively casual as the phrase went, was not in fact very deceptive.

"Sit down, Richard. Cigar?"

"Thank you." It was a huge, very special Havana.

"I suppose you realise," George said after a pause and a clearing of the throat, "that the seat is vacant?"

For a moment, Richard couldn't imagine what he was talking about and looked vaguely at the seats in the room. Then he grasped that George meant the parliamentary seat of West Berkshire. The premonition became precise and menacing.

"I suppose it is," he said. "You're in the Lords, of course."

"Just so." Another pause. "The seat has always been held by a Somers, you realise that too."

Richard said nothing.

"To come straight out with it, old boy, I'm relying on you to take over."

"You can't mean that, George."

"I'm afraid I do."

"I haven't the faintest desire to be an M.P."

"Nor had I."

"But you didn't have any other career. I'm a soldier. I don't blab about it much, but I'm in the Army seriously. I'm hoping for a captaincy any time now."

"I know it'll be a sacrifice for you, Richard. I'm afraid there are duties that can't be avoided."

"I don't know a thing about politics. Don't read the papers, half the time. I'd be a rotten M.P."

"Buck up, old boy. When you put your mind to something, you can do it. It's not so dashed difficult, either. So long as you don't make an ass of yourself, or do anything ungentlemanly, you can manage as well as the next fellow."

"Well, in that case the next fellow can do it."

"Who? Somers are a bit thin on the ground in this generation."

"Does it have to be a Somers? It's a tradition, but it isn't a law. Most seats aren't filled by family tradition, are they?"

"West Berkshire is. Where a tradition exists, you just don't break it to suit your own preferences. I don't want to preach, but surely if we don't stand for that we don't stand for anything."

Richard stared hopelessly into the fire. A log broke and fell, like the breaking of his hopes.

George said: "Mother feels very strongly about this. You see, only one thing counts with her: keeping the seat in the family would have been the Pater's wish. His wishes are sacred to her, naturally. She's bearing up not too badly now, but an injury to his memory, as she'd consider it, is a thing one wouldn't care to inflict on her."

"You might have kept this till after Christmas," Richard said ruefully.

"I'm sorry. Mother's been worrying about it."

Richard returned to London in a mood of depression. The weather was consistently nasty: no crisp winter frosts, but a run of fog, drizzle and chilling dampness. On New Year's Eve, he dined with Robertson-Haig and drank far too much. Waking up with a splitting head, he felt that he was saying farewell to his youth.

It had been a bad year, he reflected. There had been the baffling disappointment with Ellie; then the shock and sorrow of his father's death; and now the doom of his chosen career. Some good might come of it all. He had a vague sense of growing maturity, a maturity that a man had to earn through difficulty as well as success. But the meaning of this maturity was far from clear to him.

He asked for an interview with his commanding officer. The dismay on the Colonel's face was gratifying, or at least consoling.

"Resign your commission, Somers? What the deuce for?"

Richard explained.

"Well, well, well. This is really a facer. But I suppose it can't be helped."

"I'm afraid it can't, sir."

"I'm extremely sorry, that's all I can say. Fact is, Somers, I've always regarded you as one of my most promising young officers."

"It's most kind of you, sir."

"It's no more than the truth." The Colonel pondered. "So you're going into Parliament. Don't believe we've ever had a fellow from the regiment do that. I trust you won't forget us when you're ruling over the War Office, what?"

"I'll never forget the old regiment, sir. But I've no ambitions of that kind. From now on, I'll be one of the Westminster rank and file."

Then the worst day came: the day of Richard's last parade.

A lump came into his throat when the sergeant-major shouted: "Three cheers for Lieutenant Somers!" and the shakos waved in the air. He had to muster all his self-control as he went along the ranks, shaking each man by the hand.

A month later, he was an M.P. The Liberals didn't contest the seat; opinion in the county would have been offended by political argument so soon after the Duke's death. So Richard was returned unopposed. He did, however, have to go through the ritual of addressing the adoption meeting.

"What do I say?" he asked Sir Hartley Stephens, a local baronet who was chairman of the Conservative committee.

"Nothing about politics—that won't be necessary. Hope to maintain the West Berkshire tradition—first concern will be to safeguard local interests—that kind of thing."

To his surprise, Richard found that his first public speech was no great ordeal. He was nervous when he got to his feet and confronted rows of expectant faces, but the words came easily enough. When he sat down after the required five minutes to hearty applause, he realised that he had actually enjoyed speaking.

George, having inflicted the blow, behaved with generosity. He suggested that Richard might care to live in Berkshire House.

"But it's your town house, George."

"I've no wish to spend any time in London, nor has Maud. You'll need a home when you marry, anyway, and that can't be very far ahead. So you may as well have the place now. And take Simmons with you; he'll make a perfectly good butler."

Richard was grateful; he wouldn't have enjoyed settling into a strange house along with the rest of the upheaval. Berkshire House was too large for a single man, of course, but it was familiar and he was fond of it. Simmons proved extremely capable. Richard gave a dinner about once a week—

a stag dinner, of course, since there was no hostess. He began by inviting old friends like Ralph Ashton; new friends, from his new world, might come in time.

As for the House of Commons, he took to it more easily than he had expected. It was, after all, a good club. Apparently it was quite normal for members of his own party to dine or drink with Liberals. This surprised him at first. It dawned on him by degrees that something bound them together, beyond differences of party and policy. The links were subtle but real: a common concern for the standards and traditions of the House; common assumptions about the way things were done, along with customs and habits and jokes that a newcomer had to learn; and, though of course one didn't show off about this, a common dedication to the good of the country. Like any other club, or like a regiment, the House had certain expectations of those who belonged to it. There was such a thing as being a good House of Commons man, and someone who qualified in that respect could be forgiven the most eccentric opinions.

Yet, what made the House a good club—this dawned on Richard more slowly—was precisely that it wasn't like any other club. Variety was part of its character. It was less like a club, indeed, than like a big school, with its range of swots and sporting types and arty types and simple sound good fellows. Even the Members who were distinctly not gentlemen— the unfashionable-looking provincial solicitors on the Liberal side, a few dubious adventurers in both parties, and the outlandish, fanatical Irish Nationalists—contributed to the variety and fascination of the House.

Then there were the great men—or outstanding figures, at least. There was Gladstone: if you were outside the House he was simply the head of the wrong kind of Government, but if you were inside he was far more than that. Richard could sense the Prime Minister's dignity and gravity, his earnest awareness of moral principle, and therefore the trust that he inspired in masses of respectable church-going or chapel-going people up and down the country. It was useless to mock or denigrate such a man. One had to watch him in the light of his own principles; given the trust that sustained him in power, any failure in his responsibility would be a betrayal indeed.

There was Parnell: a man tainted with disloyalty, implicated in the worst excesses of disorder and Fenianism, yet once again a more impressive figure than one could imagine from merely reading the newspapers. A strange man—remote even from his followers, unsociable, unsmiling, a bachelor, absolutely a man who stood alone. A man now bent on sheer destruction, but somehow a man fitted to rule.

It was a pity, Richard thought, that there was no similar commanding personality on the Opposition front bench. Disraeli died just after Richard entered the House; never to have seen him was a matter for deep regret. The most distinguished Conservative, Lord Salisbury, was in the Upper House, and this put the party at a certain disadvantage in the Commons.

Richard's desire—it was less than an ambition—was to be a good House of Commons man. As in West End society, he soon had the gratifying feeling that people liked him. He mixed easily and joined readily in smoking room conversation, for it was definitely not done to talk politics all the time. He also earned approval by his willingness to sit and listen, to acquire an understanding of political questions from older and more experienced men. Of course, the House wasn't an academy of experts and he didn't aim at becoming any kind of expert himself. Still, his ignorance was so complete that he felt a duty to grasp the rudiments of what was being debated. Here he was, probably for the best years of his life—until the infant Marquis of Wantage grew up, he supposed. The least he could do was to put his mind to the business.

He made his maiden speech in a debate on the state of stock-farming, after going down to Severalls so that George could brief him on the facts. He said what he had to say and sat down within ten minutes—it was bad form to go on too long, and unforgivable in a maiden speech. It went off all right, so far as he could see. He had passed his initiation.

He spoke again in the debate on the Irish Relief Bill. This was decidedly a greater test. He wasn't availing himself of the courtesy traditionally accorded to a new member, but intervening as an equal among his fellows; he had to bob up three times before the Speaker called him. While a maiden speech was something of a formality, this time he confronted a real appraisal.

He had thought hard about the issues involved. The Government was proposing to compensate tenants who were evicted by their landlords. In the first place, Richard said, this was a new and questionable use of public funds, raised by taxation which had been voted for no such purpose. Secondly, if landlords could not evict tenants of whom they disapproved and replace them by others in whom they had confidence, there was a clear threat to the rights of property. The Bill proposed only compensation for eviction, but its logic could lead to a Government claiming the power to forbid evictions, a wholly unwarranted extension of the state's authority to the private domain—and if in Ireland, why not in England? And thirdly, since in most cases the tenants were being evicted not for mere fecklessness but for deliberate nonpayment of rent as a part of the Nationalist campaign for Home Rule, compensation made offenders appear as victims and implied a condonation of that campaign. It was inconsistent of the Government to propose this measure and at the same time seek to restore public order by its Coercion Bill and its Arms Bill. "If the object of Irish Home Rule is ever to be attained," Richard concluded, "an object to which I need scarcely say that I am entirely opposed, let it at least be by the legal and parliamentary means that this House exists to uphold, and not by a surrender to illegitimate methods of social disruption and subversion."

As he made his points, aided by notes on his cuff, Richard was interrupted from the Liberal benches. He hadn't reckoned with this; the experience was totally new to him. He stopped, tried to begin again, let a sentence vanish in mid-air. A Liberal rose with a question. He was in danger of getting hopelessly sidetracked. "If I may be permitted to continue, I propose to answer that question where it arises," he said with a calmness that came from heaven knew where. "Hear, hear's" from his own side gave him confidence. He forged on, now in an attentive silence; he had that elusive reward, the ear of the House. A Nationalist shouted something incomprehensible in his vile accent and was crushed by shouts of "Order!" When Richard sat down, he knew that he had passed this second test.

After the division, he was congratulated by the man whose policy he had attacked, the Chief Secretary for Ireland. "Very neat, young man, very neat," said the Liberal dignitary. Next morning, *The Times* printed three sentences of Richard's speech. It was the equivalent of a mention in despatches.

All this time, he was still consumed with love for Ellie. Her face appeared to him in the House as it had appeared to him on the parade-ground. There was no one, of course, to whom he could disclose his feelings. He had told Alice that the young lady had rejected his advances; if he had to suffer months of uncertainty, there was no reason why Alice should suffer too.

Ellie wouldn't read the parliamentary report, he knew. Yet, in a sense, he had spoken for her. How could it be otherwise, when his entire life was lived for her? To accept the duties that fate laid upon him, to try to do his best at every task, to act as a man should—this, and only this, was to be worthy of her.

Besides, he had an idea that she might look on him with greater favour as a serious person. She would value the soberness of public responsibility more than the glamour of a Hussar uniform. When at last he saw her, he tried to appear more reflective, more mature.

He hadn't seen her for nine long months, from the summer morning when she fled from him until the following March. She was in ailing health during most of the summer and autumn, he heard. He couldn't quite gather what was the matter—a proneness to headaches, to getting easily tired, the Ashtons said. She didn't come to London to resume her music lessons, but stayed at Longmarsh. He couldn't go there without an invitation, and none reached him. He bore the deprivation as best he could; endurance, it seemed to him, was a necessary price for supreme happiness.

Letters were his only contact. He wrote enquiring about her health; she replied thanking him, saying that she didn't herself know what was wrong, nor did the doctor, but it was nothing serious. Then she sent her condolences on his father's death. In January, he wrote to inform her of the coming changes in his life. Each time, he gave her fervent assurances of his love. To these, in her dutiful replies, she never referred.

Then Celia told him that Ellie was in London. She was with her mother at the house in Berkeley Square, for the season. She had been allowed to miss one season to study the piano; that concession was not to be made twice.

"Her health is restored, then?" Richard asked.

Celia made a moue. "You know my mother. Ellie will do the season if she has to do it in a wheelchair."

Partly by contrivance and partly by luck, he saw Ellie several times—at dances and receptions, at Celia's evenings, and twice when he paid formal calls on Lady Farnham. She looked quite well, although not at all happy. Once again, clearly, she detested the season. Asked how she was spending her time, she gave the briefest of answers. Doubtless she was going about, or being dragged about, a great deal, and he didn't want to add to the strain by forcing his company on her too often. Besides, he hadn't much free time himself. The parliamentary session was at its busiest, and the political scene—mainly because of Ireland—was far from tranquil. If he wanted to be a good House of Commons man, he had to be a regular attender at debates and divisions. He had dinner invitations, which were to be regarded as an honour, from older Members; he didn't like to drop his Army friends altogether; and he allowed himself at least one night a week with Alice. It would have been a full life, even without being in love.

It was particularly difficult for him to be alone with Ellie. When he paid his calls, he had the impression that she must have made her mother promise to remain in the room. At the events of the season, there was always a crowd—round Ellie, especially. But at last, one evening in May, his chance came. They were both at a ball, one of the grandest of the season, and he partnered her—the joy of holding her by the waist was ecstatic—in a waltz. She complained of the stuffy air and the noise, and he prevailed on her to sit out the next dance on the terrace. It was a warm night; the garden was a pool of darkness between the brilliantly lit mansion and the lamps of Piccadilly.

"Something has happened in this last year," he said. "Something that I should not have thought possible."

She said nothing, but looked timidly at him.

"I am more in love with you than I ever was."

She looked down at the paved terrace. He heard her sigh; the meaning of the sigh was a matter for conjecture.

"Ellie, we must talk to each other. Can we meet without this crowd, do you think? Perhaps in Regent's Park, where we had so many happy hours."

"I'll try," she murmured. "After this dreadful season is over—I'll try."

"I have waited, my dearest one. I would wait for you for ever. But the waiting is long; my heart gives me no peace."

For a moment, he thought that she was going to make an answer that would encourage his hopes. But all that she said was: "Please, let's go inside."

CHAPTER 7

A Long Engagement

THE SEASON—the dreadful season. For Ellie, it was a nightmare of noise, of crowds, of exposure. Twice a day, for the afternoon tea party and for the evening, she had to be prepared: strapped and laced into dresses with tight waists, hung about with jewellery, fussed over and intimately touched by maids, harassed by her mother because time was passing. At last her mother declared that she looked lovely, and the maids joined in a chorus of admiration. But what Ellie felt was that, with each stage of the dressing, she took on a disguise. She was being prepared, not for any kind of life, but for display. They might just as well have dressed up a doll. There were in fact clockwork dolls that performed pretty much as she was to perform.

Then she was led into the arena. It really seemed like that; she had a vivid dream, suggested by a historical novel that she had read, of being a Christian martyr in the Roman arena, and the same helpless terror came over her every time she entered a drawing room, a dining room or—worst of all —a ballroom. Merely to stand there, stared at by scores of eyes, would have been fearful enough. But she had to play her part. She had to dance, which she had never enjoyed or done well. She had to consume sherbets and little cakes and glasses of champagne which she didn't want. She had to talk, though she was sure that no one caught what she said in the incessant noise, and it didn't matter so long as her lips were seen to move. She had to smile, and smile again, and keep smiling, for no reason that made any sense.

She was performing for the men, of course. It was clear that, while the season was organised by women, men were the destined beneficiaries. The point was to get the girls, such as Ellie herself, engaged: that is, successfully delivered into the hands of the men. At the end of each season the score was totted up, like the bag after a day's shooting.

The method was to reduce her, by a mixture of flattery and intimidation, to a state in which her surrender would be inevitable and would appear—this was a strict convention—to have been made of her own free will, her so-called choice. To this end, the men gazed at her with widened eyes of adoration, whose real greed and impatience were only at times perceptible. They smiled to make her smile and talked to make her talk. They pleaded with her to dance, as if she had any right to refuse. They made opportunities to touch her—gripping her waist in the dance, clasping her hand when they talked, holding her arm to steer her where they wanted her to go. She loathed being touched, even by women and far more by men. They schemed to get her alone on a terrace or in a garden. And all the time she felt herself struggling— weakly, vainly—against an undermining of her will, of her thinking mind, of whatever she could call her essential self.

She counted the days to the end of the season. But it would be only a reprieve, she knew: other seasons lay ahead. She was twenty, and as ripe for the market as a turkey at Christmas. With every year from now onward, her continued freedom would be more of a failure, even an offence. Even Charlotte had been dragged through half a dozen seasons, despite her inadequacy as an offering, to be mercifully released only when she proved quite hopeless. And Charlotte was strong in character, able to take it all as a mere nuisance and indeed as rather a joke. Ellie didn't see how she could endure.

There was only one way of escape, and this was the surrender itself. She could agree to marry Richard. He would press her for a decision, undoubtedly, before the summer was out.

That she ought to accept Richard was obvious to everyone except herself. By failing to do so, she would condemn herself as very foolish, very annoying and difficult, altogether unreasonable. The women of the family had been telling her this ever since his proposal. They were like allies in a campaign, each employing the tactics of her choice.

There was Lady Farnham, bringing to bear all her resources of wisdom and force of character and, naturally, maternal authority. Her argument was that Ellie was in danger of missing a precious opportunity. As she repeatedly pointed out, Lord Richard Somers was a man who needn't look far for a bride.

There was Celia, whose particular weapon was to assume that it wasn't a question of yes or no, but of Richard or someone else. "Whom are you thinking of, apart from Lord Richard?" she would ask. "You can tell me, you know." She simply refused to believe that there was no one else. Once, exasperated, she said: "But, you little goose, you can't go through life without a man, can you?"

"Why not?" Ellie ventured to ask.

"Why not?" Celia stared at her with dilated eyes and said: "You know very well why not—we all know, really." Ellie was terrified. A talk with Celia always threw her into confusion and stammering, because she couldn't forget about Major Falconer.

There was Fanny, who appeared from Paris in the middle

of the season and regarded the whole business as an entertain-
ing drama, but also as a perfectly simple situation involving
no dilemma at all. "If you want to keep the men dangling a
bit longer, my dear, it's your privilege," she said. Ellie earnestly denied that she wanted any such thing. "Well then,
marry Lord Richard, for heaven's sake—you'll never do
better."

There was Grace, Arthur's wife, who made Ellie feel quite
guilty by treating her with kindness and sympathy. She said
that she'd been a shy girl herself, that saying Yes to a man
always required courage, but that saying No out of a lack of
courage could lead only to lasting regrets. Sometimes, according to Grace, it was only after marrying a man that one
knew for certain that one had loved him all along.

So they all agreed—all except Charlotte, who refrained
from giving advice and told Ellie: "You are the only one
who knows what is right for you." But probably Charlotte
agreed too, and it could be said that, being unmarried, she
lacked the qualification to hold an opinion. The rest of them
seemed to be saying: "We are women, we are married, we
know that marriage is the destiny and fulfilment of a woman
—who are you to deny it?" Surely it was both wrong and
foolish to defy them. They had always cared for her and
helped her; surely they would advise only what was for her
good. Even if she had good reason to resist them, and to resist
the rules and assumptions of her entire known world, she
didn't believe that she would have the strength. But indeed,
what reason could she have?

There was no doubt in her mind that Richard would be a
good husband. He was kind, considerate and—she felt this
strongly—sincere, far more than any of the other young men
who pestered her. She also had a feeling that he was cleverer
than people guessed. He would achieve something; his wife
would be proud of him.

Then, there was no doubt that Richard loved her. That day by the lake, and again this year on the terrace, she had felt the force of his love so powerfully that it frightened her, it seemed to overwhelm her. That was her foolishness, however. For she had also felt a strange, bewildering kind of joy. This was what a woman ought to feel, Ellie supposed, when she knew herself to be truly loved by a man. The joy frightened her, too—or it was joy and fear at the same time. Perhaps, if she married him, the fear would leave her and the joy would remain.

But did she love him? This was the question that had plagued her for almost a year. She pondered over it, she wrestled with it, and still she had no answer—no certainty. Sometimes she felt that she wanted Richard as a friend; she looked back fondly to their walks in the park, when there had been only friendship between them. But one couldn't go on having such a friendship with a man, except of course an older man like Dr. Pfaffer. Besides, Richard hadn't been only a friend to her in reality. He had loved her, and she had known it although she had refused to admit it to herself.

The source of her doubt, she thought, was that she didn't really know what love was. Other people—other women— seemed to know, and took the knowledge for granted so much that they couldn't imagine its absence. Certainly they never explained what love was. So, how could she know? How could she recognise it?

She had missed Richard during the months of separation and wanted (while also dreading it) to see him again. She found pleasure in being with him, in the sound of his voice, and in the look in his eyes when she ventured to meet them. And there was the strange joy; she was sure about the joy. Perhaps this joy was love. Perhaps, if she sought anything else, she was imagining what didn't exist. Perhaps it was all as simple as other women seemed to find it. In that case, if only she could conquer her fear and her shyness—and these, after all, were faults—she would understand that she too had been in love all along.

She thought, too, that the fear which made her tremble in his presence might be itself a proof of love. For a woman's love was submission, as a man's love was the desire to possess. And in face of submission, there must be fear.

But that was the trouble. Something very deep in her— her essential fault, doubtless—made her recoil from submitting, to Richard or to any man. Yet something equally deep wanted to submit, to know the relief and security of coming to rest in his keeping, leaving all doubts and struggles behind. When she considered the question in this way, it seemed to follow that she had only to cease her resistance, a resistance which she couldn't explain and which she knew to be wrong and unwomanly. She had only to give the upper hand to the feelings that were right and womanly. Then she would find peace.

She had to make up her mind soon, anyway. It wasn't honourable or kind or sensible to keep him in uncertainty for more than a year. Besides, although Richard had said that he would wait for ever, her mother might be right—the opportunity might pass by, and then she would be fair game for other hunters. The season was coming to an end at last. She yearned to return to Longmarsh, but her mother wouldn't let her leave London without giving Richard his answer.

He was always free in the mornings, he said. Replying to a note from him, she said that she would be pleased to walk with him in Regent's Park. She felt almost at home there, and she wouldn't come across acquaintances as in Hyde Park. Richard called for her, he made his carriage wait, and they walked along the Broad Walk or sometimes by the lake, just as they had a year ago. It was fine, sunny June weather, but not too hot for walking.

Inevitably, it wasn't like last year. Then, he hadn't declared his love for her and they could talk about everyday topics or remain easily silent. Now, his love was in the open and every meeting was a renewal of his proposal. Small-talk was an evasion, silence was awkward. He spoke of his love every day, sometimes only when they met and when they parted, sometimes all the time they were together.

She saw that he was gaining confidence. To him, evidently, it was all fairly simple: not entirely simple—he called her his little puzzle—but simpler than it was for her. She was exceptionally shy and hesitant, and this was what he had to contend with. He had to be persistent without being rough or demanding, he had to be persuasive, he had to be eloquent. He really was eloquent—it must be from speaking in Parliament, she supposed. Quite clearly, he felt that he was winning. He would win by his confidence, by his eloquence, and above all—as he deserved to win—by the strength of his love.

Somehow, it was no longer a question of her resistance. She wasn't resisting; she was merely failing to say Yes. It was a question of her courage. To commit herself, to take the great decision of her life, did call for courage. Without in any sense accusing her, he made her feel this. She grew ashamed of her lack of courage, her feebleness. She might regret it for ever, as Grace had said. She got up every day determined to make the effort. The possibility of saying No had become unreal, something she no longer thought of. There was only her inexplicable and tormenting failure, a failure that she had to overcome.

She said Yes on the Friday, for no particular reason except that the approach of the weekend set a kind of time-table (he was invited to Hatfield, Lord Salisbury's place) and thus heightened his eloquence and his urgency. She heard his voice throbbing with passion—though he never raised it unduly—as he asked once again: "Will you be mine, dear Ellie?"

"Yes," she said. She hadn't known until that moment that she would. The word seemed to have escaped from her like a breath, without her volition.

He asked: "Did I hear you say Yes, Ellie?"

Perhaps, at long last, he found it too good to be true. More probably, she had spoken too quietly to be clear. She found herself unable to repeat the word, but she nodded.

"I am the happiest man on earth," he said.

She felt, more than anything else, a tremendous relief. It had certainly been an effort. She was pale, presumably; he took her arm and said: "Let's sit down on that bench."

He kissed her, and it took her by surprise, although of course it was what a man did at this moment. She had never been kissed on the lips before. It gave her a stifled feeling, though he did it gently. It was curious, she thought: something that five minutes ago would have been unforgivable conduct, an outrage on her virtue, was now his natural right. It was the beginning of submission. But that was love—she must, absolutely must, believe in love now.

He drew away, and she compelled herself to look at him, ashamed that this was an effort too. He was smiling cheerfully.

"Oh, hang Hatfield!" he said. "Hang Lord Salisbury! I don't want to be anywhere but with you, my sweetheart."

"I'm going to Longmarsh anyway," she said.

"Can we live apart until Monday, do you think?"

She thought: how strange, I shall never live apart from this man again. Somehow this appeared to her as a new fact, which she hadn't taken into account. She was being very silly, obviously.

Richard came with her to give the news to the delighted

Lady Farnham. Celia knew within an hour; Lord Farnham and Charlotte knew by the afternoon. Ellie began to live a new life, as a fiancée, which was not that of a wife but something of the same order.

The family mustered at Longmarsh on the following weekend. Arthur and Grace came, and Ralph and Celia, and Fanny and, for once, Claude de Chaumont. Richard placed the engagement ring on Ellie's finger and kissed her (on the cheek, but publicly—an extraordinary feeling). Their future happiness was toasted in champagne. The atmosphere was more than joyful; it was jubilant, triumphant, as if a victory had been secured after a real risk of defeat. A victory for whom? Ellie wondered. For Richard, obviously. Also, and just as clearly, for the Colmore family. Also, she felt, for the institution of marriage, for the hallowed relationship of man and woman, for the proper functioning of society.

When the House rose, Richard came again and stayed for a month. Ellie found that she was living with him, more or less—rather more than less, indeed. He came down to breakfast at the same time as she (did he watch for her?), kissed her cheerfully, and set before her what he soon learned to be her favourite dishes. They discussed what they would do with the day: a walk, an outing in the trap with a picnic or lunch at a country inn, perhaps a ride. He knew that she disliked riding, but he loved it, so she sometimes rode for his sake. She would soon come to enjoy it, he said confidently— perhaps she hadn't had the right mount. She still didn't enjoy it, but she didn't like to say so. Almost every day, they did what he wanted. He couldn't be blamed for this; he always consulted her wishes, and made a suggestion only when she didn't have one. Somehow, she seldom had. It was absurd to reject what he proposed if she could offer no alternative. A pattern established itself: initiative on his part, acquiescence on hers. The pattern of marriage, she supposed.

It was assumed that she and Richard would be alone most of the time. The others—even the younger children, properly instructed no doubt—didn't join in an outing unless they were particularly asked, and even then had to be pressed. Finding Richard and Ellie in a room or a corner of the garden, they made excuses to vanish. But it was very difficult, and clearly not at all the right thing, for Ellie to be alone as she had previously understood the word—by herself. If she set out for a stroll in the grounds, Richard was at once by her side. When she played the piano, he was there to turn the pages. When she said that she wished to read, he sat opposite her and read too, saying that he wouldn't disturb her. She read novels or poetry as usual; he was reading Burke, having been told by a senior M.P. that he would thus gain an essential grounding in political philosophy. He read seriously— clearly she didn't disturb him. She, however, found it hard to concentrate in his presence. Sometimes she put her book aside and took up her crotchet-work, at which he smiled tolerantly.

When they were alone, Richard often touched her. It was in a man's nature to take pleasure in this, no doubt. He put his arm round her waist when they walked; he held or stroked her hands when they sat on a garden bench; and when he told her that she had glorious hair, or pretty little ears, or wonderfully smooth cheeks, he stressed what he was saying by touch, as if somehow this made it truer. He never asked whether she wanted to be touched. Men didn't have to ask, she had to remind herself. She felt that her face, her hair, her hands were no longer her own. They were at Richard's disposal, by the right of his conquest of her.

He also had a right to kiss her, whenever he chose and likewise without asking her. Sometimes the kisses were gentle, but sometimes they were passionate, indeed forceful, and sometimes they were repeated until she felt that he would never stop. She wished that she could enjoy it. Other women enjoyed it, she knew, though presumably not so much as men. But she hated the pressure; she hated the brushing sensation of his moustache; she couldn't get over the feeling of being stifled when his lips shut off the air from hers; and worst of all she hated the hard touch of his teeth. (He had rather prominent teeth, she now noticed for the first time.) No, even that was not the worst. The worst was being embraced, when her whole body was pressed and stifled and her breasts went flat against his chest.

She was well aware of why she hated being kissed, and being embraced in particular. It made her think of what would happen after they were married. Her body would be fully at his disposal, and he would do the thing that men did to women. She thought of this continually. Richard often said, "What are you thinking of, my love?" or, "Penny for your thoughts," and she blushed because she could not answer.

She didn't know how she could ever bring herself to endure it. She was afraid of it because it was violent and loathsome, and she was afraid of it too because it would transform Richard into a violent and loathsome creature. She loved him now—she had told him so, admittedly at his urging, but she did believe it. She hoped that, as his wife, she would come to love him more and more. But how could she love him, when her closest intimacy with him was expressed in this thing?

She toyed with the hope—the fantasy—that he wouldn't do it after all. But she knew that he would. It was a husband's right, and a wife had no right to deny him. Just as a kiss on the lips became permissible when they were engaged, so the thing became permissible when they were married. Above all, she knew that he wanted to do it. She saw that in his eyes when he touched her before a kiss; to stop at kissing, for a man, was restraint. Sometimes—when he embraced her in a lonely place, and when he kissed her goodnight at the door of her bedroom—she guessed that he would like to do the thing now, if the rules had allowed it.

During his stay at Longmarsh, Richard raised the question of the date of the wedding. Ellie had been afraid of this. She still couldn't manage to think of herself as a wife; she needed more time for that. And the thing he would do to her as her husband—perhaps time would help her to be reconciled to it, to prepare for it somehow, though she couldn't imagine how. Of course, she couldn't speak of this to him.

"I thought perhaps . . . next summer," she said.

He was displeased, as she had expected.

"That means a year's engagement. It isn't usual, unless there's a death or some such reason."

"I don't like the idea of being married in winter," she explained. "We've always been together in summer—it seems right for us. And there's the honeymoon. Wherever can one go in winter?"

Richard had been thinking of October, which could be quite a pleasant month. He looked at her reflectively. It was still true, as it had been when he began to woo her, that she took fright if she was rushed. He must accept that, since he loved her.

"Well, you've certainly thought it all out, you clever little puss," he said. "Let it be as you wish. Still, it's a very long engagement."

"Dear Richard," she said, "you're so kind and patient with me."

That struck the right note. He smiled generously and pressed her hand.

He did try to persuade her into a spring wedding. The House was in recess for Easter, and the weather might be good. But there was nothing like the summer, she said. They compromised on Whitsun, when the House rose for a fortnight and he could reasonably take another week. Calendars were consulted; the wedding was fixed for the Thursday before Whitsun, a date in the last week of May.

In September, they went to stay at Severalls. Ellie didn't enjoy this at all. She was daunted by the palatial house, the atmosphere of formality, and the large array of servants whom she never managed to recognise. She was glad that, barring unlikely accidents, Richard could never become Duke of Berkshire; she couldn't possibly live in this place.

She found the Duke very dull and soon decided that he was stupid—a quality that irritated her, and surprising in Richard's brother. The Dowager Duchess hardly spoke to her, and evidently saw the world through a triple veil of wasting health, irreparable grief and piety. Only the Duchess was at all companionable. But there was nothing to talk about, for this was a house in which no one ever read books or listened to music.

They returned to London. It was assumed that Ellie would wish to be in London, with Richard, and accordingly Lady Farnham was prepared to make a long stay in the town house. Anne, now fifteen years old, would benefit from a taste of London life and from visiting the museums and galleries. Ellie, however, said that she would be perfectly happy staying with her aunt. She would resume her lessons with Dr. Pfaffer, to keep busy while Richard was occupied.

In fact, she saw Richard every day and often twice a day. He escorted her to Prince Albert Road, and generally he stayed during the piano lesson. "I'll sit in the corner and be as quiet as a mouse," he said jovially. Ellie could see that Dr. Pfaffer wasn't pleased, and indeed she wasn't pleased either. The lessons had been her refuge, the last stronghold of her former self. But she didn't see how to object to Richard's presence. Evidently he intended it as showing a sympathetic interest in her hobby, which most men wouldn't have bothered about. And, she supposed, he had a right to be with her anywhere, now that she was his.

On two or three evenings a week, she went to dinner parties with him. She hadn't expected all this dressing up and gadding about; it was almost like the season all over again. But it was part of being engaged, apparently. She had to be displayed once more, or she and Richard had to be displayed as an engaged couple—a handsome couple, people said. Friends of the Farnhams were eager to meet him, or to entertain him if they already knew him. Richard's friends were still more eager to meet her. She met his old mess-mates from the regiment, who devoured her with their eyes and told her that Richard had always been a devilish lucky fellow. She met young M.P.'s; to her surprise, they were not much more interesting than Hussar officers. In her mind was always the thought that these were the people whom she would be inviting to dinner for the rest of her life, because they were Richard's friends.

Once, as she was leaving the dinner table with the other ladies, she heard a man saying rather too loudly: "By jingo, Somers, you're going to have some splendid rides on that little filly." She paused to hear how Richard would answer. He laughed and said: "She's a shy one, you know—didn't come to the bridle without whistling."

She noticed an odd social convention. People didn't congratulate her, although getting married was supposed to represent happiness for a woman; they congratulated Richard. But it made sense. They were congratulating him on his successful pursuit, on his capture. The engagement period was indeed like the season. The difference was this: in the season she had been made to show herself as a quarry, and now as a trophy.

She hated it. And she was bad at it; she never knew what

to say, she couldn't manage to smile and look suitably happy. But if she was bad at being a fiancée, how could she be any better at being a wife?

The engagement seemed to her like a long journey to a destination that she had not chosen. She was being carried on helplessly, against her wish. Against her wish, really? That was impossible. Yet she felt it.

When Christmas was over, preparations for the wedding began in earnest. In Lady Farnham's experience, there was always a last-minute rush no matter how early one started to plan. She arrived in London and plunged into the business zestfully. The first question was: where would the wedding take place? Ellie said that she would prefer Longmarsh parish church. The idea was charming but in practice impossible, Lady Farnham said. When the bridegroom was a Duke's brother, things had to be done in suitable style. This meant inviting everyone of a certain position in society, and when one reckoned with connections of both families, Hussar officers, Members of Parliament, and pillars of the Conservative Party in Richard's constituency, the number of guests ran into scores. Longmarsh wasn't big enough for the wedding breakfast; there wouldn't even be room for them all in the church. No, the wedding must be in London. Lady Farnham vacillated in some agony of mind between St. Margaret's, Westminster; St. James's, Piccadilly; and St. George's, Hanover Square; she decided on St. Margaret's because of its symbolic proximity to the Houses of Parliament.

Then there was the question of the honeymoon. Fanny wrote offering the loan of her country place, which was on the Seine near Rouen, an easy journey if one crossed to Dieppe. Ellie was in favour of this, mainly because she wouldn't see anyone she knew. Richard said that it would be quite an adventure; he had never been abroad, except to

India which, being British, wasn't exactly abroad. He wouldn't attempt to talk French, he said, but he could rely on Ellie for that.

Then, of course, the trousseau. Once again, Ellie had to be measured, examined, twiddled round like a tailor's dummy, repeatedly touched. The wedding-dress was a major undertaking, sketched and planned as an architect designs a house. There had to be a dress for the wedding breakfast, a going-away dress, relatively simple dresses for quiet country days on the honeymoon, but also dresses in the height of fashion because she would be in France—urgent letters went to Fanny to find out what was being worn in Paris. The assumption was that Ellie could not possibly wear anything she possessed already. She had to become, visibly, someone else.

Beyond this, she had to concern herself already with her future home. She was daunted when Richard showed her over Berkshire House for the first time. It wasn't so vast as Severalls, but it was very big for a town house. She didn't see how they could possibly use all the rooms. When she said this, Richard chuckled and answered: "Well, my love, it's a family house." Introduced to the servants, she was daunted again by Simmons, who told her with an upper servant's blend of deference and privileged chattiness that he could remember Lord Richard shaving for the first time and cutting his chin. Simmons would always know things about Richard that she did not. She would have liked to start off with a new butler, but didn't dare to say so.

She was supposed to indicate any changes in the furnishings or decoration that she would like. The workmen could be put in now, while Richard was out all day; after the marriage (when Ellie would presumably be in all day) it would be inconvenient. She was unable to think of anything. There was already a music-room with a magnificent piano, though it had not been played since Richard's now elderly aunts had

had their girlhood lessons. Feeling obliged to make some suggestion, she asked for the paintwork in her own bedroom to be blue, as in her room at Longmarsh, instead of chocolate-brown. She was daunted too by his bedroom, which was big enough to give a party in, but was in fact to be the scene of . . . what she thought about all the time.

All these preparations were repugnant to her. She hated fuss and bother, and she thought with dread of the ceremony and the wedding breakfast, when she would be displayed and stared at as never before. She was troubled, too, by a growing sense of unreality. It was foolish, of course. The marriage ought to be getting more real, not less. Yet she could not resist the wild, absurd notion that it was all a charade, that it had nothing to do with her—that the marriage wasn't going to happen.

She still wasn't ready for it, at all events. Richard had a habit of celebrating anniversaries beforehand, so to speak. He would kiss her and say: "Only four more months" . . . "Only three more months." These announcements always startled her. She didn't want the wedding to come soon, any more than she had at the beginning of the engagement.

In March, she was parted from Richard for three days. He had to attend certain functions in his constituency. "Next time, the Member will be accompanied by his wife," he said; and she was startled again, not having reckoned with this aspect of being married to him. He suggested that Ellie might care to stay at Severalls for the three days, or else to take a rest at Longmarsh, but she decided to remain in London. At first guiltily, then frankly, she admitted to herself that it was wonderful to be alone. She walked alone, despite the blustery weather, to Dr. Pfaffer's. Her lessons, which had been going badly for some while, suddenly went well. In the afternoons and evenings she practised the piano, read with concentration, or simply sat alone in her room and thought.

In these three days, she came to understand what had been happening to her during the engagement and would happen to her—increasingly, irrevocably, fatally—in her marriage. She was ceasing to be herself. She was being remade as Lady Richard Somers, and destroyed as Ellie. Destroyed gently, destroyed with love, but destroyed all the same. What confronted her was not merely submission, but annihilation.

Some women welcomed this, she thought. Some could survive, like her mother, who was so strong and positive, or like Celia and Fanny, who were high-spirited. But she, Ellie, would not survive.

She realised that, after all, she could not marry Richard. She tried to convince herself that this was merely another sign of her foolishness. But she knew that this was not true. She was releasing, from a kind of locked-away darkness, her real feelings, her real thoughts and wishes, her real nature. A strange pride stirred in her.

So there was only one thing to do. She must break off the engagement. It would call for immense courage, incomparably more courage than the effort of accepting Richard last year. It would be intensely painful for Richard, who truly loved her. It would be painful for her; for she felt, curiously, that she loved Richard now more than ever before. There would, of course, be the most terrifying scenes with her family. And she would never be able to explain why she was doing this, either to Richard or to anyone else—not only because she would get confused and stammer, but because what she felt would be utterly meaningless to them. Girls did break their engagements, true, but only because of some fault discovered in the man, or because they fell irresistibly in love with another man. She could give no such reason, so her conduct would be inexcusable.

Nevertheless, she had to do it. A curious, melancholy calm

came to her, from the knowledge that she had no choice. She doubted her courage, but she didn't doubt the decision. She was afraid of the scenes, afraid of utterly collapsing; but in her deepest self, the self that would be saved and would remain after the ordeal was over, she was not afraid.

Since she had to do it, she must do it at once. Any pretence that she still meant to be Richard's wife would be the most dishonourable hypocrisy. She began a letter, but decided that this was cowardly; for his love, he deserved a farewell from her lips.

Unexpectedly, on the day when he was due back in London, he came to Prince Albert Road to escort her home after her music lesson. He must have come straight from the station. She was thrown into perplexity; she couldn't very well speak to him in the carriage. It was raining, so she couldn't suggest a walk in the park. Nor did she want to speak to him at Clarence Terrace, with her aunt within earshot.

"It has been an age," he said in the carriage, stroking her hand.

She said nothing.

"You look pale, my darling," he went on. "More beautiful than ever, but pale. Is anything the matter?"

"I slept badly," she answered. She had scarcely slept at all.

"I had to see you today," he said, "but I'm afraid we can't be together this evening. I must be in the House until the ten o'clock division. Perhaps it's just as well; you'd be wise to go to bed early. Tomorrow we're dining at the Humphreys', you remember."

At half-past nine, Ellie said to her aunt: "I'm going out."

"You're going out, dear? At this hour? And in this weather?"

"I have to see Richard."

Mrs. Fairfax smiled. "Ah, very well. Still, you might have

thought of it before the carriage was put away. I'd better send Wilson out for a hansom. If I'm in bed when you come back, tell him to lock up."

When Ellie reached Berkshire House, Richard hadn't come in yet. Simmons ushered her into the drawing room.

"Shall I serve anything, Miss Colmore? Madeira and biscuits, perhaps?"

"Yes, Simmons, thank you."

Richard didn't come until a quarter to eleven. She thought guiltily of the cabby waiting in the rain. But it wouldn't take long, she hoped.

She heard the front door, Simmons' voice, and then Richard's: "What? Is she?" Then he came hurrying in.

"My love, this is an unexpected pleasure."

"Richard," she said, "you must listen, please, to what I have to say."

"That sounds very solemn."

"It is. I can't marry you, Richard. I've come to return your ring." And she did, in fact, take it off her finger and hold it out.

He asked: "Do you know what you've just said, Ellie?"

"Yes, I know."

Then a curious thing happened. Richard, the fluent, the eloquent, stammered: "But . . . but . . . but . . ." Almost as surprisingly, Ellie was quite in command of her words.

"I know this must hurt you, Richard," she said. "It grieves me, too, more than I can express. But I have searched my heart. I have thought long and earnestly. I did you a great wrong when I accepted your hand; I was promising what, I now realise, I cannot do. I can only try to make up for it— like this."

"I don't understand. This is impossible—meaningless."

"I was afraid you would say that."

"It *is* impossible," he cried, regaining his voice. "Everything tells me so—our love, and the happy hours and days we've spent together already, and your sweet and loving nature. You can't leave me, Ellie. We have come too close together for that. Nothing can divide us, nothing."

"You must believe me," she said, quavering a little now.

"I can't believe you. You don't give me a reason, anyway. If I've done anything to offend you, if I can alter my ways to be worthy of you, I beg you to be frank."

"It's nothing like that. No woman could hope for a better husband, truly. The reason is only . . . I can't be your wife. It isn't in me."

"You're dreaming, Ellie! Or I'm dreaming. Help me to wake!" He moved toward her.

"Don't touch me, Richard, please."

He stopped short, then paced about the room, straining to control himself.

"Something has happened while I was away," he said. "Someone has poisoned your mind. Or your old fears have returned. Tell me, darling, please tell me."

"Nothing has happened, except that I've thought seriously."

"But, dash it, what are these thoughts?"

"I think . . . You deserve happiness, Richard. If I could give it to you, I would. But I can't."

"I won't believe this!" he shouted suddenly. "You are mine, my dearest, you are mine. You belong to me if ever a woman belonged to a man. Happiness!—What happiness can there be without you? I love you beyond reason, beyond thought, to distraction."

"Please, Richard . . ."

"And you!" he swept on. "You love me, Ellie. You can't dissemble about that. Stand there, if you can, and say that you don't love me."

"I do love you," she said, faintly and sadly.

"Then this is madness, simply madness. If we love, we must marry. If we love, we must never part."

"We must part," she said still more sadly. "I must be true to myself."

"I won't let you go."

"I must go. I must go now, from this house, before we make each other any more wretched."

"I won't take the ring. Throw it in the gutter if you wish— I won't take it. We belong to each other for ever. I told you that I shall love you until the day I die. I swear that now, on my most sacred faith."

"Goodbye, Richard."

"No—you shan't go!"

He reached to seize her hands. She knew that she had to draw on the last reserves of her courage. If she yielded now, he would possess her for ever. She ran from him and pulled the bell-cord.

"Simmons, my hat and cloak, please."

She couldn't have got away if Richard hadn't, for a minute, stood like a man under a spell. But when the cab started to move, she looked back and saw him on the pavement, bareheaded in the pouring rain.

CHAPTER 8

The Peace
of Marriage

ON AN APRIL DAY in 1884, a little more than two years after
the scene described in the last chapter, Lord Richard Somers
and Geraldine Hutchison were married in the parish church
of St. Marylebone.

Richard could not have said, in retrospect, how long he remained plunged in misery after Ellie vanished from his life.
The recovery was gradual, like the recovery from grief after
a death. There was a period when it seemed unthinkable, and
it could never be complete. He knew, even in the midst of
his happiness with Geraldine, that he bore the wound with
him and would bear it all his life. The sorrow came to him,
no longer like a sharp pain but like a dull heavy ache, at unexpected times and especially when he was alone: tramping
through the Berkshire woods, or working in his study, or
waking in the small hours from a dream that he knew,
though he could not recall it any more than he could bring
her back, must be of Ellie.

The first days after Ellie went, though they proved not to
be the worst time, were very hard. He had to cope, for one
thing, with the sympathy or embarrassment of other people.
This was trivial beside his inner anguish, but it roused that
anguish as a touch can rouse a bodily pain. Men at his club

or at the House greeted him with exaggerated heartiness, evidently uncertain whether to mention what they'd heard or not. Lord and Lady Farnham hastened to London, full of regret and bewilderment. They were more overtly distressed than Richard, and he found himself trying to console them. Celia Ashton said: "I don't know if I should apologise for my sister—I believe she's utterly insane." After this, he avoided the Ashtons' house as much as he could; Ralph was a lasting friend, but Richard preferred to meet him for a stag dinner. Arthur Colmore, who belonged to Richard's club, had the tact to say simply: "I'm sorry about what's happened." Richard was grateful for this, but he was glad when Arthur was posted abroad again. Much as he liked and respected Arthur, he wanted to see no one connected with Ellie.

A couple of weeks after the first shock—again, as happens after a death—he was struck by a second and utterly overwhelming wave of sorrow. The House rose for the Easter recess, so he had nothing to do; he lost track of the day of the week, even the time of day. Simmons had orders to admit no callers, he shrank from going out, and he went from morning to night without uttering a word except for a necessary order. The weather was foul, without a hint of spring. He wandered from room to room, always feeling cold despite the blazing fires, or stood for hours at a window staring at the incessant rain. He tried to read, but in vain; often he didn't even glance at the paper. He ate what was put before him without noticing what it was. He slept heavily but for short periods, in armchairs as much as in bed. There were days when he didn't rise until noon, days when he breakfasted or even lunched before shaving, days when he didn't change for dinner. There were nights when he got stupidly and suddenly drunk on whisky or brandy—not that this helped at all—and was still dressed and downstairs, his head splitting, when a frightened housemaid came to sweep the fireplace. The servants must have thought that he was going to the dogs. But he was past caring about that.

One thought filled his mind—Ellie, Ellie, Ellie. But it wasn't really a thought. It was a vain yearning, a torment; it was the love that had obsessed him for two years, as intense as ever, but turned by loss into despair. She was always before his eyes as she had been on that last night, unbearably beautiful, holding the ring in her hand. She had put the ring down on the hall table; Simmons, eventually, informed Richard that he had locked it away.

Sometimes the memory was so sharp that it was as though he could literally see her. In his agony, he probably spoke to her and reached out to touch her—he didn't know. But she disappeared, like a vision fading into air. That she had disappeared, however, was not altogether a figure of speech. She was not at her aunt's house, nor at Longmarsh. At first, there was no trace of her except for telegrams to say that she was safe and well. Then she wrote to her parents and told them where she was, but added that she was trusting them not to tell Richard. Perhaps he could have pressed them, but he didn't. If he were ever to regain her, it wouldn't be— couldn't be—through bad faith and pursuit. He asked only whether she was in London; he couldn't have gone about haunted by the possibility of seeing her by chance. No, Lord Farnham said, she was not in London.

So she was gone, like a phantom. But there had always been something phantom-like about her, something mysterious and elusive. She had gone for no reason, or no reason that he could understand—she had simply gone. He thought of the legends in which a man fell in love with a woman of unearthly beauty, who then turned out to be unearthly indeed, and vanished into the air or beneath the waters of a lake.

Yet she had a body—the body that he had come near to possessing. He had held it in his embrace. He had kissed her lips. When he remembered her and longed for her physically, through the straining of his own body, the torment became a physical pain.

Gradually, he regained something like normality. He had believed that he could not live without her; but he did, independently of any desire to live, like a plant or an animal. Afterwards, he found it strange that he had never thought of suicide even in the depths of his suffering. He had been as wretched and as despairing as any suicide, he supposed; and if death had come to him, he wouldn't have cared. He must have been preserved by an inner vitality of which he was unaware.

However, he didn't live as he had lived before. The catastrophe had changed him, he felt, into another kind of man. There could be no more happiness for him; he recoiled from the idea, as an outrage on his love. He saw the rest of his life, if it had to last another sixty years, as nothing but endurance.

When the House reassembled, he plunged into the political struggle with a zest that was close to ferocity. There was serious trouble in Egypt. The fanatical Arabi Pasha had risen to power on a wave of hatred against white men; British residents, according to trustworthy reports, were in fear for their lives. The Government did nothing. Richard attacked this shameful passivity, this abdication of a great nation's responsibility to its sons and daughters. He made what he thought to be a powerful speech, but it wasn't well received by his own party. He realised that his friends had detected a tone of spite, where he had intended righteous anger; he was suspected of using the conflict to relieve his private troubles, and this was neither gentlemanly behaviour nor serious politics. The suspicion was justified, he admitted to himself. Eventually, the Government sent troops and they dealt with Arabi Pasha as Shere Ali had been dealt with years ago. Three years ago, in fact; it seemed an age in Richard's life.

He considered whether to change his residence. Since he was sure that he would never marry, Berkshire House was greatly in excess of his needs. But he felt unequal to the business of finding and furnishing another house. In the summer, he accepted an invitation to join a shooting party in Scotland and then stayed for six weeks at Severalls. When he returned to London, he returned to Berkshire House because he had made no other arrangements, and he stayed on. After all, it was good for the house to be lived in, as his father had once said, and George didn't want it.

Through the autumn, and through the year of 1883, Richard recovered without knowing it. For a long while, the best that could be said was that he wasn't constantly and acutely unhappy. Then there came times—moments, hours, even whole days—when he was happy. Not happy as he had been before, but capable of enjoyment. He enjoyed active pleasures such as riding, he enjoyed good talk—both lively talk and serious talk—with friends, and he enjoyed the sparring and the clash of politics. When he came home after a good dinner party, he was vaguely aware that the presence of attractive women had been part of the enjoyment. But he thought of none of them, singly, as possibly figuring in his life.

About women—in the other sense—he didn't quite know what to do. He had his desires; he suspected that they were stronger than in the average man, though he wasn't sure. He no longer had a mistress, since he had dropped Alice (with a handsome present) when he got engaged. By this time, probably, she had either a new patron or a husband in her own station in life. There couldn't be much difficulty in finding another mistress, but he was unequal to making a positive effort, just as he was unequal to moving house. And he was averse, or mildly averse, to involving himself in another domestic ménage—in any kind of simulacrum of a marriage.

One evening, while Richard and another bachelor M.P.

were drinking brandy and soda to while away the time until the ten o'clock division, the other man said: "Hang it, I wish that bell would hurry up and ring. I'm due for one of Handicott's little arrangements—rather a special one, too."

"What d'you mean?" Richard asked.

"Surely you know about Handicott, the lonely man's best friend?"

Handicott, it appeared, owned a tobacconist's shop in a turning off Victoria Street. It was a good shop, with an ample selection of both pipe-tobacco and cigars, but it was only a part of Handicott's business. Richard dropped in the next day and mentioned his friend's name.

Handicott, a dignified man with the air of a discreet and understanding solicitor, nodded sagely. "Perhaps you'd care to step into the back room, sir." There, he said: "Perhaps you'd care to glance through the photograph album, sir."

"I rather fancy this, I think," Richard said, after turning a few pages.

"There you show excellent taste, sir, if I may say so. Particularly as the young lady has only lately arrived in the metropolis to mend a heart broken in, I believe, Somerset."

Richard made frequent use of the Handicott service. One noted the address—generally in Chelsea or Pimlico—and arrived at one's own convenience. One didn't pay the girls (or young ladies, as Handicott always called them) but kept an account at the shop to which cigars could also be charged. It was the satisfaction of desire at the most elemental level, in a way that Richard had once considered distasteful. But now he preferred the satisfaction to be impersonal and devoid of intimacy, and even chose not to visit the same young lady with any regularity. He also avoided golden hair and any features that reminded him even remotely of Ellie.

Then, in the late autumn of 1883, he met Geraldine. She was the youngest, and the only unmarried, daughter of Sir

Alfred Hutchison, a greatly respected Conservative M.P. Sir Alfred was a widower, and Geraldine kept house for him with smooth efficiency, as Richard observed when he was invited to dinner.

After they were married, he used to tease her by saying that she had marked him down as a husband before he had any suspicion of it. When she was in a gay mood, she replied: "Well, someone had to look after you." When she was serious, she turned her fine dark eyes full on him and said: "I fell in love with you—I'm not ashamed of that."

What he thought about her, at their first two or three meetings, was that she would make someone an excellent wife and it was surprising that she was still single. She wasn't a young girl—she was twenty-four, as she once mentioned to him in her straightforward way. He imagined that she felt a duty to stay with her father; this turned out not to be so. As she told him later, she had made up her mind at an early age to wait for the right man and had rejected three proposals. Geraldine was always cool-headed and clear about what she wanted or did not want.

Richard found himself invited almost weekly to Sir Alfred's house in Weymouth Street. This wasn't surprising; Sir Alfred was the senior adviser, if not exactly the leader, of a group of Members who felt that the Opposition should be pressing the Government more vigourously. There was serious political talk over the port, and the ladies often had to wait more than an hour before the men joined them. Nevertheless, Richard believed afterwards that Geraldine had something to do with the frequency of these dinners and his own regular presence.

At dinner, and later in the drawing room, she asked intelligent questions about the political scene. She had an exceptional grasp of it, for a woman. Otherwise, the theatre and the operetta were her main interests.

"Have you been to *Princess Ida* yet, Lord Richard?" she asked one evening early in the New Year.

"Not yet, Miss Hutchison."

"I can't wait to see it. My sister and her husband have taken a box; we should be delighted if you'd join us."

"That's extremely kind of you."

Richard sat diagonally behind Geraldine, so that he could scarcely look at the stage without her profile coming into his field of vision. During the performance, which bored him, he found this more and more gratifying. Unexpectedly, halfway through the second act, she turned. Their eyes met. Hers were calm, not at all embarrassed, reflective.

They had supper—a party of six—at Rules, near the theatre. Geraldine was unusually animated; she talked well, in a vein that was light and amusing but never silly.

He accompanied her to her door. In the hansom she was quiet, dreamily humming one of Sullivan's tunes.

"I've enjoyed the evening tremendously, Miss Hutchinson," he said.

"I'm so glad. My sister was most interested to meet you."

"Perhaps we shall all meet again."

She turned to him with a frank, open smile. "I don't see why that should be impossible."

A few days later, he was invited to tea by the sister, Mrs. Lockhart. Not unexpectedly, Geraldine was present. The sisters resembled each other—the same rich dark-brown hair, the same clear, well-shaped features. It was intriguing to note how small differences in proportion could make a vital distinction in quality. Mrs. Lockhart—Sybil—was handsome. Geraldine was beautiful.

Richard took stock of two facts. He was becoming an intimate of the Hutchison family, as he had formerly been of the Colmore family. Far more important, something was developing between Geraldine and himself: an attraction, a creation of possibilities of which, he had no doubt, both of them were equally aware. Quite soon now, he would have to decide whether to check the development or let it gather momentum.

Was he falling in love with her? The mere posing of the question, which he would have considered unthinkable until recently, pointed to an affirmative answer. Examining himself, he recognised all the signs of love: constant desire for her company, preoccupation at surprising moments with the thought of her, delight in her beauty, and the irrepressible stir of carnal inclinations.

He had said to Ellie: "I shall always love you, I can never love anyone else."

He was perfectly certain of loving Ellie as much as ever. The agony had subsided into a ceaseless steady pain; but that, he knew, would never leave him. If loving Ellie meant missing Ellie, longing for Ellie, sorrowing over the loss of Ellie, then it was true that he would love Ellie until he died.

But it seemed to him now that, although he hadn't imagined it before, it was possible to love in different ways. Love for Ellie had struck him as a revelation. Love for Geraldine was growing in him, gently and calmly. It wasn't a consuming passion; yet it need not, for that reason, be wanting in strength and depth.

The question resolved itself into one of the integrity of asking for Geraldine's hand. That she would accept him, he felt without undue vanity, could be regarded as likely. Strictly speaking, it would not be dishonourable to marry her without love. He would be a good and loyal husband, sure of making her happy. But this wasn't enough for him. He wanted to be able to say, looking her straight in the eyes: "I love you, Geraldine." And, after searching his heart, he believed that he could say it without deceit—as a truth existing on another plane from the eternal truth of his love for Ellie.

A man changes, he thought. A man learns, and discovers the complexity of life. For instance, he had once thought that he could never be anything but a soldier, and now he was committed to the world of politics. He was no longer the same man who had loved Ellie with blind adoration—blind to the penalties of loving her—nor was he the same man who had fallen into despair from the loss of her. He had still a long time to live. The love for Geraldine, he believed, was of the kind that would continue to grow after marriage and parenthood. The love for Ellie would remain as an inner wound, always real, always true, but receding more and more into the silent depths of his being.

He saw Geraldine often, drawing nearer to her in a measured and easy way and gaining confidence that he was acting rightly. It was a winter love, altogether unlike his summer love for Ellie. Sometimes they rode in the park—she was a skilled and enthusiastic horsewoman—but mostly they met indoors: at her home or her sister's, at theatres, in the ladies' tea-room of the House. When he thought of Ellie, he would always think of sunlight and shimmering water. He came to know Geraldine against a background of glittering chandeliers, frosted windows or velvet curtains, hansoms like moving islands in foggy darkness. Ellie—motionless and quivering, or walking slowly, a white centre of beauty in the warm hazy air. Geraldine—hurrying into a room in fur tippet and muff, cheeks glowing from the cold, with a laugh and a greeting, bringing the vibrant beauty of movement.

He was grateful for the contrast between them. Resemblance would have made Geraldine a substitute instead of another love. It wasn't only that she was dark and Ellie fair. Geraldine was strongly built, rather tall, graceful certainly but not at all delicate. She dressed in bold colours, never in white. "Can I wear this?" she used to ask Richard after they were engaged. "You don't find it garish?" "I think it's splendid."

One couldn't think of her as mysterious or elusive—as a phantom. She was a presence, clearly defined and reassuring. She was always decisive, always in control of her thoughts and feelings, living not in doubts and hesitations but in certainties. The young girl—the girl he had never known—had been submerged entirely in the achieved and confident woman. In a conversation, she looked straight at anyone who spoke to her and expressed herself with fluency and firmness. Her voice was strong, always audible across a room or down the length of a table, but saved by its pleasing low register from being strident. She laughed readily and cheerfully. Shyness was absolutely not in her nature. Richard wasn't marrying her for her practical or social abilities, but he could see that she would take charge of Berkshire House effortlessly. As the hostess in Weymouth Street, she was already more like an accomplished young wife than a daughter. He had the impression (rightly) that she preferred the company of men to that of women. She had never seen herself as anything but the wife of a man who was successful in public life, who was popular and moved in society, and whom she could sustain and assist. She was trained for that, and knew that she had mastered the training.

She needed Richard, in fact, and so she loved him. He needed her, and so he loved her. Nothing could have been more normal.

He committed himself three months after first meeting her. She had mentioned an amateur dramatic performance which she had promised to attend, deputising for her father who was a patron of the charity concerned, and Richard asked if he might accompany her. The performance was lamentable; she behaved graciously until it was possible to leave, then laughed over it as he escorted her home. Suddenly she said: "I'm glad you were with me. It's good to share even things like this, isn't it?"

"There is much that I could gladly share with you, Miss Hutchison."

She looked at him thoughtfully and said nothing more until they reached Weymouth Street. Standing on the pavement, he took her hand, then pressed it.

"I shall see you soon, Lord Richard, I trust," she said.

"Very soon, I hope."

"I hope so. I do indeed hope so."

The next time he was invited to dinner, he sent her a note asking if he might come an hour early, as he had something particular to say to her. She replied, in her typically bold and legible handwriting, that this would be perfectly convenient.

He could safely assume that she was in no doubt of what he intended to say. She received him in her small boudoir on the second floor, a room he hadn't entered before. There seemed to be no sense in wasting time on small-talk, so he proposed to her at once.

"I am yours, Richard," she said in her strong, clear voice.

When he kissed her, he felt her lips warm and welcoming, her hand firm on his shoulder.

Sir Alfred made the announcement at the dinner party. The guests were all friends of Richard's, three of them M.P.'s. In their congratulations, he caught a note of relief. He was back in the mainstream of life, the proper scheme of things.

It was, in fact, a most suitable match. Had Richard still been a cavalry officer, and known primarily as the Duke of Berkshire's brother, it might have caused a little surprise in society. The Hutchisons were of the gentry, not at all the aristocracy; they had knighthoods, which they amply earned, but no link with titles. They were very much a political family. Geraldine's great-grandfather had been Speaker, her grandfather had been in Peel's Cabinet. Sir Alfred was one of those great House of Commons men who never seek office, whose speeches from the back benches are heard in respectful silence, and who incarnate the conscience of a party. For a young man in politics, he was the ideal father-in-law.

Though not a man to be flattered by a connection with a noble family, Sir Alfred was most favourably disposed toward Richard. "One can never be sure," he said in the smoking room of the House, "but that young fellow could have the makings of a Prime Minister." On the Somers side, the satisfaction was equally great. George had admired Sir Alfred during his own time as an M.P., and wrote to say that he considered the alliance an honour—gracious words from a Duke. When Geraldine visited Severalls, she earned immediate approval. Richard realised that his family had never honestly liked Ellie.

"Do you believe in long engagements, dearest?" he asked Geraldine.

"No," she replied at once. "I've never seen the point of them."

They settled on a date in April, which would allow a honeymoon during the Easter recess. A big society wedding was inappropriate; Sir Alfred was not rich, and Geraldine had no mother to make elaborate arrangements. They would be married at the parish church nearest to Weymouth Street, and invite only relatives and selected close friends to the wedding breakfast.

For the honeymoon, Geraldine suggested Ireland. She had been there before and liked it; it would be new to Richard. An Irish peer, a friend of Sir Alfred's, was delighted to place one of his residences at their disposal.

A few weeks before the wedding, Geraldine made a reconnaissance of Berkshire House. Richard showed her round, and they took tea in the drawing room, where she looked perfectly at home.

He said—the occasion seemed as good as any—"Geraldine, you know that I've been engaged before?"

"Yes, I know that," she said. "It was about two years ago, I believe?"

"About that—yes."

She put down her cup and asked: "Is the memory very painful to you, Richard?"

"It is painful. I should never ask anyone to marry me unless I were sincerely in love—I believe you know that."

"And where there has been love," she said, "something always remains. Is that what you want to tell me?"

"Bless you, my sweetheart, for your understanding. What remains is a wound; it can hurt like an old soldier's amputated foot. I love you, Geraldine. When I gave my heart to you, I gave it as honestly as a man can. But it is a heart that has suffered: not exactly the heart of a young man. That is what I want to say, I think."

"May we always be frank with each other, darling, as you have been now," she answered. "Our love need fear nothing then."

He kissed her. They were in the room where he had seen Ellie for the last time. No phantom stirred; he felt relieved of a burden.

Severalls was on the way to Fishguard, where they were to catch the boat for Rosslare, so—on Geraldine's suggestion—they spent two nights there directly after the wedding. Maud installed Geraldine in a very large bedroom used only on rare occasions, by Royalty or other distinguished guests. With its old French tapestries and curtained bed, it had a slightly museum-like air. Geraldine, however, was very pleased with it and remarked that it was a kind thought on Maud's part.

When Richard went to join her in this room, he found that he was nervous, just as if it were the first time for him as much as for her. Indeed, it was his first time, except on quite different terms with women of a quite different kind. But as soon as he touched her, he realised that she was not nervous at all.

The house in Ireland was pleasant and comfortable, though a little damp from lack of use. They strolled in the rather overgrown grounds, viewed some local antiquities, and took long rides among the green Wexford hills. There was an atmosphere of seclusion, of being away from the busy world. It had been an ideal choice for a honeymoon.

They returned to live in Berkshire House. Geraldine took charge with an air of triumphant serenity. It was many years since Berkshire House had been the regular home of a married couple, in the time of Richard's grandfather. She brought it to life, rather as an energetic new sovereign might revive a backward principality. She recruited some additional servants, dismissed a maid whom she found to be lazy, and got onto excellent terms with Simmons. She had the main drawing room and the library changed round—an obvious improvement, since the library was now at the back and shielded from street noises. She bought two new carpets; she banished some dim-looking paintings to the attic; she installed a new modern range in the kitchen.

They entertained a great deal. Richard loved to see his wife presiding at dinner, keeping a watchful eye on the servants while she maintained the conversation. He understood to the full how lonely he had been and how much he had needed her. At present, his own life was busy; the House was fully occupied, between the Budget debates, a new Franchise Bill, and continuing troubles in both the Near East and Ireland. But Geraldine, as he remarked admiringly, seemed to get through more in a day than he did—managing Berkshire House, paying and receiving calls, helping charities, keeping up her grasp of public affairs, coming to the ladies' gallery at the House when Richard was likely to speak. She throve on it, clearly.

In June, he suggested that they might acquire a country house. They were invited somewhere almost every weekend, and sooner or later this hospitality must be returned. He had a picture in his mind of a house weathered by time, not too large—a place like Longmarsh, though he didn't exactly say this to himself and certainly not to Geraldine. Furnishing and organising a second home, decidedly, wouldn't overtax her energies. She agreed in principle, but said that there was no hurry. She would be very happy to spend this summer at Severalls, and Mother—Geraldine was fully on family terms with the Dowager Duchess—had invited them quite pressingly. Had she happened to become the mistress of Severalls, Geraldine would have taken charge as readily as at Berkshire House. She would have made a good Duchess, Richard thought—rather more than he would have made a good Duke.

One night, as he was putting on his dressing-gown to return to his room, she yawned and said: "You know, Richard, before I was married I didn't imagine that this occurred every night."

"It depends on the man, perhaps," he answered.

"Yes. You're undoubtedly a man, my dear, aren't you?"

He said: "If it's too much for you, you have only to say so."

"Oh no," she said casually, as if he had asked whether some social engagement might be inconvenient. "No, not at all."

Thus they lived together: a proper marriage, a good marriage. At the end of six months, Richard found it hard to believe that they hadn't been man and wife for years. He had a great feeling of peace, of contentment, of relief after strain and suffering. Geraldine, by giving him herself, had given him more than he could ever repay.

CHAPTER 9

In Office

RALPH ASHTON—Major Ashton now—left England in August
1884 to take part in the Sudan campaign. Richard, who was
staying at Severalls, came to London to dine with him and
see him off the next morning from Waterloo. It was singular,
to say the least, that a man should spend his last evening at
home with a friend and not with his wife, but Richard was
aware that the Ashtons' marriage was less than perfect. There
were friendships of Celia's which Ralph neither shared nor
liked, there was evidently a degree of estrangement, and—
after nine years—there were no children. Richard was concerned, but asked no questions. At dinner, the friends spoke of
the coming campaign.

The situation was to be viewed with anxiety. Most of the
Sudan, nominally an Egyptian possession, was in the hands of
the Mahdi, an even wilder fanatic than Arabi Pasha, and his
bands of dervishes. General Gordon, the hero of the Chinese
wars, had been sent to Khartoum earlier in the year; now he
was besieged in that remote spot, with scanty forces immensely
outnumbered by the Mahdi's hordes.

As in the Egyptian crisis two years earlier, precious months
had been wasted by a vacillating Government. The siege had
begun in March; only now, in August, was a relief expedition
being despatched. It was a substantial force, and the command
was held by the great Lord Wolseley, who had conquered

wherever he had fought—in Canada, in the Gold Coast, and most recently in Egypt. But the distances were huge, the railway stopped hundreds of miles short of Khartoum, and the advance could be made only on foot across the desert sands or by boat up a river cursed with shallows and cataracts. An Alexander, a Napoleon might have failed to get there in time.

Richard, and his friends who gathered for regular dinners—the venue transferred, with Geraldine, from Weymouth Street to Berkshire House—were clear about what was at stake. It was the safety of Egypt. It was the control of the Sudan and the upper reaches of the Nile, on which the French were casting envious eyes. It was the maintenance of law and civilisation in the face of savagery. But above all it was the honour of England; for, if a soldier was sent to do his duty and abandoned when in danger, honour was lost.

Reluctantly—for it was a matter far beyond ordinary party controversy—Richard was coming to the conclusion that England's honour was not safe in the hands of the Liberal Government. Lord Hartington, the Secretary for War, was understood to have argued for action and Lord Granville, the Foreign Secretary, to have argued against it. Divided counsels had led to delay—perhaps a fatal delay.

What of Gladstone, the Prime Minister? His was the supreme responsibility, for uniting his Cabinet and for making the necessary decisions. And he had failed. He had sought a compromise where no compromise was possible. He had dodged the issue, in his own mind and in debate. Under pressure in the House, he had taken refuge in the ponderous generalities of which he was a master, in labyrinthine hairsplitting and legalism, in pleading lack of information, and finally in saying that other questions were more important—as if anything could be more important than honour.

So his was the final dishonesty, because he was trading on his reputation for integrity. It was Gladstone, and no lesser man, whose fraudulence must be exposed. This was partly a matter of strategy, for Gladstone's reputation was the Liberal Party's greatest asset. But, to Richard's mind, it was also a duty imposed by the standards of public life. The greater the man, and the greater the trust placed in him by his countrymen, the greater was the betrayal.

Through the long autumn, and then into the winter, people thought and talked constantly of Gordon's peril and the progress of the relief force. As a Member of Parliament, Richard was always being asked for news—by idle society ladies shaken out of their frivolity, by doctors or lawyers who would normally be immersed in their professions, by waiters, by cabbies, by his own servants. He sensed a deep anxiety, an intuitive understanding even among the simplest and humblest that something precious was in jeopardy. It was bitter to reflect that waiters and cabbies cared for the nation's honour more than Her Majesty's Ministers.

However, Richard knew no more than anyone else. Messages from the journalists accompanying the relief force reached London as quickly as messages from Wolseley. There was always a delay of about a week. While England waited and guessed, the victory might have already been won—or the blow might have fallen.

The news of disaster came on a raw, bleak day in February. Richard was leaving his club after luncheon when another member stopped him on the steps.

"You've heard, Somers?"

"What?"

"It's all over."

The expedition had reached Khartoum to find it sacked and deserted. Gordon was dead, together with his loyal Egyptians. The relief force was just two days too late.

Richard knew that he ought to go to the House, but he felt unable to speak to anyone except Geraldine. Declining a cab, he walked slowly home as if he were following a funeral procession. Newsboys were already selling special editions. The streets were full of people standing in groups and talking. In Piccadilly, a man in a raglan coat—a retired military man by the look of him—was striking his stick on the pavement and repeating: "Damn . . . damn . . . damn."

Geraldine took one look at Richard's face and said: "You've heard, then."

"Yes. You've heard too?"

"Father has been here. He was hoping to find you."

"I'll go to the House soon. Just now—I can't."

She poured him a brandy, without calling a servant.

"We are all to blame," he said. "We could have pressed Gladstone harder in the summer."

"Father says the Queen has sent him a terrible letter."

"She must feel it badly. Her flag—her uniform."

"Gladstone will be brought down now, surely."

"I hope so. But that won't bring Gordon back to life."

At the first opportunity, the Opposition moved a vote of censure. Gladstone's speech was awkward, full of prevarications, well below his usual form. The Tories were merciless, the Liberals ashamed and subdued.

Richard rose as the House was filling again after dinner.

"In our distress," he said, "in what I do not hesitate to call our shame, there can be but one consolation. It is that we are conducting tonight not a debate between parties but a solemn inquest among Englishmen. My right honourable and honourable friends, far senior to me in age and authority, have recalled the high reputation to which triumphs in war and peace have raised this ancient land of ours—the reputation now lowered in the eyes of the world. If I venture to add my voice to theirs, it is because I have worn Her Majesty's uniform. I have, with countless others, many of whom are now silent for ever, defended our interests and our dominions against Her Majesty's enemies. On the field of battle, our minds were at ease in one vital respect. We knew that we had the unflinching and undivided support of the Ministers entrusted with the conduct of affairs. Sir, when that assurance is placed in doubt, England loses the right to demand courage and sacrifice from such heroes as the man whom we mourn at this hour."

He paused. The House was utterly silent. Members returning from dinner paused at the bar rather than cause disturbance by their steps.

"Each of us tonight has the privilege and the duty to speak not to a faction but to the House of Commons, the guardian of England's liberties and England's honour. All of us—this is no time to seek exceptions—are patriots, deeply concerned to restore what is precious beyond all price, our rightful pride in our country. We have no power to erase from history the tragedy under whose shadow we stand. We can only resolve that it shall never be repeated. That, sir, is what I believe we shall do in the division lobbies tonight."

As he sat down, he heard the low rumble of assent that means more to a House of Commons man than the wild applause of crowds. He felt a hand on his shoulder; it was Sir Alfred's. He looked up to the ladies' gallery. Geraldine gazed at him, proud and loving.

Lord Hartington wound up for the Government. His speech was as awkward as Gladstone's—he had never been an orator —but it impressed by the awkwardness of honesty, for he admitted frankly that the delay had been a blunder. There had been rumours that Hartington would resign; Liberals now felt that, if he stood by his chief, they could only do the same. To waverers, he offered the assurance that the military effort would be pursued until the Mahdi was crushed. The Government survived by a majority of fourteen votes.

But it was fatally shaken, and events shook it further. In

the broiling summer heat of the desert, even Wolseley could not pin down the dervishes. The Sudan had to be abandoned. Ralph came home, looking weary and unwell; the campaign had been a misery, he said. In June, on a trivial issue—a tax on beer that in normal times would have been grumblingly accepted—the Government was beaten. Gladstone resigned. The Queen sent for Lord Salisbury.

Richard was summoned to Downing Street and offered the post of Under-Secretary for Home Affairs.

He was amazed. His acquaintance with the Prime Minister, a remote and autocratic figure, was of the slenderest. He had been invited to Hatfield with a troop of other guests, but he had assumed that he had been put on the list because of his social and not his political position. He was just thirty years old; he had sat in only one Parliament. He had made his mark, but he knew that effectiveness in debate was not always regarded as implying readiness for office.

Geraldine said: "Modesty won't get you to the top, my dear."

"The top!" Richard exclaimed, laughing. "Who's talking about the top?"

"I am," she replied calmly.

It was strange, being suddenly in office. It was strange to enter the Home Office as if it were Severalls or Berkshire House—with its marble staircases and countless rooms, it was rather like Severalls—and to sit at a huge desk. It was strange to be treated with deference by men old enough to be his father, when he knew less about Home Office problems or Home Office routine than the most junior clerk. However, there was little for him to do. The new Government had yet to win a parliamentary majority, and the civil servants indicated politely that they could manage quite well on their own for a few months, particularly in the summer; they didn't intend to take a Secretary of State seriously, still less an

Under-Secretary, until they knew whether he was there to stay. There was no need for Richard to be in London when he would normally be in the country, no need at all.

He was glad to take the hint, because he was now the owner of a country house. Geraldine had found it by means of systematic enquiry, and when they went to see it they knew at once that it would suit them. Whitstone Priory, as its name indicated, had once been a religious foundation, built in the fifteenth century. There were traces of this origin—two sturdy columns and a vaulted ceiling in the entrance hall—but the Priory had been extensively rebuilt after the Dissolution of the Monasteries to make a Tudor manor-house. In the eighteenth century, a family enriched by the slave trade had acquired the house and added two flanking wings, tastefully using the same local stone. It was the extinction of this family, or at least of its male line, that now caused the Priory to be put on the market. What most delighted Richard was the visible evidence of its history, its air of having grown as England grew. However, Geraldine swiftly demolished a verandah which had been inappropriately added about the year 1840.

The Priory was only a dozen miles from Severalls, but on the other side of the Thames, in Oxfordshire. From its windows, the view embraced a magnificent sweep of the Cotswolds. There was adequate stabling, a charming garden, and a decent amount of land.

It was a wonderful summer, rich in happiness and promise. Geraldine was with child. Because of her condition (though she said that she felt perfectly well) she didn't ride. They took gentle walks, or sat in the garden and planned improvements. Richard felt his love for her becoming stronger and deeper, as he had hoped.

Lord Salisbury, who never hurried unless he saw good reason, decided to hold the election in November. Richard had to face a contest for the first time. His seat was of course perfectly safe, but he campaigned actively—partly to make himself better known in the constituency, chiefly to explain the great issues that had arisen in the past year. He addressed meetings in all the market towns and some of the larger villages. Geraldine keenly regretted that she could not accompany him, but her pregnancy was now advanced.

The outcome of the election was disappointing. The Liberals, though reduced in numbers, were still the largest party in the House. In January 1886, the Conservative Government was defeated and Gladstone resumed office. Richard was a back-bencher again.

For him, this event was eclipsed by the birth of his first child. He fretted anxiously downstairs while Geraldine was in labour, but she managed with her usual efficiency and the doctor assured him that it was an easy birth. When he was allowed into her bedroom to kiss her, and when he held the strangely light bundle in his arms and looked at the funny, precious face, he felt that his marriage was proven and triumphant.

Geraldine had predicted that the child would be a boy, and so it was. She favoured the name of Charles, which was traditional in the Somers family but for some reason had not been used in recent generations. Richard, however, thought that calling the child Alfred would give her father pleasure, and this was decided on. "Charles next time," Geraldine said.

On the political scene, the spring saw an astonishing development. Gladstone introduced a Bill to grant Home Rule to Ireland. Richard, at first, couldn't believe it. It was well known that many Liberals, including such important figures as Lord Hartington, were firmly opposed to Home Rule; there was simply no majority for the Bill. It was an act of political suicide. Gladstone seemed to be bent on splitting his Cabinet and his party, so recently reunited after the strains of the

previous year. Or it was megalomania; the old man believed
that, when he commanded, everyone would obey him.

As all men of sense foresaw, so things happened. The Bill
was decisively defeated. Lord Salisbury took office again. Another election was held; this time, Geraldine went to all
Richard's meetings. The Liberals were in disarray, split wide
open, with Hartington at the head of a separate grouping
under the name of Liberal Unionists. The Tories won an absolute majority. Barring disasters, they would govern for the
next seven years.

The administration was made up very much as it had been
the year before. As well as being Prime Minister, Salisbury
kept the Foreign Office in his own hands. He had little interest in domestic affairs, which he left to Ministers who sat
in the Commons. Richard, once more, was Under-Secretary
at the Home Office. And now, he could get his teeth into the
work.

The Home Secretary was an elderly man, undoubtedly holding office for the last time. Richard had scarcely exchanged a
dozen words with him while they were in Opposition. He was
reserved by nature—the kind of man who is content to be
thought dull. He was seldom found among a talkative group
in the smoking room, didn't move in society, and was believed to spend all his leisure with his wife at their unfashion-
able house in Bayswater. At the Home Office, he concerned
himself only with major decisions, which he mulled over for
days at a time. Everything else was dealt with by Richard,
with the guidance of the civil servants.

For a while, Richard thought that the Home Secretary was
lazy or senile. He realised gradually that he had been mis-
taken. The Home Secretary was working in an older tradition, which cast the man with responsibility as an arbiter
rather than a high-grade official. He was really very conscien-
tious; it was simply that he didn't pride himself on reading a

hundred papers a day. In point of fact he read very slowly, pausing for reflection whenever a sentence struck him as dubious. But above all, he was deliberately allowing Richard to handle as many questions as possible. Though he was too reserved to explain this, he was watching over his young Under-Secretary's education. It was the conduct of a good and generous man. As the weeks passed, Richard came to regard the Home Secretary with profound respect.

Richard loved the work. His appetite for papers was insatiable; he didn't mind if it amused the civil servants. After a canter in Hyde Park with Geraldine, he was at his desk on the stroke of ten. For the first time in his life he was a student, and he found it congenial. But he was a student with the added zest of putting his knowledge to immediate use as he acquired it.

He considered himself lucky to be at the Home Office. It was the "odds and ends" department, taking charge of whatever didn't fit in anywhere else. The Poor Law, workhouses, lunatic asylums, orphanages, prisons, the Metropolitan Police, safety in mines and factories, notification of epidemics—there was no end to it. A panorama of the life of England seemed to unfold across his desk. Not only was he serving his country, but he was coming to know it and understand it as never before.

To this time in Richard's life, also, belonged the episode of Hannah Smith.

He never saw her, of course. She was twenty-three years old, according to the papers, and a police officer described her as the most beautiful woman he had ever set eyes on. She was the wife of Herbert Smith, a grocer in a modest but respectable way of business. He was a widower, and well over fifty, when he married Hannah; she was in effect a housekeeper, and there could have been no question of love on either side.

But he gave her a good home, raising her from extreme poverty.

John Andrews was a young man who had earned a living in a variety of ways: as an assistant in Smith's shop until he was dismissed for drinking, then as a Covent Garden porter and a billposter. He had lodgings in the neighbourhood, where he was visited by Hannah Smith. It was the landlady who told Smith that Andrews and Hannah had a guilty association. The grocer behaved sensibly. He gave Andrews a ticket to Australia and a useful sum of money.

On keeping an assignation with her lover, Hannah found that he was gone. She returned home; the shop was in the charge of the assistant and Smith, according to his custom, was in the back room for an afternoon nap. The Smiths' one maidservant, working upstairs, and the assistant in the shop heard a brief altercation—Hannah "yelling and screaming," the maid testified. Hannah stabbed her husband, who was in his shirtsleeves, with a bread-knife. The maid ran for a policeman. Still standing in the room, still with the knife in her hand, Hannah was arrested.

She was sentenced to death after a short and straightforward trial. In view of her immorality and the nature of her crime, no deputations of parsons and humanitarians made representations on her behalf. The case, indeed, attracted no particular attention.

Richard had an appointment to submit to the Home Secretary a set of amendments to workhouse regulations. The Private Secretary asked him to postpone it.

"The papers are all ready. He need only look through them and approve them."

"Quite so, Lord Richard. But he's considering the Smith case. I shan't be able to persuade him to give his mind to anything else."

"What's the Smith case?"

"A death sentence, on his desk for confirmation or re-prieve."

"I see."

Clearly, it would be impossible—even indecent—to interrupt the Home Secretary at such a time. But, two days later, there was still no chance of seeing him.

"This Smith case seems to be very complicated," Richard re-marked.

"Not exactly," said the Private Secretary. "It's unpleasant, indeed distressing. But complicated, no."

On impulse, Richard asked: "May I see the papers, please?"

The Private Secretary hesitated. "The decision is for the Home Secretary alone. That's a long-established rule."

"Of course. I shouldn't attempt to influence him. It's for my own information; I've never seen papers of that kind."

"Very good, Lord Richard."

After reading the papers, Richard asked the Private Secre-tary: "What grounds for a reprieve could there be?"

"Well, if it could be shown that Smith treated his wife badly and she had reason to hate him, that might be an ex-tenuating circumstance. However, he was a good husband. If the murder itself had been the outcome of a struggle—if Smith had used or even threatened violence—that would be a major consideration. But there's no such evidence. Finally, if she was temporarily deranged or hysterical when she com-mitted the crime, it might be taken into account. But yelling and screaming—the maid's evidence, you recall—can't be said to amount to that."

"You see no possibility of a reprieve, then?"

"Unfortunately, none at all."

"It seems terrible for her to hang. I mean, a woman—and at her age."

The Private Secretary was silent for a moment. Then he

said: "You may never have heard this, Lord Richard, but there have been distinguished men who have been eager to attain any other high position—the Treasury or the Foreign Office—and have declined that of Home Secretary."

A curious atmosphere, a blend of solemnity and nervousness, began to pervade the Home Office: perhaps, Richard thought, the atmosphere of a prison before an execution. The Home Secretary was unseen except when, grave and silent, he arrived in the morning and left in the afternoon. Richard gathered that he had read the papers in the Smith case over and over again.

Then, one afternoon, he was told that the Home Secretary would look at the workhouse regulations. He took them along. As usual, the Home Secretary was courteous and calm; he read through the papers in his careful way, asked a few questions, and gave his approval. But he looked like a man who had just returned to his desk after a grave illness.

In the outer office, Richard asked the Private Secretary: "He's confirmed the death sentence, I suppose?"

"It was his duty."

"When is she to hang?"

"Tomorrow morning."

Later, to his surprise, Richard was summoned by the Home Secretary again. The old man—he did look like an old man now—looked at him almost shyly and said: "I'm sorry if I inconvenience you, Somers, but I wonder if you're free to dine with me this evening?"

Richard was expecting guests, but he said at once: "It will be an honour." Geraldine would have to understand.

"Thank you. I'm most grateful. Be so good as to reserve a private room at some quiet restaurant."

As Richard was leaving the room, the Home Secretary asked: "Are you a drinking man, Somers?"

"I've been a cavalry officer, sir."

"Ah, yes. Good."

During dinner, as the claret was served, the Home Secretary said: "You know, I was about your age when I first held office."

"Indeed, sir?"

"Yes, I was Under-Secretary at the War Office. Lord Aberdeen was Prime Minister. A very anxious time—the Crimean War . . ."

After the meal, they began to drink brandy. The Home Secretary said: "Do you know, when I was a young fellow I travelled round the world."

"Right round the world, sir?"

"Yes. In the eastward direction. First of all . . ."

At midnight they were still drinking brandy. The Home Secretary asked: "Were you at Eton, Somers?"

"Yes, sir."

"I was at Harrow. There were some remarkable characters among the masters at that time. My housemaster, for instance . . ."

So he went on and on: delving further and further into the past, telling long rambling stories about people whose names meant nothing to Richard, talking to avert silence, talking, talking.

They drank about as much as a pair of drunkards on a spree. But sobriety held them like a curse, part of the night's ordeal.

At three o'clock, the Home Secretary said: "We must let these poor fellows close up."

"They'll stay as long as we make it worth their while."

"No, no. It isn't fair. They'll have been working since luncheon."

It was a clear night, not at all cold, but moonless and dark. London was silent, waiting for the day.

"I'll accompany you home, sir," Richard said. "We'll find a cab at Charing Cross."

"I think I'll walk, Somers."

"Walk to Bayswater, sir?"

"I used to be a great walker, you know. Don't do enough of it nowadays. Good for the constitution."

"I'll come with you."

"No, no, I shouldn't dream of it. Right out of your way. I'm very much indebted to you already."

Despite all that Richard could say, the Home Secretary insisted on setting out alone. Richard stood in the Strand and watched him, a lean upright figure, his white scarf bright between black coat and hat, his stick making a thin brave sound.

Richard didn't go home. Geraldine would wake up and ask questions; he didn't want to explain to her until later. She was steady and courageous, but it wasn't a night for her, a happy wife with a baby. He went to his club and was shown to a room by the night porter. He slept in snatches, waking twice to stare at the grey dawning sky. When he woke for the third time, it was ten minutes past eight. The time for executions was eight o'clock. It was over.

While he was being shaved by the club barber, it came to him with sudden certainty that the Home Secretary had not gone home. He thought of the solitary old man walking about, the stick tapping . . . where? Whitehall, the Embankment, Westminster Bridge: it was by the ceaselessly flowing river, somehow, that Richard imagined him.

He went to the Home Office, and to the Home Secretary's set of rooms.

"Is he here?"

"Yes, Lord Richard, he's here," the Private Secretary said.

"He was here at eight o'clock, I suppose?"

"I believe so."

Richard went to his own room. He sat for a while watching the sunlight spread across Whitehall. It was a fine day; Geraldine would be sorry that they'd missed their morning ride. People would be strolling in the parks, remarking on the good weather, hoping that it would last over the weekend.

He lit a cheroot, then threw it away. His head was heavy and his throat dry; he knew that the drink was not the reason. He had ceased to be a young man.

CHAPTER 10

The Underground River

As a man enters middle age, life becomes more settled. A year can easily pass without bringing any changes. In 1887, nothing in particular happened. Three things happened in 1888, none of them extraordinary.

Richard's second son was born, and duly named Charles. He had rather wanted a daughter, but Geraldine was pleased with her brace of boys. Boys, she remarked, were in short supply in the family; George and Maud now had four children, three of them girls.

Sir Alfred Hutchison died. A disease of the kidneys, which he bore with fortitude, had been undermining his health for a couple of years, so death came as a merciful release. Geraldine grieved, but in moderation. She was entirely a Somers by now, and saw little of her sisters. One was married to a banker and one to a clergyman, so they were outside the political world in which she and Richard moved.

Then, in a Government reshuffle, Richard was made Under-Secretary for War. It was neither a promotion nor a demotion, but a normal sideways move for a man in politics. Geraldine pointed out that it would widen the range of his experience. She had a time-table for him: he was to be in the Cabinet by the age of forty. Beyond that, it was harder to see. But, some-where round the year 1900, Lord Salisbury and his senior col-

leagues would be passing from the scene and a new generation would take their places. When that time came, all the
possibilities would be open.

She was devoted to Richard, and devoted to his career. It
was the same, to her mind. She had made their home into a
social centre of Conservatism; her dinners were the talk of
London and everyone knew what was meant by "the Berkshire House set." At weekends, her hospitality was equally
purposeful. Richard would have preferred to keep the Priory
as a private retreat, with no guests except close friends. Geraldine, however, was clear in her mind that social life was a
branch of political life and the weekend was an essential part
of both. She got her way on most occasions, but it remained a
disagreement between them. A minor disagreement, of
course; all their disagreements (the few that they had) were
minor.

They differed—differed rather than disagreed—in the way
that they thought about politics. Richard thought of making
some contribution, thought he didn't know yet what it might
be, to the guiding principles that were fundamental to the
conduct of affairs. What threads could be woven into the tex-
ture of English life? How could its quality be strengthened
and enriched as well as preserved?—These were the questions
over which he mulled during quiet days at the Priory. It
seemed to him that other men's minds passed too easily over
the surface of such questions.

Geraldine thought of politics—a woman naturally did, he
supposed—in terms of advancement. It would have been ac-
curate to call her ambitious. She was not, and would have recoiled from being, the type of "new woman" sometimes
described in the weeklies, who sought to compete with men
and equal men's achievements. All her intelligence and ability
—considerable, he knew—were vested in her devotion to him.
He was immensely grateful, immensely glad to have such a

wife. Still, if ever they had Ten Downing Street as an address, it would mean more to her than to him.

Such reflections led him, strangely, to thoughts of Ellie: thoughts that were still painful but were also a secret refuge, a dream of peace. He wondered at times how he could have loved two such different women as Ellie and Geraldine. It could only mean that in some ultimate sense there were two men in him. He was a rising Conservative politician, a capable Under-Secretary, Geraldine's faithful and contented husband; he was genuinely glad to be that man. But he was also the man who had lost Ellie and would never forget her. Through his life, the love for Ellie would run like an underground river: unseen, silent, hidden from the busy world, yet flowing as steadily as any river open to the sky.

One morning, the name "Colmore" caught his eye on the front page of *The Times*. Anne Colmore was engaged to a lieutenant in the Navy; Richard didn't recognise the young man's name. He was struck by a sudden sense of the passage of time. Anne had been a child—six years younger than Ellie, if he remembered rightly. Now she was twenty-one, the same age as Ellie when he should have married her. Ellie, therefore, was twenty-seven. She could easily be married. Quietly, without her parents' approval, without an announcement in *The Times*—it was entirely possible. Yet it wasn't only his vanity, he thought, that told him with absolute certainty that she was not.

It occurred to him that Ellie might attend Anne's wedding. He was attacked by a passionate desire to see her again, even if he didn't speak to her, even if—better if—she didn't see him. But he reminded himself that he could have seen her, or at least found out where she was, years ago. Once he was married to Geraldine, Lord and Lady Farnham would have received an enquiry as indicating no more than a vaguely sentimental interest. He had chosen to know nothing of her, and surely he had been right. There were risks that he dared not run.

So life went on: the public life, the river that ran in the open. He was not altogether happy at the War Office. He was bored by discussions of regimental reorganisations and promotions; it was curious to recall that these might have been the whole of his life. There was just enough of the cavalry subaltern still in him to make him tremble before his first meeting with Lord Wolseley, a hero whom he had adored since boyhood. But Wolseley in Whitehall was rather verbose, rather pompous, rather slow to grasp a logical point. In the War Office, of course, the Army was the world. Richard missed the variety of Home Office work, the many-sided involvement with England in all its aspects. Still, he could assume that he was doing his job well. The Secretary of State valued his opinion; so, remarkably enough, did Lord Wolseley.

Another year: 1889. In March, looking through the current Army list, Richard saw an entry that surprised him: "Ashton, Lt.-Col. R. d'A. F., transfer to Indian Army list with equivalent seniority." It was unusual for any British Army officer to transfer to the Indian Army, which had its own career avenues, and very puzzling in the case of an officer who had no connection with India and had never served there. Richard asked for an explanation, and received this minute:

> To Under-Secretary from Adjutant-General's Branch. The transfer of Lt.-Col. Ashton to Indian Army is considered advantageous to H.Q. Calcutta, which is somewhat lacking in staff officers of ability and initiative, qualities that Lt.-Col. Ashton possesses in a high degree. The transfer of this officer arises from his own request, made for personal reasons.

Yet more puzzling. Since Richard had been in office, his friendship with Ralph had become rusty. The Ashtons didn't fit naturally into Geraldine's guest list, and Richard had also got the impression—whether or not she had said it outright, he couldn't recall—that she was reluctant to receive Celia. Richard had invited Ralph to an occasional dinner at his club, but it wasn't easy to find the time, and now he hadn't seen his old friend for over a year. He sent Ralph a note without delay, and they dined at the club a week later. Ralph looked markedly older, and his manner was uneasy.

"You really did ask for transfer to India?" Richard asked.

"Yes, I did."

"It's quite a step, you know. Of course you realise that, once you're on the Indian Army list, you'll be there until retirement. Personally, I shall regret it very much."

"It's kind of you to say that, Somers." Ralph did look genuinely grateful, as if kind sentiments seldom came his way.

"I can't persuade you to change your mind, can I?"

"I'm afraid not. I have my reasons."

"How is Celia looking forward to India?" This had puzzled Richard more than anything else. Dublin—even Aldershot—had been an impossible exile for her, he remembered.

"Celia will not be coming with me," Ralph said.

Richard said nothing. It was for Ralph to explain this or not, as he chose. They talked of old times and old friends through the meal, and adjourned to a quiet corner for brandy and cigars.

Out of a silence, Ralph said with an evident effort: "I think I ought to tell you what my reasons for going to India are. When you hear, you'll understand that it's in absolute confidence. I haven't told another soul, and I never shall."

Richard waited. Ralph took a sip of brandy and continued: "My marriage is at an end, as a real marriage. My wife is unfaithful to me."

"My dear fellow, I'm dreadfully sorry."

"Oh, it wasn't a sudden shock. I really knew years ago, but

I never allowed myself to face it. About two months ago, I was confronted with evidence—I won't go into details—so flagrant that I couldn't ignore it. I questioned her. She told me everything. She didn't spare me—it was a scene I'll never forget."

"Do you mean that it had been going on for years?"

"Practically since we were married. While I was in Ireland, while I was in the Sudan, whenever my back was turned."

"Did she tell you who the fellow is?"

Ralph gave an ironic smile. "She gave me some of the names. Not the recent ones."

"Ashton, what are you saying?"

"There appear to have been at least twenty. Celia herself can't remember exactly."

"Good God! Good God!"

"If there is a good God, His ways are mysterious so far as I'm concerned."

Richard was intensely moved. Thinking of the happiness of his own marriage, he was almost ashamed of his good fortune. What had Ralph done, indeed, to deserve this sordid betrayal, this insult to manhood?

Ralph was saying: "I think that what wounds me most is that she denied me children. I'd have loved children. I could have been a good father even to another man's child. But she never intended to become a mother. She told me about that too."

"She should never have become a wife. One's obliged to say that."

"I suppose you're right. In some peculiar way, she isn't like other women. It's almost beyond blame. It's more as though she were driven—fated—to behave like this. Why, I'll never understand."

"You must put it behind you, Ashton. I know that's easy to say. But you must. You must remake your life."

"I shall put it behind me. That's why I'm leaving England. But as for remaking my life: I don't hope for that."

"You're entitled to a divorce. You've got evidence, you say. And God knows you have every right. You can marry again; you're not forty, are you?"

"No, I don't intend to divorce her. What she might become, after that public shame—it's too horrible to think of. There's the family to consider, too. Her father's in bad health."

"There's such a thing as being too generous."

"It isn't altogether that. The truth is, I love Celia. What she's done, that she's ceased to care for me, or never did care— all that's beside the point. We can't choose whom to love, nor can we give up loving from choice. So it seems to me, at any rate."

"And now you'll never see her again. Is that your intention?"

"Now that she's told me what she has, it's the only possibility. She could give any promise—not that she offered to—and be incapable of keeping it. Am I to watch her every hour? To live with her, sharing her with half the riff-raff in London? It's beyond my strength. I could be capable of murder—of killing her, perhaps. I saw that in myself when we had the fatal scene. I must leave her, and still love her. It's the only way."

They parted with a last firm handshake on the steps of the club. Richard went home in a state of acute distress. He told Geraldine that he had papers to read and she had better go to bed.

"I'll wait up for you," she offered.

"No, my love, please don't. You need sleep—you look rather tired. I shan't disturb you tonight."

She kissed him. "There's something wrong, Richard, isn't there?"

"At the War Office, yes. I have to think it out."

He went to his study, lit a fresh cigar, and sat gazing into the fire. It was as though a friend had died—not suddenly on the field of battle, not peacefully in the care of a loving wife and family, but wretchedly, pitiably. He was sure that he would never see Ralph again. A man had to take care of himself to survive the Indian climate, and Ralph would not take care of himself. This departure, this resignation, was a form of suicide.

Still, for Richard, life went on. He was looking forward to summer, to the easy leisurely days at the Priory. In May, there was a weekend that was a promise of the holidays; for once there were no guests, and the weather was warm. He and Geraldine sat in basket-chairs on the lawn and watched the boys playing with a new puppy. As usual on Sundays, he thought with distaste of Monday in Whitehall.

Then Geraldine said: "I think we should go abroad this summer, dear."

"Abroad?" he repeated. "Where?"

Naturally, she had it all worked out. "To Paris, to see the Exhibition. Then to Geneva, to make a tour of the Alps. And then to one of the German spas. The Midhursts always go to Baden-Baden, you know. Lady Midhurst tells me that one meets all sorts of interesting people there."

"It sounds very energetic. I don't think I'll be fit for anything like that when the House rises."

"Come now, Richard, don't pretend to be an old man."

"We could travel in England if you want to travel. We've always got two or three standing invitations in the North. Or Ireland? We haven't been to Ireland since our honeymoon."

Geraldine was silent for a short while. Then she said: "You know, Richard, it would do no harm for you to become familiar with European questions. You might find yourself at the Foreign Office one of these days."

"Ah," he said, smiling, "I might have known my little strategist had a plan of campaign."

And, he thought as he turned the idea over in his mind, about this sort of thing Geraldine was seldom wrong. The Prime Minister was a foreign policy man; a junior Minister with a knowledge of Europe would rise in his esteem. Richard disliked this style of calculation, but after all he was in politics seriously.

They set off as soon as the House rose. Geraldine was the guide. She had been to Paris and Geneva with her father, though not to Germany. As soon as the steamer docked at Calais, Richard felt the foreign atmosphere and was, all at the same time, bewildered, stimulated and amused. The porters in their blue blouses ran instead of walking and expected him to follow them, instead of following him in the normal manner. The attendants on the train ushered him and Geraldine into their reserved compartment with bows and smiles, like a hotel manager welcoming a wealthy guest for a month's stay. Nobody seemed to be able to do anything without talking incessantly, and at a speed which struck him as fantastic even considering that French was their native language. He didn't understand a word, of course. Geraldine's French—also of course—was equal to all requirements.

As the train moved off (hooting instead of whistling) Richard thought that he might have seen France for the first time seven years ago, with Ellie by his side. Ellie spoke French too, but the hurry and confusion would have daunted her and her quiet voice would have been unheard in the din. They would have lost their porter and the luggage, probably. He smiled at Geraldine and pressed her hand.

The fortnight in Paris was exhausting. Geraldine whirled him about from the boulevards to the Bois, from Notre Dame to Napoleon's tomb. The Exhibition involved three long visits, and they queued for two hours to take the lift up the Eiffel

Tower, the new wonder of the world. Photographs, as Geraldine said, quite failed to prepare one for it. It was gigantic, astounding—and, so far as Richard could see, totally unnecessary. Only the French, with their passion for going to extremes, could have thought of creating this monstrosity to straddle acres of their city. He tried to imagine such a thing being put up in Hyde Park—the notion was unthinkable.

There was a certain quality in French life which Richard had sensed on the quayside at Calais and which presented itself insistently wherever he went. One could describe it, taking a favourable view, as excitement or zest. As a visitor, one couldn't help responding to it; but he was perfectly certain that he could never have lived in France. For one could describe this quality, also, as instability, license, disorder. In the streets, respectably dressed men plunged into quarrels and abused one another, waving their arms and shouting, like tipsy draymen in London. In what Richard took to be the equivalent of the West End, it was difficult to tell who was a gentleman and who was not, and still more difficult to tell who was a lady. A person whom one might have taken for a Countess—driving in the Bois in a carriage with liveried servants, or occupying a box at the opera—was openly pointed out as the Count of Something's mistress. Geraldine and Richard were recommended to see a play by a writer called Feydeau, which was all about married women and their lovers deceiving the husbands with ingenious stratagems. Richard found their antics very amusing despite his ignorance of the language, and Geraldine took it all in her stride, but it wasn't a play to which one could possibly have taken one's wife in London, even if one imagined any management putting it on.

As a member of the Government, Richard was asked to dinner by the Ambassador and then invited to the homes of certain Frenchmen—a Deputy, a newspaper editor, a senior official of the Quai d'Orsay—who were well disposed toward

England. The dinner parties were conducted more or less as in London; the food was excellent, though spoiled by excessively rich sauces. With Geraldine as interpreter, Richard was able to gain some understanding of French public affairs. Instability, in this sphere, reigned supreme. There were so many parties in the Chamber of Deputies that Richard never got them quite straight. There were no proper Government and Opposition benches; a party might be supporting the Government one week and opposing it the next. The life of a Government, on the average, was about a year. Recently, a General Boulanger had very nearly established a dictatorship; he was now in exile, condemned *in absentia* for high treason, but Richard met a politician who said cheerfully that he had done his best to assist Boulanger to power. Socialists, who declared openly that their aim was revolution, played a busy part in the political system which they hoped to destroy. The Church was regarded as the enemy of the State, and the State as the enemy of the Church. There was much discussion of a recent case concerning a teacher who had been dismissed because he was seen going to church, instead of being dismissed for not going to church as one might think reasonable. In fact, everything was the opposite of the reasonable and decent way of managing a country.

By comparison, Geneva was restful. In the smaller towns along the lake, there were clusters of English people living as if they were at home, with English tea-rooms, English bookshops, Anglican churches. They took tea with an elderly lady, a family connection of Geraldine's, who had lived at Montreux for thirty years and might never have left Kensington. Geraldine, however, also kept up her relentless programme of tourism. They went all round the lake by steamer, gazed at mountains and glaciers, and ascended to viewpoints by cable-car, which Richard found somewhat unnerving.

After visiting Basel and Strassburg, both fine cities, they arrived at Baden-Baden. Richard was favourably impressed by Germany. The staff on the railway and at the hotels were polite and efficient; everything functioned smoothly; one had the sense of an ordered, contented, well-regulated society. Germans were always introduced by titles, derived from their profession if they had no hereditary rank—Mr. Barrister this, Mr. Professor that, Mr. Railway Director the other. Even a wife could be known as Mrs. Barrister. It sounded odd, but it indicated a respect for status and achievement that was surely a sound quality.

However, Richard realised that he was getting only a casual view of Germany. Baden-Baden, in summer at least, was a highly cosmopolitan place. It was curious, as one strolled in the pleasant grounds of the spa pavilion, not to know what language one would overhear next. In the town, there were cafés patronised mainly by English people, or by the French, or by the Russians. Some visitors kept to the society of their compatriots, but if one chose—and Richard did—one could use the casino or the billiard-rooms to strike up an acquaintanceship with a foreigner. There were, he observed, people of different nationalities who had never been to one another's countries but who were firm friends, thanks to meeting year after year at Baden-Baden.

He saw how wise Geraldine had been to suggest this visit. A spa was like a weekend house-party on an extended scale. It provided opportunities for relaxation, for gossip, for flirtation; mothers brought their daughters, and doubtless each summer yielded its harvest of engagements. But opportunities existed just as amply for serious conversation in a calm and leisured atmosphere. A gentleman in the hotel dining room might be pointed out as an Ambassador or even a Foreign Minister, and Richard guessed that international problems were often resolved here, very much as problems of domestic politics were resolved at Hatfield or Chatsworth. At the least,

if one used one's time profitably, one could come to understand the other fellow's point of view.

He had several interesting talks with a Count who held a
position in the Imperial Chancellery at Vienna, and who
spoke remarkably good English—as Germans and Austrians
often did, unlike the French who annoyingly spoke nothing
but French. The Count explained how the structure of the
Austro-Hungarian Empire enabled people of a dozen nationalities to live peaceably together, despite differences of language and of advancement in the scale of civilisation. It was
something like the British Empire, controlled by a similar
blend of authority and guidance. Then the Count said: "Tell
me, Lord Richard, what is this Home Rule question?"—and
it was Richard's turn to do the explaining.

At the casino, Richard got to know a Russian Prince, who
also spoke English adequately, though with an extraordinary
accent. It turned out that the Prince had been a cavalry officer,
and had fought in the Balkans at roughly the same time that
Richard had fought in Afghanistan. According to him, the
Russian drive toward Constantinople was not a mere urge to
conquer, but arose from a feeling of responsibility for people
who were considered as brothers because they were Slavs and
Orthodox believers. Richard didn't altogether take this at face
value; however, there was no doubting the fervour in the
Prince's voice and it was worthwhile understanding how an
aggressive policy—as it was considered in England—could appear perfectly reasonable to him. The talk with the Prince
ended with a warm invitation to shoot bears on his estate at
some unpronounceable place. Richard didn't mention this to
Geraldine—she might have wanted to go.

There were people, he reflected, to whom France or Germany or Russia meant as much as England did to him: a vision of familiar beauty that called for devoted love. He had
known this before, as an obvious fact. Patriotism, he assumed,

was a feeling as natural to all men as the love of women. But to know it was one thing; to feel its expression, in brightening eyes and deepened voices, was another. Surely, he thought, there must be a way of conducting affairs that allowed men of every nation to find free scope for this devotion without denigrating the devotion of others, without hatred and conflict. That was, perhaps, the supreme task of statesmanship. He began to feel that he would like to be at the Foreign Office as much as at the Home Office.

Despite the lure of the Priory, he was almost sorry to leave Baden-Baden. He had never expected that he would take to foreign travel so readily. He tried to imagine the lives of people who lived permanently abroad, like the lady at Montreux, or of those—he had met a few—who moved continually from place to place, residing in hotels or furnished villas. That would be impossible for him, he decided. To be deprived of home and homeland was a half-life, a kind of death. But a spell abroad—there was a great deal to be said for it. He reviewed in his mind what he had enjoyed in these two months. Long train journeys, with unexpected vistas presenting themselves as one rattled along; settling in to a strange hotel room and arranging one's belongings to make it comfortable; poring over maps and planning excursions; chance conversations with strangers whom one might never meet again, in which one found oneself talking more intimately than with most of one's acquaintances at home. It had been good, in middle age, to discover a new pleasure—a new dimension of life.

The next summer, it was taken for granted that they would go abroad again. "I'll let you off Paris, my dear," Geraldine said. They crossed to Ostend, visited Brussels, and travelled by easy stages up the beautiful valley of the Rhine. When they arrived at Baden-Baden for the second time, it was almost a homecoming. At the hotel, they were given the same room as before. He had mentioned that they liked the eastern outlook, toward the pine-covered hills, and the manager had remembered. Richard had little experience of English hotels, but it was hard to imagine a hotel being better run than this.

They settled into the Baden-Baden routine. It was a routine consisting chiefly of food, drink and conversation; but in the mornings, while Geraldine met other ladies at the pavilion, Richard often went for a brisk walk through the woods. Routes were indicated by white, red and green paint-marks on the pine-trees, a typically efficient German system. He came back through the centre of the town and bought the previous day's *Times* at a shop which stocked a cosmopolitan array of papers and magazines. The "English café," as it had become by custom, was directly across the street. He was able to read his *Times* either with Darjeeling tea or with coffee and cream in the German fashion, for which he had acquired quite a taste.

One morning, about to enter the shop, he found himself barring the way of a lady who was coming out. *"Entschuldigen,"* he said, standing aside and removing his hat. He was beginning to pick up some German phrases; the language came to his tongue more easily than French.

"Good morning, Lord Richard," the lady said.

She was middle-aged, rather fat, dressed in sensible clothes with no pretensions to fashion—unmistakably English, he should have realised. Suddenly, he recognised Charlotte Colmore. The foreign street vanished; he was for a moment at Longmarsh.

"Miss Colmore, isn't it?"

"It is," she said, and smiled—at his confusion, perhaps.

"I must apologise. You recognised me at once."

"You look scarcely older. And I had the advantage of knowing that you were here. You're quite a Baden-Baden celebrity."

"Oh, surely not. It's my second visit. Delightful spot. Is it your first time here, Miss Colmore?"

"Why, no." She seemed surprised by the question. Then she said: "Pray don't let me detain you. You were going to buy *The Times,* I presume."

"It can wait. May I offer you some refreshment?"

"At the English café? It will be a pleasure."

Over coffee, Richard asked: "Are you making a long stay here?"

"I have my summer routine. I stay with Fanny in Paris, then I spend a week here, and I go on to stay with Ellie at Karlsruhe."

Richard almost dropped his cup. Karlsruhe—it was not twenty miles away. It was said to be an attractive town. Geraldine had spoken of making an excursion there.

Charlotte looked at him closely. "You knew that Ellie was at Karlsruhe, surely, Lord Richard? No?"

He shook his head. He didn't feel able to speak.

"She has been there for eight years."

She was married to a German? He couldn't believe it. He didn't dare to ask.

But Charlotte said: "She teaches at the Hochschule—the High School for girls. It's an excellent position, for a foreigner in the country."

Richard managed to say: "I see."

Charlotte added cream judiciously to her coffee. "You would find Ellie greatly changed, Lord Richard," she said. "She has grown used to responsibility, to holding a place where she is valued. They say she's a very good teacher."

"Is she happy?"

"Why not? Aren't you happy, making decisions at the War Office?"

"That's one kind of happiness. I am happily married, too."

"I don't doubt it. I'm told that your wife is the most admired hostess in London and of great assistance to you in your career. You might have been less happy, married to Ellie."

"Perhaps so, Miss Colmore. I never made that calculation."

"I know something," she said, "of the way in which you parted from Ellie—or Ellie from you. I hope you bear her no resentment now."

"Resentment? I never felt that. It would have been impossible." I loved her, I love her still—this couldn't be said.

There was a silence. He made the effort to turn the conversation.

"You don't find it tedious travelling alone, Miss Colmore?"

"Oh, people are always helpful. I go all over the place. Last year I went to St. Petersburg to stay with Arthur—my brother, you remember. It's a magnificent city."

"So I have heard. Is he still there?"

"No, at present he is in England on leave. He doesn't know where his next posting will be."

Richard accompanied Charlotte to her hotel. It was a modest place in a narrow street, hardly more than a Gasthaus really. She couldn't very well be short of money; perhaps she preferred it. Leaving her, he was glad to be alone. He forgot about buying *The Times* and took another—a longer—walk in the woods.

He couldn't decide whether Charlotte was a very shrewd or a very obtuse woman. She seemed to think that men and women existed on their own and could be happy on their own, as teachers or as politicians. Of course, she had no experience of what love meant: its consuming force, its ineradicable grasp. Apparently she had believed that he knew where Ellie was; it wouldn't occur to her that he had chosen not to know. Or there was another possibility: she wanted to tell him that Ellie was utterly lost to him—even more lost, in this new life, than if she had married.

Was it so? Did Ellie never think of him as he thought of

her? Had she no regrets, no spasms of longing, no remnant of
love? Had she indeed changed as much as Charlotte said, or
did Charlotte merely wish him to think so? He tried to imagine Ellie's life: a beautiful woman without a man, an English-
woman in a foreign country, a routine of work and responsibility within a narrow compass; and, since she was a teacher,
a life among girls who were what she had been. Because he
loved her, he wished her happiness and peace. But, for that
same reason, he couldn't believe that she was quite resigned—
as if she were another Charlotte, as if love had never entered
her life.

Ellie would know, presumably, that he had married. Did
she believe that he had forgotten her? That thought was painful. He felt a sudden impulse to make her understand that he
could never forget her; the truth he had spoken to her remained truth; his love for her lived at the heart of his being.
But—married to Geraldine, parted from Ellie by an act more
irrevocable than hers—he had forfeited the right to gratify
that impulse.

The yearning to see her racked him as he tramped through
the woods: the pine-woods, the German woods, the landscape
that was now hers as the English downland had once been. It
was a yearning that he had never stifled, and it was reinforced
by curiosity, by the irritation of knowing something but not
enough. Why must she be at Karlsruhe of all places in this
big country—in this continent, indeed? He could even go
there today. Geraldine, as it happened, was lunching with
some other ladies and wasn't expecting to see him. But no, the
idea was madness.

He lunched alone at a village inn high in the hills. It took
him all day to regain any composure. In the evening he went
to the casino and played, against his custom, for high stakes.

Geraldine again mentioned the excursion to Karlsruhe.
Richard made an excuse, but could only defer it; they were

staying a whole month at Baden-Baden. As it happened, however, the problem was resolved in an unexpected way. The next letter from Nanny told them that little Charles was in bed with a sore throat. It was probably nothing to worry about, but one never knew—Geraldine recalled that there had been cases of diphtheria at Oxford, not far from the Priory. They decided to return at once.

It was the right course. Charles didn't have diphtheria, but he was uncomfortable and fretful, needing his parents. As soon as they arrived, he began to mend.

Richard settled down to restful weeks in the house he loved, an English house in the English countryside. He felt like a man reprieved.

CHAPTER 11

An Englishman's Creed

THERE WAS A DAY—a November day in 1890—when Richard found the atmosphere of the House of Commons distasteful. Although some business was being transacted on the floor of the House, very few Members paid any attention to it. Tories and Liberals alike gathered in chattering groups in the smoking room or the Members' lobby—waiting, guessing, snatching at rumours. Upstairs, in the committee room where the Irish Nationalists were meeting, Parnell was fighting for his political life.

The adultery between Parnell and Mrs. O'Shea was a proven fact, now that her husband had been granted a divorce. It was depressing, Richard thought, to find the most unpleasant tittle-tattle—whispers had gone round the political world for years—confirmed as truth. Parnell had been leading a double life, treating scandal with scorn, maintaining in his party the dignity of the autocratic leader whom none dared question, yet guilty all the time of what his followers regarded as mortal sin.

Parnell's position was desperate; Gladstone's was difficult. Whatever one might say of his politics, in private life he was the soul of rectitude—he had lately celebrated his golden wedding. He was pledged to introduce another Home Rule Bill if he won the next election. Now, that meant taking a known adulterer as his principal ally and handing over to him the reins of power in Ireland. To Liberal supporters—Low Church or Methodist family men who were the backbone of middle-class England—the prospect was abhorrent. A week after the divorce, Gladstone stated that for Parnell to remain as leader of Irish nationalism would "place many hearty and effective friends of the Irish cause in a position of great embarrassment." The Nationalists had to choose between loyalty to their chief and hope of attaining their goal.

Richard had no doubt in his mind that Parnell should have resigned when the divorce suit was filed. Instead, he had chosen to brazen it out. Apparently he believed that, unlike lesser men, he was entitled to have it both ways—to conduct his personal life in defiance of the normal code and to retain his power too. His true sin, Richard considered, was arrogance. He couldn't imagine it possible that his subordinates should challenge and dismiss him: that any other man could lead his party or govern an independent Ireland.

And yet, it was the fall of a giant. An ordinary politician would have calculated more prudently, would have chosen long ago to give up either the leadership or the woman. But an ordinary politician would not have been Parnell.

So, when the news came that the Nationalists had voted to disown Parnell, Richard was repelled by the sanctimonious smiles in the smoking room. He knew his fellow Members. Half of the married men kept mistresses or availed themselves of Handicott's service. If another man's wife—a woman like Celia Ashton—welcomed their advances, no scruples deterred them. But they would have broken off their liaisons at the least hint of risk, because love seldom entered into the matter. Richard was sure that Parnell loved Mrs. O'Shea as passionately as he had loved Ellie. It was in the nature of the man. He asked himself: if Ellie had been married to an O'Shea when he fell in love with her, could he have retreated from love by a calm act of will? No, surely not.

He left the House as soon as he could. Geraldine had the news already.

"So he's down," she said.

"He's down. It was inevitable, really."

"Of course. How a man could be so reckless, I don't begin to understand."

The events of the next year did nothing to cheer Richard up. Gladstone was still bent on Home Rule, and there were signs of a steady drift of public opinion toward the Liberals. The next House of Commons might well have a solid Home Rule majority.

Parnell campaigned desperately in Ireland to regain his position, was assailed by jeering mobs of bigoted Catholics, exhausted his strength, and died. To Richard's mind, Home Rule would be a disaster in any circumstances; with Parnell gone, it would realise the worst of fears. Parnell had been a gentleman, a statesman, and moreover a Protestant. Out of the havoc of separation, he might have fashioned at least a relationship of amity with England. As things stood now, the heirs of Home Rule would be a scattering of ignorant demagogues, hating all that England stood for, manipulated by equally ignorant priests. Deprived of English law, English social peace, English civilisation, Ireland might sink to an Asiatic level of backwardness and anarchy.

For Richard himself, there would be consolations if the Liberals won the next election. He was thoroughly tired of the War Office. The work consisted, essentially, in administering a smooth-running machine and maintaining a steady flow of troops to garrisons throughout the Empire; but any decisions to use these troops would be taken by others—by the Foreign Office, by the Colonial Office, by the Viceroy of India. In any case, there were no wars on even a minor scale during Richard's period of office. He was glad enough of this. He could no longer recognise himself in the cavalry subaltern who had found excitement at Shutargardan Pass and looked forward cheerfully to giving the Russians a thrashing. To live in peace and help others to live in peace, he knew now, was far more laudable than the most blazing of triumphs on the battlefield, and all that remained with him from the Afghan campaign was the bitter memory of young men dead when they had scarcely begun to live. However, what it all added up to was that being Under-Secretary for War was an interlude of dullness in his life.

During empty periods at his desk—there were quite a few— he thought increasingly of his future. He was at the meridian of life, not far from the age of forty when, according to Geraldine's time-table, he should be in the Cabinet. It was Geraldine, he supposed, who had set ideas of ambition, of getting to the top, geminating in him. Yet they were nothing to be ashamed of; they were legitimate and even necessary, for any man who went into politics and did not choose the path of the eternal back-bencher; and he knew, from the ease with which he handled the tasks of office, that he did not lack ability. What should he hope for, he wondered? Ministerial rank would come first, no doubt, at some not very exalted department like the Local Government Board. But after that? Home Secretary?—It was a fascinating field, despite the terrible burden of the death penalty. Chief Secretary for Ireland? Foreign Secretary? When his musings led him in that direction, he recalled himself sharply to the present.

One day, he was called to Downing Street to explain to the Prime Minister the issues involved in a War Office wrangle— one of the many trivial disputes between the Commander-in-Chief, the old Duke of Cambridge, and the civilian authorities. It was rare indeed for an Under-Secretary to come face to face with Lord Salisbury; it happened only because the Secretary for War was indisposed.

Lord Salisbury listened (or perhaps did not listen) with his

habitual expression, midway between aloofness and impatience. He really had no interest in the question, Richard
thought. Probably the Queen, who was the Duke of Cambridge's cousin, had requested her Prime Minister to deal with
it personally.

But, when Richard had finished speaking, Lord Salisbury
favoured him with a nod and something that was almost a
smile, and said: "Very clearly expressed, Somers. I'm obliged
to you."

"Thank you, my lord."

The Prime Minister reflected, or thought of nothing—one
could never be sure with him—for a couple of minutes. Richard wondered whether he ought to take his leave. However,
Lord Salisbury suddenly looked straight at him and said:
"You've been travelling on the Continent, I believe."

"Yes, my lord."

"A very good habit. Well, Somers, I'll consider this business."

That summer, however, Richard and Geraldine did not
travel. When they visited Severalls for a weekend in June,
they found that Maud was ill. It was shocking to the point of
being unnatural. Anxiety about Richard's mother was to be
expected, and George suffered from rheumatism; Maud normally looked after them. She had never consulted a doctor on
her own behalf in her life, and she wasn't yet forty. Now this
sturdy, vigourous woman was lying all day on a chaise-longue,
pallor in her once rosy cheeks, needing help to walk from one
room to another. She took it bravely and made fun of herself
—"I'm a lazy girl, I'm afraid," she said. Whether there was
real danger, George didn't know. The doctor diagnosed anae-
mia and prescribed beef tea and iron tablets, but the patient's
failure to respond to this treatment puzzled him.

The children were naturally distressed. Freddy in particular
was highly strung and exceptionally devoted to his mother.

Geraldine took them to stay at the Priory; the change of scene helped them, and her own boys were overjoyed with the company of their cousins. The six children launched into busy projects. They dammed a stream to make a paddling pool, and built a Robinson Crusoe hut out of old planks and dried reeds. Richard, when he came down to the Priory in July, enjoyed helping them.

Geraldine went over to Severalls every two or three days. It was a place of gloom, she told Richard. His mother, going through a spell of agonising migraines, was in the doctor's care too. George was in despair, scarcely able to eat his meals or give necessary orders about the household and the estate. "Thank heaven those poor children are out of it," Geraldine remarked. Maud was more cheerful than anyone else, but she was getting weaker. A specialist was sent for and was good enough to interrupt his holiday; he merely said that the case showed unusual features and medical knowledge had its limits. There was little pain, only a remorseless draining away of vitality. As July yielded to a wet and depressing August, Geraldine saw that there was very little hope.

The fatal telegram came on a morning of incessant rain. Maud had died in the night, painlessly. Richard assumed the duty of telling the children. Freddy and the younger girls sobbed helplessly; Elizabeth stared at him with grave, prematurely adult eyes.

Death, that year, kept Richard in its shadow. Not much later, he received a letter from India: sadly but not surprisingly, Ralph had succumbed to a monsoon fever. The old regiment held a memorial service, which Richard attended. Celia was a dignified figure, her expression invisible behind a thick veil. When the will was read, Richard was informed that Ralph had left his sword and medals to young Alfred, for lack of a son of his own.

At the beginning of winter, Lord Farnham died. Ellie

would come home for the funeral, Richard supposed. He
spent a miserable day at the War Office, his thoughts at Longmarsh.

In 1892, Lord Salisbury decided to risk an election. Richard
increased his majority; according to Geraldine, the voters took
pride in being represented by a man with a great future. But
the country as a whole was in a mood for change, and Gladstone campaigned with astonishing energy for a man of
eighty-two. When all the returns were in, they showed that
the Liberals would control the House with the support of the
Irish Nationalists.

As hostesses in country houses complained all over the country, the election ruined the summer. Polling was in July; the
opening of the new Parliament and the predictable defeat of
the Government on a vote of confidence kept M.P.'s in town
during August. Geraldine was as annoyed as anyone. She had
set her heart on going to Baden-Baden, after the sacrifice she
had made the year before. But, with the season over and the
Counts and Princes dispersed throughout Europe, what was
the point?

Nevertheless, the Liberals were in office and Richard was a
free man, with no responsibilities until the House met again
in January. Geraldine suggested a tour of Italy. They went to
all the famous places: Milan, Venice, Florence, Rome, Naples.
Naturally, Geraldine was in her element. She worked at her
Baedeker every evening, making crosses in the margin beside
the most important sights, noting how long each visit would
take, and also noting the recommended tips to guides—Italians were well known to make exorbitant demands when they
saw an English face. She couldn't get enough of ruins, amphi-
theatres, museums, galleries, cathedrals, churches. Richard followed in her wake, trying to remember the difference between
Caligula and Caracalla or between Titian and Tintoretto.

The antiquities were impressive; they stirred his sense of

tradition, his admiration for time-defying achievement. He felt the strength and the splendour of this civilisation that rose eternally from the assaults of barbarians. But he didn't like the cathedrals crowded with knick-knacks, the Baroque altars, the painted ceilings and painted statues. They were too ornate for his taste; he would rather have had the austere grandeur of Canterbury or the simplicity of an English parish church. He found the Italians polite and amiable, but the hotels were not run nearly so well as in Germany and the trains were unpunctual. Though he had enjoyed the break, he was glad to get back to London and to all the aspects of home that one valued only after being away from them: linen that was sure to be clean, meals that one didn't need to order, a man like Simmons who poured brandy and soda in the correct proportions without being told.

The boys were delighted with their presents—toy soldiers for Alfred, a musical box for Charles—and wanted to know all about the tour. Alfred asked when he could go to foreign countries. Geraldine said that he must wait until he was a big boy and could talk French.

"Can Father talk French?" the child asked. Geraldine reproved him, but Richard had to hide a smile. The boys were growing up fast. It was a pity to be away from them for so long, he remarked to Geraldine in the evening. They would be off to boarding school soon enough.

He still regretted that he didn't have a daughter, but Geraldine now said that she would prefer not to have any more children. She hadn't regained her slender waist after Charles was born; her figure was almost matronly now that she was in her thirties, and she mentioned occasionally that she was afraid of getting fat. Richard was aware that her body no longer excited him. The physical side of their marriage had lost its importance through a gradual and tacit change; nothing had to be said. He accepted, of course, that it was impossible to behave like a bridegroom and bride after eight years. In hotels, where they shared a room, her nearness sometimes roused his desires. At home, he went to her room far less often than before. He saw that the carnal act had become wearisome to her, and he tried to be a considerate husband in this as in other ways. He knew how much he owed her.

When the House met, the Government introduced the Home Rule Bill as the first business of any consequence. Richard spoke in the debate on the second reading. The House was crowded, and more Members hurried in when the word went round that Lord Richard Somers was on his feet.

"Some honourable Members," he said, "have made the assumption that it is only the future of Ireland with which we are concerned. If it were so, it would certainly deserve our most earnest consideration, for the destiny of an island of four million people is no light matter. But, sir, it is far more than that. It is the destiny of England that we shall shape by our decision.

"Some may wonder that I speak of England and not of the British Isles or the United Kingdom. I beg honourable Members of Irish and Scottish and Welsh birth to be patient with me. We are linked in a manner that runs deeper than any inheritance of blood. It would ill become a Member of a party that honours the name of Disraeli to claim England as the exclusive possession of those whose ancestors trod English ground. England is not a word on a map, nor a tally of acres or square miles. England is not what we inhabit, but what we are.

"England, sir, is a loyalty, a belief and an ideal. England is an honoured Queen, her forebears and her heirs, a monarchy that transcends party strife and has been strengthened rather than weakened by sharing the counsel of responsible Ministers. England is this House and another place, accustomed to candid and fearless argument but pledged to a common search for the general good. England is a political system developed and refined by the wisdom of the centuries. England is the jury of twelve good men and true, the incorruptible magistrate, the unarmed policeman on his beat. England is the citizen of whatever degree, nourishing his family by the strength or the talents that God has given him, living at peace with his neighbours, speaking his mind freely and respecting the rights of others. England is a way of living together in friendship and in trust. Such is the England that countless men have loved, served and defended: men whose names have been Smith and Jones and MacDonald and O'Brien, but men united by the principles and the traditions that I have endeavoured to describe.

"Now, sir, what is the doctrine that would break these precious bonds? In Ireland, it is called nationalism. It is grounded in no ideals and allied to no new method of government, for none has been proposed. It is based on the mere supposition that those men and women are Irish whose homes are within a certain territory, whether they like it or not— and we know well that many do not—and without any notion of voluntary compact. Ireland is diminished by this, but England is diminished too. For if an Irishman is a man who lives west of the Irish Sea, an Englishman is merely a man who lives east of it. England is deprived at a blow of her identity shaped by loyalty and belief, and reduced to the same arbitrary and mechanical definition of territorial nationalism.

"What follows then? How should we resist the claims to separation made by Scotland or by Wales, as soon as people living in those territories espouse the scheme of nationalism? By what right do we hold our Empire, if not by the extension of English law and English peace? If we confess our abandonment of that principle, the way is open to the demands of Indian nationalism, Malayan nationalism, Jamaican nationalism. Carried by word of mouth, the same doctrine may infect the smallest and most primitive tribe in Africa. And, sir, although it is natural for us to prize the English ideal above all others, we should recognise that each of the great and stable states of Europe rests upon an equivalent foundation—a common loyalty and a common system of government. Should nationalism carry the day, we may live to see the Bavarian divide from the Prussian and the Neapolitan from the Lombard, destroying a unity so lately won, while the Pole and the Balt reject the sovereignty of Russia, and the Bohemian and the Croat reject that of Austria. There may be no halting-place until the world is given over to an anarchy of petty states, a new age of barbarism in which every man's hand is raised against his neighbour.

"It is not subjection that we on this side of the House require from Ireland. We seek to impose no duty that we are not ourselves prepared to render, to Her Majesty the Queen, to the authority of Parliament, to laws freely debated and impartially administered, to Ministers whose office we honour while we oppose their policies. Our subjection, if subjection it be called, is cause for pride. It is made by virtue of a grander vision and a deeper faith than any that the tawdry banner of nationalism can evoke. In that vision and in that faith, I cannot believe that the House of Commons will be lacking."

It was the speech that had been expected of Richard, and that he had required of himself. In the gallery, Geraldine smiled proudly. An Irish Member rose and began a windy tirade; Members began to drift out.

But the commitments had been made, and the Bill gained its majority in the House.

CHAPTER 12

The Fatal Meeting

In September 1893, the Home Rule Bill was defeated in the House of Lords. The Conservative majority included peers who were rarely seen at Westminster—for instance, the Duke of Berkshire. The Liberals declared that it was an insult to the electorate and to the representative House, but there was nothing they could do.

Richard and Geraldine had been to Germany in the summer. She was determined to revisit Baden-Baden, while he wished to spend some time in Berlin and get a real understanding of German political attitudes. She drew up a plan: first Berlin, then a look at Dresden and Nuremberg, which were said to be the most beautiful German towns, then Baden-Baden.

In a rash moment, Richard remarked that one missed a certain amount by not knowing the language. Geraldine immediately engaged a tutor—a young man who worked in the London branch of a German bank—to come to Berkshire House for an hour every morning. Richard hadn't seriously contemplated learning German, but it helped to fill the time now that he no longer had an office to go to. Geraldine proved to be the better pupil, as he expected, but he made reasonable progress. As soon as they had mastered the rudiments, the lessons took the form of reading a German newspaper. When he got to Berlin, people were astonished by his knowledge of recent events there.

It was a splendid place, he thought. The streets were wide and straight, the public buildings were noble, the monuments such as the Brandenburg Gate were conceived on the grand scale like those of imperial Rome. Yet the city did not sprawl, as London and Paris sprawled. Pleasant lakes and woods were within easy reach of the centre. Berlin had grown fast since becoming the capital of a Great Power, but the growth was planned and regulated.

On the day after their arrival, an attaché at the British Embassy called at their hotel, bringing an invitation to dine with the Ambassador. Richard felt honoured; now that he was in Opposition he was a private citizen, and after all he had never been more than an Under-Secretary. He learned that the Ambassador was Lord Farnham—Arthur Colmore. Arthur had done well to reach this position in his early forties, but he had always been brainy.

Richard and Geraldine arrived before the other guests. While Grace showed Geraldine over the main rooms of the Embassy, Richard chatted with Arthur.

"You don't look a day older," Arthur said. "I wonder how you do it."

"Is that a compliment? My wife would prefer me to cultivate a statesmanlike appearance. Anyway, it's a pleasure to see you after all these years."

"It has been a long time, indeed. My sister Charlotte mentioned meeting you at Baden-Baden. She'll be here next week. She's coming on from Karlsruhe."

"I hope we'll meet."

There was a short silence; both men thought of Ellie, but neither spoke of her.

"Charlotte is a remarkable woman," Arthur said. "I was placed in a dilemma when my father died. Diplomacy is my life; it wouldn't suit me to retire to Longmarsh, much as I love it. Charlotte solved the problem. She manages the estate just like a man."

"I'm not surprised. There ought to be a special dispensation to allow her to sit in the Lords. She'd do very well."

The dinner party was small but select: a German diplomat who had played a part in the Heligoland negotiations, a Colonel attached to the General Staff, a member of the Reichstag, and their wives. As the Colonel's English was limited and two of the ladies didn't speak it at all, Richard and Geraldine tried out their German. This went down well; the Germans seemed to take it as a great compliment that anyone should learn their language. The diplomat's wife said that she would be glad to know their honoured guests' opinion of German translations of Shakespeare. *King Lear* was playing in Berlin at the moment, she informed them. Geraldine replied that they would make sure to see it. The diplomat's wife promised to see to the tickets—it would be a pleasure. Her husband said that all educated Germans admired English culture. He had offered German East Africa in exchange for Shakespeare, but had been unable to persuade Lord Salisbury.

After the ladies left the table, the serious conversation was in English. The Reichstag member said that Germans could scarcely help taking England as a model. They now had a united country with three English characteristics: a monarchy incarnating a common loyalty, an aristocracy rooted in the land, and a Parliament with a stable majority to support the Government and an Opposition to make constructive criticisms. Since the system worked in England, it ought to work in Germany too.

The diplomat said that, if one took a historical view, a weak Germany had always been a factor of instability in Europe. It had led to the chaos of the religious wars and had been an irresistible temptation to Napoleon. Modern Germany, he hoped, was a factor of stability. With the prosperity of fifty million souls at stake, war was an impermissible luxury. Turning to the Colonel, he said: "It's sad, but we are putting you out of business."

"Out of business," replied the Colonel, "will I with happiness be." He had fought at Sedan as a young man, he told Richard. The loss of life had been *schrecklich*—dreadful, yes? He hoped that the French knew that too. Was it true, he asked Richard, that the statue in Paris symbolising Strassburg was covered with a black cloth and the French had ideas of revenge? Unfortunately it was true, Richard answered. The Colonel sighed and said that one should be more realistic. Anyone who had been to Strassburg knew that it was a German town. Richard said that he had been there and certainly got this impression. Then the question should remain closed, said the Colonel; Germany at least was satisfied with her frontiers.

This was the first of a number of interesting discussions. Richard was impressed by the way in which Germans set out their ideas. A Reichstag member justified his opinions by references to history, political economy, statistical knowledge; an English M.P. would have been afraid of sounding pedantic, but the truth was that few M.P.'s could have competed on this intellectual level. At a dinner party, the company almost always included a Professor or a Doctor (which didn't, in German usage, mean a medical man) who was heard with respect while he discoursed on his subject. Germans tended to be long-winded and ponderous in manner, and a discussion was a sequence of monologues rather than a conversation. But everyone was ready both to teach and to learn. A valuable attitude, Richard thought. ↳

Wherever he went, he felt the strong manly beat of patriotism. In a café, if one saw a group of students drinking beer, they didn't sing sentimental ballads or comic songs like

English youngsters. They sang—very musically, too—songs about their Fatherland, such as the refrain which Richard heard so often that he soon knew it by heart:

Lieb' Vaterland, magst ruhig sein,
Fest steht und treu die Wacht, die Wacht am Rhein.

Even in a few weeks, one got a clear impression of what it was like to live in Germany. It lacked the ease and friendliness that marked English life at its best. Where England had grown, Germany had been planned. Strength and purpose were the dominant qualities. Everyone had a place and everyone had a job to do: the professor, the manufacturer, the labourer. (Hardly anyone was unemployed in Germany, Richard learned.) People worked to improve their family circumstances, as in England, but they also kept in their minds that they were making a contribution to the whole mechanism—to Germany.

The Army was very important to Germans, Richard noticed. One saw officers everywhere in Berlin, mainly because they wore uniform in the streets and on social occasions, instead of changing into mufti when off duty as in England. They carried themselves proudly and were treated with deference. Once, Richard saw a captain march into a shop and demand service from an assistant who was attending another customer; everyone present seemed to find this quite natural. When a troop of cavalry rode down a street, people cheered. One felt that they were joining in a ritual of devotion, not simply enjoying a picturesque spectacle. Germans in general were happiest in uniforms; even cabbies had peaked caps and coats with shiny brass buttons. Richard was ready to believe that the men in responsible positions, both in the Government and in the Army itself, wanted peace. But if war came, there was no doubt that Germany would be united in the drive for victory.

He tested his impressions on Arthur, who had been in

Berlin for almost three years. Every time they talked, he had greater confidence in Arthur's judgment.

"You've summed it up very well," Arthur said. "One does feel a tremendous potential power. No reason why it shouldn't be a power for good; there's so much constructive ability, so much respect for art and science. But as a power for evil it would still be tremendous. You know those dogs? German shepherd dogs. Good workers, very obedient, responsive to training. But, by Jove, they can bite if anyone annoys them."

"What are the danger spots, would you say?"

"One can't quite tell. There are untidy zones where the frontiers of influence are vague. Germans can't stand untidiness. There's the Baltic; Germany's very much extended along the coast, and the Russians are sensitive about the approaches to St. Petersburg. Then, if the Austrians got into trouble in the Balkans, the Germans would feel obliged to back them up. Old Bismarck once told me that he thought the next war would start in the Balkans."

When Charlotte arrived, Arthur and Grace gave an all-English dinner party, inviting the Somers, another couple from the Embassy, and an elderly bachelor who was the doctor to the English community in Berlin. The Germans were as reliable in medicine as in everything else, the doctor said. When the necessity arose, he didn't hesitate to entrust a patient to a German hospital.

Placed next to Charlotte at dinner, Richard said: "I hear that you're the squire of Longmarsh now."

"Do you consider that very unsuitable, Lord Richard?"

"Not at all," Richard said hastily. "I know Arthur's very grateful to you."

"Are you enjoying your stay in Berlin?"

"Very much, thank you. I find myself drawn to Germany more than to any other country I've visited."

"One can easily take to German ways, yes."

He lowered his voice and said: "Please tell me, Miss Colmore—how is Ellie?"

"Contented."

She did not amplify this, and he felt a difficulty in pursuing the subject.

A few days later, Geraldine suddenly fell ill. She woke one morning complaining of a violent headache, of a kind that she had never known before. She insisted on trying to get up, but lost her balance as soon as she tried to walk. If Richard hadn't supported her and helped her back to bed, she would have collapsed.

The English doctor was summoned, and diagnosed the bursting of a small blood-vessel in the brain. He gave a sedative; there was nothing else he could do.

"Is this dangerous?" Richard asked.

"Probably not. I hope to be able to reassure you completely by this evening."

Richard sat by Geraldine's bedside all day, holding her hand and watching for the slightest change. Despite the sedative, she was in severe pain. She bore it courageously and twice urged him to leave her, to go out for a walk; but he couldn't have forgiven himself if he hadn't given her such comfort as his presence could provide.

Neither she nor he had ever had a day's illness until now. His powerlessness, in the face of this sudden threat, was a torment. Like all laymen in such a situation, he thought miserably of his lack of medical knowledge. He had no idea how great the danger was—doctors always tried to avoid alarm. Every spasm, as it twisted her face and quickened her breathing to a gasp, terrified him, for he had no way of judging whether to send for help. The hotel manager had a page ready to run to the English doctor's surgery, and there was a German doctor actually in the hotel. It could have been worse if this had happened in France or Italy, where one couldn't rely on German efficiency. Nevertheless, being away from home intensified the ordeal.

Toward evening, she fell asleep. He hoped that this was a good sign; but her unconsciousness, her remoteness from him, was disturbing. Her breathing was regular—good, he supposed. But it was quiet—bad, perhaps. He decided to send a message to the doctor. At this moment, however, the doctor came in.

"She's just fallen asleep."

"Ah, that's splendid."

The doctor took Geraldine's pulse.

"She's out of danger, Lord Richard."

Richard could have shouted from joy and relief.

"I dare say she'll sleep for ten or twelve hours. The body has ways of restoring itself. She may say that she feels perfectly well tomorrow, but of course she's weakened. Keep her in bed until I've seen her."

"How long will she be ill?"

"Oh, she'll have to convalesce. That's not to be hurried."

"We'd better go home as soon as she's well enough to travel."

"Yes, I should advise that. She'll be equal to the journey in four or five days, I expect."

Geraldine agreed to go home, reluctantly but with her usual good sense. But she absolutely refused to let Richard change his plans. He had introductions, even appointments; people were expecting to see him at Dresden, Nuremberg and Baden-Baden; some of their new German friends had taken considerable trouble. Geraldine would be perfectly all right at the Priory, with Nanny to look after the boys when she needed to rest.

Even the strain of the journey was no problem. The doctor was due for his annual holiday in England; by advancing his plans a little, he could travel with Geraldine. Richard gave in.

"I hope I'll manage without you," he said dubiously.

"You'll have a rattling good time, my dear. Every man needs to be a temporary bachelor once in a while."

"I'll see how things go. I shall probably come home from Baden-Baden earlier than we'd planned."

"Not on any account. I should be furious."

In Berlin, after she had gone, he felt like a man without a limb. In restaurants, in houses to which he was invited, in the hotel at night, he missed Geraldine constantly. He was glad to resume his travels; in towns where she had never been, he found that he missed her less. With a certain sense of guilt, he realised that he was having a rather good time. Dresden was magnificent. Nuremberg, with its winding streets and gabled mediaeval buildings, was fascinating; the German past, the makings of Germany, surrounded him as they had nowhere else. The people to whom he had introductions were extremely hospitable, and an English guest was evidently an event in their lives. Geraldine had been right—it would have been unkind to disappoint them. Some of them didn't speak English, but his German was steadily improving.

Without Geraldine, he was less punctilious about the museums and monuments. He spent hours strolling in the streets, sitting in cafés, imbibing the flavour of German life. And, as a temporary bachelor, he could go into beer-halls and cellars—very authentically German, these were—to which one obviously didn't take ladies. It was a pleasure to follow his impulses instead of sticking to the itinerary made out for each day. In a way, it was a rejuvenation—something like the days when he had knocked about London, on leave after service in India.

One evening, in the lobby of the hotel, a young lady said to him: "We meet again, Lord Richard."

They had met on a Sunday, just after Geraldine had left Berlin, when he had been invited to an al fresco lunch at a villa in the Spandau woods. There had been many guests and he had exchanged only a few words with this young lady, but had been struck by her air of independence. The host told him that she had insisted on becoming an actress, much to the annoyance of her parents who belonged to the old aristocracy. Now, she explained, she was on her way to stay with relatives who had an estate near Nuremberg; they would be fetching her from the hotel next morning.

Richard invited her to dine with him. At a table in the large public dining room, it was quite proper. However, the waiter conducted them to a corner table which created a somewhat intimate atmosphere. He ordered champagne. She was an amusing companion, with a fund of gossipy stories about the theatrical world, and remarkably pretty. She was not more than twenty-five, he judged, and she seemed to regard him as belonging to her own generation, asking at one point whether he was a new Member of the English Parliament. He was aware, in fact, that he didn't look thirty-eight. Either she didn't know that he was married, or she chose not to know it. With the second bottle of champagne, he saw clear indications of an opportunity. He let it pass, of course. But the possibility gave him an undeniable pleasure.

He reserved his seat in the train for Baden-Baden. There was a change at Karlsruhe.

One knows things, he recognised later, without admitting the knowledge to oneself. One has intentions, while believing that one is resigned to the guidance of chance.

There was an hour and a half to wait at Karlsruhe. He told the porter to keep an eye on his luggage while he had a snack. Torrential rain, rattling like bullets on the glass roof of the station, turned the afternoon into premature darkness. A summer storm, but it could last for hours. He remembered that the hotel at Baden-Baden was over a mile from the station; arriving in this downpour would be unpleasant.

The Karlsruhe station restaurant proved to belong to a hotel, which was built over the booking hall like the Charing Cross Hotel in London. Richard asked for a room. It was common sense; anyone would have done the same.

He spent a restless evening, trying to read a Tauchnitz edition of a Trollope novel but unable to concentrate, then trying to write to Geraldine but failing to finish the letter. The rain went on most of the night. Trains chuffed, trams clanged their bells in the station square, students held a sing-song downstairs. He didn't sleep until the small hours.

In the morning, the sun shone in an innocent blue sky. The square and the houses gleamed as if they had been washed clean with giant mops. Richard ate a light Continental break-fast. He felt curiously happy, in a light-headed, schoolboyish, irresponsible way—presumably because nobody knew where he was.

He would take a stroll round the town, he thought. It was said to be an attractive place, so why not see it now that he was here? Anyone would have done the same. Geraldine would have done the same, had she been with him. There was a plan of the streets in the hotel lobby. To get to the Grand Duke of Baden's castle, obviously the principal sight of Karlsruhe, one followed the Kaiserstrasse. One passed the Hochschule, he noticed. One could not avoid passing it.

So he would glance—simply glance—at the building where Ellie spent her days. As it was still the summer holiday, the school was closed. He had no idea where she lived. There must be a school caretaker; he could enquire for her address. But he would certainly not do that.

And what if he did see her? It was eleven years now—time enough, surely, to come to terms with the irrevocable. He had restrained himself, deprived himself, all this time. Their lives were set now, his and hers; he had moved toward his kind of achievement and maturity, she toward hers. They could speak of that divergence calmly and in friendship. He had Charlotte's word that she was greatly changed. It could even be the path of wisdom to see her, to read the end of the chapter, to replace the phantom of Ellie lost with Ellie living.

But he didn't think much about this, partly because he was in no fit state for logical thought, partly because in any case he was not going to see her.

The school was at the angle of the Kaiserstrasse and of a small square, bisected with paths and planted with chestnut trees. He turned into the square to look at the main entrance to the school, which faced it.

Ellie, dressed in white—white against the green—was sitting on a bench and reading a book. His steps crunched on gravel. She looked up. His mind whirled, losing grasp of time and reason. She was utterly unchanged—beautiful, beautiful.

"Richard," she said.

"Ellie."

She stood up, put down her book, and walked toward him —slowly, as if she were unwilling but irresistibly compelled. He took her hand and kissed it in the Continental fashion. When he released it, it fell lifelessly to her side.

"You knew I was here?" she asked.

"In this town—yes."

"I never wrote to you. I wanted . . ." She left this unfinished.

"Your sister didn't tell you that we had met? In Baden-Baden three years ago, and last month in Berlin?"

"Charlotte? No, she didn't tell me."

Trying to speak lightly, he asked: "Aren't you pleased to see me?"

"Pleased?" She glanced up at him and quickly down again, in her old way. His heart turned over.

"I don't know," she said. "It's a great surprise."

"I must apologise for that. I'm travelling to Baden-Baden,

and I stayed here last night rather than go on in the storm. Today I took a walk to see the town and . . . well, chance has taken a hand."

"No, Richard," she said. "It's not chance."

He made no answer to this. After a moment, he said: "This is the school where you teach, I believe. It looks quite imposing."

"Yes." She turned to look at the school; it restored her self-command. "It's one of the best in Germany. There wasn't a proper girls' school here until after the founding of the Empire. Baden has always been rather a backwater, but we're coming up to Prussian standards."

"A great deal has been achieved in Germany, I know that."

Ellie now seemed quite composed. "You must let me show you the town, Richard."

"You were reading. I've broken into your day."

"Oh, not at all. I always kill a little time in the square when it's sunny. In the holidays, I mean. There's no time to kill during the term."

"Do you always stay at Karlsruhe during the holidays?"

"Nearly always. It's my home. All my friends are here."

"You haven't been back to England at all?"

"Yes, briefly. Shall we walk up to the Schloss? It's considered rather fine."

Crossing the spacious square in front of the castle, they met a lady who knew Ellie and engaged her in conversation. Richard couldn't follow the German, which was rapid and colloquial on both sides. Ellie introduced him as *"ein alte Freund aus England."*

"That's the greatest gossip in Karlsruhe," she remarked as they walked away.

"You didn't introduce me by name, I noticed."

"One can't be too careful. You're in public life, after all. Is your wife travelling with you, Richard?"

He explained.

"I saw a photograph of her once in the *Illustrated London News*. She's beautiful."

"It has been a successful marriage."

"I'm glad. Have you got children?"

"Two boys."

"Shall we go round by the park? We're quite proud of our park."

It was a typical German park, laid out to a geometrically precise plan, and with a lake in the middle. Small boys were sailing their model boats. They wore sailor hats with ribbons at the back, as in the German Navy.

"I always think of you with water as a background, Ellie," he said.

She was pensive; he imagined for a moment that she hadn't heard him. Then she said: "The lake in Regent's Park."

"And the lake at Longmarsh."

She managed a smile. "Do you remember feeding the ducks?"

"Of course."

"You had to go and buy bread. There must be a baker in Baker Street, you said."

Richard didn't trust himself to speak.

"It seems like yesterday," she said in her quietest voice.

"I can never forget it, Ellie. Did you imagine that I had forgotten?"

"No. One doesn't forget . . . things like that."

"It has made me very happy to see you again. Is that wrong of me? I hope you don't think so."

"I don't know. What is right and what is wrong . . . it's so hard to tell."

"At least, I'm happy to see you contented in your life here. That's true, isn't it?"

"Ah, yes. You must believe that."

"I should be going. They expected me at Baden-Baden last night. Shall I accompany you back to the school?"

"Please. I live close by."

They were silent all the way back to the little square. It was strange; they had so much to talk about, as old friends. But they were not mere friends. They both knew that now.

"I must say goodbye, Ellie. I shall always wish you all that's good in the world."

She gave him a quick, searching look.

"Richard, when you said that you think of me . . ." She broke off, but he understood.

"I think of you often, very often. I have never ceased to think of you from the day that we parted."

Almost inaudibly, she said: "I've never ceased to think of you."

"It's not wrong, Ellie."

"I don't know. I can't help . . . we can't help . . . You must go, Richard."

He kissed her hand again. When he turned round at the corner of the street she was back on her bench, reading.

Alone at Baden-Baden, he was shaken by regrets as fierce and raw as in the first desolating days after Ellie had left him. He made up his mind that he must never see her again. It was too dangerous, far too dangerous. And now the need to return to England—to Geraldine and the boys, to the life he had made—was imperative. He stayed only three nights at Baden-Baden, meeting the people he had promised to meet.

He sent a telegram to the Priory, so Geraldine was in London by the time he arrived. As soon as Simmons had greeted him and left them alone, he took her in his arms and kissed her passionately.

"Oh, my dear," she exclaimed, extricating herself and laughing, "has it been so terrible?"

"I love you, Geraldine. Say you love me."

"Of course I love you. You really must travel without me again. The effect is remarkable."

"No, never again."

"As you please. What time is it? We should dress for dinner."

He followed her into her room and drew her down onto the bed before she put on her evening-dress. It was years since he had done this.

"You'll settle down tomorrow, I hope," she said afterwards.

CHAPTER 13

Doomed to Love

SHE STOOD by the window of the familiar room, the music-room at Longmarsh. She had made a resolution to practise the piano every morning. But she hadn't the steadiness, the command of herself, to achieve even this small degree of discipline: she, whose life for years had been a submission to a time-table, a submission so willing that it had become entirely natural. She played a little, made discouraging mistakes, let her mind stray, then got up and wandered about the room. From the fireplace to the window, from the window to the bookcases, back to the window again.

It was so beautiful here in England. Autumn, surely, was the most beautiful season of the year. Nothing changed suddenly, yet nothing remained the same as a German pine-forest did. The beeches and oaks changed their colours and then dropped their leaves very gently, a little bit from day to day, like old friends growing older. Everyone said that this autumn, the autumn of 1894, was the most beautiful in living memory. It was now the first week in November, but the weather continued mild and calm. Only the sunlight, changing subtly like the trees, was a little softer and hazier every day.

In the music-room, and in her bedroom, and in the garden, it often seemed to Ellie that she had never gone away.

"It seems like yesterday," she had said to Richard at Karlsruhe. It seemed to her, indeed, that time was not a process but an infinitely complex scene, in which all experience—past, present and future, as one said in the ordinary reckoning—was contained at different levels of consciousness. A life was like a year, in which summer came before winter and yet also came after winter. She was standing by a lake, trying to meet Richard's eyes, captured and afraid, struggling. When was that? A dozen years ago, or last year, or yesterday?

She was in a hansom, going up Park Lane and Gloucester Place in pouring rain. She didn't know how she could face them all in the morning—her aunt, her mother, Celia. It suddenly struck her that there was one person with whom she would be safe: Dr. Pfaffer. She called to the cabby that she'd changed her mind—she wanted to go on to Prince Albert Road. He grumbled: "The other side of the park? In this weather?" Half a sovereign, she called desperately. Had she got one? Yes, in the corner of her purse, there it was.

She was drinking cocoa as Dr. Pfaffer pondered and planned. She was sobbing with relief when he methodically produced a solution to every difficulty. She had never worked nor trained for work, never imagined taking charge of her own life. But she could teach—why not? The piano, he assured her; English, obviously; French and other subjects, she could try. Dr. Pfaffer said that there was no such thing as family feeling if his sister couldn't make a place for Ellie at her little school. Ellie could travel with Dr. Pfaffer's niece, who was in any case planning a visit to Karlsruhe. She had no money of her own, had never handled more than pocket-money. But a loan would be only an advance on her salary. Her parents would never allow it if they knew. But they need not know; and after all, she was over twenty-one. Ellie saw the emerging outlines of a being that had always been led, guided, encased in protection: herself.

A pupil was playing the piano, and Ellie miraculously was

not the pupil but the teacher. She was speaking German; she really could make herself understood. She was standing in front of a class; she had never raised her voice like this, but they did hear her in the back row.

She could do it. She was needed, she was valued. She had a profession.

She was summoned to Fräulein Pfaffer's room. She trembled as she knocked at the door. Here it was, the punishment for her illusions: failure, dismissal. Fräulein Pfaffer spoke firmly, unsmiling and authoritative as always. At first the words didn't make sense: "Too good for our little school." Ellie trembled even more. Other words followed: High School, vacancy, opportunity.

She was saying: "Eva, if you do not make an effort I cannot help you." Eva bowed her head. Just as well, since she was a good four inches taller than Ellie.

She was a wedding guest. Eva suddenly was not a school-girl, but the bride of Water Traffic Under-Director Brüning. Herr Brüning said jokingly but respectfully that if he didn't get obedience from Eva he would report her to Fräulein Colmore. He was twenty-four; Fräulein Colmore was twenty-six.

She was correcting homework in the staff-room. The other teachers, standing by the door, hadn't noticed her.

"I've heard that she left England because of an unhappy experience. She loved a man and he deserted her."

"Is that why she never married?"

"She wouldn't look at anyone else. So I've heard."

"Extraordinary. She's still attractive."

Still. Thirty, but still attractive.

She was at Longmarsh. She didn't handle money, or go into shops, or give orders to the servants. She walked in the grounds, but seldom went beyond the gate. She didn't ride, because she was frightened of horses. She disliked meeting strangers and was at ease only with her big sister, Charlotte. She was a shy girl—younger than her years. No, she suddenly remembered, she was thirty-three.

Certain words, apparently simple, bewildered her. Home. Myself. Ellie. Fräulein Colmore. Life. Reality. Sometimes she thought that she had them pinned down; then they eluded her.

She had come to Longmarsh in the summer because her mother was gravely ill. Lady Farnham, consistently happy as a wife, had taken badly to being a widow. By choice, she would have died the day after her husband. Though the doctor didn't tell her that she had a fatal disease, she said to Charlotte that she wasn't fooled and she considered it a welcome release. Learning this from Charlotte's letter, Ellie assumed that she would be going to England, as on the occasion of her father's illness and death, for a week or two—to say goodbye to her mother and attend the funeral.

She was the last to arrive, and found the whole family assembled. Despite the sadness of the occasion, the fact that the old house was filled again created a cheerful atmosphere. The brothers and sisters wandered about the garden and the grounds, recalling incidents of long ago, exchanging news. No one wanted to stay indoors, partly because they had to talk in hushed voices, partly because the glorious summer weather was irresistible. One day, everyone joined in an expedition to the barrows—a sort of fond tribute to their dying mother.

"Ellie, you haven't changed a bit—how do you do it?" they all cried.

She didn't know whether she had changed or not. They were talking about outward appearance and this wasn't, she thought, what mattered. Still, as she looked at them, it did strike her that some had changed far more than others.

Arthur—Lord Farnham—walked with a stoop and was almost completely bald. Yet he hadn't changed so much, essentially, because he had never been really youthful. He was back in London as head of the Northern Department of the Foreign Office. Ellie gathered that it was a highly responsible position, concerned with the making of policy. "A Foreign Office mandarin"—that was the phrase.

Charlotte looked the same as ever, perhaps because Ellie had been seeing her every year. As a young woman she had been considered to have a regrettably full figure (one didn't like to say "fat") but now she made an impression of solid presence, of monumental sturdiness, quite suited to her personality. Kindly, calm, reliable: she was still the same.

Celia had changed, or so it seemed to Ellie. Her face, when she thought herself unobserved, expressed a weariness that went far beyond mere boredom. The others found her unchanged because her figure was as good as ever. She went riding before breakfast and played tennis energetically with the young ones—Anne and Tommy. Amid the peace of Longmarsh, she brought an element of restlessness. According to Fanny, she had a string of admirers and could marry again any time she liked. Ellie thought of Celia and Major Falconer. It seemed like yesterday; it could be today.

Fanny, however, had become disastrously fat. Four children and French food, she said—the combination was fatal. She put a brave face on it. She told Ellie that she enjoyed life, she had a flourishing *salon,* she supposed that Claude had a *petite amie* somewhere but he behaved like a gentleman. Her manner was that of the old Fanny: lively, gay, full of jokes. But there was a pathos in it, as of an actress playing a part that demanded more and more effort.

Robert was unrecognisable. Ellie hadn't seen him on her last visit to England; he had been, for a while, a missionary in China. He had caught some infection there, had nearly died, and had been ordered home by the Church. He now had a lean, ascetic look and, like Arthur, was prematurely bald.

He was the modern type of clergyman, had a slum parish in Bermondsey, and lived in a world of settlement houses, soup kitchens and boys' clubs. He hadn't married, evidently wouldn't marry. The rest of the family felt slightly uneasy with him.

Anne, more than anyone else, appeared to be perfectly happy. With the slightest encouragement, she produced photographs of her pretty house at Portsmouth, her husband, her little boy and her little girl. She and Tommy went into corners and talked about babies; Tommy's first, still an infant, was delicate, and Anne gave advice and reassurance. Tommy had bought a farm in Suffolk and intended to devote himself to country life. Little Tommy, a husband and father: he had been a mere child when Ellie had left home. But when he rowed on the lake and climbed the old beech in the paddock, he was a child again.

So there they all were, gathered to witness a death that they would genuinely mourn, but a death that they recognised as in the nature of things, a timely close to a good life.

Only, their mother did not die. The presence of her children, making the house as full and busy as in its heyday, seemed to restore her failing strength. She came down to meals, asked questions about everything, and expressed her opinions in her positive way. The doctor said that there was no question of a recovery; she had a strong constitution, that was all. She could collapse tomorrow or she could live for months.

It was rather awkward. Arthur had his responsibilities, Celia presumably had her lover or lovers, Fanny had her *salon,* Robert had his parish, Anne had her children, Tommy had his farm. They scattered, promising to return at the call of a telegram. Ellie stayed. It was a long way to Karlsruhe, the fare took a noticeable bite out of her salary, and the school holiday was about to begin.

Through July and August and September, she didn't leave Longmarsh. She was supposed to be making herself useful, but there was a nurse in the house and Charlotte was in charge. The days and weeks went by, pleasantly empty and somehow unreal. It was a warm, lazy English summer—like all the summers of her youth, or at all events like her memory of them. It was her undoing; she sensed that, but could not resist it. She was losing what she had found at Karlsruhe: herself. But whether the Karlsruhe self or the Longmarsh self was the true Ellie, she no longer knew.

To add to the unreality, the sick old woman's mind began to wander. Or that was the phrase. It could also be said, Ellie thought, that she was summing up her life by living through it again, without regard to chronology which no longer mattered to her. At all events, she would suddenly begin to talk as if it were 1860 or 1870 or 1880. She often said that she was looking forward to seeing her husband again. This might have been quite coherent, since Lady Farnham had taken to religion in her later years and believed firmly in the after-life. Or it might have meant that she thought Lord Farnham was away. In Ellie's childhood, he had gone to the West Indies on a commission of enquiry.

Two or three times, Lady Farnham planned house parties and drew up guest lists of people who were as old as she was, or dead. Again, she got worried about the children's lessons and declared that she must have a word with Miss Frayn. Charlotte duly sent for Miss Frayn, who was living at Guildford. By the time the former governess arrived, Lady Farnham was back in 1894 and asked her how she was enjoying her retirement.

Two incidents disturbed Ellie particularly. One afternoon, sitting in her own room, she heard her mother's voice raised in agitation and hurried to see what was the matter. Lady Farnham shouted: "A daughter of mine, behaving like that!

There's bound to be a scandal. And with Ralph risking his life in the Sudan, too." Then she gave a curious smile, quite unlike herself, winked at the nurse, and said: "Mind you, it's no fun doing without it"—and added a most extraordinary expression. The nurse and Ellie avoided each other's eyes.

The other incident happened when the nurse was off duty and Ellie was sitting by her mother's bed. The invalid was asleep, or so Ellie thought. Suddenly she opened her eyes, looked at Ellie with her old commanding expression, and said: "You silly child, you'd better make up your mind to accept Lord Richard. You'll never do better, mark my words."

Ellie trembled.

School was beginning in Karlsruhe. Ellie wrote to explain, and the Director replied that she was not to worry. She had worked devotedly for years; she could regard the term as a period of leave, if necessary.

Lady Farnham died on the first of October. It was Charlotte who was in the sickroom. She told Ellie afterwards that the old woman unexpectedly sat up and said in a clear voice: "I think I'll run up to town and order some dresses." Then she shuddered, and fell back dead.

The family assembled once more for the funeral. After it, the house was quiet again, indeed quieter than before. There was nothing to do. Ellie reflected on how a house can revolve round an invalid, as at other times it can revolve round a child. She would go back to Germany soon, of course.

But she didn't go. Packing, travelling—it all seemed too much for her. Teaching also seemed too much for her. She couldn't imagine how she had done it. She couldn't feel herself to be Fräulein Colmore.

Charlotte said: "You don't realise how exhausted you are. It's nothing to be ashamed of; it's all been a severe strain. You'd be wise to do what the Director says and stay until after Christmas."

"No, I can't do that," Ellie answered. She had a feeling that, if she stayed so long, she would never be able to go back at all. She would have lost herself—lost Fräulein Colmore—for ever. Perhaps she would stay as long as the fine weather lasted. That was some kind of decision.

So now she stood by the window, uncertain and afraid. There was a question that she dared not put to anyone, even to Charlotte. What was to become of her?

For there was something that she could not tell Charlotte. She was in love with Richard. Hopelessly, miserably, eternally in love. She had struggled to escape, and she had failed. She was doomed to live the rest of her life in this confusion of longing and fear.

"It's over. I'm free. I'm someone else." She had said that to herself many times. She had said it when she first crossed the Channel, and in the pride of succeeding as a teacher, and when she heard of Richard's marriage. But she had never altogether convinced herself, and now she knew the truth. She had never ceased to love him, just as he had never ceased to love her.

She felt herself sinking, as she had felt when she was engaged to Richard. She felt the captivity, the stifling, the threat of annihilation. She knew that she ought, as before, to take the train to Germany and reshape her life. But this time, though everything seemed to be the same, it was really worse. It was worse because of the vain struggle and the relentless grasp of love. She was weaker now—a woman of thirty-three, a respected teacher—than as a girl. She couldn't fight for herself, because she couldn't believe in herself.

She would never see Richard again, she supposed. He had seen the dangers that day at Karlsruhe. He had a loyalty to his wife. Never to see him again: it was right, it was wise, it was the only chance of survival. And yet it was terrible. She would always fear him, and she would always yearn for him.

She wandered out of the room, to the hall. Charlotte was visiting a neighbour, she remembered. It was strange to be alone at Longmarsh. She walked through the front door, across the lawn and along the path to the lake. She often walked this way, thinking of Richard.

She often saw him, too. When she saw him this time, standing at the spot where he had proposed to her, he appeared to her so clearly that she was afraid she was beginning to have hallucinations. She stopped and stared. He was really there.

She was still some distance away, and his back was turned to her. She could quite easily have gone back to the house without being seen and told the servants that she was receiving no visitors. But she went on, helplessly, hopelessly.

He turned, and they stared at each other for a minute in silence.

"I had to come here," he said. "I won't tell you any stories about chance or about being in the neighbourhood. I have tried, as hard as a man can try. I tried for eleven years, until that day at Karlsruhe. I've tried since then—another year, the longest and cruellest year of my life. I can't try any longer, Ellie."

"I know," she said. "I know."

"I came back to London last week from my country place, and Arthur told me you were here."

"I shouldn't have stayed."

"I told myself that I shouldn't see you, that I should only stand by the lake and remember. I try these pretences, you know. But I don't pretend I'm sorry. I am happy. You are happiness to me, now as always."

"Don't speak of happiness. What's the use? Oh, Richard, what's the use?"

"Let me only say what I must. I told you last time that I've never ceased to think of you. I meant—you know I meant— I've never ceased to love you. I love you now. Only a man who has tried to kill his love, I think, can love as I do."

She began to tremble. She would stammer if she spoke, she thought, though she hadn't stammered for all these years. But she mastered herself.

"You know it's hopeless," she said. "You know we can only torment ourselves—each other. What can we do? Why have you come?"

"Not out of good sense or reason, I know. I needed this moment as a soul in Hell needs a drink of pure water. Only let me look at you for a little while and say: 'My darling, my sweetheart, my own love.' Then I shall go. If I come again, it will be because I can't resist it."

"I should go back to Germany."

"But you haven't gone. We are both beyond doing what we should."

"I know. I should tell you not to come here. But I can't."

"And if you went to Germany—to the South Seas—I should come there too."

She said: "Charlotte will have to know, you understand. It's only chance that she's not here today."

"Very well—Charlotte will have to know."

She began to walk along the path, keeping away from him, afraid of his touch.

"How is your wife? And your children?"

"All well. I wish it were possible for you to know them, Ellie. Geraldine is a good woman—none of this is her fault. I was sorry to hear of your mother's death."

"Thank you, Richard."

He burst out suddenly: "I can't go on talking of—anything but you. I won't stay. A little of this is all that I can bear. All that you can bear, my poor darling."

"Go now, Richard. Don't look back."

They gazed at each other again, storing each other up for the time apart. Then he turned with a kind of shudder and strode toward the lodge gate, hastening like a man pursued.

He had not touched her. He had not even kissed her hand, as in the square at Karlsruhe. Yet she felt herself possessed by him.

When Charlotte returned, Ellie told her who had been at Longmarsh. She was astonished by her own calmness, her ability to deceive.

"You know we meant a great deal to each other at one time, Charlotte. It's long ago, but it's some kind of a bond. A sentimental friendship, I suppose. It was a pleasure to see him, especially as he's done so well in his career."

"I'm sorry I was out."

"Yes, he was sorry too. He wishes to be remembered to you. But he may call again, one of these days."

Charlotte changed the subject. What she thought, Ellie wasn't sure.

CHAPTER 14

A Word with Lord Salisbury

AN ARTICLE ENTITLED "Reflections on the Maintenance of Peace" appeared in the January 1895 issue of *The Nineteenth Century*.

The writer began, striking an initially happy note, by remarking that the Great Powers had been at peace for almost a quarter of a century. There was no reason why this satisfactory state of affairs should not endure; history would record, quite possibly, that war between mature nations had become a practice rendered obsolete by the steady progress of civilisation. However, international peace could not be maintained—any more than civil peace and public order—without a consistent effort by those who must regard themselves as its guardians. In that effort, it was incumbent on England to play a greater part than ever before, now that she had attained an unprecedented peak of wealth, political responsibility, and world-wide power.

For three centuries, the writer recalled, England had sought to prevent any single Power from dominating Europe and had therefore intervened in many wars, the classical case being the coalition wars against Napoleon. The restoration of the balance of power had been regarded as a satisfactory outcome. But, the writer pointed out, this action had been military rather than political. England had permitted the attempt at domination to get under way, had applied the corrective at considerable cost to herself and others, and had then withdrawn into passivity until a similar danger presented itself again. War had not been (as defined by the German theorist, Clausewitz) a continuation of policy by other means, but a belated substitute for policy.

The time had come, in the writer's view, to adopt a policy which would maintain the balance of power as a guarantee of peace, and not merely be prepared to restore it after it had been disturbed. Such a policy would make demands on England which she could not, despite her power, meet by acting in isolation, as in the past. It implied steady co-operation with other nations committed to upholding the balance, and steady restraint of nations not so committed.

Getting down to brass tacks, the writer stated clearly that France was a factor of instability on the European scene. The heritage of radical ideas and enthusiasms, dating from the French Revolution and always potent under a republican régime; the traditions of conquest and of interference in the affairs of other countries; the unstable character of French governments, tempted to enhance their popularity by demagogic appeals—these were facts that had to be recognised. In the revanchist demand for the recovery of Alsace and Lorraine, inflammable material was always at hand. At the other end of Europe, a similar factor of instability arose from Russian designs in the Balkans, urged on by the quasi-religious emotions of Pan-Slavic doctrine. Neither of these Powers enjoyed the benefits of stable parliamentary government, based on a solid educated class. The extremes of democracy in France, the extremes of autocracy in Russia—both were conducive to irresponsible and impulsive action. Hence, the Franco-Russian treaty of alliance, the major international development of 1894, must be viewed as potentially menacing in the highest degree.

Germany, on the other hand, had a manifest interest in peace, in forestalling conflicts and crises, and in restraining the ambitions of France and Russia. With this factor of stability, England should openly and unmistakably associate herself. "Anglo-German co-operation," the writer asserted, "is natural, it is grounded in plain affinities of thought and mutual understanding, and it can become the most fruitful and beneficent relationship in the international arena." He did not advocate an Anglo-German alliance; the principle of rival alliances presupposed exactly what should be ruled out, the possible recourse to general war. But he argued cogently for—the phrase at once became familiar in serious discussion—a German orientation in foreign policy.

The article caused a considerable stir. It was anonymous, because the writer did not wish to come forward as a Member of the Opposition challenging the policies of the Government, but rather as an Englishman appealing to thoughtful men in both parties. However, all informed people knew that the writer was Lord Richard Somers—*"chef d'une grande famille proche à la Cour,"* as a French newspaper said with amusing inaccuracy.

The French press was furious, full of strident headlines about *"calomnies inadmissibles"* and *"provocations inouïes."* The serious German papers confined themselves to translating long extracts from the article without comment. In England, the effect could be traced in a long correspondence in *The Times* and in countless private conversations among people who mattered: conversation at dinner tables, in clubs, in country houses, in the smoking room at the House. Speculation centred on whether Lord Salisbury had inspired the article, and whether it foreshadowed the policy that a Conservative Government would adopt. In reality, the article embodied Richard's own ideas, shaped in his mind during the five years since he had first crossed the Channel, and discussed only with a few friends—most thoroughly and most seriously with Lord Farnham.

He was pleased with the article and its reception. Until now, his greatest satisfaction in this line had come from making speeches; but he knew that a speech was a thing of the hour, effective through its tone and mood more than its content. The article was on record, durable and unambiguous. He had worked on it hour after hour, under a shaded lamp in his study after Geraldine was in bed, patiently, earnestly, testing his logic for flaws, recasting and improving the sentences, discarding every word that seemed exaggerated or meretricious. It had calmed him, somewhat, in a time of inner turmoil. It would stand—a footnote to history, at least—whatever became of him. When all was said and done, it was something he had given to England.

A month or so after the article appeared, Richard and Geraldine were invited to Hatfield for the weekend. This might mean something, or it might not. Increasingly, as he grew older, Lord Salisbury secluded himself and left his guests to entertain themselves, assuming that he discharged the duties of a host simply by doing them the honour of inviting them.

But on Saturday afternoon, as Richard was engaged in a game of billiards, a footman summoned him to the presence.

"Ah, Somers," Lord Salisbury said when he was announced, "I was hoping for a word with you."

"I trust I find you well, my lord?"

"Well enough, this beastly winter. You're in the pink, I see. How's your charming wife?"

"Very well, thank you."

"Remember me to her," Lord Salisbury said, as if Geraldine were not at Hatfield too. "Things are looking up, wouldn't you say? If we don't see a dissolution before the end of this session, I'm a Dutchman."

Richard agreed. Since Gladstone's retirement, almost a year

ago, the Liberal Government had been gradually but irreme-
diably breaking up. With Home Rule no longer on the cards,
it lacked any unifying purpose. Lord Rosebery, the new Prime
Minister, commanded little respect and had an unfortunate
knack of alienating one faction after another. One couldn't
foresee exactly when or on what issue the Government would
be brought down, but it was bound to happen. When the election came, a Conservative triumph would be a safe bet.

"It's not too soon to think about the shape of a Cabinet,"
Lord Salisbury pursued. "I've been considering seriously
whether I should keep the Foreign Office in my own hands
again or not. I don't know that I relish it as much as I used to
—all those dashed papers, seeing Ambassadors, that kind of
thing. And foreign policy is likely to call for something more
than general supervision, wouldn't you say?"

"Considerably more, in my opinion."

"Quite so. Quite so." Lord Salisbury gazed out of the window, making Richard wonder as usual whether he had lost
the thread of his thoughts. Then he said casually: "I'd be glad
if you'd take it on, Somers."

Richard had a momentary impulse to burst out laughing.
Political life was conducted informally at the highest levels, he
knew; yet it didn't seem possible that he was being offered
the Foreign Office. It was more as though Lord Salisbury
were asking some junior secretary to relieve him of a tedious
chore, such as drawing up the guest list for next weekend.

Controlling himself, he said: "I'm at your lordship's service."

"Good," Lord Salisbury said briskly. "You might think it
would be easy to find a few men in whom you can have confidence, but it's not. I should have confidence in you, Somers."

"I'm more honoured than I can say."

"Regard it as settled, then. I hope I didn't drag you away
from the ladies?"

"No, my lord. I was playing billiards."

"You're in the middle of a game? By Jove, you should have said so. I won't detain you, then."

Richard lost the game. He couldn't muster the exhilaration that the news deserved. A couple of years ago, the prospect of becoming Foreign Secretary would have been a fulfilment. Now it was a complication—a complication and an irony. Lord Salisbury had confidence in him, at a time when he no longer had confidence in himself.

But Geraldine would be happy, he thought. Assuming that Rosebery did fall this year, her hopes would be triumphantly realised: Richard would be in the Cabinet at the age of forty.

She looked radiant at dinner, her diamonds flashing, the rich darkness of her hair set off by a mother-of-pearl comb, her smile serene and gracious. He watched her admiringly from ten places away. The men on either side of her beamed when she spoke to them. What would they have said if they had known that her husband left London on weekdays, travelling inconspicuously second-class, to visit another woman? They would have shrugged and said that any man is free to be a fool.

He went to bed very late. The men joined the ladies long after dinner, then separated again. In the library after midnight, Richard and half a dozen others discussed the troubled situation in South Africa. Balfour listened to him attentively, he noticed. Lord Salisbury would have consulted his nephew about the Foreign Office, of course.

He undressed quietly, thinking that Geraldine was asleep. However, she wasn't. In her most alert voice, she asked: "What did the old man want to see you about, Richard?"

Richard dropped his studs into the box. They made a dead sound, loud in the night.

"He offered me the Foreign Office."

Geraldine got out of bed and stood beside him by the window. After a moment, she linked her arm through his.

"I'm very proud of you," she said.

"There was no other obvious candidate, once he'd decided not to hold it again himself."

She laughed. "You mean, the obvious candidate is you."

"If you care to put it that way."

She dropped his arm and started to walk about the room with a curious mannered step, rising on her toes—a restrained but nonetheless exultant dance.

"For a man in this position, you don't look very excited," she said.

"But you are?"

"I'm delighted, of course. What wife wouldn't be? But perhaps satisfied is more the word. I've never had any doubts, my dear."

He kissed her. For a moment, desire stirred in him: not exactly that, but the wish to assure her—or assure himself—that this moment belonged to them both. She disengaged herself, stifled a yawn, and said: "It must be frightfully late."

"I'm afraid so." Richard wound his watch and hung it on the hook in the travelling-case, a gift from her before their first Continental journey.

"Goodnight, Richard."

"Goodnight, dearest."

She was asleep in two minutes, breathing regularly and peacefully as she always did.

The next day, as if Geraldine had given him strength in her sleep, he felt something of the pride and satisfaction that it was natural to share with her. He rose early—early for a Sunday—and was almost alone at breakfast. Possessed by a sudden energy, unusual for him these days, he went out for an hour's tramp. It had indeed been a beastly winter after the fine autumn, one of the worst on record: hard frosts, wild snow storms, freezing fogs, everything that the English climate was capable of. Probably it was not yet over. But today was mild and still, like a remission in an illness, a gesture of hope and mercy.

He really did deserve it, he thought. It wasn't a matter of bringing the younger generation into the Cabinet, or of promoting a man who was popular in the House and in the party. Salisbury had been one of the great Foreign Secretaries; he revered the Foreign Office, he wouldn't confide it to anyone unworthy. In Richard, he recognised a man with the qualities he valued: the reflective cast of mind, the foresight, the grasp of what it meant for nations to live together in mutual respect. Characteristically, he hadn't thought it necessary to say anything about the article in *The Nineteenth Century*. But he must have read it, and made his decision since reading it.

And Richard knew that, as well as deserving the Foreign Office, he wanted it. Forty was young to be in the Cabinet, of course, decidedly young to be Foreign Secretary; but it was far beyond what a man could call his youth. It was beyond the time of learning and developing, of getting a thrill from dramatic clashes and pugnacious speeches, into the time when only achievement could yield any satisfaction. It seemed to him that his abilities had been expanding by degrees, always more or less surprising him, to match the demands made on him.

Achievement was what mattered, then, and he could be reasonably confident of it. The chief of a major Department of State, he knew, can succeed if three conditions are granted him: the support of the Prime Minister, the acquiescence of his colleagues, and the willing help of his civil servants. Salisbury must be favourably inclined toward the German orientation, or he would not have made his offer to Richard. The other leading Conservatives, for the most part, took little interest in foreign affairs. Given a Foreign Secretary who knew

what he wanted to do, and whom they regarded as capable
and clear-minded, they would be gratefully inclined to take
his policy on trust. The civil servants liked a strong Minister
and a consistent line of policy; Richard could rely on Arthur
Farnham and several other senior men, and Arthur might
soon be Permanent Under-Secretary. So the omens were good,
and the opportunity was tremendous. What he had written in
his article, Richard believed absolutely. War or peace—the
misery or the happiness of millions—could depend on a few
men in the Foreign Offices of the Powers. It could be given to
him, and to those few others, to lay the foundations of a
golden age of trust, safety and prosperity. A sense of greatness
filled his mind: not his own greatness, but the greatness of the
work that he could do.

He stopped to lean across a gate, enjoying the silence of the
winter landscape, and lit a cigar. He knew just where he
stood. He would have been the happiest man in the world if
he had not been in love with Ellie Colmore.

He had seen her within the past week, on the Wednesday.
It wasn't at all difficult to spend a day with her. The bad
weather, disorganising the train services, had been the only
real problem. He seldom lunched with Geraldine, especially
when the House was sitting; she had her own appointments
and activities, and it was normal for her not to know where
he was all day. If Ellie had been his mistress and he had
wanted to spend the night with her, that wouldn't have been
very difficult either. Like most men, he sometimes slept at his
club after a stag dinner. Besides, he was in demand as a
speaker at Conservative meetings all over the place, so a night
out of London was nothing unusual.

Nevertheless, he didn't see her often. The intensity of their
love, the dizzy wonder of meeting and the agony of parting,
made every encounter into a testing strain, a strange experience in which joy and suffering melted like two disparate

metals at white-heat to fuse as . . . he didn't know what, a nameless and confusing emotion. He went to Longmarsh, as he had told her, when he couldn't resist it. Since the first time, back in November, it had been about every three weeks.

In theory, there was no reason why he couldn't continue like this. A number of men in the public eye—Prime Ministers, Foreign Secretaries, Royalty—had kept up irregular liaisons. Sometimes, as with the Prince of Wales, it was careless, almost open; the world could think what it liked, the wife had to adjust herself. Sometimes, as with Parnell, secrecy was maintained until the explosion came. One might ultimately be destroyed. Certain disasters could not be survived—notably, of course, a divorce action. However, a man with strong nerves accepted the risk and walked the tightrope as long as possible.

But Richard didn't feel that he could do it. His love for Ellie was not an aspect of his life that he could keep apart from other aspects. It was—just as much as fourteen years ago—a consuming passion, a ceaseless yearning of body and soul. It gripped him like a fever, whether he was sitting in the House or dining with Geraldine or hearing the boys recite the poems they had learned. When he was away from Ellie, he felt that he was only half a man. He behaved in an outwardly normal way, he supposed; his mind went on working, on politics and on the daily routine. Yet he was distracted, divided against himself, locked in struggle with his own nature. He had to ask himself: How could such a man be Foreign Secretary? The work was immensely taxing, especially since he meant to impose an entire new design on foreign policy. It called for single-minded concentration, continual energy of spirit, and a foundation of inner peace. And instead of that, his hidden love was cracking the surface of his life. The underground river was close to breaking the surface. Sometimes he was amazed that it wasn't obvious to others. He would blurt it out sooner or later, he felt—to Geraldine, to

Arthur or some other friend, to Simmons—there was no telling. How could he go on like that, for years, surely for the rest of his life? No, it was beyond his strength.

What if he said to Geraldine: "There is another woman in my life, and I must see her sometimes"?

It was a possibility. It was more or less honourable, compared to concealment, and it forestalled the danger of a sudden discovery. Geraldine knew what men were like. She realised that his love for her had lost the ardour of earlier years. If he never went to her bedroom again, she would on the whole be relieved. She would retain much of what counted with her: family life, social position, the pride of being the Foreign Secretary's wife.

But what would she imagine? A physical attraction, an outlet for his desires, a slender waist and youthful playfulness of the kind that she no longer offered. An unimportant diversion to see him through a still vigorous middle age. An arrangement, in fact. To let her think this was a deceit—a far graver deceit than concealment, for it distorted the truth.

It was a deceit, moreover, that he would be unable to maintain. Once Geraldine knew that there was another woman, she would come to see the meaning of every abstracted silence, every look of longing in his eyes. She would grasp the force and depth of his love. For Geraldine believed in love, a kind of love that she took to be more than passion: a devotion of heart and mind, a lifelong sharing of hopes and achievements, an accumulation of intimacy that rendered a marriage proof against any challenge. That he loved her in that way, as she loved him, was final truth to her. She could make concessions, even sacrifices. But she could not relinquish that final truth and remain his wife.

If only, he thought, his love for Ellie were less than what it was! If it were a sentimental infatuation to be gratified by these wistful days at Longmarsh—or if it were a simple demand of his senses. But it encompassed these, and was infinitely more. It was the same old longing—fierce and tender, imperious and devoted—to possess her wholly, to fuse his life with hers, to exist only with her and through her.

Well—he wanted everything. He could see that clearly enough when he applied an observer's common sense. He wanted Ellie, and he wanted Geraldine. He wanted to float away in a dream of love, nourished only by kisses and a quiet voice. He wanted Berkshire House, and Geraldine commanding and charming at the head of the dinner table, and the summer days with the boys at the Priory, and the warmth of friendship and good talk. He wanted to be Foreign Secretary —wanted the bite of satisfying work and the consciousness of achievement. If he could have stifled one of these desires, he would have been grateful for the peace of mind. But he could not.

Ten days later, he went to Longmarsh again. He had no purpose in going except to see Ellie: literally to see her, to quench his thirst for her beauty. A kind of routine for his visits had been tacitly established. He would arrive about noon, having walked from the station if the weather was at all bearable, or else taken one of the old, creaking four-wheelers that waited in the yard. Ellie was always in the music-room. He would ask her to play the piano and sit beside her to turn the pages. For an hour, he could dream that everything was the same as in that summer when she had been his promised bride. Nothing in the room had been changed. When he gazed at the soft contours of her face, the lucent delight of her hair, he lived again in a world of youthful love and hope. He stayed to lunch, and then they sat for a while in the drawing room. When he said that he had to go, she ordered the carriage. The length of his stay didn't matter. Had it been a moment—a gazing, loving moment—it would have had as much or as little significance. Their life was measured by such moments.

Sometimes Charlotte was with them, sometimes not. Richard was not at all irked by her presence when she did stay in the drawing room. He had nothing in particular to say to Ellie. The great essential truth had been said.

Charlotte had once remarked that it was a pleasure to have a guest at Longmarsh. She hoped, she said, that there would be house parties again one day. She didn't care much for them herself, nor did Ellie, but she felt that the house was being wasted. Now that Arthur was back in England, she had told him that he could use Longmarsh whenever he liked; but he and Grace had bought a cottage on the coast and seemed to prefer to spend their weekends there.

Richard didn't know what Charlotte really thought about his visits, nor did she give any indication. She wasn't a woman who cared greatly about social conventions or went in fear of gossip. She must surely be aware that he was in love with Ellie, but she could no more grasp the intensity of his passion than an ordinary church-goer can grasp the fervours of religious ecstasy. Perhaps she felt a certain responsibility, having inadvertently paved the way to the meeting at Karlsruhe. So far as he could guess, she was trying to behave as if the situation were quite natural—to absolve Ellie from any feeling of guilt, since Ellie's happiness was clearly the supreme consideration in Charlotte's mind. If she thought that his visits were making Ellie unhappy, doubtless she wouldn't hesitate to tell him so. Presumably she did not think so, and from this he took a kind of comfort.

This time, Charlotte excused herself immediately after lunch. She was due at a meeting of school governors, she said. She would send the carriage back; one of the other ladies would bring her home after the meeting.

"It's a rotten day to go out," Richard said.

"It can't be helped," she replied stoically.

It was in fact a wild, blustery day—one of those days when, no matter how one tries to warm a house, blasts of cold air find the cracks. The fire in the drawing room burned badly; the wind, instead of helping it, blew puffs of smoke into the room. Ellie coughed.

"These stupid fires," she said. "A German stove is so much more sensible."

Richard said: "I don't like that cough, my darling. This weather is treacherous."

"It's only the smoke. I'll sit over here." She moved to the sofa.

"You'll be cold. Let me fetch a rug."

"Well—if you think so. There's a plaid in the hall."

He covered her with the plaid, tucking it in carefully. She looked up at him: tranquil, tender, beautiful. He bent suddenly and kissed her lips.

"Don't, Richard, please," she said faintly.

He sighed, sat beside her, and clasped her hand.

"Do you wish I hadn't come today?" he asked.

"I wish things were different. But they aren't, are they?"

"They can't be."

"No . . . And so, you have to come here. Where ought you to be today, Richard? At the House of Commons?"

"It isn't necessary to attend every day."

"Still, isn't that where your wife thinks you are?"

He said, rather stiffly: "I don't feel guilty when I'm with you, darling."

"You don't?" She mused over this, and then said: "All the same, you don't tell your wife where you've been, do you?"

"Please, Ellie. There's no need to worry about that."

"I don't like to feel that I'm taking anything away from her."

"My angel, there's no need to feel that."

"I do. And, all the same, I don't give you anything. I never could. I should like to, Richard, if only I could."

"To be with you, sweetheart, as we are now—is that nothing?"

"It's not enough for you, truly, is it?"

He couldn't answer.

Looking away from him now, she asked: "Do you want me to be your mistress, Richard?"

"I should never want you to do anything beyond your own free wish."

"I wonder if I could. I doubt it, somehow. I suppose, if I could, then I'd have been your wife."

He stood up and began to pace the room.

"I entreat you, darling, don't talk like this. A mistress—I could never think of you in those terms, even if we . . . You're the woman I love. That's all that counts."

"But I wish I knew what you wanted. What do you want, Richard?"

"My God, I wish I knew."

There was a noise outside. It was the carriage, back from taking Charlotte to her meeting.

"I shan't stay long this time," he said. "You're sad today—it's my fault. I know I'm being unfair to you, my poor darling."

He hadn't the strength to go without kissing her again. He knelt beside the sofa, holding her in his arms, trying to calm the trembling of which he was the cause. Miserably, he knew that she would weep when he had gone. He was close enough to weeping himself.

In the train, staring through a misted window at heavy rain, he remembered that he had said nothing to Ellie about being promised the Foreign Office. When he was with her, such things were unreal.

CHAPTER 15

A Decision
and a Promise

THE HIGH SCHOOL DIRECTOR had written to Ellie twice. The first letter, in December, transmitted heartfelt Christmas and New Year wishes from all her colleagues, with the hope that they would soon be welcoming her back. The second letter, in February, enquired more formally about her intentions. Ellie meant to answer the first letter; she meant to answer the second; she answered neither. She no longer had a job, she supposed. It was a disaster, but it was an aspect of a larger process, the disintegration and disappearance of Fräulein Colmore.

She had no excuse: that was clear. She wasn't at all unwell; Charlotte and most of the servants had gone down with heavy colds during the bad weather, but not Ellie. Probably she had quite a sturdy constitution, though people always said that she looked delicate. She had been resting, or rather idle, for months, and now she didn't even get tired. If she did nothing, it was because nothing seemed to have any point. She had resolved on various projects—serious reading, serious piano practise, gardening, embroidery. All melted away as vain intentions.

Hour after hour and day after day, she sat in front of the fire or lay on the sofa, generally holding a book which she didn't read, and lost herself in a great measureless vacancy.

Insofar as she was doing anything, she was thinking of Richard. Not thinking, really; she no longer thought in any logical or constructive sense, in the Karlsruhe way. She was waiting for him—that was all. She was longing for him, she was dreading him, but essentially she was simply waiting. It occurred to her that she could scarcely have been more dependent on him if she were actually his wife—or his mistress, it didn't matter which. For what did a woman do, when she was dependent on a man? She made herself comfortable in the house and waited for the only things that gave her life a meaning: his step in the hall, his voice, his touch. True, Richard came only every fortnight or so, instead of every evening like a husband or every couple of days like (she supposed) a man who kept a mistress. But that made no real difference because the measurement of time had become so vague for her, and because he didn't need to come more often in order to dominate and paralyse her life. As soon as they parted, they began to come together again: that is, the waiting began.

So things went on through the winter and into the spring. But she had a feeling, stronger each time Richard came to Longmarsh, that they could not go on much longer. She was not capable of making decisions, but Richard was. He wanted more of her than he now had, obviously. She accepted this life of meeting and parting and waiting because she hoped for nothing better. They were in love and they were suffering for their love—it had always been like that and always would be. But for Richard, she saw, it was a matter of errors and misunderstandings which could be put right once he found a way—not easily, not without cost, but his principle was that it could be done.

She was very much afraid. As one may sense a thunderstorm in quivering stillness, she sensed the approach of a huge catastrophe. She wanted to escape, as she had escaped before, but she lacked the strength to act. She could only wait for him, dreading what he would do. Once he was ready, she knew that he would march headlong into catastrophe, because it was his nature to prefer any risk to resignation. And she loved him for that; it had always been her fate to love him and fear him for the same qualities.

One morning in April, he arrived at Longmarsh while she was still at the breakfast table. It wasn't so very early—ten o'clock, by which time she would have done a couple of hours' work at Karlsruhe. She had fallen into the habit of lingering after breakfast, letting her second cup of tea get cold, trying in a desultory way to read the newspaper, forming plans which she was unlikely to carry out. It was early for someone to come from London, however. She was startled when he was announced; part of his power over her lay in his ability, which she had never been able to counter, to catch her unprepared.

"Should I show him into the music-room, Miss Eleanor?" the maid suggested.

"The music-room—yes."

She went to him, as she always did. As soon as she closed the door, he took her in his arms. She felt herself crushed. Strange, this pleasure of a man in depriving a woman of the possibility of movement.

"My angel, my sweetheart, my beloved . . ." She let the words pass through her; they were not words with meaning so much as a sensation, a throbbing in his throat and in her ears. Throat to ears, hands to her shoulders, chest to her breasts, man to woman. Words like these, it seemed to her, were not spoken by Richard Somers to Ellie Colmore but simply by the male to the female body. Intimate and yet curiously impersonal, they were the incantations of a ritual, like the familiar words of church services marking the course of human destiny, from a christening to a funeral.

When he let her go, she said: "I didn't expect you—I mean,

at this time. You must have left town very early."

"Yes. I slept at my club, as a matter of fact. The House sat until late."

She saw now that his eyes were unnaturally bright, with a kind of nervous intensity. She said: "You don't look as if you had slept at all."

"I don't think I did. I was thinking of you—longing for you. I'd have come here in the night if there'd been a train."

Yet he didn't look tired. He was excited and full of energy, like a sportsman on the morning of a great contest or a soldier on the morning of battle. He had some purpose, and by seizing her in his arms he had already begun to accomplish it. She was afraid of him when he was like this: afraid of his determination, his confidence, his impatience. This was not the Richard who had been coming to Longmarsh since November, the man of doubt and agony. This was the Richard of years ago, the pursuer, the man poised for possession. It was because he had a purpose, and couldn't wait to put it into effect, that he had come so early. Also, quite likely, he had planned to find her alone; he must have remembered that Charlotte spent the morning in the estate office with the bailiff.

"Darling," he said, "we can spend the whole day together—isn't that splendid? Look at the sunshine! Spring's here at last. We can drive up on the Downs. D'you remember that old inn where we used to go? They do quite a decent country lunch, or they used to. Or else we could take a picnic basket—what d'you think?"

Even his voice—a ringing voice, a young man's voice—recalled the Richard who had swept her along to picnics and excursions when they were engaged. She couldn't resist him, of course. Besides, she had a slender hope that his purpose, and his elated mood, rested simply in this idea of a day together. There might be nothing more, after all.

They took the little old trap in which all the Colmore
children had roamed about the countryside. From the ridge of
the Hog's Back, one could see for miles in every direction.
The air was extremely clear, as it is on sharp spring days.
They stopped at the highest point and she picked out church
steeples, the chimneys of a brickworks, the white trail of a
train. The expanse of fields and woods, hills and valleys,
gave her a dizzy feeling, as if she were flying in the sky. All
through these ten months, she hadn't been outside the gates
except occasionally to the village shop and to church. She had
forgotten that there was so much of the world, she said to
Richard. He laughed; he seemed delighted, as if he had
created the view for her.

However, she was troubled. She was irrationally anxious
about being so far from Longmarsh—she, who had lived for
years abroad. When he took an unexpected turning, she
asked: "You do know where you're going, Richard?" He
laughed again, carelessly rather than reassuringly. He was absolutely in control of the day, she not at all. And he drove
with his left hand clasped round her waist. Everyone in the
neighbourhood knew her—he must realise that, surely. When
they met people, he called out a cheerful greeting. This disturbed her greatly, not because she cared what anyone saw or
thought, but because of the possible meaning of his reckless-
ness.

He had decided that it wasn't quite warm enough for a
picnic, so they lunched at the inn. He found his way to it
unerringly, as if they had been there last week instead of
fourteen years ago. It still served a good simple lunch: salted
ham and pickles, game pie—mostly rabbit, but hot and tasty—
and apple tart with cream. Richard drank a pint of ale from
an old tankard, and Ellie had a glass of cider. The innkeeper
knew her and seemed not in the least surprised to see her.
He said he hoped she was back home to stay, and asked

whether Lord Farnham "as is now" intended to take up residence. He looked speculatively at Richard; perhaps he recognised young Miss Ellie's fiancé, perhaps not.

They left the horse grazing in the paddock behind the inn and strolled through a copse of tall beeches.

"Look—primroses," Ellie said.

There were only a few, but enough for a posy. Richard picked them, twisted the stalks together, and fastened them to her dress with his tiepin.

"It's so peaceful here," she said. "Let's stay for a little while."

He fetched the rug from the trap, spread it on the ground for her, then folded it to cover her. But, with shelter from the wind, it was quite warm in the copse. She gazed up at the sky, pale blue beyond the pale green leaves. He sat a yard away, leaning against the trunk of a tree.

"Are you happy, darling?" he asked.

She had to be a little bit happy, because his happiness touched her like the spring sunshine. Besides, it would hurt him if she said No.

"I believe I am," she said.

"You will never be unhappy again, so far as it rests with me."

Words, she thought. But the intensity of his tone alerted her.

"What do you mean?" she asked.

"Let me tell you, Ellie. We know with utter certainty that our lives are bound together. I have thought long and earnestly about what we should do. I have searched my heart, as I searched it when I first fell in love with you. Now I have taken my resolution. I shall speak to my wife and ask her to give me my freedom."

"You mean—a divorce?"

"Yes, I mean that."

"Oh no!" she gasped. "No, Richard, no!"

He smiled, gently and tolerantly. She saw what he was thinking: she was flinching as she had flinched before. It was his duty, he believed, not to allow it again.

"Yes, Ellie," he said. "This time, it shall be Yes."

She tried to rise to her feet.

"Don't move, darling," he said quietly but commandingly. "We shall stay here until all is decided."

She couldn't move, indeed. She lay back, as helpless as if he had thrown the weight of his body on her.

"Listen," he said. "Years ago, we were parted by fatal errors. Mine was by far the greater blunder—the greater betrayal. I was unfaithful to the only love that can ever have a place in my life. I made myself believe that I could give to another woman what is eternally yours. When I did that, I wronged you, I wronged myself, and I wronged Geraldine. She has been all that a wife should be—the centre of my home, the mother of my children. If a faithful and serene marriage could sever the bonds of love, my marriage would have done that. But it was a delusion. I had only to look once into your eyes to know that. And if I had never seen you again, I should still have loved you until death."

"Until death."

He gazed at her, wondering why she had echoed the words. She herself didn't know why; they had seemed, among all he had spoken, the most real.

"We have proved our love," he resumed. "We have tested it, we have struggled against it, we have hidden from it. It lives on—it is the whole of life for us. We are no longer young enough to imagine that our feelings are uncertain or groping. But we are young enough, Ellie, to make a fresh start. We have only to face the truth, to live by the faith that it is in our hearts. We have a clear choice. We can continue to en-slave ourselves to what we know to be a lie, and drag our way through the world in misery. Or we can seize our chance, and be happy for all the years that remain to us—happy as we deserve to be, happy as we can be only when we are together."

How eloquent he was, when his mind was made up! She had almost forgotten that, in the painful meetings when indecision had confined him to halting, broken phrases. And he was so sure of what he said, so single-minded in his faith. She gazed at him in love and pity.

"We can never be happy," she said. "We have always been unhappy—it's what we do to each other."

"That was because we never gave our love its rights. Its strength is proved by the unhappiness we have endured. If we could ever live apart in any contentment—if we could ever forget each other—surely it would have happened by now."

"If we could ever give each other happiness, surely that would have happened by now."

"Ellie, there's something you force me to say. You carry the burden of mysterious fears. How these fears arise, I've never understood. They are the penalty of your sweet nature, your quiet modesty, I suppose. They stand as a barrier to the natural course of love. Something in you is afraid of happiness—afraid of love itself. Isn't that true, my dearest?"

"It's true," she said. "It's what I am—it's myself. And it's the reason why we can't be happy. How can I achieve happiness, Richard, at the cost of myself?"

"You must let me help you. Love that answers to love has not twice but ten times the strength of love that stands alone. When you are mine, we shall banish these fears. When you are mine, we shall be brave together and happiness will be our reward."

She said nothing. What was she to say, since she could never make him understand?

"We need some courage," he said. "It's not a pleasant thing, a divorce. But of course your name won't be mentioned. We can live abroad for a while—I think that would be wise. When we're together, above all when we're man and wife, nothing else can hurt us. There will be people we can't see, but you've never cared for society. The people you care about —Charlotte, for instance—will understand, surely. And what does anything matter, weighed against love?"

"Ah, love," she said. "Love, love. It will destroy us yet, Richard."

"No—it will save us. I know it. Oh, how can I make you believe it?"

He picked up a piece of wood, torn from the tree in the winter storms, and began to break it into short lengths with his strong hands.

"You know, dear," he began again, "I shall be giving up much that the world values. I've had a certain success in public life. When there's a change of Government, I could expect—well, no matter. I shall have to say farewell to all that. It means something to a man, the wreckage of a career. I don't speak of this to make you sorry for me. I make the sacrifice for my own happiness as well as yours. I do it—I can't say with no regrets, but with open eyes, sure of gaining more than I'll lose. But could I do it if I had the faintest doubt that it is utterly right? Could I do it if my love were anything less than the blazing faith that it is?"

"And what about me?" she answered. "Do you think I have nothing to regret? When you found me at Karlsruhe, did you see nothing but the girl you had lost? I had something to value, Richard—not what the world values, perhaps, but something precious to me. I had a life, built up slowly and anxiously by attempting what I never believed I could do. I had contentment, I had peace. All that has gone. You can never restore it to me, even if you wished. It's all swept away in this whirlwind of love. And now that it's gone, you imagine that I can be happy."

She had never, in all the time that she had known him, spoken to him at such length or so boldly. It had taken all her strength. She saw that he was taken aback. He had never thought of this—never imagined that, in loving her, he loved someone who was growing, searching, aware of needs that man's love could not answer. He loved—still, at this moment —an ideal of his own creation. And so, there could be no understanding. He was making a great sacrifice; she didn't deny that, she knew what achievement meant to a man of his gifts and powers. But in the end, he would remain himself—a man. In his code, it was the essence of manhood to fulfil his ruling passion, to possess his ideal. While she—she was to sacrifice not only a career or a position, but herself.

"We mustn't quarrel, darling," he said. "We mustn't stain this moment with bitterness. What sense does it make to compete in what we're giving up? Let's look forward to what we shall gain together. We are on the threshold of a new life —think of that, Ellie, think only of that!"

"I wish I believed it," she said sadly. "I wish I could believe it."

"But in any case, Ellie, what are we to do? Are we to go on as before, frustrated in the longing that rules our lives, meeting for these brief tantalising hours, or perhaps not meeting again, yet always yearning, always loving in vain? Even if I grant that our being happy together is only a hope, with a risk of disappointment, are we not to try the chance? Isn't it our duty to hope, and to strive for what we deserve? Perhaps I don't offer you the certainty of happiness, as I once believed. Perhaps I'm calling you to a new struggle, a struggle against your fears. But I offer you love, and I offer you hope."

She smiled a little, and said: "It's always hope with you,

isn't it? Always try again, whatever the odds."

"Yes, always hope!" he cried in his ringing voice. "Because love gives hope, as the heartbeat gives life!"

He knelt beside her, grasped her in an embrace, and thrust kisses on her cheeks, on her lips, on the white flesh above her dress.

"Ellie, my own dearest Ellie," he said, "these fears of yours make me more utterly certain that I'm right. I must give you love because it's your safeguard. I must give you hope because you are in danger of despair. I shall never leave you again, my darling. You are mine, not only as my joy but as my sacred trust. I shall watch over you and care for you, fighting your fears as I never fought an enemy in my life."

She trembled. He had her now—there was no escape. He was crushing her again, hurting her, squeezing the breath from her. The thick tweed of his jacket was bruising the primroses, but he didn't notice.

"You must promise me that you will be brave and loyal, when I speak to Geraldine and arrange the divorce. Promise me that, Ellie."

"I promise," she said weakly.

"Promise that you'll come to me, or let me come to fetch you, as soon as it's possible."

"I promise."

"Promise to be mine at last—mine for ever."

"Yes, I promise."

The sky and the leaves whirled above her. She felt herself fading away, falling apart. It was the moment of annihilation, the end of herself. She missed something that he said. Then she was lying flat again, wrapped closely in the rug, and he was standing.

"It's all been too much for you, darling," he said. "Rest now —try to sleep a little. I'll take a turn along the lane, and

then we must be going. We've topped the crest, Ellie. Nothing
will ever be so hard again."

She watched him until he was out of sight. He walked with
a swinging stride—happy already, satisfied, triumphant. It
struck her that he was walking away from the inn. She could
harness the horse and drive the trap. There was a station not
far away. She could be in Karlsruhe in a couple of days.

But this was only fancy, she knew. He had said that he
would follow her anywhere in the world, and he meant it.
She was bound to him, not only by her promise but by the
strength of his purpose. She was bound to him by his hope
and by her own despair.

And, she thought wearily, what did it matter to her? Her
life—her free life, her life as herself—was over in any case.
Why shouldn't Richard have what he desired so passionately?
He was almost like a boy, so eager and impatient, with his
heart set on what had eluded him; it was a shame to disappoint him again. She couldn't be happy, but he would be
happy when he possessed her. It wasn't reasonable to insist
that they should both be unhappy. So she would be brave,
as he called it.

She was still breathing with difficulty. She undid the hooks
of her bodice, and saw a bruise on her left breast. She must
have been squeezed against something hard—either his wallet
or his cigar-case. But she bruised easily; she always had. She
would be bruised all over, she supposed, when he ultimately
possessed her. She must try not to let him know about the
bruises, she thought.

She slipped her hand under her petticoat and felt her body.
It was strange that it should be so unimportant to her and so
important to Richard. It was a pity that she couldn't give it
to him—"Here you are, I don't need it"—and herself be free,
detached from it. Most men would be quite pleased if that

were possible, she imagined. But not Richard; he wanted all of her.

She began to cry, helplessly and painfully. She fumbled for her handkerchief, but then she restrained herself from using it. Richard would notice if her eyes were red, and she belonged to him now. She lay on her side and let her tears fall on last year's leaves.

They were quiet as they drove back to Longmarsh. The wind was keener and the sky clouded over; she sat with the rug over her shoulders, shivering. Richard urged the horse along as much as he could without being harsh to it—he never treated horses badly. He paid his respects to Charlotte, who asked him to stay to tea. But he excused himself, saying that he was committed to dining out in London and must catch the next train.

Ellie had hoped that Richard would tell Charlotte about the divorce, but apparently this duty fell to her. Just at present, she was not equal to it.

CHAPTER 16

An Upheaval
at Berkshire House

"What name should I say, madam?"

"Miss Colmore."

Although of course impassive, Simmons was extremely interested. This would be an aunt, he guessed, of Miss Eleanor Colmore. He remembered vividly—as if it were yesterday, so to speak—the parting scene between Miss Colmore and his lordship. It had been good enough for a play; he would have needed to put wax in his ears to avoid hearing the words, or anyway his lordship's words. Over the years, he had often wondered what became of Miss Colmore. She had gone abroad, according to Mrs. Ashton's butler (a good friend of Simmons'), but she might have returned.

Could it be Miss Colmore, Simmons asked himself, whom his lordship had been visiting? She was a stunning creature, if she'd kept her looks and her figure. His lordship had been smitten with her and no mistake, and very hard hit when she walked out. Simmons considered that her ladyship was far more suitable as a wife for a gentleman in Lord Richard Somers' position, but he also thought that it would be quite romantic if his lordship had taken up with his old flame again. There had always been, in Simmons' view, a romantic side to his lordship's nature. He had clearly been visiting somebody, and Simmons was inclined to think that it was a real love affair and not merely an arrangement.

Anyway, it was to be presumed that her ladyship had found out about it. There had been a big scene this very morning. Simmons had overheard nothing, because the scene took place upstairs in his lordship's study. But when she came downstairs, her ladyship had looked more distressed than Simmons had ever seen her. This was proof positive that his lordship was having a serious affair with a lady of his own class, quite possibly someone known to her ladyship. Her ladyship had more sense than to distress herself about an ordinary arrangement, so long as it was reasonably discreet. As for his lordship, he hadn't looked worse since the awful scene with Miss Colmore.

His lordship had ordered Simmons to pack a bag, and left instructions that he could be reached at his club until further notice. Half an hour later, her ladyship had gone off with Master Charles (Master Alfred was at his boarding school), telling the coachman to drive to her sister's house in Kensington. Nanny had orders to pack up Master Charles's things and follow. Quite an upheaval, altogether. Confronted with the senior Miss Colmore, Simmons was relieved to be able to say truthfully that no one was at home. Though Miss Colmore, naturally, had not asked to see her ladyship.

Charlotte strode away along Park Lane, looking for a hansom. She realised that it was no use going to Richard's club; barred by her sex, she wouldn't even get inside the door. When she found a hansom, she directed the driver to the Foreign Office. It belonged to the world of men just as much as a club or the Houses of Parliament, but women were not absolutely excluded. She sent her name up to Lord Farnham with a pencilled note assuring him that her call was dictated by genuine necessity, and was conducted to his office within five minutes.

"My dear Charlotte, this is an unexpected pleasure."

Charlotte took this as a courtesy; Arthur was obviously busy. Having offered her a chair, he said with a faint smile: "You haven't come to see me on a question of foreign policy, I take it?"

"No, indeed."

At a glance from Arthur, the young secretary left the room. There was no point, Charlotte decided, in beating about the bush. She stated the facts of the situation straightforwardly.

"This is astonishing—simply astonishing," Arthur said. "You're certain that he intends to ask for a divorce?"

"He told Ellie so, quite definitely. She told me this morning, and I took the next train to London."

"I had no idea . . . You know, I count Richard and his wife as among my closest friends. They dined at our house last week. Everyone who knows them regards their marriage as a model of fidelity and happiness."

"You have to remember, Arthur, how much he was in love with Ellie."

"I do remember. But, dash it, that was a dozen years ago. Are you telling me that they continued to meet, all that time?"

"No, not until fairly recently. He has been to Longmarsh about once a fortnight through this last winter. I can't quite explain . . . One had the impression, seeing them together, that the intervening years had ceased to exist for them. As if they were in a make-believe world—a sort of dream."

"It appears to be real enough now."

"Unfortunately, yes."

Arthur stood up and began to pace about the room.

"It would be the most appalling scandal, of course. The ha'penny papers—you can imagine. But that's far from being the worst of it. I suppose you're aware that we may see a change of Government at any moment. Richard—in confidence, I need scarcely say—Richard is tipped for Foreign Secretary. A man of his abilities, a man with his clear and fresh ideas, is badly needed. To be deprived of him by this fatal step—it's virtually a national disaster."

He came to a halt, staring gloomily at a portrait of the great Earl of Chatham.

"Really, Charlotte, I'm compelled to say that you might have given me some warning."

"I blame myself, Arthur, more than anyone can blame me. I believed—I wanted to believe, no doubt—that these visits were leading nowhere. There was nothing improper, you understand, no assignations; Ellie never leaves Longmarsh. It all seemed to be a dream, as I've said—a sentimental indulgence. I knew that he had prospects of high office. I couldn't imagine him throwing that away. My life hasn't provided me with many illustrations of how a passion can affect a man."

"Well . . ." Arthur returned to his desk and sat down slowly, stroking his chin. "At the point things have reached, it's difficult to see what can be done. Richard has made a decision; he's a very strong-willed man. Ellie has fallen in with it, I assume. Divorce and remarriage are within the law of the land. They hope to be happy, when the whole wretched business is over. By what right, exactly, can anyone intervene?"

"Ellie will never be happy with him," Charlotte said.

"What d'you mean? Doesn't she love him? She must know her mind, at her age."

"She was miserable when she told me this morning. She trembled, she clung to me—she was like a sensitive child being sent to boarding school. This I really can't explain, Arthur. She loves Richard, but not as your wife loves you. She isn't strong enough to go through with this. I have terrible forebodings, Arthur, though I can't give a name to them. I feel that it will break her, somehow."

"But what does she say?"

"She says, Richard wants her so much, he must have her."

"I see. No, frankly, I don't see; but I'll take your word for it. If only she'd married him in the first place—I never understood why she didn't. Still, that's water over the dam. What do you want me to do, Charlotte?"

"I'll be grateful if you would persuade him to let me talk to him before he does anything irrevocable. He may be reluctant. But he does realise, I think, that no one else cares for Ellie as I do."

"Very well." Arthur seemed relieved by the prospect of action. "He's at his club, you say? I'll go now. I have the Danish Ambassador coming, but I can be back in time. Perhaps you'd care to wait at my house. Grace was proposing to spend the day at home."

Grace was not quite so astonished as her husband. Richard was a bit of a ladies' man, she said. There had been rumours in Germany—something about an actress he'd been seen with. One could well imagine that he must be irresistible, didn't Charlotte agree?

Arthur telephoned. He had seen Richard, but too late. Richard had spoken to Geraldine before leaving Berkshire House this morning.

"Poor Ellie," Charlotte said softly. "Oh, poor Ellie."

Grace urged her to look on the bright side. It appeared that Grace had never liked Geraldine; she considered that a managing woman was a trial to a man like Richard. Divorce was an ugly business, but it was sometimes necessary—though she wouldn't say this in mixed company—to sort people into the proper pairs. A sweet, gentle woman and a strong-minded man, in Grace's view, were very much a proper pair. Ellie's great mistake had been to attempt a career and set up as a "new woman"; it might be all right in plays by Ibsen, but not in reality. The disruption of Richard's career was obviously the most serious aspect of the matter, but Grace thought that he might be able to return to public life after the dust had settled.

Charlotte said: "I really don't see how a man who has been through the divorce courts can ever hold office under the Crown."

"Well, not under the Queen, of course, but she won't live for ever. I have a feeling that standards are going to change in the twentieth century."

Geraldine, meanwhile, was telling her sister about the scene with Richard. It had been extremely painful. As she described it, Geraldine still had difficulty in believing that it had really happened. Feelings that she had never expected to experience —bewilderment, outraged love, and a bleak, hollow sense of loss—were given an extra twinge by the humiliation of being taken utterly by surprise.

She heard her own voice, sharp with fear: "Richard, you can't mean this!"

"Could I say it if I didn't mean it?" he asked. "Could I inflict this on you, if I were not driven to it by an absolute necessity? The heart is not subject to the will, Geraldine, nor to the reasoning mind. I love another woman. I don't love her because I choose; I have struggled, believe me, against loving her, but I have struggled in vain. And now I have reached the breaking point."

She moved restlessly in the chair he had set for her. It was not a comfortable chair and she was ill-at-ease in his study, a room she seldom entered. She had felt a premonition, a first anxiety, when he had asked her to go there with him. There was a good reason, she saw now; it was at the far end of a corridor, where neither Charles nor the servants were likely to come. But it was a place apart from their life together.

She said—wonderingly, as if she had to say it herself before she could grasp its meaning—"You want me to give you a divorce? To bring our marriage to an end? Is that it? Is that really it?"

"It must be. I can't help it—it must be."

"I don't think I have deserved this, Richard."

"You have deserved nothing but honour and loyalty. It is I who am undeserving—unworthy of a wife like you. But . . ."

He shrugged his shoulders, a gesture that was rare with him.

But what, she wondered? Did he mean that what she deserved—along with his marriage vows, his obligations, the compact of their life together—had become irrelevant in his eyes? That he could toss all that aside simply by saying "I can't help it"? That was what he did mean, apparently. However, why should she allow this?

Her mind began to work again, pitting itself against this absurdity. To give up, as though she had no rights and no resources, would be contemptible. She rallied herself to fight—for herself, for their children, for Richard.

For what he was doing, she thought, was a crime against his true nature. She stared at him; he was toying unhappily with a paper-knife, avoiding her eyes. She saw him as the victim of a malignant obsession, a poison in his soul. There must be some way to save him, to set the disorder to rights.

"It's almost our wedding day," she said. "Eleven years, Richard. Eleven years, during which I can honestly say that I've never had a thought but how to help you and contribute to your happiness. I gave myself to you for life, not for a term of years. I merged my own life into yours, as a wife must. I bore your children; I made this house into a home. I believed, until this moment, that we had grown closer together, bound by everything we've shared, by our hopes and strivings, by the happiness we gave each other. I believe that still, Richard— I believe it still! Do you tell me now that it's a mere illusion?

I cannot accept that. I should be false to all that I know and all that I believe—false to you too—if I accepted it."

"My dear," he said, "I owe you all that a man can ever owe to a woman. I know that I am wronging you, shamefully and ungratefully. If you choose to reproach me, you have every right. I had hoped that we could part without bitterness, but I can't ask you to forgive me—it would be a presumption. I can only say—and perhaps one day you will believe it—that I honour and respect you now more than ever in our life together."

"Then how can you do this?" she cried.

"I do it because I love Ellie Colmore. Try to see what that means, Geraldine. Should I continue living as your husband, benefiting by your devotion, while my heart is elsewhere? What would you feel, seeing in my eyes the longing that I can't suppress—the longing for another woman? Just because of everything I owe you, I can't subject you to that."

"Eleanor Colmore," she said. "How strange—that it should be Eleanor Colmore."

He said nothing. He was longing for her now, Geraldine saw—he was impatient to go to her.

"It's very wounding, Richard. You must see that it's particularly wounding. When I married you, I understood that you had loved Miss Colmore. I didn't understand, nor did you give me to understand, that you still loved her. And now, after eleven years with me: well, if you were smitten by some new passion, if some young charmer had appeared from nowhere, I suppose that's a risk that any marriage must face. But to go back to Miss Colmore . . . Tell me the worst, Richard. Does it mean that you never loved me? Does it mean that she was always first in your heart?"

He sighed; evidently he had hoped to be spared this question.

"I loved you, Geraldine. I told you the truth. There was a

remnant of love for Ellie; I believed that it would die away, and I was too hopeful. So long as I didn't see her, I was safe. I met her again by chance, and it was fatal."

He evaded her eyes again. It couldn't be true, she thought, that he had met Ellie again by pure chance. It wasn't important, but the detail angered her.

"What has Miss Colmore done to deserve you?" she demanded. "I'm sorry, Richard, but I must say this. She had her chance to marry you, and she threw it away. What has she sacrificed for you? What has she given you? While I lived for you, she lived for herself. What can she give you now, to compare with what you are losing?"

"I have never loved for advantage, Geraldine."

"But what can your life be, after this? Have you thought of that at all?"

"I realise that I must leave public life."

"You say that as if you were giving up an avocation— getting too old to ride, or something. I know you better than that, Richard. You are a man—not any woman's slave, not an idle pleasure-seeker. You need full stretch for your abilities. You need the House of Commons—the arena of action—the great world. Why, you chafe in Opposition, let alone idleness. You want to be Foreign Secretary—how can you deny it? It hasn't come to you by luck, but because you're ripe for it. What can any woman offer you in exchange for that? Her body, I suppose—will that content you, when your powers of mind and spirit are condemned to rust away?"

"I don't claim that I am wise to take this decision, Geraldine. I know what I must do—that is all. I don't ask for approval, either yours or anyone's."

"You won't get it," she cried at him. "Approval—good heavens, it's a disgrace! Certain things aren't done in a family like yours, whatever the law may allow. What will your mother say? The shame will kill her, I shouldn't wonder. I'm only glad that my father hasn't lived to see this day. He believed in you, Richard. It's a blow to everything you stand for. The ha'penny papers will make a cheap sensation of it, the Radicals will spout about the morals of the aristocracy, the canting parsons will have a field-day—oh, just think of it!"

"Please, Geraldine, try to calm yourself. Do you think I haven't faced all this, in the months of struggling against what I know to be my fate? You only tell me how overpowering my love for Ellie is. There is a heavy price to be paid, and I shall pay it. I don't expect you to understand. I can scarcely understand, myself, the passion that I must obey. I ask you only to give me my freedom, to make of it what I can."

She didn't understand, indeed. She stared at him as at a stranger; he seemed to be possessed by this mad, self-destroying passion—possessed and transformed. It was not love, she thought. How could love be at odds with loyalty, with family feeling, with everything that sanctified it? Mixed with her dismay and her righteous anger, there was a sense of sheer irritation. When they disagreed, he had always met her with logic and persuasion. Now he offered her nothing but this obstinate repetition. He wasn't trying to convince her—only telling her that she must yield, as he had yielded, to the damnable stupid infatuation.

"You speak of freedom," she said. "A divorce isn't freedom for a man like you. It's ruin—it's banishment from the place where you belong. Once you've been through the courts, the damage can never be undone. Rather than that—listen to what I say now, Richard." She made a supreme effort; the words were odious to her. "You can be unfaithful to me—perhaps you already have been, I don't care to know. I'll bear it as best I may. I'm not so innocent as to imagine that I'll enjoy a rare distinction. But if you must have a mistress, remember that I am still your wife. And try to remember that only a wife who truly loves you could have brought herself to say what I've said."

He sighed once more. "It's a generous offer, my dear. But we're beyond the point at which it could be possible. Ellie is not my mistress. Ellie is my whole life."

She felt afraid again, just as at the beginning of the interview: afraid of his strength of purpose, afraid of the mysterious passion. To prevent herself from weakening, she said: "You know my feelings. There's no need to prolong this scene, is there?"

He stood up, as if bidding goodbye to a visitor.

"I shall go to my club," he said. "I can't remain here, after what has passed between us."

"This is your home, Richard. You will return here whenever you choose. But I think I'll take Charles to Sybil's house; he's quite old enough to notice that something's wrong."

"We must talk again, Geraldine. You're overwrought. I don't take your natural reaction as a considered answer."

"I have nothing more to say," she declared. It was a good exit line. But, as she went downstairs, she was not confident about it.

She would have liked to leave the house at once, but Charles was in the park with Nanny. Shutting herself in the drawing room, restlessly moving and replacing the ornaments on the mantelpiece, she heard Richard give orders to Simmons and watched him step into a hansom with his valise. When Charles came in, she ordered the carriage and took him to the Lockharts'. The child was puzzled, naturally. She told him that one of the maids had an infectious disease.

Once in Kensington, she felt at a disadvantage. She had not been close to Sybil for a long time, if ever, and she was embarrassed by having to explain the situation. At first she was tempted to keep up the story about the maid's illness, but it was unlikely to deceive another wife.

Sybil was faulsomely sympathetic and loudly indignant. Richard's conduct was outrageous, she declared. Telling a wife to her face that he loved another woman—it was an insult. But, unhappily, one had to remember what men were like. Forty was the dangerous age. In strict confidence, there had been an episode involving her husband and a young woman in his employment. Sybil had pretended not to notice, of course. No doubt, she said rather cattily, Geraldine had been lucky up to now. But there could surely be no question of giving Richard the satisfaction of a divorce. A wife had to endure these things; time was on her side.

Geraldine found that she disliked her sister more than she had realised. This shallow tolerance, this avoidance of trouble —it was beneath the standards that she and Richard had set themselves. In Sybil's eyes, apparently, Richard's frankness was his greatest offence. The attitude was very Kensington, very middle-class.

She spent the afternoon reading to Charles and playing Beggar-my-neighbour with him. He didn't fret much; he was a placid child, compared to Alfred. In the evening, declining dinner with the Lockharts, she returned to Berkshire House.

Alone in the drawing room, she considered the situation with resolute calmness.

Everything she had said to Richard was completely justified; she was sure of that. The divorce would be a disaster. His life after it could be nothing but a tragic waste. But he knew this. He had known it before she had opened her mouth. His passion for Ellie was not a whit diminished by the fact that it was beyond reason. Geraldine didn't understand this passion, but she felt its strength. Neither her devotion nor her generosity meant anything to him, so long as it ruled him. It would never leave him, she thought despondently. Why should it, since the whole course of their marriage had not sufficed to overcome it? Naturally, she had been unable to accept this terrible truth; naturally, she had been impelled to fight. What could she achieve, however, by fighting on against hopeless odds?

She tried to envisage Ellie, whom she had never seen. Maud had once described her. A shy, strange little thing; beautiful in an ethereal, Pre-Raphaelite kind of way. Not at all suited to be the wife of a man like Richard, Maud had said, but one could see how she had bewitched him for a time. That had been Maud's word: bewitched. Maud's only mistake—and Geraldine's—had been to imagine that he had freed himself from the spell.

It was probably true, Geraldine thought, that he had tried to free himself. She recalled the evening when, arriving home from Germany, he had embraced her like a lover, almost in front of Simmons, and possessed her in a sort of frenzy before they dressed for dinner. He must have been with Ellie; that was obvious now. Ellie couldn't be young—Geraldine's own age, more or less—but presumably she had kept her cursed ethereal beauty and her figure. When he possessed her, or kissed her, or merely gazed at her (it didn't matter which), he relived the dreams of youth. There was nothing, now, that Geraldine could do about that. What was it that a man wanted, she asked herself, in the depths of his heart? Not really a woman's body, or not only that; not even a woman at all; ultimately, a dream. A wife could not be a dream. So much the worse for wives.

One thing was dreadfully clear: time was not on her side. It was the loyalties of marriage, already grievously weakened, that would fade—not the passion, not the dream. She remembered his moods of abstraction during the past year. He had been moving away from her, steadily, inexorably. And that had been the time when he had been torn by rival forces, when the issue had been in doubt. Perhaps she could have held him if she had seen the danger: perhaps not. By now, it was too late. The debate was closed in his mind, doubtless with relief. He had made his decision, and surely he had made promises to Ellie. He had been immoveable this morning, she realised, because she had merely been presenting him with appeals and arguments that he had repeated to himself for months and in the end rejected. What reason had she to imagine that they would sway him in another month or another year, any more than now?

He might return to her, she thought, when he was reduced in vigour of heart and mind, drained of the power to conceive such a passion—an old man seeking only rest and comfort. But she didn't want that old man. She wanted the Richard she knew. And the Richard she knew was the man who burned with desire for the other woman.

He had always loathed concealment and deceit. Her offer to tolerate a liaison would have been easily acceptable to another man, but not to Richard. Not even if it meant being Foreign Secretary, she thought sadly and yet also proudly. If she refused him a divorce, he wouldn't submit and stay with her; he would leave her and live in sin with Ellie. At this, Geraldine felt a spasm of horror. It would be a worse scandal than a divorce. Perhaps Ellie would shrink from this open defiance of the conventions—she was a lady, after all. Probably they would go abroad. Still, people were sure to find out. And if they didn't find out, was that any better? If he hadn't left his wife for another woman, the only other explanation was that he found life with her intolerable. But no one would really suppose that Richard was living as a single man. His reputation and his career would be ruined in any case. What could she achieve, therefore, by refusing him the divorce? She would be refusing to "give him the satisfaction," as Sybil put it. Surely that was unworthy of her.

She examined herself with all the honesty that she could summon. The words she had spoken this morning had sprung from her sense of outrage, her dismay and her anger. Natural and justified feelings, to be sure. But if she persisted in them, they took on a different guise. Anger became vindictiveness, the mean resolve to deny him any chance of future happiness. Dismay became self-deception, a blind clinging to a legal fiction emptied of all reality. She could call herself his wife as long as she pleased, but she could not compel him to be her husband.

What had she to look forward to, then? Today's interview had been painful; the next might be a mere wrangle. And the next, and the next? They would descend into a misery of mutual bitterness, of accusations and reproaches traded like blows. He was aware now that he had wronged her; but, as she continued to refuse him what he called his freedom, he would feel increasingly that he was the one who was wronged. First he would resent her stubbornness, and by degrees he would come to detest her. He would forget that he had respected her and owed her gratitude. He would forget altogether that he had ever loved her. She could not bear that—no, it was too much.

She had not much left to carry her through the remainder of her life, she thought miserably. But she had her dignity. She had the cold, hard integrity of facing facts.

She wrote a note, requesting him to meet her at eleven in the morning, and sent a footman to catch the midnight post. Then she went to bed and slept soundly. Her decision had brought relief, but also utter exhaustion.

There was not much more of the ordeal. They met for less than ten minutes. She saw that what she told him made him happy; he had to check the beginnings of a smile. That hurt, but she told herself that it was a part of the new reality.

She hadn't the strength to discuss what was to be done with their two houses, or any details of that kind. She would write to him, she said; and of course the lawyers would see to the repugnant processes of the divorce. He offered to make the necessary explanations to Alfred and Charles, but she replied that she considered this to be her responsibility.

There was an awkward silence.

"You are a noble woman, Geraldine," he said. "I can't leave this house without saying that, with all the sincerity that is in me. I knew you would act generously—it is the essence of your nature. I repeat what I said yesterday; it is I who have been ungrateful and undeserving."

"Perhaps," she answered. "But it is I who must suffer."

And with that, she did begin to suffer. She felt, as directly as the onset of a sickness, the descent into a suffering that could never be relieved and could never end. She might receive sympathy. She might—of course, she would—devote herself to her children, fatherless as they were now. But when she heard Simmons close the front door, she could feel only the bleak hopelessness of living without Richard.

He would suffer too; she knew that, even if at this moment he did not. What they had shared could not be cancelled as though it had never existed. A part of him—the best part of him, she believed—would regret what he had cast away. Yet he was going to the woman who waited for him. He had his passion, whether it sufficed him lastingly or not. He had his triumph, his knowledge of a purpose achieved. And she had only defeat and loss.

Suddenly, the empty drawing room seemed enormous. Berkshire House seemed enormous. It had been the right size for the life that she and Richard had led; but that life was over, with all her hopes and all her happiness. What did she want with Berkshire House now? She would find a smaller place, she supposed.

Her eye fell on her engagement book. It was full, as usual. It was surprising, though lucky, that yesterday had been an empty day. But today, she and Richard were to dine out. She sat down to write a note of apology—"an unforeseen family emergency" seemed to be the best formula.

Two ladies from Berkshire, who organised social functions in Richard's constituency, were coming to lunch. She would have to go through with that; they must be already in the train. They would never lunch at Berkshire House again, but they would find that out in due course. In the afternoon, she was to preside at a charity committee. She would go through with that too. And then, she would have to go and see how Charles was getting on.

She felt a thin assurance of returning strength, of suffering at least contained. She rang for the cook to give the orders for lunch.

CHAPTER 17

The Cruellest Trial

RICHARD SIGNED THE REGISTER, as he had been instructed: "Mr. and Mrs. John Smith, 88 Thayer St., London W.1." Evidence would show that there was no such number in Thayer Street. They went upstairs: first the page carrying the suitcases, then Mabel Porter, then Richard.

Mabel Porter, he thought—what a name! What a profession, come to that. An odd profession; the woman had no more reputation than a street-walker, yet in a sense she might be perfectly respectable. She was generously built, with a swelling bosom, a florid complexion, and—as he saw when they entered the room and she removed an enormous hat trimmed with violets—fair hair done in ringlets. The whole effect was distinctly coarse to a discriminating taste, but attractive enough to make adultery plausible.

He was still trying to think why the hotel had struck him as familiar. It was in a narrow street, shielded by run-down buildings from the Regency terraces and the sea-front. Looking out of the window, he suddenly remembered. He had stayed here when he took Alice to Brighton for a weekend. He must have asked some other young fellow—Smythe, Robertson-Haig: the names had to be plucked out of the past —for a hotel where no questions were asked.

It was a warm night. With the window open, he could just hear the cheerful noise of a band. Through a gap in the buildings, he caught a glimpse of the fairy-lights on the pier and of the broad white path marked by the full moon on the placid sea. Brighton Pier hadn't changed, no doubt. He remembered the crowds of working-men with their wives or sweethearts, for whom a day at the seaside was a great event; the redcoats and the bluejackets, the pert little Cockney girls with ribbons streaming from their boaters; the band, the pierrot show, the hucksters crying their whelks and jellied eels. It was noisy and vulgar, to be sure. Ellie would have detested it, and so would Geraldine. But it had been fun with Alice.

What a treat it had been for her, that weekend! And Richard had enjoyed it too—the beach in the sunshine, and the pier at night, and kissing in the gardens behind the Dome. How carelessly happy he had been then, as if there could be no more to life than the pleasures of a cavalry subaltern with a pretty mistress! It seemed to him that he was remembering someone else, a man as remote from his present life as Alice was remote. It was before he was in love with Ellie. Not to be in love with Ellie—he could no longer imagine what that was like.

"I say, you're miles away," Miss Porter remarked.

Richard apologised.

"That's all right. But it's a bit early to turn in, don't you think? How about getting them to send up something to drink?"

"Certainly."

He rang, and ordered a bottle of champagne.

"Thanks ever so," Miss Porter said. "That's doing it in style, I must say. I've known some who'd jib at coughing up for a port and lemon. Look out of the window again for a minute, d'you mind?"

He obeyed. She slipped out of her dress and into a loose, revealing gown.

"You know, if you don't mind me saying so, you might be a bit more sort of *en déshabillé*."

"Ah, yes. Of course."

He removed his jacket, undid his waistcoat buttons, and exchanged his boots for slippers.

The waiter, a suitably sharp-looking fellow, brought the champagne.

"Will there be anything else tonight, sir?"

"No, thank you."

"Tea at what time in the morning, sir?"

"Don't disturb us until we ring."

"Very good, sir."

Richard tipped the man half a sovereign, another point to be remembered.

"Thank you kindly, sir. A very good night to you—er, Mr. Smith. And to you, Mrs. Smith."

"It's a pleasure making your acquaintance," Miss Porter said over the champagne. "I do like a gentleman who is a gentleman. I suppose you're somebody distinguished, though. I'd know if I weren't so ignorant."

"If you haven't heard of me, I'm not distinguished."

"Oh, I never read the papers."

For the life of him, Richard couldn't keep up a conversation. Miss Porter said: "I hope you don't mind me asking, but is your wife ditching you or are you ditching her?"

"I'm leaving my wife."

"Thought so. I can always tell. The gents who're getting ditched are all bright and breezy, and the ones who're ditching their wives are as glum as a wet Sunday. Funny, but that's how it is."

"I'm sorry to be such poor company."

"It's natural. You'll feel better when you're with your ladylove. I don't mind if we settle down for the night, if that's what you'd prefer. The gentleman usually tucks up on the sofa. There's a rug and a cushion. Sort of roughing it, but it's only for once, isn't it?"

"I shall be perfectly comfortable."

"Pleasant dreams, then, Lord Richard."

"Goodnight, Miss Porter."

She went straight to sleep, breathing heavily. A clock just behind the hotel chimed every quarter of an hour. Alice had laughed about it, he remembered, saying that people obviously didn't come to Brighton to sleep. However, it didn't disturb Miss Porter.

Richard slept in snatches on the badly sprung sofa. When morning came, he found the room unendurable. He wasn't obliged to spend half the day here, surely. He stood it until nine o'clock, then rang for hot water and shaved. Miss Porter slept on. He rang again and ordered breakfast. She was awake by the time the waiter brought it, but still in bed—all to the good, no doubt.

"What are we having?" she asked with interest.

"Porridge, haddock, ham and eggs, toast and marmalade."

"Just the ticket."

She ate heartily, and so did he. The beginning of a new day restored his spirits.

"You'll want to get back to town," she said. "Don't wait for me. I expect I'll stay till the afternoon. I love dear old Brighton."

"Very well, then. Everything went off all right, I believe."

"Oh, Lord yes, don't you worry. There's enough evidence to divorce an archbishop."

"I'm extremely obliged to you, Miss Porter."

"Glad to have been of service, Lord Richard."

"I suppose the lawyers will . . ."

"They'll see to my remuneration—yes, that's all taken care of."

They shook hands. A sordid experience; he was glad that it was over, he would never speak of it to Ellie. But, in retrospect, he would find it amusing. Though he would never wish

to see Mabel Porter again, he found to his surprise that he
rather liked her. It was not for him to despise her, at all events;
he certainly was obliged to her.

Now that this distasteful business was over, there was
nothing to do but wait. He hadn't seen Ellie since the day
when she had given him her promise. He ached for her, but
the lawyer had warned him that, unless one were careful, a
wife sometimes named the real object of her husband's affec-
tions instead of the person selected for the purpose. It was unthinkable, of course, that Geraldine would stoop to such an
action. However, he was determined to be scrupulous in doing
whatever the lawyer said.

He found it hard to control his impatience while the legal
preparations moved slowly forward, and did his best to think
only of his reunion with Ellie. They were to meet in Paris. He
didn't like the city, but Ellie would be travelling separately to
join him—the lawyer advised against fetching her from Longmarsh—and it was an easy journey for her. Then they would
leave Paris almost at once for Switzerland. He had made some
enquiries and learned of a little place, very peaceful and practically unknown to English tourists, where they could rent a
house and live under an assumed name. The divorce action
could not be heard until the autumn, and then there was a
further delay before the decree nisi became absolute. After
that, they would be married quietly by the nearest British
Consul, and in a couple of years they would return to England.
They could never be received in society, and he must guard
against Ellie's being subjected to any unpleasantness, but they
could live quietly in the country. He couldn't reconcile himself
to living abroad for ever.

He had told the lawyer that Geraldine was to have both
Berkshire House and the Priory. Berkshire House, strictly
speaking, was not his to dispose of. It was the property of the
Duke of Berkshire, and the Marquis of Wantage—fifteen

years old already—might need it within the measurable future.
The Priory cost Richard a wrench; he loved the house, and he
had always expected to end his days there. But he considered
it his duty to let Geraldine have it, and to leave his sons the
home that they had known since infancy. As for Ellie and
himself, his secret hope was that they might live at Longmarsh. She would be happier there than anywhere else; it had
seen so much of their love that it was their natural home;
Charlotte would be a welcome companion. However, Longmarsh was the Farnham family residence and Richard had no
idea what view Arthur would take of the divorce and remarriage. Perhaps, after all, it would be best for him and Ellie
to find a new home for their new life together.

Geraldine had gone to the Priory and apparently intended
to stay there indefinitely. Simmons and a few of the upper
servants were being kept on at Berkshire House pending final
arrangements, but the footmen and maids had been paid off.
With Geraldine away, Richard was free to select the belongings that he wished to take, but he could not bring himself to
enter Berkshire House again. He sent instructions to Simmons
to pack up his clothes and the political papers from his study.
Geraldine could have everything else in the house, so far as
he was concerned. Simmons sent, along with the papers, a
photograph of Ellie that had once stood by Richard's bed,
and had been put at the bottom of a drawer when he married
Geraldine. He wondered what Simmons knew. A good deal,
probably.

Living at the club, Richard was in limbo between the normality of marriage and the outer darkness—that is, in relation
to society and public life—which he would soon inhabit. People
doubtless assumed that there was a rift between Lord and Lady
Richard Somers, if only because Berkshire House was closed
at the height of the London season. But Richard told no one
that there was to be a divorce. It would have been painful to

impose on old friends the necessity of avoiding him. Besides, as soon as the news was out he would have to resign from the club, and it was convenient to live there for the time being.

He saw as few people as a man feasibly can who is living at a club in Pall Mall. The House was in recess for Easter, then for Whitsun; when it was sitting, he appeared only to obey a three-line whip. Every morning, he walked to the London Library and studied the history and constitution of Switzerland. It seemed reasonable to learn something about a country where one proposed to live for a while, and the project occupied his mind. He lunched and dined alone, in small restaurants more often than at the club. In the evening, he retired to the writing room and wrote to Ellie. His letters covered pages and pages, and he never missed a day. Her answers came irregularly and were tantalisingly brief; but, he told himself, she had never been much of a one for words.

At last, after what seemed to him a ridiculous length of time, he was informed by the lawyer that the evidence had been taken, the petition drawn up and approved by Geraldine. Only a few tasks remained. He saw his banker and drew letters of credit for use abroad. He secured a reserved compartment on the trains and a cabin on the boat, and the same for Ellie two days after his own journey. He wrote three letters. One was to old Sir Hartley Stephens, still chairman of the Conservative committee in West Berkshire, to say that he would be unable to contest the seat at the next election. The new member would not be a Somers, Richard reflected; that would be a blow to George, but it couldn't be helped. The second letter was to Lord Salisbury, regretting that he would be in no position to serve Her Majesty in his altered personal circumstances. The third was to his mother, to break the news to her and George before they read it in the newspaper. "I cannot hope for your sympathy," he wrote, and thought: how true that was. She would be utterly appalled. Still, he didn't believe that it would kill her. Like many people who have been semi-invalids for years, the Dowager Duchess had revealed a remarkable toughness in later life.

Richard left for Paris on a scorching day in June. It was twenty years since he had first set eyes on Ellie, fifteen years since he had proposed to her, fourteen years since she had become his betrothed. Always June.

Boarding the steamer, he thought sadly of the period of exile that he was beginning. He went straight down to his cabin, avoiding even a glance at the white cliffs. Pictures of England came hauntingly to his mind's eye: the sweep of the Cotswolds seen from the Priory, the lake at Longmarsh, the little wood where he had picked primroses for Ellie. Ellie and England: he must have both, to be truly happy.

Geraldine was there, at her home in the heart of England. She had much to endure; he was glad that she need not face exile as well as solitude. He was glad too that she would be at the Priory when the newsboys shouted: "Lord Richard Somers' sensation!" in the London streets. It would be hard for little Alfred at his school—boys could be merciless. Perhaps Geraldine would have him sent home before the news broke, and keep him at home until the autumn term. By now, she must have told the boys what was happening. She was too noble to speak harshly of Richard, but they were bound to blame the parent who had deserted them. When they grew up, they would know how a man could be possessed by love for a woman and perhaps they would blame him less. But that was far away.

It was painful for Richard to lose his sons, just when they were beginning to disclose the outlines of manhood. He had started, in the last year, to explain to Alfred what the Government did and what the House of Commons was for. The boy was exceptionally intelligent; his school reports were splendid. Exceptionally handsome too, with the regular Somers features and Geraldine's large dark eyes. Charles was quieter, less precocious, but he showed a quality of steady persistence. Richard would have found deep satisfaction in helping and guiding them. He wondered if they would remember that, so long as he had been a father to them, he had been a good one. He didn't deserve to be remembered, but he hated the thought of being forgotten.

But he might be a father again. Ellie was quite young enough to bear children. She had found joy in caring for children as a teacher; the greater joy of motherhood was something he could give her, a rich addition to the happiness that waited for them. He imagined her cradling a baby in her arms, smiling her gentle smile as a toddler took his first steps, teaching a child to play the piano. Perhaps Ellie would give him a daughter—he had always wanted a daughter. Another golden-haired and blue-eyed Ellie, known and loved from infancy. The thought did a great deal to cheer him up.

By the time the train approached Paris, his mood was buoyant. Action and movement—the clatter of the wheels, the streaming of the smoke past the window—never failed to raise his spirits. The vacant, inert period of waiting was over, or almost over. The old life was behind him; the losses and regrets were behind him too. The new life was about to begin. He thought only of Ellie—of clasping her in his arms, of calling her his own at last, of the attainment of his heart's desire.

He had taken two rooms at a hotel in the Rue de Rennes. Since English visitors always stayed on the Right Bank, presumably it was sensible to be on the Left. But he wasn't sure that it would be all right; nobody who came to London could possibly stay south of the river, after all. His main reason for travelling two days before Ellie was to make sure that the hotel was passable, and change it if necessary.

It was, in fact, passable. The rooms were rather small, but they would be making a very short stay. The atmosphere of the hotel was of middle-class gentility. The other guests, he observed at dinner, seemed to be people of the substantial shopkeeper class from the French provinces. He heard not a word of English. He was treated with deference through the mere fact of his nationality, although he had given his name as Mr. Somers and suppressed his title.

Forty-eight hours passed peacefully. Now that he had crossed his Rubicon, his impatience left him. He strolled in the streets near the hotel; he bought a couple of presents for Ellie; he sat under café awnings looking idly at the passers-by. A whole morning went in reserving places in the *wagon-lit* for the journey to Switzerland. Dozens of people were preparing to travel, and there was the inevitable French confusion and inefficiency.

When the time came to meet Ellie, Richard was at the Gare du Nord an hour too soon. He thought of her sitting in the train, coming closer and closer. Even now, he was not impatient. He drank a cognac, smoked a cigar, and puzzled his way through an afternoon paper.

The train arrived. Ellie was not on it.

Richard couldn't believe it. He stood at the barrier until all the passengers had passed through, surrounded by an atmosphere of greetings and kisses; at first he felt that he was sharing in it, then it gradually excluded him. He strained his eyes, scanning the length of the platform. One figure after another seemed to resemble her—a white dress, a flash of golden hair —only to become completely different as it approached. He remembered that she hated crowds; she would wait until the rush was over. She had a good deal of luggage. She might have had difficulty in securing a porter. He ought to have gone to her aid already. He pushed his way onto the platform, silencing the ticket-collector's protest with a coin, and hurried along the entire length of the train. Then he came back, slowly, peering into every compartment. No Ellie.

A railway official, though evidently of responsible status, proved unhelpful. There was no way of finding out whether a compartment had been used, even a compartment reserved by name.

Richard insisted on a search for the guard. The man was unhelpful too, almost insolent. *Une dame anglaise, cheveux blonds, assez jeune? Crois pas, monsieur. Mais on verrait une dizaine comme ça chaque jour, n'est-ce pas?*

Could he have missed her, Richard wondered? She had the name of the hotel, so she might be there by now. He rushed out of the station and hailed a fiacre. At the approach to the Pont-Royal, the traffic was at a standstill: coachmen yelling abuse at one another, horses rearing and panicking, gendarmes blowing whistles and gesticulating, a typical French muddle.

Reflection told him that he couldn't really have missed her. There could be any number of simple reasons why she hadn't come. She might be indisposed; one of her brothers or sisters might have visited Longmarsh at the wrong moment. There would be a telegram at the hotel. Possibly a telegram or a letter had gone astray; one didn't expect the post to be as reliable as in England.

There was a telegram: "Ellie unwell. Please do not worry. Letter follows. Charlotte Colmore."

The manageress asked whether the second room would be occupied. Not tonight, Richard said, but he wished it to be reserved until further notice; he would pay for it, of course. In the evening, the staff treated him with greater deference than ever and addressed him as "milord." Charlotte had used his title for the telegram, he supposed.

The next day was a blank, hollow space in his life. The weather was stifling. He closed the shutters on his windows to keep out the sun and didn't leave his room, except for meals and to go down to the lobby whenever he thought that post might have been delivered. Nothing came.

The day after that, Charlotte's letter was brought up to his room with his shaving water.

Ellie has suffered a nervous collapse. The strain of the present crisis in her life, doubtless, is sufficient explanation. When I say that you are not to worry, I mean that there is no sign of any illness in a medical sense. But she is quite unable to travel or to risk any exertion whatever. The doctor has prescribed complete rest.

You may perhaps feel a desire to be with her, but I must tell you that it would be most unwise. The doctor is quite emphatic that she must receive no visitors, particularly a visitor who might excite her emotions. Rest assured that I shall inform you immediately when her condition improves. I shall assume that you are staying in Paris unless I hear to the contrary.

Richard stayed in Paris; he had no option. One day followed another in leaden succession: days of agonised yearning, but also of maddening tedium. He was unprepared for this further period of waiting and found it much harder to bear than the waiting in London. There had been a set limit to that, and a confident expectation of happiness to come. He had envisaged Ellie waiting like himself, sharing his hopes; he had rehearsed in fancy the joyous meeting in Paris and the pleasures of settling into the new home in Switzerland, and placed them on fixed dates. He looked back to that period, almost, as one of enjoyment.

He had nothing to do in Paris. He took a daily walk, but soon wearied of the nearby streets. The weather continued sultry, discouraging exertion yet making him tired without it. Anyway, he didn't like to be away from the hotel for long, for fear of missing a letter. Hour after hour, he stayed in his room. Time seemed to stand still; often he was sure that his watch had stopped. Whispers followed him when he appeared downstairs. The English lord travelling incognito, the lady who hadn't arrived—it was rich material for gossip, obviously.

It was a time of miserable brooding and of baffling uncertainty. What did it mean, a nervous collapse? He had very little idea, and re-reading Charlotte's letter yielded no enlightenment. Was Ellie in pain, was she in distress? Or was it rather a paralysis of feeling, as well as of the will and the power to act? The nerves, so he took it, supplied the mind with its strength. One spoke of steady nerves, strong nerves, weak nerves. People with weak nerves flinched from difficult tasks and were shattered by unpleasant experiences. A soldier with weak nerves couldn't hold out under bombardment; a Home Secretary with weak nerves couldn't order an execution. But Ellie, after all, hadn't been required to do anything like what he had done—speaking to Geraldine, spending the sordid night at Brighton. She was required merely to travel to Paris and join her lover. Travelling abroad was certainly no problem for her. Years ago, she had travelled alone to Germany and established herself as a teacher. Whatever one might say of the wisdom of that decision, she had carried out a difficult task with—surely—cool nerves. Why should her nerves collapse now? It didn't make sense.

He himself, probably, had gone through some kind of nervous collapse after Ellie had broken the engagement. He remembered being unequal to putting his mind to anything, even to the ordinary day's routine. Still, that had been a reaction to a dreadful blow—to the deprivation of happiness. Ellie, on the contrary, was now on the brink of happiness. No, it made no sense. But then again, there was her strange inability to believe in happiness. Could it be her mysterious, irrational fears that put the strain on the nerves?

The immediate question was: How long did a nervous collapse last? He took comfort from Charlotte's assurance that

Ellie was not actually ill. On the other hand, this increased the uncertainty. A doctor could treat an illness and forecast, more or less, the period necessary for recovery. Except for advising rest, which anyone could think of, there was nothing a doctor could do about a nervous collapse. Richard had an uneasy feeling, though he couldn't recall a case, that rest might be necessary for several weeks. This didn't prevent him, every morning, from expecting a telegram summoning him to the Gare du Nord.

The Times announced that Lady Richard Somers had filed a petition for divorce, alleging her husband's adultery. The ha'penny papers didn't reach Paris, but their headlines were easily imagined. Richard couldn't remember a divorce petition ever receiving such prominence in *The Times,* except for Captain O'Shea's.

The Government was defeated at last and the House dissolved. He read the news with an irrepressible hankering for the excitement in the division lobbies, the bustle of the election campaign, the satisfaction of office. Later, when the Conservatives returned to power, he read that Lord Salisbury was again keeping the Foreign Office in his own hands.

He had been in Paris for a week, then a fortnight, then a month. The oppressive heat continued with scarcely a break. It was a rotten time of year to be in a city. The aristocratic mansions in the Boulevard Saint-Germain were deserted, like the great houses in Park Lane; restaurants and theatres put up notices to say that they were closed for the summer. Such restaurants as remained open, however, were packed with tourists. Richard longed for the countryside, for the relief of fresh air and space. He thought of spending a few days at a resort in Normandy, or making a short trip to Switzerland to look at houses for rent. His room, absurdly small for an extended stay, gave him a feeling of being penned in. But he was chained to Paris by the daily recurrence of hope.

After a week, he had given up keeping the room for Ellie. The manageress appealed to him; Paris was full, she didn't like to turn people away, she would let the room only to transients and he could have it at a day's notice. Richard was obliged to agree. He felt the renunciation as a bad omen, as if he were no longer expecting Ellie.

He wrote to her almost every day, perhaps for his own sake as much as hers. Letters of love and devotion, letters of comfort and tenderness, letters in which he tried to divert her with such news as he could think of. He was careful never to reproach her, never to show his impatience. He even urged her to rest as long as necessary and not to travel until she was quite recovered. All he asked in return was a word to say that she was thinking of him. But no letters came from her. After a time, he wrote to Charlotte begging for news. Charlotte answered, politely but rather tersely, that there was no change.

The idea of going to Longmarsh began to work on Richard irresistibly. He told himself that he had no right to defy a doctor's orders merely to assuage his own longings. Yet the doctor really had no more competence in this situation than Richard himself—less, indeed, for no doctor had an insight into Ellie's troubled soul. It was her fears that had struck her down; the more he pondered, the more he was convinced of that. He had said to her at their last meeting that something in her was afraid of happiness and afraid of love. And she had replied: "It's true."

Very well, then; he must help her to overcome these fears. Had she not yielded to them all those years ago, her life and his would have been tranquil and painless. He had beaten them back on the day when she had given him her promise, but they had returned in his absence. Now he must inspire her to confront them again. She needed his strength, his guidance, his protecting love. Far from having a duty to keep away from her, he had a duty to go to her. He blamed himself for having been so slow to see it.

Besides, he couldn't count on it that he had the full truth of the matter. He regarded Charlotte as a friend, and she had been broad-minded about his visits to Longmarsh, but he didn't really know how she viewed his intention to secure a divorce and marry Ellie. At Baden-Baden, her description of how Ellie had changed (untrue, as it turned out) had surely been designed to dissuade him from seeing her. Certainly, Charlotte had no conception of the needs and powers of love, nor of the happiness it could bring. She was a strong-minded woman, with a good deal of influence on Ellie—an influence, he suspected now, thrown into the scale against him. She couldn't actually have lied to him; there must have been a nervous collapse, or Ellie would have come to Paris. Still, her letters were remarkably uninformative. The ban on his going to Longmarsh (imposed, it now struck him, before he had suggested any such thing) could well have been Charlotte's idea as much as the doctor's. And it was very strange that Ellie had not written. Nervous collapse or no, she couldn't be incapable of writing a line. Could Charlotte have stopped her letters from reaching the post? Or intercepted his letters? Such suspicions might be unjust, but—once conceived—he could not dismiss them from his mind.

He decided to wait for another week. The prospect of action, and a definite time-table, relieved him considerably; he went out one night to a *bal musette* and quite enjoyed it. Above all, the idea of seeing Ellie at last made him feel that happiness was once more within his grasp. He cautioned himself that he must not excite her or press her to go away until she was well again. He would sit patiently by her side, soothe her fears, allow his love to do its healing work. All would be well —he was certain of it!

He did not tell Charlotte that he was coming. He reflected, too, that he ought to avoid being recognised on the journey, especially near Longmarsh. The petition was safely filed, naming Mabel Porter; but he was now the centre of a sensation, and gossip would pick up whatever it could. He thought of shaving off his moustache, but couldn't reconcile himself to that. He went to an optician and asked for spectacles, saying that he couldn't pick out objects at a distance so well as he would like. The man insisted on testing his eyes and told him that he was wise to take remedial action in time. His sight really was deteriorating . . . *"à l'âge que vous avez, monsieur, c'est normal."*

To avoid staying a night in London or reaching Longmarsh late in the evening, he travelled by the overnight boat. Dawn touched the white cliffs as he came ashore; he had not expected to see them again so soon, and couldn't resist a leap of his spirits despite his anxieties. He breakfasted at the Charing Cross Hotel, took a cab to Waterloo, and caught the nine o'clock train. At the little station, he left his valise with a porter. He would walk to Longmarsh, he decided. But he hadn't gone more than fifty yards along the village street when a familiar voice called: "Lord Richard!"

Charlotte was coming out of a shop, carrying a parcel.

"Miss Colmore," he said, taking off his hat.

"You're not . . . Oh, it's lucky I saw you!"

For Charlotte, she looked quite agitated. There was something in his suspicions, he thought grimly.

"It's not altogether surprising that my concern should bring me here, is it?" he asked.

"I must talk to you, Lord Richard. Let me think. Yes, The Crown will give us a private room."

He was obliged to go with her to the inn. The landlord ushered them into a decently furnished parlour.

It was for Charlotte to speak first, he felt. She seemed to have regained her composure.

"Are you wearing spectacles now, or are you trying to disguise yourself?" she asked.

"My sight is not what it was," he replied with dignity. However, he put the spectacles in his pocket.

"Well . . . It appears that you didn't believe me when I said that it would be unwise for Ellie to see you."

"I naturally intended to speak to you first. I hope to see her, I admit."

"It is impossible."

"With respect, Miss Colmore, I wonder that you can be so positive. Ellie is no longer a young girl, and I am the man whom she intends to marry when I am free. I shall then have certain rights in law. In humanity, I feel that I have them now."

"I fear that you have no idea of Ellie's condition."

"If I may say so, your letters have scarcely been enlightening."

"I know. I've been meaning to tell you more—you'll see that it's far from easy. I was waiting for the visit of a neurologist from Harley Street. He came only this Monday."

"Perhaps now you would be kind enough to tell me all."

Charlotte was silent for a while. A pendulum clock on the wall ticked loudly, indifferent to his impatience.

"I will tell you the full truth, Lord Richard. You will find it hard to bear, I warn you. But you must know sooner or later."

"Tell me, please." Fear began to catch at him. The room seemed chilly, though it was a sunny morning.

Charlotte looked straight at him and said deliberately: "The truth is that, if you saw Ellie, you would see a helpless child. I dress her in the morning and undress her at night. I feed her with a spoon, when I can coax her to eat. Yesterday, for four hours, she was occupied with tearing sheets of paper into little pieces."

Richard stared at her, horrified.

"Is this . . . Has this . . . Has she been like this all the time?"

"Since the day of her intended journey, yes—all the time. If there is a faint improvement, it doesn't last."

"But what does she say of how she feels—of why she behaves like this?"

"You don't understand yet. She can't see herself with the eyes of the Ellie we know. She can't express what is going on in her mind, nor can we interpret it. Her talk is a mere babble —absurdities, words repeated fifty times, unfinished phrases. Sometimes, for a whole day, she doesn't speak at all. Once I copied down everything she said; I had a hope that it would be useful to the neurologist. He made nothing of it except that it is typical of her condition. You may read it if you wish."

"Has she spoken of me?"

"No. I should tell you if she had, truly. She no longer inhabits the same world as before her collapse. I don't think she recognises me. She knows that I'm Charlotte, a person who cares for her, but I doubt if she remembers me as her sister. Memories—connections—are what she has lost."

"Let me see her, Miss Colmore, I beg you. She will remember our love—she will, she must!"

"You still think of her as you know her. You must bring yourself to realise this: if Ellie had no one to care for her, she would be committed to an asylum."

"You are telling me that she's mad!"

"She could be certified. A magistrate would not hesitate. I shall never allow it to happen, of course."

"This Harley Street man—does he consider her mad?"

"He has a name for her condition: dementia praecox."

"What advice does he give?"

"Rest and good care. What else is possible? As he explains it, the mind can cease to function normally, as your right arm might cease to function if you had a stroke. If you rest, you may recover the use of your arm. If Ellie rests, her mind may recover."

"When?"

"It's not possible to say."

"Tell me the worst. She may never recover?"

"The doctor's words were, 'One can always hope.' "

Richard looked out of the window, which overlooked a mean little yard. Untouched by the sun, the room really was cold. He felt frozen to the heart. Something—either Charlotte's sturdy presence, or a fading remnant of his hopes—still protected him from the agony that would rend him. It would come, he knew.

"It is hard to bear, indeed," he said.

The clock ticked. Charlotte said nothing.

"Miss Colmore: I have loved Ellie all my life, ever since I was a man. I have thrown away all that I had—marriage, home, career—because I could not live without her. I implore you to let me see her."

"You must not ask that, Lord Richard. It's more than I dare risk. I think I know, so far as one who has never loved can know, the intensity of your feelings for her. That intensity— that passion—is the reason why she must not see you. I don't condemn your love. I shield her, as weak eyes must be shielded from the sun."

"But . . ."

"Please, Lord Richard. Love—what is it? It is a venture into strange regions, a turmoil of the spirit. I wonder at it, even while I am thankful to have been spared it. You have the strength to glory in it—Ellie has not. She lacked that strength even when her mind was unclouded. She lacks it now—utterly, pitiably. It is for me to plead with you, not you with me. Leave her in peace. Her recovery, her very survival, depends on that. It is a further trial for you, I know: the cruellest trial, yes. But if you truly love her, you will bear it for her sake."

Richard bowed his head.

"I will bear it," he said. "If I have the strength, I will bear it."

She collected her parcel and her handbag. They were both anxious to escape from the confining little room.

"I have kept your letters, unopened. She will read them when it's possible for them to mean anything to her. You have my solemn promise that I will let you know at once of the least improvement in her condition."

"Thank you, Miss Colmore."

"You will be in Paris?"

"I don't know. I'll write to you."

He offered to carry her parcel and wait while she completed her shopping, but she said that she was returning to Long-marsh almost directly. They shook hands. She went into a shop across the street, while he paid the landlord of the Crown something for his trouble.

He had just missed a train to London. Standing about at the station or in the village seemed unendurable. He strode rapidly, almost like a man pursued, into the open country, not caring where he went, just able to choose the opposite direction to Longmarsh.

A carriage, filling the narrow road, forced him to stand close to the hedge. He climbed the next stile and struck across a field, then followed a lane leading uphill. He didn't know where he was: how could it matter? The lane petered out in a wood, unusually dense and dark for this part of England. He was hidden, at least, from the mockery of the sunlight.

A carter, on his way to gather firewood, was surprised to see a man lying under the trees, tearing at the earth, howling like a beaten dog.

CHAPTER 18

Living
on the Continent

IN THE YEAR 1900, Lord Richard Somers (once a cavalry officer, with battle experience in Afghanistan) wrote to the War Office and offered his services in any capacity in South Africa. He received a routine letter of thanks, then nothing more. It was what he expected.

Living on the Continent—even, as he lived, in a secluded manner—was unpleasant for an Englishman at that period. Foreigners regarded the South African War as a bullying assault on a small nation and rejoiced over the British Army's humiliating defeats. Even Rhoda, who was English herself, thought that it would have been the decent thing to leave the Boers alone.

Could it be, Richard wondered, that this new century would see the decline and evanescence of England's greatness?

> *Far-called, our navies melt away,*
> *On dune and headland sinks the fire.*
> *Lo, all our pomp of yesterday*
> *Is one with Nineveh and Tyre.*

The lines haunted him. Lines written—strange!—at the climax of the pomp, on the occasion of the Queen's Diamond Jubilee. Poets, perhaps, had the longer and truer vision.

The tumult and the shouting dies,
The captains and the kings depart.
Still stands Thine ancient sacrifice,
An humble and a contrite heart.

So be it. The distant future would not remember a man who had been Foreign Secretary—let alone a man who had not.

Richard contemplated the twentieth century gloomily. The mere numerical change created a sense of uncertainty. One had written the date '99 on a cheque or a letter; it seemed absurd to write '00. Suddenly, the past was snatched away. The year 2000 would be worse, he supposed. He had read somewhere that most ninth-century people had expected the world to end in the year 1000. It was not surprising.

And one had to look ahead so far. In the seventies, one thought of the eighties; in the eighties, one thought of the nineties. Now, the word "century" compelled the mind to face vaster distances. Beliefs, loyalties and ideals would dissolve or be discarded. Others would replace them, no doubt. Without beliefs, loyalties and ideals, man cannot live—Richard was sure of that, if of nothing else. But what they would be, he could not discern.

Material change worried him less. Motor-cars, chugging occasionally through the streets and leaving a trail of smoke, stink and ugly noise, repelled him; but that kind of thing was merely the current form of mechanical ingenuity, and his grandfather must have been equally repelled by trains, which Richard took for granted and indeed rather liked. What did disturb him, when he saw a car, was not the thing itself but the crowd of excited schoolboys running after it. Perhaps these inventions—motor-cars, and the flying machines which were forecast in magazine articles about the new century—would themselves be the prime focus of beliefs and values. That was indeed a dispiriting thought.

He, Richard Somers, would be out of place in the twentieth century. The jolt of history stressed that he was a man of the past. The irony was that he didn't feel old; his hair was only grey at the temples and his spectacles were not at all a necessity. He was forty-five, in unfailing good health, still attractive to women, capable of a hard day's work had there been any for him to do. Yet, in every respect that mattered, his life was over. It was no use complaining, but it was hard to get used to. Mind and body, in their undiminished vigour, rebelled.

It was strange how things had turned out for him. He had never expected to be a wanderer in foreign countries, living in hotels or at best in provisional homes. Up to a point, certainly, he enjoyed travelling. The plans and decisions, the new scenes, the encounters and discoveries—these provided a simulacrum of purpose and activity. On the other hand, he missed England terribly. Even while he admired a dazzling vista of the Mediterranean coast or the Alps, he would have exchanged it gratefully for a lane edged with primroses. He missed English faces, English voices, the natural use of his own language. And he felt, more severely with every year, the lack of a place to call his own, a home that he could be sure of until death.

The first phase after the catastrophe of 1895 was a ghastly memory. During the journey back to Paris, a grim reversal of his journey of hope, and during the one night that he had to spend at the hotel in the Rue de Rennes, he writhed in helpless agony. Then he went to Switzerland, simply because he had to get out of Paris and he wasn't equal to making any alternative plan. He rented a house—the loneliest he could find—took on a couple of village girls as cook and maid-of-all-work, and did absolutely nothing for six months. It was painful to be in the very place that should have been the scene of his happiness with Ellie, but just that pain seemed to be the inevitable condition of his life. Except for the servants, whose dialect he could barely understand, he spoke to no one. When the winter snow surrounded the house, he felt only relief. Alien, colourless and forbidding, the outlook from the small double-glazed windows reflected the misery in his heart.

Misery—and guilt. Day and night, the tormenting questions beat at his mind. Had he demanded of Ellie, as Charlotte said, more than her strength could bear? Would she be sane and happy today if he had not drawn her promise from her in the little wood—if he had not sought her out at Karlsruhe —if he had utterly forgotten her when she broke the engagement—if he had never loved her in the first place? Was it his love that had driven her mad? Was his love nothing but cruelty?

He could not believe it. Thousands of men and women throughout history had been driven to suffering by impediments to love or by a lover's desertion; none, surely, by love's loyalty and persistence. What did a woman need, if not a man's love? He had offered her, first and last, the purest devotion. It was her happiness that he had sought: his own happiness, yes, but that had no meaning without hers. If her strength failed, he had tried to fortify it. If her fears held her back, he had tried to overcome them. The disaster was that, without him, they had captured her at the end.

Yet the sense of guilt would not leave him. He had blundered somehow; and a blunder, when its consequences were so dreadful, was a crime. Good intentions—love itself—supplied no defence against that charge. He could not understand how he had sinned, but his lack of understanding was the sin itself. Hour after hour, he sought to recall every word he had spoken, every thought that had shaped his actions, every look in her eyes that he might have interpreted more truly. Hour after hour, he gazed at the photograph which was all that he still had of her, as if it could tell him something that the living

Ellie had never told. He was left with nothing but a tragic, heart-rending mystery.

He wrestled with this mystery, amid the snow and the silence, until he was overcome by a despairing exasperation. Before winter ended, he left Switzerland suddenly. An urge to get on the move—to flight or evasion, perhaps; he didn't care to analyse it too closely—seized him as completely as, hitherto, he had been seized by the need for solitude. He took ship from Venice and made a long journey in wholly unfamiliar countries: Greece, Syria, the Holy Land, Egypt. A chance meeting with a German antiquarian led to an interest that stirred his mind. He spent weeks living in a tent and sifting the desert sand with a trowel, and was lucky enough to find a scarab which the antiquarian declared to be valuable. But in summer he found the heat intolerable and returned to Europe.

He was pursued wherever he went by the longing for Ellie, the wretchedness of having lost her, the racking uncertainty of not knowing whether she was lost for ever. When he received a letter from Charlotte, every two months or so, he opened it with quivering fingers. The news was always the same. His life was a burden, a matter of mere endurance; he had been tempted by suicide, had weighed the logic of it consciously. But he clung to hope, or hope clung to him. To kill himself while there was a chance of her recovery—and there was always a chance—would be not only an absurdity but the profoundest infidelity. His duty was to suffer for love, not to make his escape. Meanwhile, he was not a saint but a man with the instinct for life. He would always suffer, unless happiness came to him at last, but it was not in him to be a pure embodiment of suffering. Gradually, just as when he had lost Ellie the first time, he became capable of living normally. Whenever he enjoyed a stimulating talk with a new acquaintance, or eagerly explored a strange town, part of his mind reproached the other part for straying from Ellie. Yet what was he to do? If paralysis of the mind was Ellie's affliction, sanity—the inescapable attachment to the real world—was Richard's burden.

After his return from the Near East, he wondered where he could settle. It was too soon to think of living in England again, especially as he had not regularised his position by re-marriage. Germany had always been more congenial to him than any other foreign country. He didn't wish to renew old friendships, based on his status as a figure in the Conservative Party (and a respectable husband), but he wanted to make new friends. That meant living in a town. He decided on Munich, and took a lease of a small house, ready furnished and convenient to the main streets. Here he lived, though he continued to travel from time to time, for almost two years.

Though he hadn't realised it beforehand, he was living in a district of Munich where social habits were relaxed and infor-mal and it was easy to make friends. These friends were not like those whom he had known in the past; but he wasn't a snob, he hoped, and he was in no position to be morally cen-sorious. In every city in Europe, evidently, there was a kind of society living on the fringes of what Richard had hitherto understood by "society." The people who belonged to it were educated, they were often of good birth, but they chose to live in a way that diverged from the governing code. In London, it was people of this sort who had gathered at Celia Ashton's house. In this alternative society, it was permissible for a gentle-man to pay court to a lady with a view to an affair, just as with a view to marriage in ordinary society. The gentleman and his mistress were then received and invited to dinner, like a married couple. Richard had never imagined that he would move in such circles. However, once he did so, he couldn't see that manners were any less courteous or well bred than in his former sphere.

He was not a saint but a man. He had to live, and he found it hard to live for long without a woman. The first time that a pretty face and a darting glance aroused his desires, he reproached himself harshly and went home to do penance in the contemplation of Ellie's photograph. But, just as his nature urged him toward new friendships and new interests, so it drove him irresistibly in this respect too. He had to recognise that, unless he shunned the ladies of the alternative society—which meant shunning the men too—one or another of them would soon be his mistress.

They were, quite distinctly, ladies. One didn't swear in their presence, one didn't snatch kisses in corridors, one didn't offer them money or presents that could be construed as bribes. Sometimes they yielded quickly and sometimes after a long courtship, but that was also true of other ladies when they were sought in marriage. Some of the liaisons known to Richard were clearly temporary; others had lasted for years and might well last for life. The motive might be passionate love, or a lighter attraction, or a mutual wish to replace solitude by companionship—it varied, but then motives for marriage varied similarly. Richard found it difficult at first to regard a lady as a potential mistress, having always assumed that mistresses came from an inferior social class. But he adjusted himself.

Sophie was the daughter of a Hamburg banker. Afflicted with consumption at an early age, she had spent years in a Swiss sanatorium. She was now virtually cured, but had been warned not to return to the damp climate of the north. Inclined to be sentimental about her delicate health, Sophie maintained that she could never marry. In pensive moods, she said that she was destined to an early death, a forecast which Richard doubted.

A doctor at the sanatorium had fallen in love with Sophie, had begged her in vain to marry him, and had then begged her —not in vain—to enter into what Sophie called "marriage in the sight of Heaven." The doctor, however, really wanted a home and children, and eventually he married someone else. Sophie contracted other marriages in the sight of Heaven, one of which had brought her to Munich. She lived in a small pension conveniently near Richard's house. "Dear Richard, I have never known a man like you," she used to murmur as she awaited his kiss. He knew that she would say the same, just as sincerely, to his successor. He went on a walking trip in the Austrian Alps, and found her gone when he returned.

Tanya's father was a Russian nobleman who hated leaving his estate while her mother preferred more sophisticated parts of Europe. As a child, Tanya had trailed about from Paris to Nice and from Venice to Vienna, fed by her mother's lovers on sweets and éclairs and seduced by one of them when she reached a suitable age. A few years later—they were in Munich at the time—news came that her father had died with his wife's name on his lips. Stricken by remorse, Tanya's mother returned to Russia to devote herself to piety and good works. Tanya, unmoved by her mother's tears, stayed in Munich; she spoke German and French better than Russian and had no wish to conceal her charms in the province of Nizhni Novgorod. When she met Richard she was still young, but—her tastes shaped, probably, by her mother's lovers—she preferred older men. Sitting up in bed and munching sweets, which she still liked, she would tell him how distinguished she found his greying temples.

Richard was making the best of his ruined life, but it was always wearisome. It was empty, above all, because of the longing for Ellie which no casual affairs could begin to assuage. It was empty, too, because he had no work to do. His existence was purposeless; it was bound to be, he had foreseen it, but that made it no easier to bear. When he had sacrificed his career, he had counted on Ellie as a recompense. Many a clerk or factory-hand, no doubt, dreamed of rising when he pleased and strolling to a favourite café to pass the hours in undemanding idleness; Richard could not resign himself to it. He contributed a few articles—unsigned, of course—to *The Nineteenth Century,* whose editor was still a friend. From time to time, he thought of undertaking a major project: perhaps a contribution to political thought, perhaps a historical work or a biography. He could have books sent from England, but being unable to use an English library was a big handicap. Really, he doubted his ability. He had learned a fair amount in his life, but he had no pretensions to being a scholar. Each project that entered his mind revealed the limitations of his knowledge. However, thinking about the possibilities gave him some illusion of purpose.

He grew weary, too, of living among foreigners. He liked many of them and found their friendship rewarding, but it was always a conscious effort to adapt himself to their customs and speak their language, though his German was quite fluent by now. He remembered wryly that, on his first visit to the Continent, he had wondered how English people could stand living abroad. No wonder they clustered together and built up their own communities. This reflection gave him an idea: why not go and live in such a community? There would be an English circulating library, an English doctor if he fell ill, and above all English homes. Perhaps some of these English people would remember about the divorce, but that could not be helped. Those who chose not to receive him would not receive him: that was all. He made up his mind.

Where to go? He thought of the English settlements on the Lake of Geneva, but rejected them. Some people would remember meeting him with Geraldine—indeed, her relative might still be living at Montreux and might be a person of influence. The Riviera was a possibility, but he preferred not to live in France. He decided on Florence. The heat might be a drawback, but he could always spend the summers in Germany.

The scheme was a success. Staying initially at a hotel run by English people, Richard soon heard of a villa he could rent. It was fairly expensive by local standards, so his immediate decision to take it made an impression. English residents, including a doctor and even a clergyman, left their cards. Before long, he was a member of the community. The people were in general rather dull: retired Army or Navy officers and civil servants living on their pensions, small investors living on their dividends, attracted by the mild climate and the favourable rate of exchange. But he would find out by degrees which of them he wanted as real friends. Meanwhile, simple familiar things—tea with milk and sugar, brandy and soda—gave him a surprising degree of pleasure.

It was after he met Rhoda that Richard made Florence his home for the indefinite future. The decisive step was buying, instead of renting, a house. It was a villa with ample rooms and a deep loggia, high up on the road to Fiesole with a magnificent view and no close neighbours. Establishing himself kept Richard pleasantly busy. The stucco was cracked and the paving on the loggia was in disrepair, calling for weeks of work by not very energetic Italians. Buying and installing furniture was a delight; he couldn't imagine how he had lived for years with furniture that was not of his choice. He had an acre of land, and he devoted himself ardently to laying out a garden and finding out which flowers and shrubs would do well. Rhoda was extremely helpful with all this.

Richard was always scrupulous—with Sophie, with Tanya, and now with Rhoda—in explaining his position. He was divorced, but he couldn't marry. He could offer affection, but not love. His heart was given to a lady suffering from a serious disease. She might recover; if she did, he would go to her without hesitation. This was as much as he felt obliged to say, but he was clear that not to say it would have been dishonest.

After a time, and at the cost of a considerable effort, he told Rhoda the full truth about Ellie. Rhoda, as a mistress, was on a different footing from the others. He could not love her, but he felt a deep regard for her. She was English; the fond words and little jokes that men and women exchange in a bedroom had never come easily to him in a foreign language. She loved and missed England, as he did. On torrid afternoons in the shade of the loggia, they would talk of places in England they both knew, English sights and sounds, English trees and flowers. She was near to his own age— thirty-eight, as she told him frankly, although her unlined skin and supple figure could have deceived him. She had suffered, as he had suffered, and she was anxious to find a resting place. Richard had not lived with Sophie or Tanya, nor wanted to; but when he bought the villa, it was to make a home for Rhoda and himself.

Unlike Sophie and Tanya, Rhoda was reserved about her past. He felt that she did not belong by nature in the alternative society; this was another bond between them. But, after he told her about Ellie, she reciprocated with her own story.

With her silky auburn hair and her retroussé nose, she must have been entrancing at the age of eighteen when she visited Rome with her mother. It was all a wonderful dream, she told Richard—the antiquities, the azure sky, being abroad for the first time. At the Forum, they couldn't find an English-speaking guide. A gentleman offered, in French, to show them round. He was part of the dream, too: tall, sinuously elegant, with flashing dark eyes. The eyes caught and held Rhoda's when she ought to have been examining inscriptions. She had never been looked at like that by a man before. He presented his card. Prince Carlo Montamare—the very sound was magical. He was at their service any time, any day.

In the gardens round the Terme di Nerone, while Rhoda's mother rested from the heat, the Prince kissed her passionately. She had never been kissed before. She could find no words; her French was not very good, nor indeed was his. He burst into a flood of Italian. *"Amore, cuore, bella, bellissima"*—her mind whirled, her heart leaped.

They were engaged. Her mother wept at the prospect of Rhoda living abroad, but she was madly in love, wonderfully happy. And it was a good marriage; Rhoda's people were Herefordshire gentry, not aristocratic, not wealthy. Carlo's father owned a huge estate in the Abruzzi, a palace in Rome, a villa near Naples. Rhoda took instruction in the Catholic faith—she would have embraced voodoo, had it been necessary. Before the altar, she thought that she would swoon with joy. On the wedding night, she felt that she was giving her soul with her body.

When it was too late, she understood. It was Carlo's clever, malicious sister who told her. Carlo was over thirty; his father had threatened to stop his funds unless he married and produced an heir. He had swooped on an English girl because his reputation among good Italian families was scandalous.

The old Prince died a year later, reasonably satisfied but grumbling because Rhoda was not pregnant. By that time, Carlo and Rhoda no longer had carnal relations.

He took women wherever he could find them: peasant girls on the estate, the wives and daughters of shopkeepers in the nearby town, actresses and dancers in Rome. A month after their marriage, Rhoda saw him coming out of a maid's bedroom. When she wept, he laughed at her. He was utterly incapable of considering his wife otherwise than as one woman among all the others, to be enjoyed so long as she had the charm of novelty and then ignored.

There was nothing she could do. Italians, apparently, believed that women had to be content with their fate. Of course, there was no divorce in Italy. She had no friends— scarcely anyone to speak to except the sour old maid of a sister-in-law. The Counts and Princes of the Abruzzi had no social life of the English kind, and many of them were absentee landlords. She recoiled from distressing her parents, and doubted if they could rescue her in any case. Carlo was away half the time, in Rome or at the seaside villa. She stayed in the Abruzzi; it was a primitive and impoverished region, she discovered. Seven years of her precious youth were lost in this wretched existence.

Then an engineer, a northerner—that is, a man from the civilised world—came to survey a route for a new railway. Rhoda heard of him through servants' gossip and rode to the town at once. It was the siesta time; no one saw her as she looked in all the rooms of the miserable, dirty *albergo* until she found him. She had come to ask if the line would pass through the Montamare estate, she said. He was bewildered until their eyes met; then he grinned. When he took her on the creaking bed, she felt happiness returning to her life.

By good luck, the engineer was unmarried and had an adventurous temperament. The night after his survey was completed, he met her with two horses in a wood near the castle. She lived with him in Turin for the next three years. She never particularly liked him, but she was free, or as free as a woman in her predicament could be. They parted on good terms when he wanted to get married.

Carlo, furious, tried to use the law to force his wife to return. He was within his rights, but a Turin lawyer—a friend of the engineer—kept him at bay with delaying devices until he gave up. "Dear Rhoda: if you wish to be a whore I don't care," he wrote eventually. Naturally, he sent her no money. She lived with men—how else could she live? Richard was her fourth lover. There had been the engineer in Turin, the Argentine Consul in Genoa, and a museum curator in Florence. The Consul had returned to Argentina; the curator had been promoted to a senior position which required respectability.

Richard was moved by this story, and still more by Rhoda's telling of it. He had never heard a woman, still less an English lady, describe what her feelings had been when she gave her body to a man. Her total candour seemed to bring a profound reinforcement to their intimacy. He reached out his hand—they had been sitting on the loggia while the sun plunged into a warm, dense night—and held hers in a long moment of affectionate silence.

As for Rhoda's experiences, they illustrated for him what he took to be a law of life: a woman needs a man. It was illustrated again when he received a letter (through his bank) from Geraldine:

> *I write to inform you, before you learn of it from the newspapers, that I propose to marry again. The gentleman whom I have accepted, Mr. Horace Greig, is an American who resides in England. He is kindly and honourable, and I have every confidence that we shall be happy.*
>
> *Let me say at this time, in all sincerity, that I wish the same happiness for you. I was shocked to hear of Miss Colmore's breakdown, and I earnestly hope that she will recover and will be united with you. There is no bitterness in my heart, Richard, over the past.*
>
> *I have been grateful for the generous financial settlement which you made in my favour, and which of course will now cease. Mr. Greig is a wealthy man, with extensive industrial interests in the United States. We shall live quietly in Devonshire, where he has purchased a beautiful house overlooking the moors. I am putting the Priory on the market and should wish you to benefit*

from the sale; the bank will see to this. Berkshire House,
where I have not lived since the divorce, naturally re-
mains the property of the Somers family.

Alfred has made an excellent start at Eton, and Charles
is doing well at his preparatory school. Both, I am cer-
tain, have inherited many of your gifts.

In closing, let me repeat that I wish you nothing but
good in the years that lie ahead.

Richard was genuinely glad, for Geraldine's sake, to get the
news. He was only sorry about the Priory; he had loved the
house, and hated to think of strangers living in it. But Geraldine was being sensible, as usual.

He had his house in Florence; he had Rhoda. Geraldine
would approve of Rhoda, he thought, far more than of Sophie
or Tanya. He was living in sin, but his settled life had almost
the respectability of marriage. Among the English community, a few people didn't invite him, some invited him without Rhoda (which she didn't mind), some invited them both.
Uniform moral standards were not so easily maintained as at
home. Major A was referred to as a bachelor, or Com-
mander B as a widower, but it was known that he had an
Italian mistress conventionally disguised as a housekeeper.

This settled life would go on, he supposed, for years. He
sat on the loggia in fine weather reading *Blackwood's* or the
Cornhill. He meditated on books he might write, though he
was no nearer making a start. He watered and pruned his
shrubs. In the evenings, he played Bezique with Rhoda. Only
at night, sometimes, did he descend into the pit of suffering,
tortured by a yearning for Ellie as raw and keen as ever.

Charlotte still wrote dutifully. There was no essential
change. Ellie was calm and peaceful; she no longer had
spasms of weeping and screaming. (Richard read this with a
start, for he had never been told of such spasms.) She had

even made a kind of life for herself. She played the piano, looked after part of the garden, sewed and knitted, all quite like a sane person, or at least a sane child. One could not know, but these might be steps toward recovery. Gradual steps—it was necessary to be infinitely patient.

Richard thought of going to Germany in the summer of 1900, but decided against it. Rhoda showed little enthusiasm, and he preferred not to go without her. The rooms were cool, and there was often a breeze at this height, so the hot weather was endurable.

In October, a telegram came from Severalls. Richard's mother was dead. If he took a train at once, he could attend the funeral.

It was raining at Dover, and still raining as Richard crossed London to Paddington. All the same, it was good to be in England again. In Berkshire the rain had stopped, but it was still a grey, chilling day.

At the station, he was met by Simmons.

"Simmons—this is a pleasant surprise."

"Thank you, my lord. I trust that I see your lordship well."

"Yes, I'm well. Are you back at Severalls?"

"No, my lord, I am in service with Lord Mitcheldean."

"Lord Mitcheldean?"

"Lady Mitcheldean is your lordship's niece—Lady Elizabeth. I beg pardon; I thought that your lordship would have been informed of the marriage. Lady Mitcheldean was kind enough to suggest that I might wish to attend the funeral, particularly in view of your lordship's presence."

"I see."

"May I venture to enquire, my lord, whether there is any better news of Miss Colmore?"

"I'm afraid not, Simmons."

"Extremely distressing, my lord."

"Yes."

George was ensconced in an armchair, close to a blazing fire.

"My dear fellow, I'm so glad to see you. You must excuse my greeting you like this. Blasted rheumatism—I can hardly hobble in wet weather."

He didn't appear too badly stricken, all the same. He looked older than his years, but he always had. Perhaps, through living with his mother all this time, he had acquired the habit of constantly worrying about his health. Richard tried to repress the unkind thought.

The Duke embarked on the family news.

"Freddy's in the Guards. Enormous fellow he's grown into —big as a church steeple. Elizabeth's married. You'll meet her husband, first-rate young chap. Mary's engaged to Harry Doddington; I'm sure you remember his father. He's in South Africa with the Lancers. We're hoping he'll soon be back— the Boers seem to be thrashed at last. When they're married, that'll leave only little Vicky at home. Not for long, I daresay —she's the prettiest of the lot." George stared into the fire. "I don't look forward to their all leaving me, I can tell you. Not very cheerful living alone, is it?"

"No, it's not." Richard didn't mention Rhoda, of course.

"You know, Richard, I was expecting you to marry again."

"I haven't been fortunate."

"I never understood what went wrong between you and Geraldine. None of my business, of course. Well, there we are. Life hasn't been altogether kind to either of us."

The funeral took place next morning. Rain fell in torrents; the mourners and the Rector stood under umbrellas, shivering, their feet trapped in mud. George leaned on Freddy's arm; his face was a mask of pain.

Richard had cherished a hope that his sons would come for the funeral. The Dowager Duchess had meant very little to them, but she was their grandmother. However, they were not there.

He made an effort to behave like an uncle to his nephews and nieces, though he was really a stranger to them. Meeting a new generation of adults made him feel, more than ever, that he belonged to the past. He liked the youngest girl best, perhaps because she was scarcely more than a child. Try as he would, he couldn't like Freddy at all. Freddy was indeed enormous, standing six foot three and broad in proportion. But there was something flabby about him, suggesting inchoate mass rather than strength. He was a lazy young man; he was last down for breakfast, and one might see him lounging on a sofa at any time of the day. The sight of a young man so obsessed with comfort made Richard uneasy. When James Mitcheldean chaffed him, Freddy scowled resentfully. Besides, he seemed to be interested in nothing in particular. Any topic that Richard attempted—the Army, politics, the estate—failed to strike a spark. He wouldn't make much of his life, Richard decided.

"Will Freddy be going into Parliament?" he asked George.

"I doubt it. The fellow we've got now makes an excellent Member. It's a pity the seat had to go out of the family, but once the tradition's broken—well, it's broken."

Nevertheless, it was plain that George doted on his son. "Freddy thinks . . . Freddy says . . . Freddy likes . . ."—the phrases kept recurring. He hated losing a moment of Freddy's company; the girls smiled, as at a regular family joke, whenever he rang for a servant and asked: "Where's the Marquis?" At dinner, he smiled proudly every time Freddy made a remark. When Freddy had to return to London two days after the funeral, George was downcast. "Ah well, duty calls," he said sadly.

The Mitcheldeans left the same day, taking Simmons with them. Mary went to pay a visit to her future parents-in-law and discuss wedding plans. George was insistent that Richard should make a lengthy stay. "Dash it, you've no reason to hurry off," he said petulantly. There was indeed no reason that Richard could give. He was bored, he missed Rhoda, the huge house was gloomy, the sodden countryside was looking its worst. But, feeling sorry for George, he stayed for a fortnight.

Vicky lightened the atmosphere somewhat. She was small and dark—an inheritance from her grandmother—and really very pretty. Sixteen a few months ago, she was an eager enquirer on the threshold of life. Richard saw that he was a fascinating figure to her. She sensed that he had a story: romantic or scandalous, in any case exciting.

When the weather allowed, they went riding together. She had a natural touch on the reins and was absolutely fearless.

"You can't take that gate, Vicky. I forbid you."

"Oh, Uncle Richard, it's easy!"

And she was away; it was a delight to see her clear it. Stung by the defiance, he followed. It wasn't so easy as she imagined, but he hadn't forgotten how to manage a horse and he cleared it too. They both burst out laughing. For a moment, he was young again.

"Tell me about where you live, Uncle Richard," she said as they rode home.

He described the house and the view.

"Can I come and stay with you?"

"I doubt if your father would approve."

She smiled saucily. "I'm sure you've got a gorgeous mistress."

"I'm sure you read too many novels."

Girls were changing, he reflected. But Vicky would belong to the twentieth century.

He wrote to Charlotte, informing her that he was in England. "If I may come to Longmarsh, you know that I should be inexpressibly happy. But, as ever, I defer to your judgment. If you still consider it unwise, perhaps you would do me the honour of lunching with me in London." Charlotte answered by return; they would lunch in London.

He stayed two nights at a quiet hotel in Knightsbridge. It was strange to stay at a hotel in the city that had been his home, but there was no alternative. Charlotte came there to lunch with him. She looked distinctly older, he thought; the task that she had unquestioningly shouldered had left its mark.

There was nothing that she could tell him—nothing that he didn't know from her letters.

"But you do think that she's progressing toward recovery?"

"I don't wish to mislead you, Lord Richard. So it seems to me, but my hopes naturally incline me to think so. There have been cases of slow recovery, and also cases of sudden recovery at an unexpected moment. It is all guesswork—all mystery."

"You'll continue to consult the specialist?"

"He sees her once a year. He still makes no forecast."

Richard asked suddenly: "Do you believe in prayer, Miss Colmore?"

"I don't think so. A God who can make this happen is a God who can make it last."

"I have tried to pray. I have prayed that at least I may understand."

"That, probably, is the last thing that's ever granted to us. If we could understand everything, we ourselves should be like gods."

Richard escorted her to Waterloo. It was raining again. He had thought vaguely of going to a theatre in the evening, but he lacked the spirit.

The next day, perversely, was clear and beautiful: one of those days that, in England, persuade one that October is the best month of the year. Richard gazed out of the window of the train all the way to Dover. On the ship, he stood on deck, staring astern until the cliffs had melted into a haze. When would he see England again, he wondered? There was nothing but guesswork. No, he said to himself: there was also hope.

CHAPTER 19

His Grace

NOT LONG AFTER Richard's visit to England, Berkshire House was destroyed by fire. The circumstances were mysterious. The house was locked and shuttered, as it had been for years. Freddy had shown no desire to use it; he had a flat in one of the new blocks built by the Cadogan Estate. Nowadays, it was considered quite proper to live in a flat, even for the Marquis of Wantage.

The police believed that tramps had climbed the garden wall and forced an entry. Tramps, especially if they were drunk, had a practice of lighting a fire not in the fireplace but in the middle of a room, breaking up the furniture for fuel. If this theory was correct, the culprits had fled when their fire got out of control. At all events, the shuttered windows prevented anyone from seeing it until it had a fatal hold. By the time the alarm was raised and the fire brigade arrived, the great house was ablaze. It was a memorable sight; dinner guests in other Park Lane mansions came out to the street to watch. Nothing could be done except to keep the fire from spreading. Berkshire House was burned to the ground.

Richard was saddened by the news. He had removed very little from the house, and Geraldine probably not much more. The noble mahogany dinner table round which so many friends had gathered, the graceful Sheraton chairs in the drawing room, his library—all were reduced to ashes. Of the houses in which he had known happiness, Longmarsh was barred to him, the Priory was sold, and Berkshire House was no more.

The insurance had been arranged decades ago by the fifth Duke, Richard's grandfather. It was discovered that he had understated the value; besides, building costs had slowly but inexorably risen. The expense of replacing Berkshire House would be enormous, perhaps necessitating a mortgage on Severalls. After a while, a property company made a tempting offer for the site with a view to building a hotel. Staying in Park Lane would make an appeal to the increasing numbers of American visitors. George hated the idea, but decided in the end that he could not refuse the offer.

Every event in this period seemed to be a melancholy sequel to the nineteenth century. The death of the Queen ended what people now called the Victorian era. Her funeral echoed the pomp of the Jubilee, but in mourning instead of celebration. The war in South Africa dragged on, the Boers resorting to irregular warfare. To deprive their commandos of support and supplies, it proved necessary to herd the population into concentration camps, a measure that increased the opprobrium heaped on Britain in foreign countries.

Rhoda generally read the newspaper and gave Richard the news, as her Italian was much better than his. One morning, she gave a gasp.

"What's the matter, darling?"

She translated: "Sensational suicide of an English nobleman. The police in London have discovered the body of the Marquis of Wantage, heir of one of the greatest aristocratic families of England and an officer in the select regiment of Grenadier Guards. The Marquis, a young man of only twenty-three years, was shot in the head with a revolver in his apartment. The discovery of the weapon and other circumstances make it certain that he took his own life, although the reason remains a mystery."

"It can't be true," Richard said. "Anyway, it can't be suicide. You know what these Italian papers are like."

But when *The Times* reached Florence, it was equally positive that Freddy had killed himself. He hadn't seemed the type to fall into despair because a girl had jilted him. Yet it must be that; at least, Richard could think of no other reason.

"Do you think I should go to the funeral?" he asked Rhoda.

"It's for you to say. I imagine they would have sent a wire if they expected it."

He didn't go, but of course wrote a letter of sympathy to George. James Mitcheldean replied, explaining that the Duke was prostrated by grief and had asked his son-in-law to deal with all letters.

A phrase in James's letter—"the loss of an only son"—jolted Richard into seeing something that had not occurred to him before. If a peer died without a son, the title passed to his brother. It was an unwelcome thought. Richard hadn't the least wish to be the eighth Duke of Berkshire or the owner of Severalls. Besides, nothing could be more unsuitable than a Duke who had been the guilty party in a divorce action and who lived in sin with a married woman.

But he refused to worry about it. George was in sound health except for his rheumatism, and one didn't die of rheumatism. The Somers, barring accidents, were a long-lived race. True, George was the elder brother by eight years and must be expected to die first. However, that could well be when he was seventy-eight and Richard was seventy. Long before then, if Richard's hopes were borne out, Ellie would have recovered and would be his wife. If not, nothing else mattered.

In 1905, he was fifty. Looking back, he reflected that his

life had been marked out in illusions. At twenty, all the illusions of youth; at thirty, the illusion of marriage; at forty, the illusion of having won happiness at last. But at fifty, he still lived in hope. He would not believe that it was the ultimate illusion.

Six months later, George died. He had lived to be only fifty-eight.

Richard was astounded by the telegram. There had been no word of an illness. He stood at the door of his house in thin December sunshine, reading the words over and over again. Then he went inside to tell Rhoda.

"I'll have to attend the funeral," he said.

"Yes. Of course. I'll pack for you."

He sat in the drawing room and waited. She didn't speak, except to give a few necessary orders to the servants. And he found it difficult to speak to her; this he had never felt before.

The regular post arrived, bringing a letter from Vicky. Delayed by the unreliable Italian postal service, it was ten days old. She wrote that George had contracted a heavy winter cold, leading to a congestion of the lungs which was causing anxiety. Vicky was married now, but evidently she had gone to Severalls because of the illness.

Rhoda said: "I'll come to the station with you."

While he bought his ticket and booked a sleeping compartment, she did a little shopping for him: an English book to read, cigars, a flask of brandy in case the Channel was rough. She was calm and efficient, concealing whatever she felt. When he boarded the train, there was enough time for her to come into the compartment and say goodbye.

"It'll be cold in England, I'm afraid," she said. "Don't you catch anything, Richard."

"I'll look after myself, I promise."

Other travellers, encumbered by luggage, moved slowly along the corridor.

"I must go," she said.

He kissed her tenderly.

"Richard . . ."

"Yes, dear?"

"You will come back, won't you?"

"What an idea! Of course I'll come back."

She smiled, with an effort. Standing on the platform, she waved as the train began to move. He waved back, then watched as she turned away. She was holding a handkerchief to her eyes.

Richard stayed a night in London and completed his journey next morning in time for the funeral. The stationmaster greeted him deferentially.

"May I be the first to present my humble respects to your Grace?"

At the church, Richard shook hands with various people whom he didn't know: the Rector, the M.P. for West Berkshire, the Colonel of the Berkshire Yeomanry. All, naturally, addressed him as "your Grace." He stood bare-headed by the grave, thinking of the other funerals he had attended at the Somers family church. There would be no more, in the natural course of events, until his own.

At Severalls, the presence of three young couples gave him a sense of being the head of the family. Vicky was married to a young barrister named John Townsend; he was extremely handsome and it was obvious that they were deeply in love. There was some good-natured chaffing at the dinner table because Townsend was a strong Liberal. The House had been dissolved and Townsend was confident that his party would come in with a good majority. Richard viewed this with apprehension; the Liberals contained a dangerous admixture of Radicals and pro-Boers. However, he liked Townsend and it wasn't the occasion for serious discussion, so he contented himself with saying that a restless mood among the voters was to be expected after ten years of Conservative Government.

The day after the funeral, the estate bailiff asked to see the Duke. Three leases had to be renewed and an eviction approved. The bailiff apologized for his intrusion on family grief, but George's illness had prevented the papers from being signed at the proper time.

"You're sure this eviction is necessary?" Richard asked.

"If I may explain the circumstances, your Grace . . ." The bailiff did so at some length, apparently grateful for Richard's attention.

"Well, there seems to be no alternative."

The bailiff gathered up his papers, but lingered.

"Er . . . your Grace will be taking up residence, I trust?"

"I really don't know," Richard said. "My brother's death was a complete surprise to me, so I've made no plans."

"Quite so. Your Grace will let me know, of course? There are several matters which have been outstanding for a considerable time."

"I see. Yes, I'll let you know."

The following evening, during a game of billiards, James Mitcheldean asked: "Will you be spending Christmas here, your Grace?"

"Uncle Richard, please."

"Thank you. I was going to say that, if you decided not to spend Christmas at Severalls, Elizabeth and I would be delighted to have you as our guest at Mitcheldean."

"That's very kind of you."

Richard had intended to be back in Florence in time for Christmas. But now it would be difficult to do that without allowing the family to deduce the existence of Rhoda.

"Shall we have a brandy?" he suggested after the game. They adjourned to the small drawing room. Everyone else had gone to bed.

"The bailiff came to see me, you know. It seems that my brother rather let things slide, even before his illness."

"Very much so, I'm afraid," James said. "He lost all interest in the estate—well, he really lost all interest in life after Freddy's death. It was a shattering blow to him."

"Do you know why Freddy killed himself?"

"I gather that you don't know, Uncle Richard."

"No."

James offered cigars, and didn't answer the question until they had been pierced and lit.

"He was being blackmailed."

"Blackmailed?"

"By a Guardsman. If you understand me."

"Heavens alive! Are you sure of what you're saying?"

"I'm afraid so. A letter was found by the police: a very explicit and very unpleasant letter. I had the task of ensuring that it wasn't read out at the inquest."

"My dear James, you haven't chosen the easiest of families to marry into."

"I never liked Freddy, I have to admit. *De mortuis,* but I never did. I liked and respected Elizabeth's father. I like and respect you, Uncle Richard. Please allow me to say that, with complete sincerity."

Richard drank his brandy and refilled his glass. He had received a severe shock. But he was grateful for James's words.

"I have to decide whether to live at Severalls," he said. "It's not easy. I never expected to inherit the title. I'm not a young man, and I'm settled into my quiet way of living."

"I can't presume to advise you. I can only say that the estate and the county . . . It's hard to imagine Berkshire without a Duke."

"More brandy?"

"Thank you."

"These are first-rate cigars."

"I'm glad you like them."

There was a silence, invested with a significance to which everything in the room contributed: the aroma of old brandy, the aroma of first-rate cigars, the deep leather armchairs, the flames licking an oak log.

James said: "There is something . . . Perhaps it isn't for a younger man to speak of this. It ought to be said, however. You should not be deterred, Uncle Richard, by past events in your private life. Believe me, you will command the liking and respect of many others as well as me. Time does make a difference; it's ten years, isn't it? What counts, surely, is your position and your acceptance of the responsibilities attaching to it. Dash it, His Majesty's past doesn't bear very close examination. He is the King, nevertheless. You are the Duke of Berkshire—there can be no other. That's how it seems to me. Forgive me if I've spoken too freely."

"No, indeed. I'm greatly obliged to you, James. Well, I shall have to think it over."

Richard accepted the Mitcheldeans' invitation for Christmas, writing to Rhoda that he had felt unable to decline it. The young couples dispersed. For a week, he was alone in the enormous house.

Curiously, he didn't feel lonely. The family portraits, the chandeliers and the grandfather clocks, the guns in their rack, the dozens of things (from fire-irons to decanters) that had been in use for decades—all these provided a kind of company. One had to reach a certain age to feel that, he reflected. He spent the evenings mainly in the library. Nobody had taken an interest in it for a long time; it was the third Duke who had been a collector in an eighteenth-century way, chiefly of fine editions of the classics. By building on this foundation and buying judiciously it would be possible, Richard thought, to create a really good private library.

Two or three of the local landed gentry, and also the

Rector, called to wish his Grace a merry Christmas. The Rector was disappointed that Richard would not be attending the carol service or reading the lesson on Christmas Day. "Next year, I trust." Clearly, people were assuming that he would live at Severalls.

The weather was crisp and clear. Richard rode for an hour or two every day, consulting the head groom about the horses and trying out three of them. The man was delighted; the horses were standing idle, he said, except when the young ladies and gentlemen came to visit. At certain moments, in familiar places, Richard was overcome by a remembered sense of the beauty of the English countryside. How could he leave it again, he wondered? How could he have borne to live away from it for so many years? A man, ultimately, had to be where he belonged. The thought of living the rest of his life on English soil, under English skies, gave him a deep feeling of contentment.

He had not felt like this the last time he had been at Severalls, riding with Vicky. But he had been a visitor then; now, if he chose, he was coming home. These fields and woods were his own. Wasn't that the farm where the tenant was to be evicted? It did look badly neglected. Wasn't that the wood where old trees were rotting, so that the bailiff wanted to clear-fell and replant? He rode round it slowly, considering the question.

It seemed to him—more and more every day—that, although he hadn't wanted this inheritance, he now had no right to renounce it. James had hit the nail on the head: inescapably, he was the Duke. That fact overshadowed his character as a man, his fortunes and misfortunes, his inclinations. Born a Somers, he stood for traditions and obligations that were intrinsic to his conception of England. He had flouted certain standards of conduct, but here was one that he could not reject. There had been eccentric Dukes, tyrannical and detested Dukes, scandalously licentious Dukes; but there had never been a Duke who refused to be a Duke.

Then, he was only a link in the inheritance. If Severalls belonged to him, it also belonged to his sons. Alfred and Charles were almost men by now; they had been brought up by Geraldine and her husband, of course, but surely Geraldine would no longer object to their seeing their father. He could welcome them to Severalls; he was scarcely likely to see them in Florence. He would transmit to them the tradition that he embodied. If he was inescapably the Duke of Berkshire, Alfred was inescapably the Marquis of Wantage.

He would be a good Duke—he was confident of that. He had energy, the will to make decisions, and sound health. It wasn't the same as being Foreign Secretary; he would not make history; but he would have work to do, responsibility, purpose. He felt a lift of the heart at the regaining of so much that he had thought lost for ever. He would take his seat in the Lords and perhaps speak in debate, though there he must tread warily and test the atmosphere. With the ending of his exile, Richard had a warming sense of re-entering the stream of English life.

As he moved toward making up his mind, he thought constantly of Ellie. Logically, so long as he couldn't see her and so long as her shattered mind remained oblivious of his devotion, it didn't matter whether he was at Severalls or Florence or Fiji. Yet he could not help feeling that they were brought together by sharing the same sunshine and rain, the English summer and the English winter. The idea of homecoming— the end of his wanderings—associated itself with an end to his trials and sufferings. Surely his love too would enter upon its inheritance. Surely Ellie would sense, if she couldn't consciously know, that he was waiting for her nearby, offering her not flight and concealment but a secure and lasting English home. These thoughts were irrational, but not the less potent. The more cheerful he felt about living at Severalls, the more confidently he imagined living there with his always promised wife.

It was the thought of Rhoda, of course, that made him hesitate through the week. A distressing thought. He believed in loyalty; yet, for the second time in his life, he was preparing to desert a woman who had devoted herself to him. He couldn't do it without feelings of pity, of uncertainty and—it had to be faced—of guilt.

He could make out a solid case in his defence. Rhoda had always known about Ellie. She had known that Richard could not give her his heart nor the central position in his life, nor could he marry her even if she herself became free. But what had been stated at the outset had never been repeated. It was buried in a recess of her mind, probably, under thousands of kisses and tender words, under the habits and assumptions engendered by years of living together. In Rhoda's eyes, Ellie was a part of his past. Rhoda probably didn't believe that Ellie would ever recover—it took faith and love to believe that, Richard supposed. So she counted on his staying with her; she thought of herself as his wife. And, as truly as Geraldine, she had been a good wife.

It was hard, he knew, for Rhoda to be discarded yet again. She was unlikely to acquire a new lover. Italian men cared only for youth, she had once remarked; she'd been lucky, at thirty-eight, to find an Englishman. Of course, no such thing would be necessary for financial reasons. Richard would see to that. But money was no remedy for loneliness.

He had to steel his heart. Rhoda simply did not come first, when all was said and done. He would have to tell her as gently as he could. The easy course would be to write a letter, but it would be cowardly and dishonourable; literally at least, he must keep his promise to come back.

Once he had made up his mind, he was sorry that he had

deprived Rhoda of a last Christmas with him. However, he
was committed to James and Elizabeth. He went to Mitcheldean when he was expected. With children enjoying their
presents, James carving a magnificent turkey, and the local
hunt meeting on Boxing Day, it was a traditional English
Christmas. Simmons presided with dignity over the staff. He
was to retire from service in another year and had been
promised a cottage on the estate. Richard was sorry; he had
thought of bringing Simmons back to Severalls.

He was pressed to stay longer, but decided to be with
Rhoda for New Year's Eve. Italy, as sometimes happens in
winter, was colder than England. Snow, whirling down from
the Alps, threw a disguise over the landscape. The train
reached Florence two hours late, but Rhoda was waiting at
the station.

They were invited to see in the New Year by a certain
Colonel Clark. Getting to his house and back over icy roads
was unpleasant; Richard would have preferred to be alone
with Rhoda. He didn't enjoy the company—the over-hearty
Colonel, who had served in the Indian Engineers and was
scarcely a gentleman; his sullen Italian mistress with her
broken English; a retired civil servant who told boring stories
in laborious detail; and the latter's wife (if she was his wife),
a blowsy Irishwoman given to risqué remarks and shrill bursts
of laughter. Already Richard had moved away from these
people, whom he had found tolerable for years.

Next day, he tried to be cheerful despite a headache. Rhoda
was quiet and pensive. She had chilblains and a snuffling cold;
she always suffered in a bad winter. He found himself noticing
her dry lips and the crows' feet round her eyes. For the last
couple of years, she had looked fully her age. He told her
something about Christmas at Mitcheldean, but didn't like to
stress its pleasures. Confined to the house by the bad weather,
they passed the hours uneasily.

That night, he took her in a sudden burst of indefinable emotion: perhaps affection, perhaps pity, perhaps regret for lost youth. She clung to him with a kind of desperation; he had to loosen her hands when he had finished. Then she buried her face in the pillow and wept.

"What is it, darling?"

She sat up and stared at him.

"It's the end, isn't it?"

"My dear, you're overwrought . . ."

"Why not say it? D'you imagine I don't know?"

"We'll talk in the morning, Rhoda."

"Say it now. Why not?"

He said what had to be said. She wept again, her body heaving and shuddering. He tried to embrace her and give her comfort, but she pushed him away. Finally, she fell into an exhausted sleep.

When he woke in the morning, she was already up. She kissed him on the cheek when he appeared for breakfast.

"I'm sorry I lost control of myself last night, Richard."

"My dear, I know what you must be feeling. It was wrong to speak of it at that time. Let me try to explain . . ."

"There's no need, really. I quite understand."

The maid poured the coffee.

"I have one request to make, Richard."

"Please tell me."

"Would you go soon? As soon as you can pack your belongings. It would be best, believe me."

Guiltily, he felt a spasm of relief.

"If you think so . . ."

"I do think so."

When everything was done, they stood on the loggia and gazed at the familiar view. The snow was melting, the sunlight filtering through high white clouds.

"I shall never forget this place, Rhoda. I shall never forget you."

"We have been happy here, haven't we?"

"The house will be yours, of course."

"No, Richard. I don't want to live here without you."

"Well, it will be yours to dispose of, anyway. And you will have an income. I'll make arrangements."

She managed a smile. "I must say that's more than any of the others did."

"Why don't you return to England, Rhoda? It's your country, after all."

"Perhaps, some day. I'd rather return as a widow. Women in an ambiguous position don't do very well in England, do they? Carlo's health is ruined, I've heard. No wonder, after the life he's led."

He saw what she had been waiting for.

"Is there better news of Ellie?" she asked.

"There are grounds for hope."

"I'm very glad, Richard."

She remained calm until his train left. There were no tears this time; she waved from the platform, transmitting nothing but good wishes. The last he saw of her was a small, brave figure walking briskly back to the barrier.

At Dover, he stepped ashore jauntily. He was home at last. One could never tell, but he knew of no reason why he should ever leave England again.

The next few weeks were busy for the new Duke. He worked in his study every morning, getting to grips with the art of estate management. Decisions awaited him, but he was determined not to make them until he had a thorough knowledge of the problems. He could scarcely find time for a daily ride, or for going out with a gun and a dog for a little rough shooting.

At the request of the Conservative committee, he took the chair at an election meeting. Political passions seemed to be running high, even in the small towns of Berkshire. As he emerged from the hall, a gang of young louts booed and one of them shouted: "Down with the idle rich!" The cry had its amusing aspect, Richard reflected. The seat was held easily, as usual, but the Liberals won the election with a landslide.

Imperceptibly, the weeks turned into months. As James had predicted, the old scandal didn't prevent the Duke from assuming his proper social position. The secretary of his old club wrote to ask whether he wished to resume his membership. Richard accepted; presumably the secretary had taken soundings and he wouldn't be blackballed. After he was elected, he went to London and stayed at the club. Old friends greeted him warmly. He received invitations to spend weekends at the great country houses—some of them, at least. Certain families held aloof, perhaps because their principles were immutable, perhaps because the lady had been a particular friend of Geraldine's. Richard didn't mind; but when he had an invitation, he felt that acceptance was both courteous and wise. In any case, he enjoyed the weekends. He had always enjoyed weekends.

He thought often of his sons. According to Elizabeth, who was vaguely in touch with her cousins, Alfred was in his second year at Oxford and Charles in his last year at Eton. Oxford and Eton—no distance at all! Richard wondered whether he should write to them or whether it would be more correct to write to Geraldine first. While he was trying to make up his mind, Alfred wrote. Could he come and pay his respects, now that he had a father within reach? The letter was written with a certain social grace and not without a touch of humour; evidently Alfred appreciated the oddity of the situation.

Next to being reunited with Ellie, there could have been no better news for Richard. He replied at once, inviting Alfred to spend as much as he liked of the Easter vacation at Severalls.

CHAPTER 20

The Death
of the Heart

Looking up from an early edition of Pope's Homer, Alfred asked: "Well, Father, how does it feel to be Duke of Berkshire?"

"I think I'm getting used to it," Richard said.

"You are? I'm having difficulty with being Marquis of Wantage. I'm afraid it doesn't really suit me."

Richard thought, though he didn't say so, that it suited Alfred very well. The young man's bearing was authentically aristocratic: not haughty—far from that—but indicative of natural excellence, aristocratic in the true Greek sense of being the best. He was also a remarkably good-looking young man, with the best of both the Somers and the Hutchison features, notably Geraldine's fine dark-brown eyes.

"This is a splendid library, Father."

"It is, isn't it? I hope to add to it. You're fond of books?"

"I decided to read English at Oxford."

"I knew nothing about books when I was your age. A brainless cavalry subaltern. Do paintings interest you?"

"Very much."

"I'll show you the gallery."

It was the beginning of giving Alfred his inheritance.

"That's a Romney. It's Lady Hester Somers, a daughter of

the third Duke. She was considered one of the great beauties of her time."

"The family has produced quite a number of beauties, apparently."

"Either produced them or married them. That's your grandmother—my mother."

"She was lovely."

"Exquisite, as a young woman. Always in bad health, unfortunately. That's your great-grandfather, the fifth Duke. He fought in the Peninsula. Here's your grandmother again. She was painted several times."

"It's a pity she didn't live in Romney's time."

"This one is by Watts. But I daresay you don't care much for Victorian artists."

The inspection of the gallery developed into a tour of the house. It really was like a museum, as Richard had always thought. But Alfred seemed to take a genuine interest. He said at lunch: "It's a magnificent place."

"Of its kind, yes," Richard said. "You're not obliged to like it, you know. A place this size—it's difficult to give it the feeling of a home. I didn't like it at all when I was younger, but now I find that I do. I suppose it's a matter of age; it's not a young man's house."

"Oh, I like it. There's a joy in space. I have a habit of walking about when I'm trying to think. Rooms at Balliol don't provide much opportunity for that."

"And what else do you do at Oxford, besides reading English?"

"Not very much else."

"I mean, d'you row? Or play cricket?" Alfred was tall and well built, with the arms and shoulders of a good fast bowler. But somehow he didn't look like an athlete; there was grace rather than power in his movements.

"Nothing like that," he said, smiling. "I write poetry."

"Poetry? Do you really? By Jove, that's a new departure in the family."

"I hope you approve. I don't think Mother altogether approves."

"I fancy that disapproval wouldn't deter you."

"No, it wouldn't."

That appeared to close the subject. Richard said: "Tell me about your mother. I know nothing about the kind of life she leads."

"Oh, she's quite a figure in Devon. Charities, committees, improvement of amenities, preservation of the countryside— all that kind of thing."

"She was always a very active person."

"She's certainly that. My stepfather is quite different. She tries to get him onto the committees, but he says that it wouldn't be suitable because he isn't British. He cultivates his garden, both metaphorically and literally."

"I thought he was a captain of industry."

"No, he's just rich. It was his father who made the money, I suspect by not very scrupulous methods. Mr. Greig attends a board meeting once a year in New York, draws his income, and otherwise prefers not to think about it. He's a very nice man. Although"—Alfred hesitated—"I feel that you must have been a much more suitable husband for my mother."

"But she's happy with Mr. Greig, I trust?"

"Contented, I should say. How many people are positively happy? Happiness is the rarest of conditions, wouldn't you agree, Father?"

"Yes, alas, that is true." But it was a singular remark from a young man, Richard thought. At Alfred's age, he had believed implicitly in happiness.

"And Charles?" he asked. "Does he write poetry too?"

Alfred laughed. "Charles disapproves completely. We get along very well, but we haven't much in common. Charles considers me frivolous, I'm afraid. He's a very serious person."

"At eighteen?"

"He has always been serious. His interests are different from mine, too. He intends to take a science degree at Cambridge."

Alfred stayed for a week, then went to Devon for the rest of the vacation. Richard grew fonder of him every day, but wasn't quite sure what to make of him. He gave an impression of gentleness, of reluctance to impose his will on the external world—very much like a poet, Richard supposed. He never had any plans for the day and was content to do whatever Richard suggested, almost like a girl. Yet, with the gentleness, there was a quality of absolute assurance. When he stated an opinion, though his manner was quiet and even tentative, Richard saw that he had thought it out and would not be moved from it. He had a kind of strength that was unlike his father's or his mother's, but was strength nevertheless.

Ambitious, apparently, he was not. Writing poetry seemed to mean a great deal to him, and reputation as a poet very little. Richard couldn't imagine him in public life; his comments on political questions were perceptive but detached. He had no plans—had made none, even before becoming the heir to a dukedom—to pursue any career. Yet the words that had applied to Freddy—words like idle, aimless, apathetic—were the very last that could be used to describe Alfred. He was sure of what he was; the question of what he might become, therefore, didn't arise. A most remarkable young man, for twenty years old.

The countryside was a delight, coming to life in a sunny, breezy English spring—a sight that Richard hadn't seen for eleven years. Father and son walked for miles along the lanes and across the meadows. Alfred sat a horse capably, but preferred walking to riding.

One day, they climbed a hill that commanded a view

sweeping down to the Thames. England showed itself at its best, fresh and green under a sky of pale blue and scudding clouds. They stopped for a smoke—Richard a cigar, Alfred a cigarette.

"It's beautiful here," Alfred said.

"Indeed, yes. Happiness is rare, you said rightly. But you must admit that this is the setting for it."

"Yes . . . Father, why is it that you didn't marry again after the divorce?"

"Has your mother told you nothing about that?"

"It's always been understood that we ask no questions—Charles and I. She never speaks of you. Of course, that's because of feelings that remain."

"You know that there was someone else—a woman I loved."

"I don't know it; I assume it."

"Well, I'll tell you."

The essential facts could have been stated in a few sentences. But Richard found himself going through the whole story in detail, trying to make Alfred see each event as it had appeared at the time: his courtship of Ellie, the broken engagement, the good intentions of his misguided marriage, the fatal meeting at Karlsruhe, the decision and the promise made on the Downs above Farnham, the waiting in Paris, the dreadful news given by Charlotte. Living again through the emotions that he evoked describing his hopes and illusions, confessing his failures of understanding, he had the feeling of creating a bond between himself and his son—between two men.

Alfred listened without an interruption or a question, and at the end he was silent for a full minute. Then he said: "It's terrible. And it's beautiful."

Richard said nothing.

"It's a poem."

"It happened, Alfred."

"Yes. The greatest poems are lived."

Alfred turned to look at his father and asked: "This dementia praecox—what is it?"

"How can one say? Doctors always have labels, but they explain nothing."

"You still hope, Father, don't you?"

"I do hope, indeed. Her sister says there are good signs; sometimes she talks quite rationally of everyday matters. There have been cases of sudden recovery, like the emergence from a hypnotic trance. And then, it's natural to hope—or natural for me."

"You must always hope," Alfred said with sudden intensity.

"I shall. Ceasing to hope is something I can't really imagine. It would mean ceasing to love Ellie, and that's an impossibility."

"Father, have you a picture of her?"

"I keep one by my bed. You shall see it. Let's go back home."

Alfred gazed at the photograph as he had gazed at the Romney.

"Was this taken when you were engaged?"

"Yes."

"I think I should have fallen in love with her, too."

"You haven't fallen in love yet, have you?"

"It's not encouraged at Oxford. I believe I'm already in love with an ideal. The woman comes along and is identified with the ideal—that's my theory. The colour of her hair and so forth isn't important."

"Ellie's hair is golden and her eyes are blue. You have to imagine that when you look at the photograph."

"Her hair may not be golden now, Father," Alfred said gently.

"What? D'you know, that's never occurred to me. But I'm sure it is. It sounds ridiculous, but I'm sure."

When Richard was alone he thought of Ellie almost all the time, from the moment that he woke and saw her photograph until he fell asleep. Yet, while he longed for her as much as ever, he no longer felt the impatience of years ago. Perhaps, through years of waiting, he had learned to wait; perhaps the hopes of her recovery created a kind of tranquillity. Above all, he was in a place where she had been. Though she had spent only a month at Severalls and hadn't liked it, she had planted memories here. Her face across the dinner table, her white-clothed form walking in the garden, her eyes turned toward a familiar view—these were realities. In a certain sense, Richard was living with her now.

A letter came from Geraldine. "I am glad that you are living at Severalls," she wrote. "It must surely be more congenial to you than residing abroad." She was glad, too, that the boys—"I ought to say the young men"—should be able to know their father. Accordingly, both Alfred and Charles came for a week in August.

Charles was as tall as Alfred but more sturdily built, on the lines of Richard's father. He was, as Alfred had said, a serious person. Richard was even less equipped to discuss physics than to discuss poetry, so he found little common ground with his younger son—except that Charles was a keen cricketer and had kept wicket in the First Eleven. The fact that he had been only seven at the time of the divorce, while Alfred had been a precocious nine, made a difference. He had difficulty in addressing Richard as "Father"; the relationship wasn't natural to him, as it was to Alfred. Richard saw that he must not expect to be on close terms with Charles. Still, he was proud of both his sons.

In the autumn and the winter, Alfred came to Severalls about once a month, either for a weekend or simply for a day. Charles didn't come; the distance from Cambridge provided sufficient reason. Gratifyingly, Alfred really enjoyed being with his father. He regarded Richard not as a figure of authority but as a friend of mature years—rather as Richard, when he was a young M.P., had regarded Sir Alfred Hutchison. Once, Alfred asked if he might bring a couple of other undergraduates. They arrived on bicycles, much to Richard's surprise. Alfred's friends were quiet, intelligent and self-assured, as he was. They were interested in poetry, in philosophy, and very faintly in politics. Alfred, so Richard gathered, was the accepted though unassertive leader of a certain set at Balliol. One of the young men said that he was sure to get a brilliant First.

His character still held surprises for Richard. It was his nature, evidently, to contain paradoxes and complexities without any sense of strain. For instance, he was unimpressed by material achievements. A civilisation was judged by its thinkers and artists, he said, not by its steelworks. On the other hand, he was intrigued by mechanical devices. He used a cigarette-lighter instead of matches and was quite upset when it failed to work. When Richard asked what he wanted for his twenty-first birthday, he said that it was his dream to own a motor-car. Richard made enquiries and bought a Rolls-Royce, which was said to be the best make. On his visits, Alfred spent hours tinkering with the engine or driving along the country roads. So far as Richard could make out, he regarded machines as fascinating toys—things of no serious importance, but a source of pleasure.

Then again, he made jokes about dons who were so absorbed in pedantic scholarship that they had never learned to live, but it was clear that the values of Oxford had a hold on him. In the spring of 1907, he said that he wouldn't be able to come to Severalls again until after his finals. He had neglected his studies to write poetry, and now he must put his nose to the grindstone. Getting a First, Richard saw, really meant a great deal to him.

He promised to come for a weekend in June, at the first opportunity after the examinations. On the Saturday, he arrived
on his bicycle just in time for lunch.

"Ah, there you are, my dear boy. You must be famished."

"Parched rather than famished, Father." A sudden heat-
wave had marked the onset of summer.

"Hawkins, a hock and seltzer for the Marquis. Well, the
ordeal is over, what?"

"It's over."

"What were the papers like?"

"I've done well," Alfred said calmly.

Lunch was served—cold salmon and cold roast beef, in view
of the weather. Richard wanted to ask what Alfred's plans
for the summer were, and whether he could make a long
stay at Severalls. But it didn't seem right to press this yet. The
weekend, at least, stretched comfortably ahead.

The telephone rang. The butler came in from the hall and
said: "Miss Colmore wishes to speak to your Grace."

Ellie? That would be a miracle—yet it was in a miracle that
Richard had always believed. However, it was probably
Charlotte.

It was Charlotte.

"Could you please come to Longmarsh at once?"

"What's happened?"

"I'll explain—not on the telephone. If you could manage to
come . . ."

"Of course. I'll start this moment."

Alfred said: "I'll drive you in the motor."

Richard hesitated. It was probably fifty miles by the most
direct route. They were unlikely to make the journey without
mechanical trouble or a puncture. But Alfred would be able
to make the repairs. Otherwise, a train to Paddington, crossing
London, another train—no, the motor would be better.

The sun glared at them as they went south, and clouds of

white dust rose from the chalk roads. Alfred drove intently, his eyes narrowed. They didn't speak, and Richard didn't dare to think.

There were no breakdowns, and they reached Longmarsh in less than two hours. Richard was seized by a tremulous joy as he directed Alfred past the lodge, past the lake, up the rise to the house. Whatever awaited him, he was here.

"I'll wait outside," Alfred said.

Charlotte was in the drawing room with a man in dark clothes. Richard realised that he was a doctor. He looked more agitated than Charlotte, who was keeping an iron control of herself.

"May I present Dr. Sargent? The Duke of Berkshire. Doctor, I think you had better describe what has happened."

Ellie's lifeless body had been found in the lake. Hampered by her dress, and by reeds which grew densely at that point, she must have been unable to struggle. Some time, probably, had passed before the lodge-keeper had seen her. Efforts at resuscitation had been made, but in vain.

Richard felt his whole world of faith and hope falling apart. He forced himself to realise that Charlotte was speaking.

It wasn't unusual for Ellie to walk by the lake, she said. The water level had fallen in the dry weather, exposing soft mud. It was possible to slip. No one could know; no one would ever know.

"Let me see her," Richard said.

She was lying on the sofa in the music-room. Charlotte had removed her wet clothes and dressed her in a simple white shift. Her bare arms were crossed over her body, like those of a sleeping child.

Her hair was golden as ever. Richard hadn't seen it unpinned since her childhood; at full length, it adorned her like a frame of sunlight. Her face, scarcely lined, showed nothing but innocence and tranquillity. All doubt, all striving and all suffering had been taken from her now. As at the first, she offered him her pure unclouded beauty.

He knelt down and kissed her cold lips. It seemed to him that she was not utterly delivered to death until after this parting. In the kiss, in the last sacrament of his devotion, they were not divided.

He never knew how long he stayed with Ellie. In one sense, perhaps ten or fifteen minutes. In another sense, a lifetime— the course of a marriage that he had lived only in his heart.

He was disturbed by a sound that was as final, as deadening, as any that he had ever heard. Charlotte was closing the keyboard of the piano.

"It is all over, Richard," she said. It was the first time that she had called him simply by his name.

"Yes," he answered, "I know." He got to his feet and followed her out of the room, closing the door quietly.

"You will stay here a few days?" she said. Until the funeral, she meant, but didn't say so outright.

"Thank you. May my son stay too?"

"That's your son, in the motor? Yes, of course."

Richard walked through the garden and down to the lake. He didn't go to the place where Ellie had drowned; nothing was to be gained by inflicting that on himself. He stood where he had clasped her hand and spoken to her of love.

"This I must say: whatever your answer may be, I can never love you the less, I can never love anyone else, I shall love you till the day I die."

He saw her glancing up at him and down again, drawing her hand away, and running from him along the path to the house. She was as real to him, as beautiful and as beloved, as on that other hot summer day. And yet, he saw her as a phantom—always eluding him, granting him only the illusion of hope, the illusion of possession. On that day, at the moment when he had counted on holding her in his arms, he had

found himself staring at the turn of the path past the rhododendrons where she had disappeared. Now the illusions were
at an end. The phantom was gone from him for ever.

Twice in his life, after the broken engagement and after the
waiting in Paris, the loss of the phantom had plunged him
into wild and frantic despair. That could not seize him now.
Despair had been a product of hope, of unavailing struggle.
Now there was no hope. A terrible and irrevocable regret: a
grief beyond utterance and without limit: these had closed
upon him and would remain until his own death. But he felt
them as a cold, still emptiness.

The emptiness was within him—deep within him, as deep
as love. The passion that had ruled his life, wrenching it this
way and that, destroying it as most people would say: this
passion was dead, dead with Ellie. He had known all the
emotions to which man was open. Love, hope, joy at times,
the vision of true happiness; longing, fear, despair, utter
misery—these had exalted him and tormented him, in all
their power and their frenzy. He would feel none of them
again. His mind and his body lived on, functioning as they
had functioned yesterday, and might live on—not that he
cared—for years or decades. It was his heart that was dead.

He was aware of an unfamiliar sense of resignation, a
strange kind of peace. A peace without inspiration or beauty,
without understanding or wisdom. But peace, nevertheless.

The sun was still hot, the long June day far from ended. It
surprised him that so little time had passed, when the world
had been transformed for him. After a while, he heard a foot-
step. It was Alfred.

"Was Miss Colmore wondering where I'd gone?"

"No. I wanted to be with you. But if you wish to go back
to the house . . . the undertaker has called."

"I see."

"Is this where she died, Father?"

"No. Over there—you can see the reeds." Richard paused, then said: "This is where I proposed to her."

"A perfect place."

"I did think it was the right setting. But she didn't accept me then. I told you about that."

"Yes, Father."

"I told her that I'd always love her, whatever happened."

"Yes."

Richard gazed across the still surface of the lake.

"And if I had foreseen that she would never be my wife— if I'd had the power to choose, which God knows I never had—then I should have chosen to love her, all the same."

It was strange to be staying at Longmarsh after all these years—twenty-five years, the period that for other men had divided a marriage from a silver wedding. Richard was very glad of Alfred's presence. Without the young man, he and Charlotte would have been obliged to speak of the past or to spend the evening in silence. Tactful beyond his years, speaking enough and not too much, Alfred sustained a conversation about the history and architecture of Longmarsh. So he continued, a source of unobtrusive strength, up to the day of the funeral.

The family gathered, and the house took on a semblance of its old life. However, the Colmore family wasn't what it had been. Celia had been dead for three years, a fact that Richard hadn't known. Fanny no longer travelled. Anne and her Navy husband were in Shanghai with the China squadron. Robert, the clergyman, had many duties and came only for the day of the funeral. Only Arthur and Thomas, with their wives, stayed at Longmarsh.

Robert avoided shaking hands with Richard—the sinner, the seducer—and stood beside the grave with his eyes cast up to Heaven and his lips moving in muttered prayer. Arthur, however, spoke to Richard as if nothing had happened to interrupt their friendship. He walked with an old man's stoop, though he was still under sixty. To Charlotte, he said: "I've never understood this ghastly business—the less said about it, the better."

After dinner, as the port went round, Richard said: "When I first came here, I thought that Longmarsh was everything that an English country house ought to be."

"Yes." Arthur sipped reflectively. "It's a fine old place, isn't it? Grace and I may come to live here. Charlotte tells me that she'd be happy with a smaller house."

"I suppose you could go up to town every day quite easily."

"I may decide to take my pension. I've been Permanent Head for five years; there's nothing after that. And I don't find myself altogether in sympathy with Grey. I've dodged being the Earl ever since my father died; perhaps I shouldn't dodge it any longer. Charlotte has done wonders with the estate, but the tenants like to deal with a man."

"It's satisfying work, an estate," Richard said. "I didn't expect to find it so, but I have."

"I've no doubt. What's your view of it, young man? Are you thinking of going into politics like your father?"

"I'm afraid that doesn't attract me, Lord Farnham," Alfred said.

"Pity. The promising young fellows all seem to be Liberals these days. Your father was very highly thought of when he was in the Commons, you know. He was tipped to be Foreign Secretary—did you know that?'

"No, I never knew that. It doesn't surprise me, however."

"It could have made a deal of difference. Well, it was not to be. Life's full of upsets."

Richard decided to return to Severalls by train, leaving Alfred to take the motor-car. He left his valise at the station and walked to the church. Ellie's grave looked very new. The flowers, refreshed by a shower, had not begun to fade. He knelt, though not in prayer; the time for that was gone, if there had ever been a time. He was kneeling in farewell, as he had knelt in the music-room.

Celia's grave, by comparison, had lost its raw and recent look. Richard thought of what he knew of her, of what would not be remembered. Time, neither cruel nor kind but impassive, was doing its work.

CHAPTER 21

Before the War

LATER, it would be called the Edwardian period. It would also be designated, from the far side of a terrible chasm, by the adjective "pre-war." It would appear as an age of comfort, elegance and pleasure, something like the Regency a century earlier. The hot tranquil summers would be remembered, the shooting parties and the race meetings, the delectable women in their huge flower-trimmed hats. A time when, until the sudden fall of the curtain, life was carefree and secure.

To live through, it was not like that. The old certainties and the old harmonies were gone. Each year brought changes, unexpected questions and challenges, conflicts of uncompromising ferocity. Even the hours of pleasure had a quality unknown in the nineteenth century: voracious, hectic, brittle —as if every moment counted.

DUKE'S NIECE ARRESTED. Lady Victoria Townsend, niece of the Duke of Berkshire, was among those taken into custody during an attempt by suffragettes to break into the House of Commons.

Vicky was charged with assaulting a policeman; he showed his bandaged hand in court and she didn't deny having bitten him. Refusing to pay her fine, she stayed in prison for a month.

Richard was profoundly shocked. He could scarcely believe

that women of any type or class were behaving like this, let alone ladies. Little Vicky—so sweet and charming, such an adornment at a dinner table, such a pretty girl, though now a wife and mother. What did Townsend think of his wife battling in an unseemly rough-house, being frogmarched along the street for anyone to see, and then serving a prison sentence like a common criminal? He could have paid the fine, even if she wouldn't. Perhaps he didn't wish to frustrate her yearnings for martyrdom. Richard ceased to invite the Townsends to Severalls. This wasn't exactly to show his disapproval, although as a member of the House of Lords and the senior Conservative in the county he did have a certain responsibility. It was more because he felt, sadly, that he and the suffragettes were not living in the same world.

To judge by their speeches, they were unable to see why men resisted giving women the vote. With rare exceptions, however, men did resist it—even the Liberal Ministers, even Radicals like Lloyd George. This seemed to Richard altogether natural. It was not a matter of justice, as the suffragettes claimed. It was a matter of one's conception of womanhood.

He found that Janet, although she was herself no suffragette, also couldn't see this. Janet Willis was the young lady whom Alfred brought to Severalls, and whom he would marry in time. Richard liked her very much, so he was sorry to differ from her. Probably he didn't understand the women of the twentieth century. For a lover of women, this was a melancholy thought.

"I don't see why women shouldn't have it if they want it," Janet said. "It doesn't matter to me; I don't expect I'd vote anyway. But since there are women to whom it does matter, why not give it to them?"

"Because it would promote conflict between men and women," Richard explained. "If a woman can vote, presumably a woman can be a candidate. In a keenly contested election a candidate attacks his opponent—tries to make him look ridiculous, if possible. Is a man to do that to a lady? And what about debates in the House? They get pretty warm, I can tell you. I've shouted: 'Withdraw, sir! Sit down! Resign! Disgraceful, sir!' I shouldn't fancy shouting: 'Disgraceful, madam!' No—to be serious, a man has certain feelings toward ladies, ranging from courtesy and respect to affection. They don't, or shouldn't, include hostility."

"Can't one conduct public life without hostility?" Janet asked.

"Not without argument, to say the least. A man—I speak for myself—a man doesn't wish to argue with ladies."

"But you're arguing with me now."

"I was answering a question."

Janet and Alfred both smiled.

"I don't like arguing with men, really," Janet said. "But that's because they're always sure they're right."

It dragged on all through these years—this angry, often violent, often hysterical campaign for women's suffrage. When the police had to strike women demonstrators, and when women in prison had to be forcibly fed, Richard felt a painful revulsion. It was more than regrettable—it was unnatural. But it had to be done; ultimately, what was most contrary to nature was the demand of these women.

Nor was it the only conflict. There was a new bitterness between the labouring classes and their employers. Strikes and lockouts took on the ferocity of tribal wars; men who stayed at work were assaulted by their neighbours; the police were hard put to it to maintain law and order, and troops had to be sent to pacify a Welsh mining valley.

The Government proposed to bring in a scheme to pay men from public funds when they were not working—to encourage idleness. Meanwhile, vindictive taxes were imposed on landed property and on the rights of inheritance. The Budget was contested in the Commons for eight months and then rejected by the Lords. This had never happened before. But then, no Government had ever set out deliberately to arouse social envy and hatred, to incite the ignorant against those who enjoyed a higher station in life. The Chancellor—Lloyd George, showing his true colours—set the tone in speeches of a vulgarity that Richard found scarcely credible.

Balked in its irresponsible financial schemes, the Government then introduced legislation to make the will of the Commons supreme over that of the Lords. It meant a constitutional crisis, something that had not been seen since the First Reform Act. The Parliament Bill, as the measure was called, passed the Commons and came before the Lords. There, the overwhelming Conservative majority had the power to kill it. The power, yes—but not, apparently, the will.

To Richard, the issue was clear and surrender was disastrous. He had been proud, in the best years of his life, to be a good House of Commons man. But he had always considered the Upper House, equally with the Lower, an essential part of the English system of government. Unchecked by the Lords, an unscrupulous Government—controlling the Commons because of a demagogic success at the polls—was free to destroy the foundations of society. The cry of "The peers or the people?" raised by Lloyd George and his kind, was fraudulent. It was the right and duty of the peers, fortified by their long devotion to the inner strengths of English life, to stand firm in the fundamental interests of the people.

The Duke of Berkshire—"a figure cast in the traditional mould, complete with ramrod spine and steel-grey moustache," as a reporter described him—spoke in the great debate of 1911. It was, he knew within himself, as cogent and eloquent a speech as he had ever made. It went to the roots of the question, to the final truths, to the imperatives of conscience and loyalty. But—Richard knew this too, with bitter clarity—it was only an incident in the drama. He wasn't known in this House as he had been known in the Commons. He had begun to attend regularly only as the crisis loomed; he was labelled in the public mind as a "backwoods peer," the derisive term for those who lived mainly on their estates.

And he knew already that the battle was lost. It was a time of shabby manoeuvres, of evasion and self-deception, of cowardice assuming the guise of prudence. The peers who were determined to vote against the Bill were known as "ditchers," men committed to the absurdity of dying in the last ditch. The compromisers were called "hedgers"—a deservedly mean word, Richard thought. When the official leader of the Conservative peers emerged as a hedger, others followed him with relief. On a stifling August afternoon, the Bill went through and their lordships were free to escape from London and brood on their humiliation at leisure.

At Severalls, Richard brooded more gloomily than most. He was convinced that he had done his duty, but he didn't like the figure that he cut. The ditchers were seen as obstinate and unreasoning, as old men clinging to the remnants of a vanished past. Richard had always thought of himself as simply a Conservative. Now he was a reactionary—a word that was coming into fashion. A cartoon had depicted him, his coronet askew on his head, riding a rocking-horse and waving a wooden sword. He had to admit that it hurt.

On top of this, there was Home Rule. Asquith, like Gladstone in his day, depended for a majority on the Irish Nationalists and had to pay them in their chosen coin. Richard forced himself reluctantly to speak in the Lords again when the Home Rule Bill was debated. It was depressing to repeat the arguments that he had deployed in 1892; all that had happened in the meantime was a further advance of nationalist fanaticism. He was disregarded, of course. Home Rule was going through, and the only resistance was that of Ulster.

However, this resistance was quite as fanatical as the pressure of the Nationalists. Irishmen of both factions, still subjects of His Majesty, drilled in private armies. Fratricidal strife seemed to be the only possible outcome of the mad Home Rule policy. British officers, sympathetic to Ulster, declared their intention of resigning their commissions. Richard was on their side; and yet it was a nasty jolt to see officers in revolt against Ministers of the Crown. What might have happened next . . . But it was August 1914.

Year by year, Europe had been moving toward a war on a scale unknown since the age of Napoleon. In England, most people's minds were occupied by Home Rule and the suffragettes—or by sensational murders and financial scandals which also seemed to Richard to be signs of the times. But the warnings were clear to anyone who followed international affairs. The nations grouped in opposing camps: the Triple Alliance of Germany, Austria and Italy against the Triple Entente of Britain, France and Russia. One crisis followed another. The Balkans, as old Bismarck had predicted, were the most likely flashpoint. Sooner or later, Austria would lose patience with the turbulent Serbs. In a deadly chain of commitment, Russia was linked to Serbia, France to Russia, and Britain to France.

Two men who understood were the Duke of Berkshire and the Earl of Farnham. Twice every summer, at Severalls and at Longmarsh, they paced the lawns, deep in earnest discussion. An observer would have seen two dignified men enjoying their leisure, at ease in the beauty of the English summer. The anxiety was within them. Each had two sons.

The error, they agreed, had been the decision to put England on the side of France, against Germany.

"We missed our chance," Arthur said. "There was a time when we might have made the right choice—the German orientation. Of course, if you'd become Foreign Secre-

tary . . ." He coughed. It was the nearest he ever came to a
reference to Richard's private life.

"Well," he resumed, "after the Boer War there was a general desire to end our isolation and find a friend. The Germans were violently pro-Boer, as you know, so the German
orientation was a non-starter. Friendship with France—the
Entente Cordiale, a nice innocent phrase—seemed attractive."

The first fatal step had been taken in 1904, under a Conservative Government. The Foreign Secretary had been Lord
Lansdowne, a man of good intentions but poor judgement, the
same who now led the Opposition in the Lords and was responsible for the surrender on the Parliament Bill.

"I blame myself," Arthur said. "I advised against it, but
not forcibly enough. To be fair to Lansdowne, he never intended a real commitment. With the Liberals—with Grey—
we've edged closer to an alliance. Now it's a question of staff
talks between our military men and the French. The public
won't be informed, but that's what is happening."

Richard looked forward to seeing his old friend, and especially to staying at Longmarsh. The memory of Ellie was
poignant, but he tried to think only of the time when she had
given him a taste of happiness. Here, in this arbour, he had
kissed her; here, she had shown him her favourite flowers and
chosen one for his buttonhole; here, they had hidden behind a
hedge while her mother was looking for her.

The friendly old house had lost its loneliness and was once
again the Longmarsh that had welcomed him in 1875. In a
world of change, that was reassuring. Grace, like the earlier
Lady Farnham, loved filling the house. Sometimes, strolling
in a secluded part of the grounds, Richard and Arthur saw a
young couple absorbed in each other; the elderly gentlemen
smiled and tactfully retraced their steps. The years were
marked by engagements, weddings and christenings. By 1914,
the Farnhams' two sons and two daughters were all married.

But Longmarsh was still a home for them. They came often
—"dropping in" in the new fashion, chugging up the drive in
their motors—and brought their friends.

Charlotte had a house in the village; a brick-built modern
house of the kind that had begun to appear in the neighbourhood since the turn of the century. She dined or came to tea
at Longmarsh from time to time, but was quite happy with
her own company. In summer, she resumed her habit of
travelling in Europe—Paris to see Fanny, Baden-Baden, sometimes as far as Rome or Vienna. Richard envisaged her sturdy,
indomitable figure impressing itself on hotel managers and
wagon-lit attendants. He never went abroad himself. He had
had enough of it.

Arthur still avoided any allusion to Ellie, but once he asked:
"Have you thought of marrying again, Richard?"

"Vaguely. I seem to manage all right, though."

He had thought of it, yes. He had also thought, though he
didn't say so to Arthur, of setting up a mistress discreetly in
London. The sixth Duke had found that desirable in his
fifties, so why not the eighth Duke? But the need for women
—the fire in the blood, the demanding twitch of the body—
was fading in him. He was glad to see it go, to be at peace at
last. It would not have seemed right, after the death of the
heart, for the mere carnal urge to survive.

As for marriage . . . The logic of events, the symmetry
that ought to govern human life (though it seldom did),
pointed to his marrying Rhoda. It would make her very
happy, and he felt that he owed it to her now that he was
free. Provided, of course, that she was free. He made an enquiry at the Italian Embassy, and was told that Prince Montamare was still alive. In general, he thought wryly, those who
die are not those who can be dispensed with. But he hadn't
really wanted to marry Rhoda. The past was the past.

If he wished to marry, there need to be no problem. It was

odd to be an eligible man again, so long after the first time, but glances in drawing rooms told him that it was no delusion. He showed few signs of advancing age, except that he wore his spectacles all the time. Society wasn't lacking in attractive widows in their forties, even in their thirties, who were charmed by his Victorian courtesy and intrigued by rumours of his romantic history. Besides, he was a Duke. Many a lady would have accepted far worse things than grey hair and spectacles to call herself a Duchess.

On winter evenings, drinking his brandy alone, Richard felt the lack of another face and another voice. On summer weekends, he reflected that Severalls ought to have a hostess. Yet, in the end, he couldn't bring himself to marry for such reasons. A man should marry for love, and only for love: he had believed it all his life and he believed it still. And he knew that he could never love again.

On the whole, he didn't feel unhappy at Severalls. He had never loved the house and he didn't love it now, but he had a wry affection for it, as an old soldier might have for the barracks. It was too big and too quiet, but it always had been. He kept busy enough, what with the estate, the dogs and horses, the library—and, beyond these, the social duties of his rank, the Conservative Party in the constituency (he was honorary Chairman) and the Berkshire Yeomanry (he was honorary Colonel). There was never a day without appointments, letters to answer, and telephone calls.

And there were visitors. The Farnhams came to stay, the Mitcheldeans, the Doddingtons. Alfred came often, usually with Janet. Alfred had left Oxford with the anticipated brilliant First and was offered a Fellowship, which he declined. It was hard enough to write good poetry, he said, and becoming a scholar would spoil whatever chance he had.

"So you'll devote yourself to poetry?" Richard asked.

"Does that seem strange to you?"

"Not at all. I wish I'd had your gifts. I suppose you'll live in London. It's a pity we no longer have Berkshire House."

"Oh, I don't think Berkshire House would have suited me."

At that time, Richard was looking for a London house on his own account. Now that the estate was running smoothly, he was attracted by the idea of spending part of each winter in town. He found what he wanted—a Georgian house with an air of quiet distinction, not too large or pretentious—in the part of Mayfair where he felt at home. One could see the Berkshire House Hotel from the top windows, which amused him.

"This is a lovely house, Father," Alfred said enthusiastically.

"D'you really like it?"

"I think it's perfect."

"Why don't you have it? You need a place. I shouldn't have much difficulty in finding something else."

"Oh, that's absurd. But if we could share it, I'd be delighted."

Richard hesitated. "Don't you want a place of your own?"

"We get on reasonably well together, don't we?"

"We do. Well, I should be very happy. And after all, I'm at Severalls most of the time."

He insisted that it was to be Alfred's house, and that Alfred should choose the furniture and decorative scheme. Through the years, Richard scrupulously avoided staying in the house for long periods. He came for a few weeks at a time in winter and spring, and when there were important debates in the Lords. If he had to go to London at short notice, he stayed at his club.

Though he tried not to obtrude himself, he enjoyed meeting Alfred's friends. Some had come to Severalls from Oxford; others were newer friends, the numbers increasing as time passed. As in his undergraduate days, Alfred had the effortless knack of being the leading spirit in a circle without any show of dominance, the first among equals.

The servants, Richard noticed, didn't quite know what to make of the young men who came to the house. Some were obviously gentlemen, a few with titles. Others had jobs— which they didn't conceal—in banks or offices, and their vowels were far from irreproachable. Presumably the servants decided that it must be all right, since the young gentleman was a Marquis and the Duke was prepared to greet everyone affably. The friends gathered informally, sometimes drinking whisky but often only tea. They joked and laughed a good deal, but fundamentally they were far more serious-minded than any young men whom Richard had known in his twenties. They talked about plays they had seen—serious plays, not merely shows—about exhibitions and lectures, and chiefly about poetry. Sometimes they read poetry aloud and discussed it: not their own, though most of them wrote, but the work of poets they admired. The names—Flecker, de la Mare, an Irishman called Yeats—were strange to Richard. The young men never talked about politics or sport or horses. Also, he never heard them talk about women, or not as the subalterns had in his regiment. Perhaps this was because of his presence, but he didn't think so.

Young ladies also came to the house—not so many as the young men, but a sprinkling. The servants must have been even more puzzled. The ladies might be genuinely lady-like, or of more dubious social origin, or of the blue-stocking type —teachers, perhaps. Few of them seemed to be attached to any particular young man. They read and discussed poetry, just like the men.

Richard couldn't remember afterwards exactly when he first met Janet Willis—either in 1909 or 1910, he thought. To begin with, he had the impression that she arrived and left with another young lady. Then he noticed that Alfred escorted her home. She lived in Paddington, Alfred mentioned.

It was in 1910—Richard remembered that definitely, because it was just after King Edward's death—that Alfred said that he would like to come down to Severalls for a week or so.

"I'd be delighted, my dear boy."

Alfred paused, then asked: "May I bring Janet?"

"Miss Willis? You know that you may bring any of your friends."

This was easily said, but Alfred had never brought a young lady before. In the nineteenth century, a young lady could never have accompanied a young man on a visit without a chaperone. But on this question, Richard was not a reactionary.

Janet did not conform at all to the style of beauty popular in 1910: bold features, ample bosoms, generous figures. She was slender, the lines of her body almost boyish; her face revealed beauty only when one looked at it carefully. By accepted standards it was too narrow, the nose too long and the mouth too small. But Richard could see that, to a man who was captivated by it, all other faces would seem banal and unsubtle. Certainly, it was a face full of character. And Janet, as he came to know her, had a character with the special quality of Alfred's circle: easy and relaxed, yet shrewd and discerning in judgment, capable of quiet self-confidence and purpose.

Richard showed her the portrait gallery. As one might expect, it was clear what interested her and what didn't.

"That's a remarkable picture."

"D'you think so? The artist isn't at all well known. It's the first Duke."

"He looks like a most determined person."

"I dare say. Quite a figure on the political scene in Queen Anne's reign."

"It's an old family," she said, with a touch of awe but a touch of gentle mockery too.

"Not really old," Richard answered. "Not a trace before 1600."

Alfred said afterwards: "Janet was amused that you don't consider the Somers to be an old family."

"Well . . ." Richard was slightly embarrassed. "I was comparing it with families like the Howards. It's all relative, I suppose."

"Janet's family isn't a family at all in that sense, you see."

"My dear boy, you don't think that matters to me, do you?"

He meant it. One was a gentleman, or one was a lady—or one was not. Possibly, in 1880, Janet wouldn't have been exactly a lady. But in this changing world, she was. In any case, he liked her; and even if he didn't, Alfred would marry whom he chose.

Janet became an established figure in Alfred's life and therefore in Richard's, both at the town house and at Severalls. An engagement, to Richard's mind, was in the natural course of events. But there was no sign of it.

Eventually—on an occasion when Alfred had come to Severalls without her, and Richard had asked how she was— he took the opportunity to say: "You know, it's quite a time since an engagement has been announced at Severalls."

"Yes." Alfred smiled. "I have pointed that out to Janet."

"You do wish to marry her, I imagine?"

"Certainly. We were discussing it only last week." Richard was baffled by this phrase. Discussing it? Had Alfred proposed to her, or not?

Alfred explained: "Janet's work is just beginning to be recognised. She gives a great deal of time to it; that wouldn't be possible with a household to manage, and perhaps children. It's important to her to achieve something before relapsing into domesticity."

"Yes, I see."

Janet was an engraver, making illustrations for books and magazines. It was also her father's profession. Richard had seen some of her work—exquisite, he thought. But he found it hard to understand how such a consideration could take precedence over the course of love toward marriage.

"We're both aware that an engagement would give you pleasure, Father," Alfred said. "If you wish it, we'll declare ourselves engaged. However, it wouldn't really alter the situation."

"Well . . . it's for you and Miss Willis to decide, not for me."

So there was no engagement. How could a young man be so patient and so coolly rational?—Richard wondered. Alfred was in love; there was no doubt of that. Surely he must be eager to make Janet his own, in every sense. Young men had passions, young men had bodily desires—no one knew that better than Richard. Perhaps Alfred had a discreet arrangement, an Alice. On the whole, Richard thought it unlikely. Perhaps he and Janet were already conducting themselves as man and wife. It would have been unthinkable a generation ago, but there was no telling what young people considered acceptable nowadays, especially in literary and artistic circles. Anyway, they seemed to be perfectly happy. He let the situation drift, as they did.

In 1912, Alfred published a book of poems. The title-page read simply: "Poems. By Alfred Somers."

"You're making a name for yourself," Richard remarked.

"Not as the Marquis of Wantage," Alfred said. "You'll have to live a long time, Father. A Duke could never be taken seriously as a poet."

The reviews, by critics whom Alfred respected, were good. "He's very pleased really," Janet told Richard. "But then, they're very good poems."

Of course, Richard was no judge of that. The poems didn't go with a swing; Alfred went in for something called broken rhythm. And there were some that Richard, after several careful readings, quite failed to understand. Now and again, however, a note of pure beauty—beauty that didn't depend on understanding, like the beauty of music—came clearly through. There were several nature poems, reflecting the green landscape of England, and several love poems, inscribed "To J—"; these were tender rather than passionate, marked by the cool and reflective quality of Alfred's love. There was also a haunting poem called "Quest," about a love that had not come to fruition. Perhaps it had been inspired by Ellie, or perhaps Richard read that into it.

When congratulated on the book, Alfred shrugged and said: "It's an apprenticeship." He was encouraged, at all events, to write more. Poetry was the core of his life, as politics had been of Richard's. He was ambitious after all, in his own way.

"The dream is to bring it off—just once," he said.

Richard asked what this meant.

"D'you know the line: 'A rose-red city half as old as time'?"

Yes, Richard vaguely recalled it.

"D'you know who wrote it?"

This, Richard couldn't say.

"Someone called Burgon. His other poems are forgotten. The rest of that poem is forgotten. But that line remains. It was worth living, to have written that."

During these years, Richard saw little of his younger son. After leaving Cambridge, Charles had shaped his life with decision. Industry was his chosen sphere; his stepfather owned mines and factories in England as well as in America, and Charles was making himself familiar with management problems before becoming a director. He was the first Somers to be involved in business, or trade as Richard's father would have called it. But it was acceptable nowadays, and he wasn't the heir to the Dukedom. Really, while Alfred was Richard's heir, Charles was Horace Greig's. That was fair, doubtless.

Charles lived in the industrial North for a couple of years, then took a flat in London. He visited Severalls for a few days about once a year; Richard was told nothing, and asked no questions, about his personal life. He said, according to Alfred, that he had no time for women. But in June 1914 he wrote to say that he was engaged—rather surprisingly, to the daughter of a Viscount.

Alfred was at Severalls at the time. He was considering another book; he had written enough poems to make a volume, and the publishers were pressing him. But, as Janet explained to Richard, he wasn't satisfied with them; they needed further work. He came to Severalls in June to apply himself to the work without distraction. He didn't even want Janet there, and in any case she was detained in London by her own work.

At Richard's urging more than at Alfred's, she came at last for a few days. One fine afternoon, Richard looked out of a window to see the young people walking slowly along a garden path, loosely holding hands, deep in talk. He had a sudden sense of their human beauty, of their immense and precious value. He was grateful to them for being here, and for living.

They returned to London. Richard was alone at Severalls when the war broke out. Both Alfred and Charles had been in the Officers' Training Corps at their universities and held reserve commissions; they joined their regiments at once.

CHAPTER 22

Heavy Losses

ON A CLOUDY September afternoon in 1916, the Duke of Berkshire—a spare, upright figure, sixty-one years old and looking
no more—came out of Bumpus's bookshop in Marylebone
Lane and looked for a taxi. He found one at the corner of
Wigmore Street and waited for a lady who was paying her
fare. The lady was dressed in black, a mourning veil over her
face. At that time, it was a common sight.

She turned and said: "Uncle Richard."

"Vicky, surely!"

"How are you, Uncle Richard?"

"Pretty well, thank you. And you . . . I'm afraid . . ."

"Yes, I'm a war widow," she said.

"My dear, I'm terribly sorry . . ."

"D'you want this taxi, sir?" the driver asked.

"Just a moment, my man. Let me give you some tea, Vicky.
Or were you going somewhere?"

"I had a bit of shopping, but it doesn't matter."

Richard gave the driver his address. He had only a house-
keeper-cook and one maid at the London house; even at
Severalls, the war had taken most of the menservants. But he
wasn't quite reduced to making his own tea.

"When did it happen?" he asked.

"A fortnight ago. I'm not really used to it yet."

"These are ghastly days we're going through. I suppose it
was on the Somme?"

"Yes."

"I don't know what I can say."

"Please don't say that I can be proud of him. People keep saying that—I can't bear it any more."

Through streets with little traffic, they drove in an uncomfortable silence. When they were in Richard's house and the tea had been served. Vicky said: "I'm sorry. Grief makes one selfish. I heard about your son."

Charles had been killed at Ypres in 1915, just when he was expecting to come home on leave and get married.

"Your other son—the Marquis—is he all right?"

"Yes, he's all right. He was wounded once, but not seriously."

"It's better to be wounded seriously and get out of the trenches."

"Alfred is out of the trenches, as a matter of fact. He's on the staff."

"Oh, good. John was hoping to get on the staff. He knew I wasn't interested in his being a hero. Well, there it is."

Now that Vicky's veil was raised, Richard saw that she was still very pretty; the laughing, bright-eyed girl had matured but had not been transformed. She was thirty-two, he worked out. It was miserably young for what had happened to her.

"One is so awfully selfish, isn't one?" she said, speaking quite calmly now. "I do realise that it's the scale of the thing that matters. Do you know how many men were killed just on the first day of the big push? Twenty thousand. We're not supposed to know—a friend at the War Office told me. Imagine twenty thousand people being killed in an earthquake. It would go down in history. But they just go on and kill thousands more the next day, and the next . . . It's more than two months now. The offensive is still going on."

"It's appalling," Richard said uneasily.

"Is it? Nobody seems to be appalled, though. Everybody

accepts it. Carry on, chins up, keep the home fires burning. I think something has happened to us—people in general. I don't suppose we'll ever be the same again. The twentieth century—it looked so nice, so progressive and hopeful. A new age of barbarism, more likely . . . Could I have some more tea?" she asked in the same calm tone.

Richard filled her cup.

"But one is so selfish," she repeated. "If I'm honest, I know that I'd see twenty thousand men die just to have John alive again. He was my man, that's all. And people say such useless, useless things. I've got to remember how respected he was, he was so gifted, he had such integrity. I shan't remember that at all. I'll only remember being in bed with him—that's what I want to have back. I'm shocking you, Uncle Richard, I'm sure."

"Please say whatever you wish, if it helps."

"It doesn't help—nothing helps. Still, it's what I'd say to General Haig if I could. General Haig, why did you kill my man? It's what all of us would say, all the thousands of war widows."

"You're overwrought, my dear," Richard said. "It's very natural. This may seem a cruel thing to say to someone in your position, but war always means casualties. And, regrettably, the casualties are always men who are loved."

"No, I'm not overwrought," she answered. Indeed, he had done her an injustice; she wasn't. She looked at him directly and asked: "Do you believe it's doing any good, this offensive?"

"We can only hope."

"That's what doctors say when their treatment doesn't produce results, isn't it? It's gained four miles, I believe. That works out at fifty thousand deaths a mile. How many miles is it from the Somme to Berlin? It seems to me that it's completely pointless."

"My dear, it doesn't do any good to speculate about that."

"Doesn't it? One would naturally prefer not to realise that one's husband's death has been pointless. But one of the things I learned from John was to use my intelligence, and I can't get out of the habit. And as I've met you . . . You're an intelligent man, aren't you?"

"I'm somewhat rusty. I have been considered intelligent."

"You see, I'm in the company of John's mother most of the time, and she happens to be particularly stupid. But at a time like this—I don't mean only John's death, I mean the war—one finds that most people either are stupid or prefer not to think."

"That may be because there isn't much scope for thinking. In peacetime there are choices: we could have followed a different policy, we could even have kept out of the war. But now we can only go through with it."

"What for?"

"I'm sorry you should ask that, even in your bereavement. For England, surely. If we're defeated, it's the end of us as a Great Power, perhaps as an independent nation."

"So it's wave the Union Jack and die for the King."

Richard said stiffly: "I know I'm an old reactionary, of course."

She smiled. "Oh, yes—you were a ditcher, weren't you? How long ago all that seems."

"Really, Vicky, using your intelligence—do you see any alternative?"

"I don't think that's the right question. I ask myself: what is the purpose? It isn't about Belgium any more. It's to defeat Germany—the enemy, the Huns as we call them now. To knock them out and stand on their chests. And the purpose for them is to knock us out. In fact, the purpose of the war is war. What's the sense of that?"

Richard tried to argue, not very effectively. He was inhibited by arguing with a woman, and far more by arguing with a woman in the shadow of her husband's death. He had a feeling, too, that he was merely repeating the exhortations of politicians and newspapers, which she had already heard and rejected.

To wind up the unpleasant conversation, and to reach a point of harmony, he said: "Well, I think the Western Front strategy is wrong. I've never believed that England ought to commit a large Army to the Continent. It's not our way of fighting; the Navy is our trump card."

"Yes," she said, "but people don't think much about that either. It's this awful fatalistic acceptance that has gripped us all. Meanwhile—it goes on. Fifty thousand men for a mile."

She stood up and gazed out at the darkening sky.

"Oh, God," she said. "Oh, God, Uncle Richard—how long does it have to go on?"

The battle of the Somme went on until November. It was a rainy autumn, and the troops were floundering in mud as they stumbled toward the German machine-guns. After four months, the gain in territory was insignificant. Vicky, a woman knowing nothing of military affairs, had been right: the offensive was completely pointless.

Richard stayed at Severalls all the winter. Wherever one went in London, one saw women in veils and men with black armbands. People who were not in mourning were haunted by anxiety: women for their husbands and brothers, people of Richard's generation for their sons. Everyone had someone in daily peril.

That was not quite true, however. Some faces were marked by an anxiety of another kind—the furtive guilt of those who had secured "cushy jobs" for their loved ones. Arthur confided to Richard that he felt a certain embarrassment, though he was merely lucky. His elder son, who had followed him into the Diplomatic Service, had tried to volunteer but had been told to stick to his responsibilities at the Embassy in Washington. The younger son had joined the Navy; in other wars it had been more adventurous and dangerous than the Army, and no one could have expected that it would develop into a relatively safe option. Arthur was not to blame, nor were the young men. But the division between those who were in the trenches and those who were not had become one of the bitterest, ugliest aspects of the war.

Richard felt some of this embarrassment about Alfred. True, Alfred had done his share of service in the trenches—over a year—and had been wounded. And of course he hadn't intrigued for the staff post. His comment was that he'd been given it because he was such a rotten soldier; at Headquarters, he couldn't do much damage. But Generals were snobs, and it was possible that being a Marquis had improved his chances of being picked out. At all events, malicious remarks about staff officers—living in French châteaux in greater comfort than if they'd been in England, berating their servants for stains on the linen while front-line troops wallowed in mud—were part of the talk of the time. Meeting a friend with a son in the trenches, Richard disliked having to say that his own son was on the staff.

When he came on leave, Alfred had to divide his time between Devon, Severalls, and being in London with Janet, who had a wartime office job. There was little opportunity for serious talk. So far as Richard could see, Alfred regarded the war as a vast nuisance. Essentially it didn't touch him, as politics hadn't touched him in peacetime; it was irrelevant to his real life, the life of a poet. He stood apart both from patriotic enthusiasm and from Vicky's kind of protest. Everything that mattered to him was simply suspended for the duration. He and Janet were still not married; it was meaningless, they considered, until they could live together. And he loathed the idea of leaving her as a widow. He stuck to this attitude, even though he was now safe.

Richard knew that he was utterly selfish about Alfred's safety. Alfred had to survive because of his inestimable value. To save Alfred, he would have seen thousands die; the fact that Vicky had felt the same about John, and everyone else about their loved ones, affected his logic but not his secret feelings. He would never forget the dreadful suspense of the first year of war, nor the anxiety caused by the telegram: "Wounded in action." Now, he interpreted the wound—it had turned out to be a broken jaw from a shell splinter—as somehow guaranteeing future immunity. One got irrational notions in wartime, that had to be admitted.

Another irrational idea, causing a guilt that he could not dispel, was that he had paid for Alfred with Charles's death. One son killed out of two at the front was about the statistical probability. He was aware that losing Charles had been a terrible blow for Geraldine. He had written to her, and her answer had been distracted, almost incoherent—entirely unlike her. Steady, conventional, bent on success in the world, Charles had been truly her son. She still had Alfred; she loved him, of course, though Richard gathered that she wasn't enthusiastic either about poetry or about Janet. But with Charles dead, she probably felt as Richard would have felt if Alfred had been the victim.

Richard was alone far more than in peacetime, for the social life of the county was in abeyance and it didn't seem right to entertain much. In gloomy winter evenings, Vicky's words germinated in his mind. He tried to dismiss them as the emotional outpourings of a distraught woman, but he knew that this was an evasion. She had been thinking about the war, and she had challenged him to think. It was true, as she said, that people had given up thinking.

He recognized, in the first place, that the Somme offensive wasn't merely pointless in itself; it was the ghastly price of a fatal commitment. He had always believed that the alliance with France was wrong, that it was bound to lead to war. Because the predictable consequences were now being endured, that did not make it right.

And the deaths on the Somme were probably only an instalment of the price. Richard had foreseen war—had foreseen this war, with these allies and these enemies—but he had not foreseen anything like this appalling slaughter. There had been bloody battles—Austerlitz, Waterloo, Sedan—in other wars; but one could make sense of those wars in terms of limited campaigns and decisive victories. Now, each battle went on as long as a campaign or an entire war and, as Vicky said, it settled nothing. England, in particular, had always fought by striking at unexpected points with well-trained professional regiments, and by using the unique asset of sea-power. In Richard's day at the War Office, no one had ever imagined that England would copy the Continental Powers and commit a vast army to sledgehammer fighting. This business of hurling masses of men at a fortified enemy line, trying to break through by sheer weight and reconciling oneself to heavy losses, was new. Conscription was also new; it meant reluctant soldiers, ill-trained soldiers with no skill in the art of survival, sacrifices valued only for their numbers. The acceptance of a massacre like that of the Somme was utterly new, and Richard could not help feeling that it was utterly wrong. He asked himself whether any rational man—Liberal, Tory, pro-French or anything else—would have entered into the commitment with advance knowledge of what it would bring. Surely, the answer was No. Again, the fact that it was happening did not make it right.

He could not make himself believe, now that he was allowing himself to think, that the slaughter could be justified by any aim or purpose. But in any case he was far from convinced of the validity or the honesty of the aims of this war. It had been said in 1914 that England was going to war in defence of Belgium. But the French were fighting to recover Alsace-Lorraine, and this was now said to be an Allied—that is, an English—war aim. Richard knew perfectly well that Strassburg was a German city. If the French wanted it, they had no right to call on the lives of Charles Somers and John Townsend. He also knew that the vital interests of Germany were in the eastern borderlands, and those of Austria in the Balkans. If the Germans won the war, they would control Poland instead of the Russians. No one had the right to call on English lives in order to keep a Russian Governor in Warsaw. It would have been ridiculous, had it not been tragic.

He thought of the Germans who had been his friends. They were not Huns, whatever that meant; they were servants of a social order admirable in many ways, and German patriots. He had no doubt that they were supporting their national war effort and that, if widows asked them what it was for, they answered that defeat would mean the end of Germany as a Great Power. So it would. But when had Charles Somers—or his father—desired that Germany should cease to be a Great Power?

Richard was revolted by the vulgar anti-German feeling that had taken hold of the country: orchestras afraid to play German music, people of German descent changing their names, denunciations of the Kaiser as if he were some savage chieftain. The Government, now headed by Lloyd George, was stirring up hatred as it had once stirred up class envy. But, he was coming to think, it showed what the war was about. Vicky was right—it was a war without definable purpose, a war of nations set on destroying one another.

What then? Suppose that Germany were "knocked out": one couldn't establish a British or French Protectorate, as if it were the Sudan. One would simply be left with chaos—a nation in a state of collapse, a hole in the fabric of Europe. Russia, in the spring of 1917, underwent a revolution and seemed to be plunging into boundless uncertainties. This was deplored because Russia was an ally. Richard saw that it was far graver than that. It could be the beginning of a general collapse among the states of Europe, weakened beyond repair by the bloodletting. If one aimed to destroy, one could set no limits to destruction. And destruction had always been the guiding spirit of men like Lloyd George, men blind to the values of stability and tradition.

In wartime, one naturally thought in terms of victory or defeat. A compromise peace seemed like a confession of failure. No one could tell, however, what might be the cost of victory. Another year of war—two—three? Another battle like the Somme, and another, and another? A million English dead? That wasn't impossible; half a million had died already. Perhaps, long before victory came, mutual exhaustion would make a compromise peace inevitable. Might it not be better to compromise now, while some of the young men were still alive?

In July 1917, the Farnhams came for their annual visit to Severalls. It was a miserable time. Rain fell steadily; in the peaceful English countryside this was merely regrettable, but across the Channel it was a disaster, for once again men were driven to the attack through a morass of mud. Another big push was under way, this time in Flanders. After a fortnight, after a month, there was no sign of a breakthrough.

Richard found that he and Arthur had been thinking along the same lines. So had others; although nothing had leaked out in public, Lord Lansdowne had submitted a paper to the Cabinet urging an exploration of possible peace terms. He was making up for his past blunders, Richard remarked.

But Arthur was pessimistic. "He won't get any support,

you know. History may say that he's right, but that's all. He's beating his head against a brick wall."

"What if the idea were brought out into the open? I've been turning over in my mind the possibility of some kind of statement, signed by men whose names carry weight. Yours, I need hardly say, would count for a great deal."

Arthur shook his head. At this moment, he looked like a really old man.

"When one retires from public life, it's wisest to stay retired. And I don't advise you to get involved in this kind of thing, Richard. You'd only make yourself unpopular. Passions run very high in wartime."

Probably Arthur was right. But for Richard, hope and activity were impulses that could not be finally stilled.

In the autumn, the Flanders offensive petered out. It was the Somme once again: frightful losses, an advance about as far as from Severalls to the lodge-gates. Alfred, home on leave, said that Haig hadn't wanted to give up; he had been convinced that his plan would achieve the breakthrough. Now the Germans were in a position to transfer troops from the eastern front, for Russia was definitely out of the war. An extremist party with the odd name of Bolsheviki had seized power and asked for an armistice. Whether the man Lenin was a German agent, as some people said, or a revolutionary fanatic, the Russian collapse was complete. The one redeeming feature of the situation was that it created a rational basis for a compromise peace. Assured of huge conquests in the East, Germany could surely be persuaded to withdraw from occupied territory in the West.

At the end of November, Lansdowne came into the open with a letter to *The Times*. The editor, so Richard heard from Arthur, refused to print it—refused to print a letter from a former Foreign Secretary! The letter appeared in the *Daily Telegraph*.

Richard made up his mind and went to London, with the intention of speaking in the Lords at the first opportunity. It was now a matter of honour; when the hedger had found his courage, the Duke of Berkshire could not remain silent.

He made his speech to a thinly attended House. A few peers muttered: "Shame!"; most of them merely looked embarrassed. An octogenarian Earl—always a fool, Richard recalled—interjected: "What about our boys?" Richard turned in his direction.

"Not one of us in this House, nor in any sphere of civilian life, has the right to invoke the men at the front—I do not choose to call them boys when they have given signal proof of manhood—as a counter in debate. As their suffering and their heroism are beyond our experience, even beyond the experience of those who have fought in other wars, so their thoughts and feelings are beyond what we can know. I say only this of them. They are heroes indeed, but they are also men. They are men with hopes and dreams, whether in public life or in any craft or trade, in the arts or in the sciences, and always in human happiness and the love of women. Their hopes are what for most of us in this House are past satisfactions. If we fail to explore any means whereby these young lives may be spared and these hopes fulfilled, then indeed we fail the men at the front."

The House remained calm. But in the week that followed, the ha'penny papers—penny papers now—raised a hue and cry. One article, headlined "The Duke Who Wants to Shake Hands with the Kaiser," alluded to Richard's long residence abroad and his German friendships. Another mentioned that the heir to the Dukedom was a Headquarters staff officer. Yet another, digging up Richard's 1895 article in *The Nineteenth Century,* quoted triumphantly: "Anglo-German co-operation is natural, it is grounded in plain affinities of thought and mutual understanding." A cartoon showed him hauling down the Union Jack to run up the white flag.

One evening, as he was changing for dinner, a crowd gathered outside his residence. He went to a window and showed himself. The shouting rose to a frenzy, and soon a stone shattered the pane. Richard continued to stand in full view. After five minutes or so, the police cleared the street. What irritated Richard was that the house was really Alfred's; probably the window would still be broken when he came on his next leave.

The war went on. Richard had achieved nothing, as Arthur had warned him. He returned to Severalls; country people were at least civilised.

In March 1918, the Germans attacked. The result was the first breakthrough since the beginning of the war. The offensive rolled on for forty miles, punching out a massive salient and threatening Paris. Staring at the maps in the newspapers, Richard confronted the possibility that the war would end neither in victory nor in compromise but in defeat.

The blow fell directly on the British Fifth Army, shattering it into a chaos of struggling units. With the telephone lines cut, the headquarters of this Army and General Headquarters were out of communication. It was vital to find out what was really happening. There was only one way: to send a staff officer on a motor-cycle. The road was under enemy shell-fire, but the risk had to be taken.

Alfred would have liked another hour before setting off. He was halfway through a letter to Janet; he had to end it with a hasty signature and address the envelope. The incomplete, inartistic piece of work displeased him. At the last moment, he decided to enclose the draft of a poem. He had written very little poetry during the war, but in the last few weeks he had felt the sudden pressure of accumulated ideas. The poem, like the letter, wasn't in final shape; however, the annoying distraction of the military emergency would leave him no time to work on it, so it seemed better to let Janet see the draft and discuss it with her when he went on leave.

He started the motor-cycle, rode away, and was never seen again.

That summer, Richard used to wander aimlessly about the grounds of Severalls, dazed and helpless, like the survivor of a shipwreck. Too much had been demanded of him: too much loss, too much suffering. This final grief left him in a state of utter incomprehension. He sometimes found himself muttering, like a child whose trust had been betrayed: "It's not fair. It's not fair."

The bitterest injustice, the last refinement of cruelty, was uncertainty. Alfred had been reported missing. He might conceivably have been captured, but months could pass before the names of prisoners reached England through the Red Cross. Hope, the twitching reflex of Richard's nature, lived painfully on and expired only after the Armistice.

He had always followed the war news carefully, but in 1918 he could scarcely make the effort. The German advance was stemmed and the Allies went over to the offensive, but it seemed to be merely a battle like all the other battles. Victory—the unseen exhaustion and collapse of Germany—took him by surprise. Afterwards, he learned that the Allied generals had been surprised too; they had been planning the big push of 1919.

On Armistice Day, Richard summoned all the servants to the large dining room and told Hawkins to serve champagne. It was a duty—he could still do his duty. Within himself he felt nothing, not even relief. He drank a token glass, left Hawkins in charge of the celebration, and walked down the drive. The church bells were ringing; the sound struck him as discordant, the cheerfulness as a mockery.

But on Sunday, when the service of thanksgiving was held, he read the lesson in a firm voice. When he sat down, he heard a satisfied murmur from the neighbours and tenants. They would have cheered if they hadn't been in church. They had forgotten the controversy of a couple of years ago, so far as it had reached Berkshire at all; they admired the courage with which he had surmounted the loss of his sons, and those who had had such losses in their own families took it for an inspiration; they knew nothing of the emptiness within him. The final irony, he thought, was what they must be saying of him as they went home: a fine old man, and in wonderful shape for his age.

CHAPTER 23

A Pity Beyond
All Telling

AT THE TURN of the year, Richard went down with influenza. The doctor told him that it must be taken seriously; this was an epidemic of a particularly virulent type. Thousands of people were dying, as if the time had come for civilians to match the toll of the war.

Richard was soon gravely ill. He sent for the solicitor and made a new will, settling legacies on his nieces and leaving Severalls to a trust. He was the last Duke of Berkshire, so at long last the house really would be a museum. As for his dying, he could see from the faces of the nurse and the servants that it was more than likely. His lungs were congested, he supposed—that was how George had died.

And it would be fitting to die now, at this time of dissolution. He had earned the right, surely, to be spared any more years of living without Ellie. He wasn't a religious man and he was unable to believe in being united with her in another world. But the thought of being as she was—of release from all desire and all endurance, of peace even if it were the peace of nullity—this thought was real, and joined him to her.

Yet some deeper force—the innate vigour of his nature, or simply the unthinking reaction of the body—overcame resignation and compelled him to struggle for breath and for life.

He passed the crisis and began to recover. "You can thank your magnificent constitution, your Grace," the doctor said jovially. "I expect you'll see us all in our graves."

Sitting up in bed, he read his letters. There was one from the bank, notifying him of the cessation of his allowance to Rhoda, who had died of influenza. There was also a letter from Geraldine.

My dear Richard,

I write to you in farewell, since my husband and I have decided to make our home in the United States. Now that the dear boys are no more, there is nothing to keep me in England. The house, and even the country, in which they grew to manhood are mere reminders of grief. We sail next week.

Both you and I must try to forget the sufferings that have been inflicted on us and to remember the happiness that we once shared. I do not expect to write to you again, and so there can be no harm in parting from you with this abiding truth: dear Richard, I have never ceased to love you.

Yours, despite everything, always yours,
Geraldine.

Time resumed its course. Outwardly, Richard's life had the same components as usual: the estate, responsibilities in the county, an occasional appearance in the House of Lords. His life was over, but he was not really old—only in his sixties. With his magnificent constitution, he was likely to live to eighty.

One day in 1920, he had a strange experience. He was returning from London by train, and was alone in his compartment, gazing out of the window at the familiar countryside. And then—not suddenly, but quite gently and slowly—he was

possessed by an absolute conviction that Ellie was sitting opposite him. He didn't need to turn his head; it was a matter
of feeling her presence, not of seeing her. But she would
have been—no, she was—perfectly still, pensive, and unalter-
ably beautiful.

The train stopped at Didcot, and two strangers got into the
compartment. Ellie was not there, of course. Yet he was
certain that, in some sense, she had been there. If she had
vanished, phantom-like, it was to be expected; it was what
she had done in life.

Richard did not rack his mind for an explanation. Perhaps
it was some kind of "phenomenon"; there was a lot of talk
about spiritualism nowadays, probably because of the war
losses, and Richard was inclined to keep an open mind on the
matter. Perhaps he had conjured up the presence with his
unconscious mind—another phrase that was coming into
fashion. That did not matter. It had happened, and he was
profoundly grateful for it.

He wondered why it had never happened during their
separation, nor in the years following her death. Then, he
had simply missed her and longed for her. But in those years
he had had attachments: a mistress, and later a son. In whatever way this visitation came about, it was a solace for being
alone.

For he was being deprived, one by one, of all the people
who had meant anything to him. Janet, after one visit, married someone from her artistic circle and drifted away. Vicky,
at about the same time, remarried. Richard did not condemn
these marriages, nor consider in his thinking mind that women
had a duty to consecrate themselves to the dead; yet in his
heart of hearts he found something displeasing in them. So
no one remained out of those who had in any sense been
part of the family at Severalls. He was still in touch with

James and Elizabeth Mitcheldean, but this had never been more than a conventional relationship.

There was still Arthur, his old friend. Charlotte, however, had left Longmarsh. Always strong-minded and outspoken, she had become sharp and crotchety with increasing years. She also suffered from arthritis and found it difficult to get about or do anything in her house, which did not improve her temper. Eventually, after taking offence from something that Grace had said, she decided to sell the house and live abroad. She settled in a hotel at Menton, on the French Riviera; it was unlikely that Arthur and Grace, let alone Richard, would see her again.

Richard had to admit that he didn't look forward to staying with Arthur so much as in the past, except for the wistful pleasure of being at Longmarsh. Arthur, now past seventy, was an old man in the full sense; Richard heartily hoped that he himself would die before reaching this stage. He shuffled about the garden, leaning on a stick, and took Grace's arm to go upstairs. Worst of all, his mind had lost its old keenness and reflective power, and often his conversation was frankly boring. He resented every aspect of the changed world in which they were living since the war, and indulged himself with gloomy diatribes against modern casual manners, people who smoked in drawing rooms, and women who cut their hair short. These complaints always ended with: "Ah, well, it doesn't matter what I think, I'm just an old fossil"—to which it was Grace's invariable duty to reply: "Of course you're not, dear."

It was true, of course, that there was plenty to depress and bewilder Arthur in the field of diplomacy and international relations to which he had devoted his life. He was not at home in a world in which the three great Continental Empires had vanished, problems were referred to the so-called

League of Nations (which he viewed with suspicion), and the United States and even Japan had to be ranked among the Powers. The map of Europe showed unrecognisable countries with extraordinary names: Bohemia had become Czechoslovakia, Serbia had become Yugoslavia. Richard too saw this as a change for the worse. Under the slogan of "self-determination," the absurdity of nationalism was in high fashion. And it was already being overtaken by a worse menace. The Bolsheviks—the word was familiar by now—had attempted to take power in Berlin, in Munich, in Budapest. They had met defeat in these places, but they seemed to be firmly in the saddle in Russia. A terrible virus was rampant in the world.

Arthur was very worried by Bolshevism, but he was no longer able to analyse the menace with his old acuity, and his diatribes were so repetitive that it wasn't always clear from his vocabulary whether he was talking about Bolshevism, Christian Science, psycho-analysis or women with short hair. On the whole, he preferred to retreat into his immediate environment. Such energies as he retained were devoted to struggling against the spread of suburbia to the neighbourhood, and to vain efforts to get the Hog's Back closed to motor-cars.

The annual visit to Longmarsh (Arthur and Grace no longer came to Severalls) was a part of Richard's outward life, a life of habit and routine. He was sustained by what really mattered—by the moments when Ellie was with him.

What had happened in the train happened again, several times. He could not make it happen by exerting his will, nor could he foresee it even a minute before; but he was confident that it would go on happening. Sometimes she was lying beside him at night—a wakeful night, for it was not a dream —and then he switched on the bedside light and gazed at her photograph, but only when the experience was over. Sometimes she was walking with him in the grounds. Sometimes she came to him in absolutely commonplace surroundings, such as a London shop.

Her presence was real; indeed, it was the only real thing in his life. It was not a literal reality, nor even an illusion in the customary sense. He did not imagine that he could see her with his eyes nor touch her with his hand, and the thinking part of his mind was aware all the time that he was alone. Had he been forced to describe the experience, which of course he never spoke of to anyone, he would have said that his thinking mind, while it continued to function, yielded its predominance to another kind of reality. It was an experience —to avoid modern psychological jargon—of the emotions.

While it lasted, he felt a happiness so complete and intense that it wiped out age and time, for such a happiness could come only from being with Ellie. Yet he also felt a deep and irreparable sadness, the sadness that had always clouded his life and hers. It was as though he were living again through the whole sequence of his passion, from his first vision of her at Longmarsh to the last. Over the years, happiness and sadness had alternated. Now, at long last, they were fused into pure love.

Alone—truly alone, after Ellie had gone—he pondered about happiness and sadness. There were some people, doubtless, who knew the one and not the other. But they were few; it wasn't the normal human condition. Not much was needed for happiness: a man's love requited by a woman's, a home, the beauty of the countryside and the pleasure of cities, work to give purpose and satisfaction. It was strange that so few achieved this. Among people he had known well, there was only Arthur; and Arthur, at the close of his life, didn't seem to be grateful for his good fortune.

There were so many threats to happiness: the checking of love, the fading of love, early death, the cruelty of war, survival in loneliness and grief. For all that Richard had seen, he felt a great and lasting pity. A poem that Alfred had cherished still came to his mind:

> *A pity beyond all telling*
> *Is hid in the heart of love:*
> *The folk who are buying and selling,*
> *The clouds on the journey above,*
> *The cold wet winds ever blowing,*
> *And the shadowy hazel grove*
> *Where mouse-grey waters are flowing*
> *Threaten the head that I love.*

Still, he reflected, there were also people who never knew either happiness or sadness in any true sense. And that, after all, he would not have chosen. It could only mean that they had never known love.

When he went to Longmarsh in 1922, he was shocked to see how Arthur had gone downhill since the year before. He had been old, and anxious about his health in perhaps a valetudinarian way; now he was obviously ill. His complexion was yellow, his skin hung from his face in fleshless pouches, his lips quivered when he spoke. He no longer walked round the garden, despite the beautiful June weather, but merely let himself be assisted by Grace from the door to a nearby deck-chair.

He gave continual orders to Grace—who looked tired and far from well herself—and hated to be left alone, but in the afternoon he dozed in the sun and she was able to take a short walk with Richard.

"He's so obstinate," she complained. "He's supposed to be on a special diet, but he insists on being given chops and steaks although he never finishes more than a few mouthfuls. And making him take his medicines—well, Richard, it's like dealing with a child."

"What do the doctors say?" Richard asked.

"Oh, well, they want him to go into hospital and have some kind of tests, but he won't hear of leaving Longmarsh. I don't know—does it really matter if they get him scientifically ticketed or not? He'll never be really well again, I've faced that."

Probably, Richard thought, she had also faced the fact that Arthur was unlikely to survive another year.

Arthur nibbled at his dinner and put it aside, saying that the meat was tough. Neither Grace nor Richard contradicted him, though it was a beautiful piece of English beef. After dinner he smoked a cigar, which was strictly forbidden by the doctor.

"D'you hear they're putting up one of these cinemas in Farnham?" he asked Richard. "It's a disgrace—it'll attract all the idle roughs from miles around. But it's all part of what they call the march of progress, I suppose."

Richard woke early next morning. It was going to be fine again—probably hotter than yesterday, to judge by the mist. He got out of bed, stood by the window and enjoyed the view. Despite Arthur's grumbles about the country being covered by nasty little houses, there was no change yet in what could be seen from the house. Everything was beautiful in the calm English way, and the colours were soft and gentle: the green of the lawn and the fields, the grey of the old church tower, the white of the mist rising from the lake.

No change—no change to the eye since he had woken here for the first time, a young man happy in the illusion that life could be secure and easily shaped. His mind went back to that first time. He had breakfasted with Ralph Ashton and made cavalry jokes about his marriage to Celia; he had gone to church with the whole house party; and in the afternoon Lady Farnham had made them walk to the barrows. But to begin with, before shaving and dressing, he had stood by a window of the east wing and been touched, as he was touched now, by the abiding beauty of what he saw.

Only . . . a girl in a white dress with golden hair had come out onto the lawn.

It occurred to him that he might well be staying here for the last time. Grace would live quietly as a widow and perhaps would not invite him again; besides, probably she would not survive her husband for long. Even if their son decided to keep up the house, Richard scarcely knew him.

He breakfasted alone. Grace appeared briefly and made her excuses; Arthur got up late, so she had breakfast with him in his room.

Richard walked down to the lake. The mist dispersed at about nine o'clock, and the water was clear and still under a blue sky. Here too, nothing had changed to the outward eye. He stood for a while at the place where, on a sunlit summer morning, he had asked for Ellie's hand.

He had hoped then, and he hoped now—hoped for her presence. If she stayed only for a moment, if she vanished as she had always vanished, he would not mind. These moments with her were the utmost that he could still expect from life; and her presence at this lovely place—this place of supreme happiness and supreme sadness—would make the moment the most precious of all.

It did not happen. Of course, it had been too much to expect. It had never happened when he was thinking about it beforehand. He had never governed nor possessed her, in life or after death.

But he had been faithful to her; and sometime, somewhere, she would come to him again.

A Note on the Type

This book was set on the Linotype in Granjon, a type named in compliment to Robert Granjon, type cutter and printer—in Antwerp, Lyons, Rome, Paris—active from 1523 to 1590. Granjon, the boldest and most original designer of his time, was one of the first to practice the trade of type founder apart from that of printer.

Linotype Granjon was designed by George W. Jones, who based his drawings on a face used by Claude Garamond (1510–1561) in his beautiful French books. Granjon more closely resembles Garamond's own type than do any of the various modern faces that bear his name.

Composed, printed and bound by
Kingsport Press, Inc., Kingsport, Tenn.
Typography and binding design by
Virginia Tan